GODS OF TIME

A NOVEL BY DANIEL ANDIS

GODS OF TIME

copyright © 2021 by Daniel Andis

SECOND EDITION | MMXXI
4 8 15 16 23 42

Lv426 2.3am

Book Design and Cover Art by D.G. Sidna
Title Font by Rizal Khurasan

ISBN 979-8-9854267-00 | paperback
ISBN 979-8-9854267-48 | ebook
eBook available at amazon.com

EDELMUS BOOKS
contact | books@edelmus.com

"If I have seen further, it is by standing upon the shoulders of giants."

A grinding of metal wheels, a tilt of the train car, the crackle of the third rail—when the lights finally go out, we can't help but squeal. One would think we'd be used to this by now; the screeching, the hurried turns, the dark tunnels and curious smells, and, of course, the lights, which cut out whenever the fancy strikes. But we're not. We're subway riding amateurs.

The lights flash back on and Leah, sitting next to me, giggles at our ineptitude. Three young women, and we're spooked by flickering lights. How embarrassing. Perhaps this is why our parents generally frown upon us crossing the Hudson River into New York City on our own. But the way I see it, every little bird has to leave her nest sometime.

"Why do the lights do that, you reckon?" Parvathy asks. She's the third member of our little gang, and always the most serious.

"Probably happens every time we run over a rat," I tell her.

Leah and I both laugh at the face she makes.

Leah changes the subject. "So are you two coming tonight?"

She turns first to me. She must believe that I'm the most likely to bail. Not because I don't like parties, but I can be quite the glum sour apple when I've let myself down. And this has been a week of defeats, nothing short of a disaster, really.

First, my high school crew team lost our annual competition, and being out on the water is one of my only true loves—well, that and photography and martial arts practice, which we're just now coming from, and a million other things. Then I got word that I didn't make it into the academic program in Providence that I had applied for.

That lab program, scheduled for two weeks over winter break, was supposed to be the cherry on top of my college application, guaranteeing me a spot at a top university, which in turn would pave my way to becoming the next great American optometrist. Or civil rights lawyer. Or international diplomat. Or some amazing thing. I haven't quite worked out all the specifics of my life plan just yet. I am only seventeen, after all. But at the very least, it was going to get me out of my house for a few weeks.

And now? Without the Rhode Island program crowning my resume, what is my future to be? Not to sound dramatic, but I think it's pretty clear—I'm ending up stuck in my hometown in New Jersey forever. That's a fate worse than death. Oh, what would not I give for a do-over, dear universe! A chance to turn back the hands of time, to repeal this improbable fiction, undo this outrageous fortune, a chance to replay my life as the better version of myself.

But, seriously, Isabel, how silly a wish is that?

Leah must sense my frustration. She takes my hand and holds it tightly. She's always been such a good friend. Which surprises me at times. We're sort of opposites. She's so tall and elegant, with straight red hair and piercing blue eyes and a smile as wide as the Hudson River. She's one of those people who will be both prom queen *and* valedictorian, the sort you'd think you should be jealous of because the universe obviously plays favorites, but who is so kind and caring, so genuine in her demeanor, that any thought of envy is quickly washed away.

I could be described as a bit more rough around the edges. I am kind of tall, but not like her. And I doubt I glow like she does. Let's call my aura more of a glower than a glow. And my hair is definitely not straight like hers—as much as I've always wished otherwise. What I have is a black tangle of long, unruly curls, kind of like a mop, one entirely too big for my head.

Sometimes I think my nose is too big for my head as well, but these days I just pretend that it gives my face meaningful character. My nose freckles are cute, though. And my eyes are a nice, uncommon shade of green. Those have gotten a few compliments over the years. You work with what you've got.

"Yeah, I'm going," I finally tell my friends.

She smiles and Parvathy clasps her hands in joy. Apparently they were both worried that I'd sulk at home tonight. Am I really that bad? I don't think so.

"But I'm not heading home with you guys right now," I inform them. "I want to ride the train for awhile, maybe walk around. Clear my head, you know? But I will be there at your sister's apartment tonight. I promise."

"Fair enough," Leah tells me.

The lights flicker off and on again.

Parvathy looks around.

"Those poor rats," she whispers.

We all have a chuckle. Finally, it's time to transfer to the PATH, that tireless train joining the city of New York, the very center of the universe by some accounts, with the state of New Jersey, *literally* the most boring place in the cosmos.

At times, I think I could see myself living here on this side of the Hudson, the New York side, perhaps going to NYU next year. My parents would be thrilled, their little girl, and incidentally only child, sticking around close to home for a bit longer. But then I realize that it's just too close to home. I want to get away. I need to get away. I'm seriously considering applying to schools in Seattle. Or Arizona. Or Tokyo.

The other day, my mom did suggest that I apply to her alma mater, Middlebury College, which is in Vermont. We vacation in Vermont every year, and have been doing so since I was little—so I'm standing on solid ground when I say that I'm something of a Vermont expert. Which is how I know that Vermont is literally the *second* most boring place in the cosmos.

Tokyo it is.

Leah and Parvathy stand as our subway train pulls into the station. Leah, all rosy cheeks and genuine smiles, asks, "Do you want us to take your bag back with us?"

How is this girl so nice?

"Yeah, that would be great," I tell her.

My two friends take my gym bag, with all my jujitsu gear from today's practice at our academy in Manhattan. This is one of the hobbies that binds us together, and one of the few things that hasn't let me down lately. Leah and Parvathy exit the train, leaving me to myself and my moody thoughts. Just before the doors close, Leah turns and blows me a kiss, yelling, "See you tonight, JCVD!"

I take it all back.

I hate her.

Nicknames drive me up the wall. I shout back in protest, "I only did that splits punch once, and I was nine!"

They both wink as the doors finally separate us and I'm carted off underground, to where I don't know. Where do New York subway trains ultimately go? To the underworld maybe? To purgatory? Is this train's final destination to the edges of the astral void, that arcane land found on no map, unknown but remembered in every heart, the place that lies, for each of us, at the end of all our exploring? My question is finally answered when an announcement is made over the intercom—

We're headed for Brooklyn, apparently.

Fair enough. My cousin Shira lives in Brooklyn. Maybe I'll stop by her place. She's two years older than me and opted for the NYU route, though I have to give her some credit. Her apartment in Brooklyn is *two* rivers removed from Jersey.

Now, technically, I'm not supposed to wonder around the city alone. My parents still have flashbacks from when they used to live here, which was, I don't know, eighty years ago or something, and the city was a lot more dangerous back then. So it's a pretty strict rule. But today there's a Starbucks on every corner, and people pay tons of rent just to live in teensy closets, so I really think their concern is overblown. Still, I'll be a good girl and make a beeline for Shira's place. Then I can at least say that I have a chaperon.

Oddly, once we depart the Jay Street station, I look around and notice I'm alone on the train car. Is that normal? I suppose it might be. After all, this early in the day, the flow of traffic is still heading into Manhattan, not away.

The city is like a heart, it beats.

Speaking of which, my pulse quickens a little as we speed up under the city and the lights flicker. My whole life I've had this fear of falling to my death. I don't know why. As a child, I'd wake from horrible dreams—me, reaching for something, anything, while plummeting into darkness. As I'm left here alone on this noisy train car, screeching and shaking as it goes, I'm reminded of those nightmares.

I try to think of something else.

Fortunately, I'm distracted when the sliding doors connecting to the adjacent car open up beside me. One is not supposed to travel between cars while the train is in motion, but people do it all the time. I expect to see a transient emerge, asking for change. But instead, it's a frumpy old woman. She's wearing a long cream-colored overcoat, sort of quilted, kind of folksy, with big pockets. It really doesn't match her flower-printed capri pants.

This lady's hair is mostly grey and haphazardly pulled together with a cheap scrunchy. Taking it all in, I can't tell if she's a hobo about to hit me up for a dollar or an eccentric socialite on her way to some new Brooklyn gallery show. I've put on my imaginary detective hat, but the hint of whiskey on her breath is a clue that does little to settle the question either way.

She's about to pass me on her way down the train car and onto the next, but she stops and turns. Her accent might be British. "Have you got the time, deary?"

I check my watch. "Yeah, it's one-o-eight."

I always give the precise time.

I consider it rude to do otherwise.

The old lady leans in close to look at my watch, a little too close for my comfort. And she's definitely drunk.

"Excuse me, lady!" I shout.

"Sorry, sorry," she says. "That wee device of yours, shows the time, does it?"

I roll my eyes like any good teenager.

"Yeah, obviously. It's a watch."

"Shows the year too?"

"The year?"

"Aye."

"No. It's one of those expensive ones."

"Bollocks," she curses.

"You don't know the year?" I ask.

"No, why, do you?"

"Of course."

I inform her of the year.

She looks surprised. "Forkballs! I best be going."

I'm genuinely curious now.

"You have somewhere to be?" I ask.

"Well, not so much that, no," she says. "You see, it's just I'm being followed by a very superficial, ignorant, and unweighing fellow. And I'd rather not be around when he pops by, if you know what I mean."

"Men are trouble," I tell her, thinking of my ex.

"You got that right, Freckles. But you can't kill them, yeah? Wish you could. Actually you can, forget I ever said that. Now, if you'll excuse me."

She looks around, as if it's only at this moment that she's realized she's on a moving subway train. "By the way, where in the bloody hell am I?" she asks.

"You're on the A train," I tell her.

"The A train? That's Lunar City, yeah?"

"Um, no, Brooklyn, actually."

This unfortunate news has truly upset her. "Brooklyn! Fork me! Of all the terrible places in the universe, of course I end up in Brooklyn."

"Could be worse," I tell her. "You could of ended up in Jersey."

She ponders this for a second before asking, "What's Jersey?"

"You know, lady, you're a little strange."

I get a finger wagged at me. "No, no, no. Hedgehogs are strange, deary. You ever seen one? I have. Just a stuffed one, though. In some history museum somewhere. They're like little hamsters with spikes. Can you believe that? Downright unnatural, if you ask me."

With that bit of cryptic wisdom, the woman continues down the train car, vanishing into the next.

A few moments later, the sliding doors between cars open again, only this time it's a man, and he's not nearly as whimsical or quirky as the old lady. He's dressed in black, with a strange dark vest over his hoodie. It looks like something a weightlifter might wear at the gym. His face is a shadowy scowl under his hood. All I can see of him is a triangular chin beard that's sharp as a knife.

He glances down at me with eyes blue and cold. He's caught me staring. I immediately look down at my feet, afraid to even breathe, all the while pretending the meeting of our eyes has never occurred, hoping that I can will him away, much like the monsters living in my closet as a child could be willed away simply by closing my eyes tightly enough.

But this man is no imaginary beast. And he certainly doesn't vanish. I hear his breathing. Time seems to have slowed.

My skin crawls.

Thankfully, I'm not the one he's after. As quickly as he came, he leaves, continuing down the train car and into the next. I let out a sigh of relief once he's gone. I will say this, though, that kooky old lady was sure right about one thing—he was indeed a very unpleasant fellow.

2

A few minutes later, I reach my destination. Coming up from the subway station, miraculously I even remember which building is my cousin Shira's. When she doesn't answer her buzzer, I use the key she gave me a few months ago to let myself into the building.

As to why she gave me a key, I'm not entirely sure. She's a bit of an odd duck. But we're close, and even though I told her that I didn't actually need a key to her place, that I doubted I could even find her place without her guiding me through the wilds of Brooklyn, she merely placed a hand on my shoulder, mustered her most sagely voice, and said that yes, one day I would need the key.

I suppose she wasn't wrong.

I head up the stairs of her building to her apartment. The inside of her place smells like cheap, apple-scented aerosol spray and weed. A few candles have blackened the paint where they've been left too close to the walls, creating these odd, impressionist shapes that are clearly going to cost that nutty girl her deposit. There's a note on the table, addressed to *whom it may concern*, which makes me wonder just how many keys she's been giving out lately. According to the note, she's in Prague for the next two weeks to visit her boyfriend.

Both these developments, Europe and mysterious boyfriend, are news to me. Probably to her parents too. But if you knew Shira, the suddenness of their arrival, and the fact that they are scribbled on the back of a takeout menu, would not surprise you.

At least she lives alone, so I have some privacy. And I do like her Brooklyn neighborhood. It's a collection of worn row houses, neat and orderly, most with simple stoops, filled at all hours with children playing and the grandparents who watch over them. There's a real community here, a vibrancy, something that is sorely lacking in the sterile, middle-class suburbs of America.

Don't get me wrong. Brooklyn has its own quirks. Juxtaposed against the row houses are districts of low-rise factory buildings. Some are still humming along with industry, but most have been converted to other uses as the neighborhood, for better or for worse, gentrifies. There's now everything from yoga studios to art galleries to boutique cafes, all sitting alongside dollar stores and international remittance shops.

Some of the old factories have even been transformed into fancy loft apartments. Shira's is one of them, though you'd never know it from the simple, beat-up exterior of the building. But I suppose that's part of the aesthetic. Shira says you have to pay extra for that.

Needing some fresh air, I throw my purse on Shira's sofa, leave her apartment, and head up the staircase to the roof, which, being an old factory, is no more than a large flat landing. There are graffiti tags everywhere and long ago some industrious resident dragged a filthy couch up the stairwell, leaving it out to weather the elements, something that it's done rather poorly.

I'd sit, but I'm pretty sure I'd catch an STI.

The rooftop does have one redeeming quality, however. Stretched out before me like a painting is the entirety of the Manhattan skyline, filling nearly all the western horizon. It's a city of glass and steel skyscrapers, of great stone and concrete towers, of buildings that sparkle in the afternoon light like quartz and crystal.

It truly is an enchanted metropolis, one that both grants and plunders dreams, often in equal measure.

I walk over to the edge of the roof. I climb up on the tiny brick ledge to look down five stories. It's a foolish thing to do, I know, but my body craves a hit of anxiety, a dose of fear, anything that can ebb the pain away from all my self-inflicted defeats this week. Even my parents tell me I'm too hard on myself, that I pursue too many things, from jujitsu, to crew, to debate team, to photography. But they don't understand. My dad is an urban planner, and my mom a lecturer and AI ethicist. They've already made a mark on the world, they've already succeeded. My future is much less certain.

Looking down works. The vertigo makes my stomach turn. An ill-timed gust of wind and I'd be gone. *Just like in my dreams,* I realize with a start. People might even think I did it on purpose. That bothers me a little. I may be glum today, but I'm certainly not suicidal.

Still, I can't look away from the sidewalk below.

"That there's a quick way to dusty death, Freckles."

I nearly jump out of my skin.

It's a miracle that I don't *actually* fall off the side of the damned building. I turn and see that the crazy old woman from the subway train is standing next to the battered couch. How is that possible? Did she follow me? She's still dressed in that frumpy quilted over-coat and the tacky flower-print pants from earlier.

I climb down off the ledge. "I thought I was alone up here," I tell her with a touch of embarrassment. "Do you live here? How did you get in the building?"

The woman holds up her hand. "I've a magic ring, yeah. Does tricks for me. Sometimes, anyway."

"You know, lady, I'll say it again. You really are nuts."

"Better to be a witty nut than a nutty wit," is all she says.

I wipe the brick dust from the ledge off my knees. "I don't know what that means. But really, why are you following me?"

"Ah, yes, about that. Well, I had a bit of trouble on the metro now that you mention it."

"You mean with that man who was following you?"

The old lady nods her head. "Aye, bit of a tosspot, that one."

"So, what happened?"

"We had a proper go at it."

"What? Like a fistfight?"

"Not quite. I blew his head off with Old Bessie."

"You what?"

"Stupid forkface was quick on the draw, though."

At first, I don't follow—it doesn't help that she's using some odd words, not all of which are even British, but then I see the wound under her overcoat.

I yell. "Oy! You've been shot!"

The woman collapses, falling toward the couch, missing it by a few inches, and ending up on her bottom.

I run to her.

She huffs and makes an introduction. "Careena J. Smith, at your service."

"Don't talk." I pull back the long coat only to find a wound unlike anything I've ever seen before, not that I've seen a lot of gun-shot wounds in my day—I don't really live in that part of Jersey. But this one is more like a fist-sized crater, black and charred, the edges of which glow red like rice paper burning into embers. I can't be sure, but I think it may be growing.

"What did this?" I ask.

She doesn't answer. She can't. First there are the whites of her eyes. Then she's gone completely. I panic.

"Hey, crazy lady! Don't pass out. My phone's downstairs. I'll be right back."

I turn for the stairwell door, which earlier I had propped open with a brick, but inexplicably there's a voice speaking from behind me—and it's not the old woman.

"Don't," the voice says. "You can't make any calls."

I scream. I jump. I clutch my chest. Turning, I'm faced with a slim woman, with handsome features, dark skin, and short, neatly cropped hair. She's not even three feet from me, but how she got up here on the roof all the sudden, I have no idea. The old lady and I were alone just a moment ago.

This new woman is only a little older than me and dressed in what I can best describe as a naval officer's uniform, dark blue with modern silver trim.

"Who the hell are you?" I ask reflexively. "And how do you people keep getting up here?"

The young officer has a kind but serious face. "That's not important right now. I'm a friend. We have to get Agent Smith somewhere safe."

I point to the old lady's wound. "She needs a hospital. I have to call an ambulance."

"They could be monitoring the hospitals."

"Who?"

"Whoever did this." The officer steps closer to the old lady Careena. "Can you pull back the coat? So I may see the wound?"

I do as asked, though I'm not entirely sure if I should be trusting either of these two strangers. Careena is completely out, slumped against that disgusting rooftop couch. Her breathing is faint.

"Damn," the officer whispers. "I've never seen mercenaries with this level of sophistication."

"Mercenaries? You mean, like, someone put a hit out on this old lady?"

The officer's expression is unironic. "Yes. And not just her. Several of our field agents. I don't know who they are, but we can't let them find her here."

I argue again, "She needs medical attention."

"Agreed, but there's nothing your hospitals will be able to do for her. Her QDD should have sent her back to us automatically. I can only assume their weapons used some sort of jammer that prevented the jump. Whoever attacked her knew what they were doing. And that scares me. Can you turn over her hand, so I may see her ring?"

I hesitate a moment, but again do as asked.

On the old lady's hand is a simple bronze ring.

"That's her QDD," the officer explains.

"She told me it was magic."

"Agent Smith is prone to hyperbole."

"You don't say."

"It appears undamaged," she tells me. "We may be in luck. By now it should have respun. I need you to take off the ring and put it on your finger."

At this point, I decide I have to put my foot down. "Look, soldier girl, I don't mind helping, but you seem a lot more qualified to do all this than me. To be honest, I'm not even supposed to be up here. Can't you do this?"

"No."

"No? Why not?"

"I can't touch her," the young officer says matter-of-factly.

I'm confused. "Why not?"

"I can't touch anything. I'm not actually here."

"That's ridiculous. This is a prank."

"It's not a prank."

Instinctively, I reach out. My hand passes through the young officer without resistance. If there are moments in life that completely alter how we understand the universe, that force us to question our assumptions of reality, well, as far as I'm concerned, such a moment has just whacked me upside the head.

"You're a ghost," I whisper.

"No. But she will be if you don't do exactly as I say."

I swallow hard. "All right. What do you need?"

"Take the ring and place it on your finger."

I do as told, first sliding off the ring before placing it on my finger. I can already tell it's going to be much too large. To be generous, the old woman didn't seem very concerned about her waistline. Yet the ring ends up fitting snugly. "This is no ordinary ring," I realize.

"No," the officer says. "Agent Smith calls her Hecate, but I find it wise not to personally identify with inanimate objects."

"Fair enough. What now?"

"We need to get her back to our facilities on Tegana. That's where I am now. Unfortunately, after these attacks, the entire planet has been placed on lockdown. The Defense Force is not allowing me to drop the tachyonic shields, even for a moment. Which means I can't bring back Smith directly here. I'm looking for alternatives. I just need a moment."

The young officer starts typing on a pad.

I'm trying to process what I've just been told. "Did you say planet? Like another planet?"

"I'm sorry to involve you in all this. I know it's a lot to take."

I'd really love to question her credibility, after all, this is insane— but the truth is she's a hologram and the old lady's kidney looks like the wrong end of a Cuban cigar. Sometimes in life you just have to roll with the punches. It also occurs to me that my parents are not as clueless as they often act. I mention this to the officer lady. "This is exactly the reason my mom tells me I'm not allowed to come to Brooklyn alone."

For a moment, I think I may have detected a smile.

"My name is Story Beckett," she offers.

"I'm Isabel."

"Yes, I know. Isabel Tzofiya Mendelssohn, seventeen years old, of Oradell, New Jersey."

I'm shocked.

"How the hell do you know all that?"

"A background check. I had to be sure I could trust you."

"You might want to check it again," I tell her. "I've not been very trustworthy lately."

"That's not what I've seen so far, Miss Mendelssohn."

I suppose I appreciate the vote of confidence. "Please, call me Isabel."

"Very well. But now I must warn you, Isabel. It's only going to get stranger from here. Believe me, however, saving Agent Smith is very important. She may be our last line of defense against very dark forces to come."

I give a forced laugh. "If this kooky lady is supposed to protect anybody from anything, I think you're screwed."

"She'll grow on you, I promise. All right, I found the alternative I was looking for. Take Agent Smith's hand. You'll be traveling together. Until you've had some practice with the QDD, it's best if you're in physical contact."

I take the old woman's hand. "Now what?"

"The QDD isn't magic, but it may seem so to you."

"I watch a lot of sci-fi with my dad," I tell her. "Don't worry about me."

Story nods. "Good. Then this will be easy. The ring can read your thoughts. To make it work, you simply think of the place you would like to go, and it will take you there."

"All right. So where do I want to go?"

She looks down at her pad. "Room 1701 aboard the *NMS Stellar Pearl*. It's a luxury cruise liner just a few days out from Tegana. They'll have the facilities aboard to stabilize Agent Smith until she's home with us."

For a moment, I can't bring myself to believe what's happening. Spaceships and other worlds? Could they all really be out there? Imagine the look on my dad's face, the Star Trek nerd that he is, when I tell him where I spent my day. *Oh, you know, dad, just another Saturday. On a fricken starship!*

It occurs to me that I'm taking everything I'm told rather calmly. This is likely just my mind choosing to ignore the actual gravity of my situation. At some point, all of this is going to catch up with me. Shake a can of soda and it seems fine. Until it's opened. That's me right now. And I'm not looking forward to the moment when my lid gets popped.

"What about you?" I ask.

"I'll be there when you arrive. I'll still be a projection, though. So you'll need to use the room's callbox to ring a medical team. But don't worry, I'll walk you through it. Oh, and one more thing. Reach into Agent Smith's pocket and take out her pistol. She'd kill me if the medics confiscated Old Bessie."

I reach into one of the large overcoat pockets and find an antique-looking derringer pistol, small enough to fit in the palm of my hand, probably capable of only a single shot. I place it in the pocket of my own autumn jacket. "Anything else?"

"Yes. It's not enough to tell the QDD where you want to go. You'll also need to tell it *when* you want to go."

"Well, now, I guess."

Story gives me a very professional smile.

"No, I mean to which year," she says.

My jaw drops. "What? You're kidding, right?"

"I'm afraid not."

"This whole time I thought you two were aliens."

"No, Isabel. We're from the future."

That does it.

That really does it.

This is the last time I'm ever visiting Brooklyn.

"All right," I say. "So *when* do I want to go?"

"That part is easy. Just tell the QDD you want to return to the present."

I look around. "Isn't this the present?"

"Technically, no," she explains. "You're just perceiving it that way. The real present, what we call the cosmological present, has already come and gone for you. Think of this now like a frame in a movie that's already passed. The audience is off watching the rest of the movie, but we're here in the backroom making edits. Those edits, however, will affect the outcome of the movie later. Anyway, that's all an oversimplification, and it's not important. Just think of it as the ring's present."

"All right, but I feel awful silly talking to a ring."

"Don't talk. Just think."

I nod. I close my eyes and focus on the destination this young officer from the future has given me. I imagine a ship in a present that is not my own. At first, nothing happens.

But then there's a tinge of confirmation coming from the ring, as if it has somehow invaded my thoughts. The sensation is not unlike the dialog box on a computer, wishing to confirm whether I really want to delete a selected file. Only this dialog box is inside my mind.

Yes, I tell the ring.

Yes, I want to go to the present.

And like that, without the fancy swirl of effects one would expect, I, Isabel Tzofiya Mendelssohn, and the old woman, Careena J. Smith, vanish from the Brooklyn rooftop. Silence returns to the world. A few moments later—an unusually strong gust of wind passes by.

3

All at once the daylight of Brooklyn is gone. What had seemed like a surreal sequence of impossible events only moments earlier is now all too real. I'm no longer afforded the luxury of denial. Impossibly, I'm somewhere else—a large room darkened by heavy shadows. Everything the soldier girl told me was true.

And yet, something is wrong.

Careena is still beside me, sprawled on the ground, unresponsive and dying. Looking around, though, we're not in a cabin aboard a cruise ship. The lighting is too dim and industrial. We're in a cargo bay, some sort of massive hangar with high ceilings and rows upon rows of heavy shipping containers stacked floor to ceiling.

I place my hand on the steel flooring. It pulsates. Some great engine is beneath us. A warp engine? Like in my dad's favorite science fiction shows? Or something else perhaps, something I could never come to understand? Does it truly mean that we're in space? In the future?

I look up. Each of the shipping containers is stenciled with the name *STELLAR PEARL*. So, we're on the right ship. I'm not sure how much that comforts me. To make matters worse, Story Beckett, my holographic aid, is nowhere to be found. Did I do something wrong? What should I do now?

"Hello?" I call out, though I'm afraid to use too loud a voice.

Someone must have still heard me. A voice calls back from further down the rows of containers. "You there! This area is off limits to passengers."

I call back. "I'm sorry, but my friend, she's hurt."

The man runs over to us. "Hurt, you say? I'll have the medics down here immediately."

He speaks into his sleeve, requesting a doctor.

Having arrived so abruptly from the outdoor rooftop and now finding myself in this darkened cargo bay, it takes my eyes a moment to adjust. At first, all I can see of this man next to me is his outline; he's short, much shorter than me, but stocky in a strange way. He's in a uniform, though it's different to the one Story wore. Hers was blue and silver. His is crimson and grey. But that's not the only thing about him that's different. As he reaches down to pull back Careena's overcoat, my eyes have adjusted enough to see his hands.

My mouth slowly drops open.

His skin is the color of shale and has the rough texture of oak bark. On each of his hands are only four digits, two in the middle, with an opposable thumb on either side.

The alien man is focused on Careena's injury. "I don't know what could have caused an injury like this here. What happened, miss?"

I can only whisper the words. "I'm not sure." I'm instead trying to summon the strength to look up, to see this man's face. When I finally do, I see a brow like a rocky ledge shadowing two all-black eyes. A dull ivory horn protrudes downward from his chin.

I should be terrified, but there's a gentleness in his eyes, a caring nature to his demeanor.

"Miss, you're staring," he says.

I catch myself. "Sorry... I'm sorry. Will she be all right?"

"I hope so. I believe this to be a nanite wound. I've never seen such a thing myself, but Dr. Heinlein was a medic during the Second Khelt War. She's dealt with every manner of injury you can think of. If anyone can help your friend, it's her."

The medics arrive only a moment later. They're all human as far as I can tell. One of them places a small metallic bead on the floor. The bead melts into silver liquid and expands under Careena like a rectangular pool of water. All at once it hardens into a cloth material with chrome handles. The truly astonishing part happens next—the silver cloth levitates upward, with Careena on it. A medic takes the rear handle and hurriedly pushes the floating stretcher out of the cargo bay.

"They're taking her to sick bay," the alien man tells me.

"I should go with her."

"You'll see your friend soon, miss. My name is Lieutenant Chimat. I must tell you, an injury of this kind, and your access to this area, is a most strange occurrence. The captain will have a few questions for you."

I go cold.

"Let's start with your room number," Lieutenant Chimat says.

I stammer. I don't know what to say.

"You do have a room aboard the ship, correct, miss?"

"Uh…"

"Miss?"

"1701," I say.

It's the room Story gave me. It's worth a shot.

He pulls a black card, not unlike a credit card, from his jacket pocket. He holds it out to me. "I just need to verify that."

I stare at it dumbly.

"Put your thumb on the scanner, please," he says.

All at once I go from cold to sweating. My stomach is churning knots. I know that once I place my thumb on the card, the jig is up —they'll discover I'm a stowaway.

And who knows what alien space people from the future do to stowaways. Toss them out of the airlock into a supernova? Feed them to cosmic alligators with three heads? I've seen enough movies with my dad to know that the possibilities are really quite endless.

"The thumb, miss."

I have no choice. I place my thumb on the black scanning card and ready myself for alarm klaxons and heavily armed security guards with futuristic rifles to hurl me to the floor. But nothing happens.

Lieutenant Chimat looks at the results on the card, though as far as I can see, it's still a matte black card signifying nothing.

"Ms. Isabel Overhill from Cawdor III," he says. "Room 1701. Premium package, paid in full. Sharing with your aunt, a Ms. Careena Overhill. That was her, I take it?"

I let out the biggest sigh of relief in my entire goddamn life. "Yes! Yes, it was. Oh, my poor aunt. My poor, poor aunt. How could something so terrible happen to such a nice lady? I mean, she's not, like, that nice —super annoying actually, and a bit foul-mouthed. But having her guts turned into nano-vomit stuff? I mean, no, that's not, like..."

I realize he's staring at me.

If he's capable of facial expressions, I certainly can't read this one.

"Follow me," is all he says.

I come to discover that the *Stellar Pearl* is a beautiful ship— long, slick, and modern, with white and grey paneling running down long, wide halls occasionally punctuated with windows peering out into space.

But it's not until I'm led through the central atrium that I truly appreciate this marvel of future design. A single, oval-shaped glass dome dominates the vessel's topside, protecting a wide arcade of shops and cafés. This boulevard must be nearly a quarter-mile long, and is accentuated by statues, trees, small plazas with outdoor seating, and fountains. I could just as well be in Paris and not the central artery of a space-faring cruise liner.

Though we head in the opposite direction, with a quick glance back, I see that the boulevard ends behind us in a large, circular park, complete with English-styled gardens—it's as if a piece of Mother Nature has been scooped up from some idyllic planet and lovingly placed inside this massive floating terrarium.

We leave the atrium and Chimat leads me to the bow, where the bridge is located on a triangular disk protruding ever so slightly ahead of the rest of the ship. I imagine if I could see the *Stellar Pearl* from some distance, it might resemble a hammer-head shark navigating through the currents of space.

There's a checkpoint before entering the command portion of the ship and I'm scanned for weapons, which causes another moment of anxiety as I remember that I still have Careena's tiny gun, Old Bessie, tucked away in my jacket pocket. Yet I pass undetected. Perhaps the gun is so rudimentary and antiquated that modern scanners simply pass right over it. Perhaps that's why Careena uses it.

I'm asked to sit in a small waiting room while Chimat briefs the captain. It does not escape my attention that a guard is placed at the room's exit. He looks to be in his mid-twenties, which, really, summarizes just about everyone I've seen aboard so far. Not a lot of old fogies in the future, apparently.

At least there's a window here. Stars are passing by outside, some more quickly than others, each a solar system, each home to their own worlds, their own planets, each holding the possibility of life. I can conjecture that some of those worlds have been colonized by now. But surely there are others still awaiting discovery. And, impossibly, one must be Earth.

Must be home.

The waiting turns out to be terrible for my nerves. I'm not sure if it's my hangover or my anxiety, but I want to wretch. My hands tremble and I can't keep my knees from shaking. I'm going to be found out, of that I have no doubts.

What then? What will these people think of me? I'll be like a Neanderthal, thawed from ice, more a curiosity of science than a sentient being. I can't even fathom half of what I've seen so far in this brave new world in which I've found myself.

My eyes well up.

It's everything I can do not to cry.

And then there's a comforting voice beside me.

"You're doing great, Isabel."

It's Story Beckett.

She's standing beside me, though I know she's not really here.

"Story, where the fricken hell have you been?"

"I apologize. There's something wrong with the QDD's uplink. It took me a moment to find you again."

"I did exactly what you said."

"I know. The ring's processor must have been damaged when Agent Smith was attacked. There could be some minor quirks until we have it looked at on Tegana. We're still three days out. I've already checked on Smith. It looks like she's going to pull through. So, for now, our best course of action is to keep a low profile."

I almost can't help but laugh. "A low profile? Really? Your buddy Careena was shot with some sort of gun that little rock dude has never even seen before. And I probably don't have to tell you that I stand out like a Victorian washerwoman here. You do realize I'm sitting here waiting to talk to the captain, right? I'm sure the captain of a fancy ship like this isn't a complete idiot."

"I know you're stressed, Isabel, but you can do this."

Again come the tears. "I really can't."

"You can."

I plead. "Can't you speak to them? You're with the military, right? I mean, that's a military uniform, right? You have to."

"I'm military, yes, but it's more complicated than that. They are a different federation. Think of them like France and me like Canada. I really have no standing with them. In fact..."

"In fact what?"

Story's lips tighten. "It would be something of a diplomatic situation were they to know that I was here, seeing how I've hacked their systems to give you and Agent Smith a room."

"What do you mean, *knew you were here*? I know you're a hologram, but there are cameras all over the place. And the guard is right there at the door." I wave to the guard to make my point. He's rather handsome now that I look at him again. Unfortunately, he pretends not to see me. Which is not the most unexpected reaction when it comes to me and boys.

Story explains. "The projection doesn't work that way. The ring isn't projecting my image in front of you for you to see. It's projecting a signal directly into your brain. This conversation is happening entirely in your head. You're the only person here who can see me."

I'm horrified. Absolutely mortified. Now I understand why the cute guard is ignoring me. *Because he thinks I'm fricken nuts!* "So you're saying I look like a crazy lady talking to myself! Oh babe, that's going to make for a great first impression with the captain, believe me."

"No, no, don't worry," she says. "You're not talking to yourself. Your responses to me are also being generated in your mind by the ring. As far as the guard can tell, you're just minding your own business. You'll get the hang of it soon. We call it SI, *sensory intervention*. It's simply a matter of convenience, nothing more. If you take a moment to notice your attention, you'll see it's quite easy to distinguish what is you in the real world, like when you just waved, and what is taking place only with SI, like this conversation."

"The ring does all this?"

"Yes. It acts like a receiver for my signal. But the QDD serves many other functions as well. It also acts like a translator. For example, I'm actually speaking Ugandan Acholi. And earlier Lieutenant Chimat was not speaking English to you either. In reality, he can't even produce the correct sounds."

"What was he speaking then?"

"One of the languages of Thane, his homeworld. We call all of them Thanish, but I'm sure they're just as varied as the languages of Earth. But you perceived English. And even his lips matched, as do mine, which is one of the conveniences of SI, replacing what you're really seeing with something... less awkward. Otherwise, we'd look dubbed, which is how it was in my parent's time."

Again, I'm somewhat appalled. "And you people are okay with that? With machines that invade your brain and trick you into hearing and seeing things that aren't even there?"

"I understand how it might seem a little strange to you, but for us it's second nature. Translators are very common tech. I imagine nearly everyone on this ship is using one. And there are safety precautions to prevent abuses, but the truth is all technology, no matter how beneficial, carries both risks and moral implications. I assure you, however, this technology is safer than the radio waves you're using back home."

Back home.

How I wish I was there now.

"So where are we?" I ask. "What year is it?"

The ebony skinned officer takes a deep breath. "Are you sure you're ready for that?"

"No, but tell me anyway."

"Isabel, it's 3021."

"Oy vey," I whisper.

Lieutenant Chimat returns to inform me that the captain is ready to see me now. I understand, without being told, that the rabbit hole only gets deeper from here.

Captain Wilhelmine Gernsback is a serious-looking woman with straight blonde hair, chiseled features, and an air of authority. She wears the same crimson and grey uniform as Lieutenant Chimat, who has left us in privacy here in the captain's ready room. With a wave of her hand, the captain instructs me to take a seat across from her handsome oak desk. I hardly even notice the gesture.

I'm still stunned that I'm a thousand years in the fricken future.

"Ms. Overhill, I appreciate your coming to see me."

If I were brave and clever, like a hero in a Hollywood action movie, I'd quip—*I wasn't aware that I had a choice, captain*. But in reality, I'm too intimidated by this woman to do anything other than nod meekly and take my seat.

At least Story is with me, standing beside me, visible to no one but myself, holding a thin tablet in her hand. The young officer is without a doubt the most calm and composed person I've ever met. It's a little annoying, actually. I'm realizing a pattern. Everything in the future is annoying.

"First things first," Captain Gernsback begins as I sit. "I'm told your aunt is quite the fighter. She'll pull through, you needn't worry."

"Oh, thank goodness," I say.

"Now obviously we have some questions."

"Of course."

"Do you know how your aunt received her wound?"

Story has promised to coach me through the entire meeting, though until I understand this mysterious SI better, I'm not supposed to look up at her, lest I make a mistake distinguishing the real from the purely mental and give away our little charade.

I wait for my prompt from Story, but she seems distracted by her pad. Her fingers are moving with amazing speed and precision. What she's typing I have no idea. If she's smart, it's my obituary.

"Tell her you don't know," she instructs me, without ever looking up from her pad.

That's it? That's how I'm going to fool this scary captain lady?

I give it a shot. "I'm sorry. I don't know."

"Are you aware of what manner of wound it was?"

"No, ma'am, I don't know that either."

"Weaponized nanites," the captain informs me. "Which is very troubling. As you probably know, offensive nanites were outlawed by the Bishkek Convention centuries ago. Our natural immune system is useless against such an enemy. These microscopic robots break apart the chemical bonds in organic cells to power themselves until a person is turned into ash, quite literally, from the inside out. Normally it happens in a matter of minutes. And yet, I'm told your aunt's wound never grew beyond the size of a fist."

"Lucky, I guess." That part was unprompted, but Story doesn't seem to mind. Or notice. She's still banging away on her pad.

"Oh, it wasn't luck, Ms. Overhill," the captain says. "Your aunt has previously been inoculated with a military grade nanite defense system of her own. The little bastards fought it out, creating quite a show, I'm sure. Dr. Heinlein tells me we got to her just in time. Your aunt's defensive nanites would have eventually been overwhelmed. The fact remains, her own nanites, while not strictly illegal for therapeutic uses, are highly regulated outside of medical quarantine. They are dangerous and, if hijacked, difficult to defend against. She should never have been allowed aboard a civilian passenger ship with this type of military technology in her blood. So I'm a little curious how she got passed our sensors at boarding. But I supposed you don't know anything about that either?"

"No, ma'am. I'm sorry."

The captain looks down at her own thin tablet. Everyone's got a fricken tablet but me. "It says here you two are Cawdorian. You boarded six weeks ago at Cawdor III. Is that correct?"

Story looks up from whatever she's doing. "Tell her yes."

"Yes, ma'am."

"Not that it's any of my business, but may I ask, what is the nature of your visit to Tegana? I see you have no onward ticket. Tegan immigration is notoriously strict about such things."

Story coaches me on what to say. I repeat verbatim, "We have invitation visas from the Tegan Ministry of Science. My aunt is the mandate's foremost expert on earthworms and, as you may have seen in the news, Tegana is currently experiencing a massive die off. Most people don't realize just how important worms are for the ecosystem."

"This is the cargo you have in the hold? The manifest says *Lumbricus rubellus*, nine hundred million. *Eisenia fetida*, sixteen million. Those are worms, I take it?"

I continue my repetition, even though worms creep me the hell out and this is obviously the worst cover story ever. "Yes, ma'am. We went down there because my aunt wanted to check the stasis settings. Then there was a bright flash and my aunt was wounded. That's when your officer found us."

"You were not supposed to access the cargo bay without an escort, Ms. Overhill. That was clearly spelled out when you boarded."

"I understand. My aunt can be... eccentric."

"There's a reason we have these rules."

"I've learned that. May I ask what happens now?"

"Well, you have admitted to entering the cargo bay without permission. For that, I will give you a strong verbal warning. Otherwise, I see no evidence you've done anything more serious, despite all the questions I still have. Lieutenant Chimat believes one of the other cargo containers must have been booby trapped. Your aunt must have triggered it by accident. It's a logical theory, I suppose, as we do occasionally have issues with smugglers. Anyway, it seems futile to hold you any longer. Your aunt's nanites are being quarantined and destroyed, but you should be able to visit her now. You're free to go."

I let out a long, thankful breath. "Thank you, ma'am."

Captain Gernsback lifts her pad. "Oh, before you go, a question. I see here a receipt in the records. You had dinner last night on the arcade. Butternut squash ravioli at Tellers Lounge. I've been meaning to check it out. How was it?"

Story's chin jerks up. "She's trying to trick you. That's not what I entered in their system. Tell her pizza. At Harich Pizzeria."

"We had pizza, actually, ma'am. At Harich Pizzeria"

"Ah, yes, so you did." I notice now that Gernsback has a slender stylus in her hand, something like a pen, I really don't know. She clicks it twice, almost absentmindedly. "And last question before I let you go. What color is the Cawdorian sun?"

I await my answer from my coach. But no answer comes. I wait another second, but still nothing. I have no choice but to turn my head and look.

Story Beckett is gone.

My holographic savior has vanished.

"You must know the color of your own sun, Ms. Overhill."

It's that damned pen. It has to be.

The charade is up.

Mercifully, Captain Gernsback isn't the sort for games, and she doesn't make me squirm in my chair too long. Instead, she looks at me quite seriously. "Your friend, whoever it is, can't help, Ms. Overhill. I assume they are with the Tegan Defense Force? Or dare I guess, the Tegan Ministry of Temporal Affairs? I can think of several intelligence agencies from several governments that could hack my computers, but there's only one that could get you aboard my ship mid-flight undetected. It's the reason the whole universe loves to hate the Tegans. Though, I'm betting you probably don't know about that."

"You know who I am?" I ask.

"Not exactly, but I can venture a guess. We're sort of slaves to technology these days. Take the universal translator, for example. Why study a foreign language when you can understand every language as clearly as your own? And yet, there's so much subtlety in the way languages are spoken. It's what makes them such beautiful things. We've lost our ability to appreciate that, I feel."

"You could always turn it off."

Gernsback smiles at me. "I like you, Ms. Overhill. I really do. Yes, I could turn it off, but I doubt you speak Flemish, my mother tongue. And I don't speak English, so we'd be at something of an impasse. You are speaking English, am I correct?"

"Yes, ma'am."

She looks again at her pad. "Ah, yes, you are. And how interesting. The language algorithm says you're speaking an Earth-based dialect of English. We don't get many Earthers this side of the galaxy. Let's see, it also says with 98 percent certainty that you're speaking a North American dialect. I assume that's a continent? And if we trust this program, there's a 64 percent chance you're using an Eastern Seaboard Mid-Atlantic United States dialect dated between 2000 and 2040. My, my... If that's true, it would make you a very, *very* long way from home, Ms. Overhill."

"It's not what you think."

She puts down the pad. "Believe me, you don't want to know what I think. The Tegans are not to be trusted. I disrupted your friend's signal to give you that bit of warning in private. They almost succeeded in this little ruse. I have to give them credit. They have some of the best hackers in the mandate. Did you know they inserted footage of you and your aunt going all the way back to your arrival on Cawdor III? Amazing, really. But there's one base they couldn't quite cover."

I put a hand to my lips. "My accent."

That stupid Jersey accent.

"No, it wasn't that," she says. "As I told you, we're slaves to technology. A normal investigation would rely on the security footage and your shopping receipts, all of which your chaperon manipulated expertly. But sometimes I enjoy reading those Old Earth detective novels, you know, where they have to look for clues the old-fashioned way. So in that spirit, I had Lieutenant Chimat take a peek in your room, only a minor violation of our privacy policy. And imagine his surprise when he found no luggage, no clothes. Nothing. Not even a toothbrush. Which tells me you were never passengers aboard this ship."

I'm like a deer in the headlights.

I don't know what to say.

She then gives me some advice. "Whatever you've gotten yourself wrapped up in, Ms. Overhill, I suggest you exit while you still can."

"I'm not sure I have much of a choice at the moment," I admit.

She nods. "You may be right about that. I'm not sure if you're aware of the dynamics of the technology that brought you here, but it was engineered by a man on Tegana named Jonathan Baker. He founded the Ministry of Temporal Affairs not long afterward. He could have shared this new wonder with the world. He could have changed humanity. But instead he and his disciples deemed it unfit for anyone but themselves. They treat us like school children who must be kept from the box of matches."

"They told me it was dangerous."

She laughs. "Why, of course it's dangerous. What technology isn't? But we can harness the power of the atom without being destined to use it as a bomb, can't we? And we're not asking for the power to alter time. But just as the atom can do more than make a weapon, their tachyon technology can do more than take one back in time. It can move matter across the universe in the blink of an eye. As a ship's captain, perhaps I should be more concerned about my job security, but just think what that could mean for humanity. We've conquered the speed of light with our ships, but there are still limits. Travel time between worlds, just in this mandate alone, takes weeks. And Earth? Earth is a place so far away that few of us out here feel any connection to it at all. But the Tegans refuse our pleas. Their secrets could save lives, could reconnect our species in ways that we haven't experienced since our days on Old Earth. But they turn a blind eye to us."

"So no one else can take me home then?"

"I'm afraid not," she tells me. "Officially there's a non-proliferation treaty, though I'm sure some governments secretly dabble here and there in tachyon manipulation. If you have deep pockets, and I mean very deep, you could try the black market, but good luck there. They use vests for the jumps, which don't hold a candle to what the Tegans have. With the black market, it's fly by night. You're just as likely to end up in the belly of a Triceratops as you are to hit the year you're aiming for."

What she seems to be telling me is that, until all of this is over, I'm attached at the hip to Careena. Great.

"So now that you know," I ask her. "What do you intend to do?"

The captain sizes me up. "Nothing."

"Nothing?"

"Look, Ms. Overhill. I'm not your enemy here. To anyone who might ask, your story checks out. On paper at least. I'm inclined to sweep the matter under the rug. And not because I enjoy any of this, but what's the alternative? Quarantine the ship because of possible nanite contamination? Not so good for our reputation, as you could imagine. Lieutenant Chimat and Dr. Heinlein already want to tear the *Stellar Pearl* apart to find the weapon that injured your friend. But you and I both know that blast didn't originate here. So I'm left with the option of keeping quiet or starting a diplomatic incident with one of our neighbors. Count yourself lucky that I'm choosing the former."

I'm speechless. I thank her and rise from my chair. But I only get halfway to the door before I stop. Something bothers me, something I can't put my finger on.

I turn back to her. "Pardon me, Captain, but you don't strike me as the type of woman who takes the easy road out. In fact, from everything you've just told me, I would think you'd love to stick an incident in the eye of Tegana. Why are you really letting me go?"

"You think I'm tricking you?"

"I don't really know."

She leans back in her chair. "It's no trick. I feel for you, in fact. But that's not why I'm letting you go either. You see, when I was about your age, I was conscripted as an assault trooper in the Second Khelt War. That probably doesn't mean anything to you, but just know that it was the worst war in the history of all wars. Bad enough that we had to draft girls your age. And we weren't ready for it. Humanity had grown soft, even in space. For too many centuries, we'd relied on drones and robots to do our dirty work for us. And what good were they against the Khelts, who were so technologically superior that they could turn our own automated weapons against us with a snap of their fingers? So we had to fight. The old-fashioned way. And we had to die, the old-fashioned way. I can't tell you how many friends I lost. Which is another reason so much of the universe hates the Tegans. They had their tachyon technology even back then. They could have ended that war before it ever started, could have prevented us from having to send children to the front lines. Yet, even faced with the threat of human extinction, the Tegans refused to violate their prime directive. They've taken an oath to protect the timeline, to never alter it. They're fanatical about it. Like religious zealots. They think they've inherited the keys to eternity. But I want to know, just who made them the damned gods of time?"

"So they didn't fight," I venture.

"Oh, no, they fought. But only with weapons and ships and soldiers and blood. And I can't say that they didn't sacrifice every bit as much as the rest of us during that war. Perhaps more so. I've always had this suspicion that they felt a need to atone for what was so clearly their sin. And so they volunteered for the front lines without hesitation."

"I don't understand what this has to do with me," I tell her honestly.

"During a massive retreat sometime during the middle of that war, my company was cut off from our evacuation point. We'd been tricked and funneled into a trap, a kill zone, just waiting to be bombed into oblivion by faceless enemies up in the heavens. We should have died. I should have died. It's not a moment you ever forget. One of the last support ships remaining in orbit was a Tegan destroyer. They were ordered to retreat, to leave us behind, and with good reason. They were packed to the rafters with rescued colonists, including many children. They needed to get out of there. They were just waiting for three of their fighters to return from the surface to give them cover. And then the most brazen thing happened. On their way back, one of those fighters broke formation for exactly three minutes and twenty-four seconds. The pilot came in fast on our position and downed the bombers sent to finish us off. It was reckless, it was against orders, but it gave us the opening we needed to escape."

Gernsback bites her lip in reflection. "You better believe that I made it my mission in life to find out who that pilot was and thank them. It's part of our culture on New Mahshad. We repay our debts. I'd say it's as close to a religion as you'll find with us. But the war was too hectic, so I had to wait. After the war concluded, I went to Tegana to repay my gratitude to this pilot. There's a bar I heard about where all the pilots meet to trade stories. I started my search there. Like I told you, I'm something of a detective. I found out my pilot's name and I went to search the records. Unfortunately, they'd been killed in a training accident during the final days of the war. Tragic really. I never found out the exact details, but I was heartbroken nonetheless."

I'm still unsure why she's volunteered this story.

"I lied to you earlier, Ms. Overhill. I told you I knew your story was a sham because I checked your quarters. The truth is, I knew you and your friend were Tegan agents the moment the incident was brought to my attention. I knew because the pilot who saved my life all those years ago on Verdun IV is now laying on a bed in my sick bay."

"Careena..." I whisper.

"It would seem she hadn't died in a mysterious crash after all," the captain says. "That was only the cover story they created for her. The truth is that she'd been recruited—as a damned temporal spook. Well, good for her, I suppose. Ironically, it appears, after all these years, the universe has finally offered me my chance to repay my debt. I'm grateful for that. So go tend to your friend, but don't thank me."

"Why not?"

The captain gives me the honest truth. "Because I think you'll see soon enough, Ms. Overhill, that all I'm doing is sending you back into the lion's den."

5

A thousand years into the future and little about hospital rooms has changed. They are still white and sterile, a sort of purgatory where matters of life and death are decided by invisible courts, by juries that ignore evidence and pass judgment on whim and fancy alone. My grandfather died in a room like this one—powerless against the humiliation of an aging mind, helpless against the ravages of time.

I'm lost in those thoughts when Careena finally wakes. How long I've been sitting by her bedside, I'm not sure. But I felt someone should.

The old woman's voice cracks. "By the pricking of my thumbs, what the bloody hell are you doing in the future, Freckles?"

I squeeze her hand and smile. "Someone had to look after you."

"Hah! Ain't that the truth." She looks around. "Where the fork are we, anyway?"

"On a ship. Called the *Stellar Pearl*."

"That stupid cruise liner they're always advertising? I take it we're on our way to Tegana then?"

"I think so."

"Quite the forking mess this is going to be."

"I think it already is, to be honest."

Careena smiles warmly back at me. It's what I take to be a rare moment of honest emotion from the old lady. "Hand me that glass of water, won't you? I take it Beckett had a hand in getting you here?"

"She did," I say as I hand her the glass.

"You know, she's normally a proper stickler for the rules. A real pain in my arse. So believe me when I tell you, some serious poppycock has transpired if Beckett is the one breaking the rules now. Where is that tart, anyway?"

"The captain blocked her out somehow."

"Brilliant. Well, it's her own bloody fault for putting us on a Mahshadi ship. The Mahshadi are wankers, every last one of them. You spend some time on this ship, you'll see what I mean." She tries to get up from her bed, but then groans in terrible pain. "What is this injustice! They can't even treat a simple wound?"

I try to explain. "The nurse told me they have to treat you with more conventional methods until Dr. Heinlein determines it's safe to turn off the quarantine field. They're worried about stray nanites. Apparently, those could hijack more advanced forms of treatment, or something like that. Maybe even make copies of themselves. I don't really understand any of it."

"I see. And how are you holding up, deary?"

It's a good question. "Well, this morning I thought the world literally ended I didn't get into a fancy lab program for next month. That all seems a bit trite now."

"And I suppose you have some questions."

"You could say that," I tell her.

"Well, don't hold them in, deary. You might explode. Ask away."

"Where are we?"

She takes a sip of water.

"That's an easy one. We're in what they call the Outer Colonies, though like the Wild West, it's a bit of an outdated term. This hasn't been the proper frontier for some centuries now. But if you want to know the specifics, we're in the Ghent Mandate of the Sagittarius Arm of the Milky Way Galaxy, which likely doesn't mean much to you, but just know that it's really forking far. Tegana is about 11,664 light-years from Earth if I remember correctly."

"So it's true what Captain Gernsback told me, these ships can travel faster than light?"

"Technically, no," she says. "But technically we can't travel back in time either, yet as you may have noticed, we have a way of playing fast and loose with the laws of the universe. Hah! Fork physics. But imagine space as a tightly stretched band of cloth. If you could loosen the tension between two points, those points would appear closer together, even though the amount of cloth has never changed. Assuming you can prevent your ship from shrinking along with the cloth, you'd have shortened the distance considerably."

"So how far away is home in one of these ships?"

She takes a thoughtful breath. "You must understand, there's only so much wiggle room to play with before you start ripping the cloth."

"How far?" I press.

"Aboard the fastest ships? And I mean the fastest. Fifty-four years, give or take. But most ships would take closer to seventy or eighty."

My eyes widen in shock.

She continues. "The only realistic way to make the journey is in suspended animation, sort of like freezing yourself. Not many do it. You'd be younger than your grandchildren by the time you arrived, and any skills you had would be obsolete. If I'm honest, I'd wager you're one of only a handful of souls in this entire mandate who has ever seen Earth."

"But you and I got here in a matter of seconds."

"We did indeed."

"So that's why no one here seems to like you."

Careena laughs. "Hah! And yet they're all on this fancy bucket of bolts just so they can holiday on beautiful Tegana. I told you they were wankers."

I push her.

"It's more than that."

"I suppose it is," she admits. "They're upset that we didn't use our tachyon technology during the war. I don't blame them, I suppose. But they don't understand how it works. The truth is, there wasn't much we could do, even if we wanted to. First, you have to understand how we cheat the physics. The amount of matter and energy in the universe is constant. And it's perfectly balanced. Sending you back in time would be like adding that final straw to the poor camel's back. Or more precisely, the Gosset-polytope dimensional membrane that we sit on would fold up into some new configuration, which not only would fundamentally alter all of the current laws of physics, it would most probably annihilate all matter as we know it."

"So how do you do what you do?" I ask.

"There was a man on Tegana named Jonathan Baker. He discovered that every particle has a bond with itself in the past. He realized he could use that bond like a road map, to find where a particular particle was at any point in history. You see, since nothing is ever created or destroyed, every particle that makes me up right now also existed in your time. Back then, of course, those particles and energies were scattered all over the place, maybe still inside stars or in different forms, who knows. But they were there. And each one has a unique fingerprint. So with his road map, a tachyon-template we call it, Baker could sort of tug on them from here, like puppets on a string. He could literally change the past."

"That's remarkable."

"Indeed. At first, he could only affect changes on an atomic scale, like moving a single atom around. But eventually he was able to pull together entire collections of matter and energy in the past and hold them in place for a few hours. It wasn't long after that that he was able to use an entire person as a template, pulling all the same particles that make them up in the present together at some point in the past. So that's how we jump back in time. We basically hold matter and energy already existing in the past together for the duration of the jump, in a shape and form that is, for all intents and purposes, me."

"Like a temporal golem," I say, finding the concept odd.

"Well, I never looked at it quite that way," she admits. "But it's all the same matter and energy that will eventually make me up anyway. So I prefer to think of it as really me. I mean, are you the same person as yesterday's you? I should think so."

That brings up another question I wanted to ask. "Story told me there's only one present."

"Aye, the cosmological present. When we jump back in time, we don't actually go anywhere. We're still here, but we're untethered from this dimensional membrane. We're placed in a higher dimensional plane, a sort of holding dimension, which is how the tachyon-template is created, how the strings are pulled. A consequence of that is that from the frame of reference of the present, you can't see us here during the duration of the jump. Nor do we have any awareness of time passing here in the present. But time does pass. An hour spent there in the field is an hour that is also passing here."

"And you remember everything when you come back?"

She nods. "Once the bond is created it becomes a two-way street. We can tug on it from our end to make changes, but the other end tugs back too. Which I'm reminded of every time I come home with a forking bullet wound."

"And what happens to your past self?" I ask. "When you come back? You just vanish?"

"In a way," she says. "For the duration of the jump, the particles in the past are being artificially held together, but they're always fighting against it. They want to fall back into their natural tachyon wells, form back up their original quasi-crystal structure. Which is good, because it's that process that gives the universe an arrow of time. So when we let go of them, they snap back to wherever they were before, like an elastic band."

"All right, but none of that explains why you couldn't intervene in the war."

She explains. "Well, there are a few more caveats. The most important being, the closer a particle is to itself in time, the stronger the bond. So, if you imagine us as performers pulling on the strings of a puppet, there comes a point where the strings are simply too tight for us to pull. There's nothing we can do to alter them."

I try to process what she's saying. If I understand her correctly, she's saying she can't go back to the immediate past because the bonds between now and then are too strong to affect. There needs to be some distance between the jumper and the year being jumped.

"So what's that distance?" I ask. "How much time needs to pass before you can jump somewhere?"

"The record is three hundred and twenty-four years," she tells me. "But that's only for a single electron. Safety protocol states a minimum of four hundred and thirty-two years for an adult jumper. Meaning everything between now and the last four and a half centuries is impossible to jump into. The physics simply don't allow it. We call that block of time the *blackout dates*."

"So that's why you couldn't prevent the war," I say.

"Exactly. What could we have done centuries before the outbreak of the war to stop it? Nothing. At least, nothing that wouldn't have had such a dire cascade of snowballing effects as to make all of history unrecognizable. Or potentially even worse. This is not a power to be toyed with lightly."

"And what about the jumping in the here and now?" I ask. "Captain Gernsback told me that you can jump between worlds in an instant. That seems to be all that her people really want. They're not asking for the ability to travel in time."

The old woman sighs. "It's an unexpected part of the technology. As I told you, in order to form a template, we have to pull you off this dimensional membrane and place you in another. When we bring you back, Baker discovered the laws of physics don't really give a hoot where we put you. We can slap you down just about anywhere."

"That's incredible."

"Certainly. I mean, we could jump home to Tegana right this instant, if they didn't have that dumb planetary force field preventing us from doing so. And look, deary, I'd love to give everyone in the universe this power, the ability to travel any distance in the blink of an eye. It could reunite families spread out across the stars, destined to never see one another again."

"Then why don't you?"

"Because this technology doesn't differentiate between space and time. We can't offer the world the keys to one without giving up the keys to the other. As such, we must remain the guardians of both."

I suppose I understand.

Still, it seems unfair.

Careena looks down at her glass in a moment of honesty. "I'd gladly cast Hecate into the fiery abyss of a star and absolve myself of all responsibility as the gatekeeper of time and space. Believe me, I'd be the first to throw away this blasted sorcery. But people are figuring out the science on their own. We do what we can to stymie them, to shut down their operations when we find them, but the black market is still expanding year after year. And with that comes those who would use this witchcraft to gain power, at any cost. Not to mention, there are a fair number of blockheads out there who think this is just sport, who don't understand the consequences of their actions. Simply put, someone has to be there to stop them."

"So you're like a cop?"

"Something like that," she says. "But it's not as glamorous a job as you'd imagine. Most times I'm chasing down some wealthy buffoon who bought a black market vest just to hunt a dinosaur or take a selfie with Genghis Khan. We practically have a permanent agent assigned to birth-of-Jesus duty. Once we had a guy who simply wanted to attend a Nirvana concert. I didn't mind that one so much. But still, ambition should be made of sterner stuff."

I can't say that I haven't considered what I, myself, might do with such a gift. "Any plots to kill Hitler?" I ask.

"Fewer than you'd imagine. Education is the best prevention, as our wonderful portreeve likes to say." I'm not sure what a portreeve is, but I detect some sarcasm in her voice. Careena goes on. "In this day and age, even schoolchildren are taught about the explicit-negation paradox. You can go back three million years in time and punch an *Australopithecus* in the face, if that's your jollies, but you can't make changes in history that would explicitly negate your reason for going back in the first place. So, if you killed Hitler, he'd never appear in your history books. But then you'd never know about him, so you'd never go back to kill him, which means he will exist and he will be in your history books. And around and around it goes."

"A loop," I say.

"Aye. A real nasty one. Remember how I told you the universe was like a sheet of cloth? Well, a temporal loop is like raking the same spot over and over with an eraser. Eventually it will tear a hole in the membrane of our dimension. And that would be bad."

"How bad is bad?"

"Bad enough that our universe would collapse through the fissure. So basically, the end of everything, past, present, and future."

I think on this a moment. "I see. But wait, how can *you* break the loop? Wouldn't you be caught in the same paradox? If you stop the jumper before they do the thing that got your attention, then they never do the thing that got your attention, so you never have any reason to go back and stop them. You'd end up trapped in your own endless cycle."

Careena winks slyly. "You really are a clever girl, Freckles. Beckett was smart to bring you along. But tachyon-grounding is a topic for another day. All you need to know is that we have a few tricks up our sleeves. Right now, we have more pressing concerns."

"Like?"

Her face goes serious. "Like why some tosser shot me, for starters! I mean, I can't say I never have it coming. But something screwy is going on. Like, why are you here? Don't get me wrong, I'm glad you got me off that rooftop. But the whole damned reason we have seven agents is precisely for times like this, when we need forking backup."

"And backup never came."

"No."

"Maybe they couldn't find you."

She shakes her head. "I'll admit I've made myself somewhat hard to find these last few years. There's some politics about my situation that I'd rather not get into. But if Beckett knew where I was, then the others did too. They could have come, and they didn't."

"So what do you think?"

"I think that my location in the field is very sensitive information. Someone told that forker where I was. Someone in the ministry. Mark my words, luv, whoever planned my attack had help from the inside. We may have to watch our backs once we arrive on Tegana."

Great, just what I wanted to hear. "So maybe now is a good time to send me home then?" I suggest.

"Wish that I could," the old woman says, though not with as much conviction as I'd like. "Hecate's power cycle is shot. We're lucky we made it here in one piece. But on Tegana, we can have her fixed up and you can be on your way. In the meantime, I need your help. Call it a *mission* of sorts."

"Of course. Anything. It would be good to have something to do, to get my mind off all of this. The waiting around has been killing me, to be honest."

She claps her hands together. "Brilliant! So listen. Somewhere on this damned Mahshadi canoe must be a liquor store. Fetch me some Cawdorian whiskey, will you?"

"Are you serious?"

"Don't be such a prude. And no matter what they tell you, don't get me any of their Mahshadi piss. I'd rather choke to death on my own dry tongue. Oh, and let's not mention this to the nurses, shall we? They're liable to have silly rules about this sort of thing."

"This really doesn't seem like the time for a drink, Careena."

She shrugs and lays back into her bed, staring up at the ceiling. "I never claimed to be a saint, luv."

"Well, I don't have any future space money. I'm sorry."

"Charge it to the room Beckett gave us, genius."

I give up.

"Fine, I'll get you your stupid whiskey. But you better get me home. And soon!"

"Believe me, Freckles. If I don't get you back, they're going to hang me for temporal treason. I'm trying not to think about all the directives we've violated in just the last hour alone. Which is exactly why I need a drink. Now get going!"

6

I leave sick bay and wander the corridors of this mighty ship. It isn't long before I'm hopelessly lost. The wide hallways seem to go on forever. Yet, the truth is I hope the maze never ends. I enjoy strolling these decks, passing fellow passengers on their way to and from their destinations, most making their way to the terrarium a few decks above, with its boulevard of shops, restaurants, and manicured parks. But I enjoy exploring these lower passenger decks. There are occasional surprises even here—an old-fashioned barbershop where two corridors intersect, a simple bakery, a café, a daycare. The future is different, but it isn't so different as I had first imagined.

Occasionally there are tourist banners placed on poles in the corridors, advertising the most popular destinations here in what Careena had called the Ghent Mandate. I take it that a mandate is a sector of space with a group of colonies near enough to one another to form a sort of community of nations, able to trade, interact, and apparently, squabble among themselves like annoyed siblings.

How many mandates there were in the galaxy, I don't know, and I'm not so sure it matters. I imagine one mandate is likely so far from any other that they become little more than abstract notions to one another, curiosities discussed in magazines like *Galactic Geographic* and *Lonely Cosmos*.

I marvel at a few of the posters displaying the colonies of the Ghent Mandate. This being a Mahshadi ship, quite a few of the cities on New Mahshad are advertised as vacation getaways. Each has distinctive cylindrical towers, apartment buildings by the look of them, lining neatly organized, s-shaped canals, a seemingly common architectural motif on their world.

Despite Careena's abrasive attitude toward the Mahshadi, I can't say that I'm not intrigued by their landscapes and city designs. Some of those canals cut through dense urban districts only to flow out into national parks, into rivers that weave their way through valleys with sharp limestone peaks and exotic greenery. I can only imagine rowing with my teammates in such a magical place. Indeed, there are a few kayaks in the photos. Good marketing, if you ask me.

I also come across a poster for the city of Dalat on Cawdor III, which I need to remember is my homeworld, at least as far as my cover story is concerned. I'm like a spy now, a secret agent on assignment, which is a little exciting, I have to admit. And apparently the Cawdorian sun is turquoise, giving the planet a bright but perpetual twilight, along with a pink and lavender horizon.

Remarkable.

Last, I find a poster for our current destination, Careena's homeworld, the Republic of Tegana. Shown here is New Harmony, the white and regal capital. The city sits on a peaceful plain, with great, snow-capped mountains far in the distance. The entire city is circular, like a porcelain plate set on a lush Mongolian steppe. It's beautiful in its simplicity.

I continue to wander the ship's halls. To think, all in the same day I've graduated from exploring Brooklyn on my own, to exploring the farthest reaches of time and space. Not bad for a simple Jersey girl, if I do say so myself. And while I admit I've forgotten entirely about my *mission* to find a liquor store, I do eventually stumble into a bar.

It's more of a lounge really, and sits at the stern of the ship, the end of the road as it were. Like a modern ballroom, it has great curved windows staring out into the emptiness of space, offering a view of the Milky Way the likes of which I could never have imagined. She's like a band of light made of a hundred colors, cut from a billion twinkling stars.

And beyond that band, looking only like stars themselves, are a billion more galaxies, each surely as beautiful, each surely with their own stories to tell, each with their own hometown girls lost in an expanse beyond comprehension. It's enough to take my breath away —to look at the edge of reality and realize that I am but a speck in space and time. It makes me wonder if I haven't been sleepwalking through my life, focusing on silly things like an extra pair of shoes, a new phone, or, dare I say it, which school I'll get into next year.

How could any of that compare to the questions those glittering lights, those foreign suns numbering more than all the grains of sand on Earth, pose to me now? Why are we here, they ask? Why is there something rather than nothing? Why should it be, that despite being no more than collections of boring, inanimate dust easily found on any rock anywhere, when lumped together in just the right way, when molded like clay into the shape of a person, those clumps should suddenly have deep and meaningful inner lives, conscious experience, the ability to come to tears in the presence of awe? Are we not such golems? And if we are, how then was life breathed into us?

Maybe I need a fricken drink.

"Welcome to Rear-Ten," the rather dapper bartender offers as I enter the lounge. "May I get you a spirit?"

I take a seat at the bar and stiffen my back, aware that at seventeen, I may be underage here. Was this region of space conquered by prudish Americans? Let's hope not. Or let's hope the fake ID Story gave me at least tweaked my age a bit.

I look up at the wall of liquors. The bottles on display are fancier than whatever cheap booze my friends manage to acquire from the corner bodega back home. I'm out of my depth here, to be honest. But if I'm going to be Jane Bond, time-traveling super spy, I should at least try to play the part.

"A whiskey," I say coolly. "Something Cawdorian."

Maybe Careena has good taste.

I fold my hands as the strapping young man in his black suspenders turns around to take a bottle down from the wall. He sets a small glass before me, and with silver tongs places a large square of ice in it before pouring an amber shot with the grace of a ballerina.

He spins the bottle around so that the label faces me. "Unearthly Child," he says. "They say it's the best on Cawdor."

I try not to act too impressed, but I think I'm ready to marry this man. "And what do you say?" I ask.

"I say it's the best damned whiskey in the galaxy."

He winks; my heart melts.

Unsure of proper fancy whiskey bar etiquette, I slam the entire shot down in one go. I mean, that's how we do it at house parties in Jersey. For a moment, my entire body goes warm.

Embarrassingly, I'm sure my face has gone quite red.

But damn, if that's not the best liquor I've ever had.

"Another?" the bartender asks.

"Oh, yes."

He again pours the amber-colored sorcery. "Take this one a bit slower there, Cowgirl," he tells me. "Breathe it in. Play with it. Enjoy it a little."

I could listen to this man and his devilish dimples instruct me on the finer points of whiskey etiquette all day, but I'm an awkward flirt and one shot likely won't overcome that sad fact. So I decide to take this second one over to an open couch closer to the windows.

I like this lounge because it's spacious and wide, with couples enjoying their time in comfortable seats and sofas, while soft, old-timey French tunes play in the background. And that view.

That fricken view.

Eventually, a server comes to me. I hope Beckett gave me a worthy spending account, because I plan to drink and dine the government of Tegana into poverty. With a press of my thumb on his black card, I order a Mahshadi coffee, whatever that is, and butternut squash ravioli, because that sounded really good when the captain mentioned it.

While I wait for my food, I fidget with the ring I'm wearing before realizing that Careena never asked for Hecate back. I have a hard time imagining her as some highly trained super spy, hunting down criminals across time and space, when she can't even remember that she's left one of the most powerful devices known to humankind with a befuddled teenager.

At my table is a small, simple tablet. Every table seems to have one. At first, I can't figure out how to get mine to come on. And I'm horrified to ask for help. Not that I'd mind another opportunity to chat up the bartender, mind you, but I really don't want to come off looking like some rural peasant who wandered onto a glitzy starship by mistake.

Fortunately, it doesn't take me long to realize that, like Careena's ring, the tablet responds to thought. I need only send a mental signal and the screen lights up. Once that's figured out, the rest comes easy, too easy in fact. It's almost unnerving. The tablet seems to know what I'm going to ask for before I do. I try to ignore any implications that might have for free will, mainly because I don't want to see what the tablet has to say on the topic.

Luckily for me, there's no end to what other information is available. I'm enthralled for hours, which is easy to do when you're on a starship and there's no indication of day or night.

I'm also pretty sure I'm violating one of Careena's ministry's fancy directives by reading up on the last thousand years of human history, but I reason that, since from my perspective those laws haven't been written yet, they don't really apply to me.

Two whiskeys, two coffees, a ravioli, and a nap later, I'm still on the couch reading. I've completely forgotten about Careena. But that's okay, because these future encyclopedia articles are fascinating. Nerd heaven.

As best as I can figure out, sometime in the 2200's a federation of nations on Earth bombarded hundreds of uninhabited worlds with what they called seed engines. These seed engines were satellites the size of aircraft carriers, each containing self-replicating robots the size of army ants.

Only goldilocks planets were selected, planets the right size for Earth-like gravity and the right distance from their stars for a hospitable climate. Additionally, each seed engine had a kill switch that would send it into the nearest star should long range sensors and cameras aboard detect life upon approach. Humanity wanted to be good neighbors and not continue their long tradition as ruthless colonizers.

Once arriving on a world, the tiny, solar-powered, insect-like robots mined the planetary surface for the raw materials needed to create massive atmospheric converters the size of cities. Depending on the conditions at the time of arrival, the process to make the atmosphere habitable could take as little as two decades to as long as several centuries.

The seed engines also contained genetically modified lichens to do some of the conversion work, along with an array of specially adapted plant life to introduce when ready. After the planet was made livable, those giant atmospheric converters would tear themselves down and reconstruct themselves as ready-made, self-maintaining settlements—ghost towns dozens of light years from Earth, simply awaiting human arrival.

Initially, interplanetary travel was limited by the speed of light. Settlers during those earliest years were frozen in stasis and undertook journeys of tens to hundreds of years to reach their destinations, knowing full well that they'd never see Earth again. But the spirit to know the stars, to push on to the next frontier, to touch the feet of the gods, was baked into humanity's DNA.

Faster than light travel was pioneered in the mid-twenty-fourth century, leading to a precarious situation where some of the earliest settlers sent to the furthest colonies arrived after younger generations with faster ships had already been calling those planets home for decades.

Now, in the year 3021, humanity inhabited almost four hundred worlds in fifty-four different mandates, with another six hundred planets in the seeding the stage.

Even so, the Milky Way is so indescribably large that no human has yet been to the other side of the galaxy, though some wide-eyed pioneers have illegally shot themselves in that direction, frozen in stasis, making a slingshot around the galactic core, destined to wake up after many centuries of space flight, should they be fortunate enough to wake up at all.

More locally, I begin to read about this little corner of the galaxy, the Ghent Mandate. Many of the colonies here are now centuries old. Each planet is home to dozens of city-states, each with their own histories, their own cultures, their own unique identities. Their populations, meanwhile, run into the hundreds of millions.

As Careena had told me, the peoples here are many generations removed from their pioneering forefathers and foremothers of yesteryear. And in truth, their titles as outer colonies have long ago been seceded to newer, younger worlds farther out on the horizon.

Unable to put my tablet down, I delve into the topic of aliens, before noticing a real, live alien standing alone at the bar. I call over, perhaps buzzed still from that last whiskey.

"Lieutenant Chimat," I say. "Join me for a drink?"

The stocky alien man with his bark-like skin and ivory chin horn walks over but shakes his head as he places a hand over what I assume to be his stomach. "I'm sorry, ma'am. The fermentation does not agree with my anatomy."

"That's too bad," I tell him. "I'm sure the captain wouldn't mind you having a little fun while you spy on me."

"Spying, ma'am?"

"I saw you hanging around sick bay too."

"Only to ensure your safety."

"I'm sure." I put down my tablet. "So if you can't drink, what is it your people do for fun?"

Lieutenant Chimat takes a seat on the edge of an armchair next to me. His face has lit up. "Oh, we Thanes are excellent caretakers. If you entered a typical Thanish home, you would be amazed, absolutely amazed, at the array of vegetation you would find."

"So... you grow plants?"

"Yes, ma'am. A joy to watch!"

"That's... something, I guess."

Lieutenant Chimat beams with excitement. "Actually, you'd be happy to know that one of the most treasured possessions on all of Thane was a plant we imported centuries ago from your Earth."

"I think I can guess. Orchids?"

"No."

I try again.

"Roses?"

"Oh gosh no, ugly things those. Don't you think so?"

"What then?"

"These are a type of ambulatory vegetation."

"Ambulatory?"

"Yes. I believe you call them cats."

I lean back on my sofa. "Ah. I guess some things never change. Though if you met my mom's cat, Mr. Kerfluffle, you might change your opinion about cats."

Lieutenant Chimat's eyes widen.

"Why, ma'am, that is a most brilliant name."

"My mom certainly thinks so." I try to change topics. "So are you married, Lieutenant?"

Again the little alien man lights up with enthusiasm. "About that. You see on Thane—"

I have to cut him off. Something is happening outside the window. I point toward space. "Hey, look. The stars aren't moving. I think we've stopped."

Lieutenant Chimat's expression turns to one of immediate concern. He looks down to the left, as if listening to a voice in his head. He stands. "I apologize, I must leave you."

"Why? What's happened?" I ask.

His solid black eyes blink twice.

I realize it's the first time I've seen him blink.

Finally, he tells me.

"The *Stellar Pearl* has been sabotaged."

I am left alone on my couch with a sudden sense of worry. I should return to sick bay and warn Careena—it can't be a coincidence that the *Stellar Pearl*'s engines have been wrecked, stranding the ship adrift in dead space. Whoever is after Careena may have followed us here. I collect myself.

That's when the first explosion rocks the ship.

It comes from somewhere far off, but it's enough to rattle the chandeliers and knock a few bottles off the shelves. The lounge becomes deathly quiet as the patrons stop their conversations and look around at one another with worried glances. Most have only now realized we have stopped.

"What was that?" someone asks.

"We've struck an asteroid, maybe," another offers.

By the second explosion, however, it's clear that the ship is under attack. Several of the guests approach the windows, hoping to see what's happening.

I stand to get my own view. Off the starboard side of our ship is a long dark vessel, roughly equal in size to the *Stellar Pearl* but somehow more menacing. Its hull is husky and battered with age, like a rusted ocean vessel barely seaworthy. There's a decidedly industrial aesthetic to its architecture.

A crew member approaches the window and stops alongside me to get a look. She's young, in a neatly pressed uniform. She's South Asian maybe, though in truth there's a great deal of ambiguity in the faces of the people of the future. Fortunately, she knows a thing or two about ships. "It's a mining dreadnought," she says to me.

"Who are they?" I ask.

"Hard to say. Pirates maybe. But I can tell you that's a very old ship and those blasters they're firing are designed to break rock, not pierce reinforced hull. They can knock us around, but unless they have something else up their sleeves, Captain Gernsback is going to blow them out of the stars. We may not be a proper warship, but we still got some pep in our punch."

Almost on cue, the *Stellar Pearl* returns fire with a battery of cannons. The back-and-forth volleys are not unlike eighteenth century frigates trading cannon fire on the high seas.

The *Stellar Pearl* shakes with every hit she takes but remains steady. The same can't be said for the mining dreadnought, which is taking unsustainable damage. While the shots themselves travel too fast to register, each time they strike they light up the enemy ship. Entire sections and compartments are blown into space. But the pirate ship continues to fire.

"She can take a tight slap, I'll give her that," the woman says.

Even so, something seems off. I may not be from this time period, but I have my intuition. I turn to the crew woman. "Don't you think something is wrong here? They must have known they were outmatched. I can't believe space pirates are that stupid."

The crew woman shrugs. "Could be they're desperate, maybe. Could be an end of days cult. You can never know what those fanatics are thinking. But it looks like it's over."

She's right.

As quickly as the skirmish had started, it was finished. The mining dreadnought, now powerless, turns dark and drifts lazily into the cold oblivion of space. Without a nearby sun to illuminate it, the vessel is nearly invisible in the darkness. The patrons of the bar watch the ship drift in solemn silence, as if a great and wild animal has been put down.

"Were we damaged?" someone asks the crew woman.

"Only our sensor array," she answers. "Got blown to hell, unfortunately. Lucky shot, I reckon."

"Great," someone else says. "So not only are we dead in space, but we're blind as a bat."

"There's no need to worry, sir. The Tegan Defense Force has been notified. They have a patrol ship less than three hours away."

"A lot can happen in three hours," a mother barks.

"The situation is under control," the crew woman says. I feel a little bad for her. She's the only figure of authority in the room. She goes on, "I suggest you all return to your rooms. Updates will come shortly. For now, all you need to know is that their ship has been disabled and their saboteur has already been apprehended. It was a clever stunt, but it failed. We'll have the engines running soon and a military escort. There will be no further problems."

There's some more back-and-forth arguing, and a deluge of questions for the poor woman, but I ignore it all. Instead, I walk over to the window. Something catches my attention. The stars in one region of space are distorted, like wet paint slightly streaked. It's strange, I can't explain it. I place my hand on the window and feel a low hum. Our engines? But our engines have been cut. It has to be something else.

"Does anyone else hear that?" I ask.

The crew woman turns, sees the distortion, and shouts. "Miss! Get away from the window!"

Too late.

A perfect circle in the center of the window, the size of a doorway, explodes into a million fragments of glass, throwing me backward across the floor.

I climb to my knees, prepared to be sucked out into the coldness of space, which is what always happens in my dad's sci-fi movies—but when I look up, there's a vessel the size of a sailing yacht attached to the hull like one of those creepy sucker fish. Its own hull is cloaked in some sort of stealth material, showing the stars behind it, and making it nearly invisible to the human eye. Perhaps the *Stellar Pearl's* sensors could have detected this ship, but as the young woman just said, they've been blown to hell.

The dreadnought was only a distraction.

All at once, several men step out of the opening. They are serious and dangerous looking, armed with rifles and dressed in black. A few are tattooed. The leader of the group, however, is the one who makes the greatest impression on me.

"It's the Red Man," someone nearby whispers.

His name fits. He's burly, with a wide chest and fingers like knotted steel. His eyes are smeared carelessly with dark mascara. Blood-red scripts are tattooed along the right side of his bald scalp. He wears black like the others, but the shoulders of his long trench coat are decorated with the red fur of some wild animal.

It's his beard, however, from which he receives his moniker; red like fire, greased with tight, angry curls. It hangs to the base of his neck, trimmed with great square edges. He possesses the presence of a biblical king.

And the icy stare of a heartless and indifferent god.

In the silence of his arrival, he eyes everyone in the room, one after another, slowly and deliberately taking us all in. He caresses his beard with mighty fingers, many of which are adorned with large rings. When his eyes finally make their way to me, my soul shakes, but then they move on to other patrons.

He speaks to us in a battered voice. "There's hell. There's darkness. There's the sulfurous pit. None of these compare to me. Cross me and I will burn you. Move against me and I will scald you. Defy me and I will consume you."

Saying no more, he leaves the lounge with his entourage. There's a purpose in their step that sends shivers down my back. Two of his men remain behind to watch us. We are hostages now —and it goes without saying that we will be executed without hesitation the moment Captain Gernsback attempts a move against this Red Man.

I want to warn Careena that they're coming for her, but I don't know how. The two guards corral us into the center of the lounge, forcing us on our knees while we wait out the confrontation. They carry ugly rifles and pace back and forth impatiently. One of them is clearly high on some sort of future chemical. His face is a mask of anger and boredom.

A woman in front of me whispers to her boyfriend. "What do they want?"

The nastier of the two guards strikes the boyfriend with the butt of his rifle. "Quiet!"

The young man drops to the floor like a sack of rocks, despite having said nothing. The guard smiles at the woman, exposing rows of tattoos along his gums. No one speaks after that.

Minutes pass like hours as we wait in silence. A thousand thoughts are flooding my mind. I start to notice everyone's shoes. Why shoes? What's wrong with my brain? I look toward the exit. There's no way I can get out to warn Careena. She's on her own. I think we all are.

The man with tattooed gums catches me looking toward the door. He's been leering at me—how long, I'm not sure. I immediately look down to my knees but it's too late. His boredom is the most dangerous thing in the room. And now I've caught his attention.

"What? Our company ain't good enough for you, luv?" he says mockingly. "You got somewhere better to be?"

I shake my head without looking up.

I'm in trouble and I know it.

He walks over and caresses my curly hair with the back of his hand. My skin crawls.

"Are you a princess, luv?"

I stammer. "No, sir."

"Good. Then no one will care what we do with you."

Without warning, he grabs a fistful of my hair and yanks me to my feet. Everyone watches but there's nothing anyone can do to help. They can only look on in horror and thank whatever gods still remain in this world that it wasn't they who caught this man's attention.

He marches me toward the washroom. I try to resist but his grip on my head is like iron. Tears of pain flood my vision.

The other guard shoots a worried glance. "Tyson, what the hell are you doing?"

"What's it look like, mate?"

"He'll kill you."

This man that holds me, Tyson, eyes his companion with utter contempt. "Then we shan't tell him. Because then he'd kill us both. And don't worry, I'll save you some if that's what you want. Now bugger off."

I beg this other man to intervene with my eyes. I see the disapproval in his face. He's a thief, yes, ruthless even, and perhaps some part of him enjoys directing his pain and anger at the wealthy and the elite who travel the galaxy in their shining starships filled with every luxury imaginable. But he's not this.

Please, I beg.

But in return in his eyes is only cowardice.

My fate sealed, Tyson forces me into the washroom. We're alone now. My heart is racing like a frightened rabbit. He still has me by the hair and the pain is like hot steel on my scalp. I can feel the grime of his fingers, the flakes of blood falling on my head from fingernails he's gnawed to stubs.

I can see both of us in the washroom mirror as well, can see the twisted lines of his face. What I see scares me. It isn't lust. I'm not even sure it's sexual. To him, I'm not a person. I fear I'm merely a proxy for a lifetime of rejection and humiliation, an empty vessel to fill with all his worst thoughts.

I try to reason with him. "Look, sir, I—"

His scream shakes me to my core. "Quiet!" He pulls harder. "You don't get to speak to me! You think just because you're born with a silver spoon in your mouth, you're better than us? Think you can get by in life on those pretty looks alone, yeah?"

"No—"

"How about we take out that spoon, luv."

He slams my face into the mirror.

When he let's go of my hair, I crumple to the ground. My lip and nose are busted. Blood and drool flow freely down my chin, onto my clothes, and pool on the tiles. I see two of my front teeth on the floor.

I'm blinded by the pain.

I just want to stay here on the hard floor and die.

He takes my forearm and yanks me back up with such violence that it dislocates my shoulder. He then pins me against the wall with the full weight of his body as his crooked knob presses against my thigh. His rancid breath condenses on my cheeks. The stench of his body burns my nostrils. The look in his eyes, that unblinking, feral look, that glint of what he believes this to be, a great and righteous victory for his frail and pathetic ego—it will haunt me for all my days to come.

I try to push him off—it's instinctive from years of jujitsu train-ing, to get a hold, a lock, the upper hand. And in doing so I catch him off guard, wrapping the inside of his leg with mine, which brings us both down hard to the floor. As he tries to grab me and roll me over, I catch his arm in the triangle of my elbow. I latch my wrist to complete the lock and with all my weight I bend his forearm backwards, against the joint.

I should hear the snapping of bone, a scream of pain, *something* —but nothing happens. What I come to realize in that moment is that his arm is augmented, robotic, something I can't understand. I might as well be trying to break an iron lamp post. All I've done is enrage him. Suddenly he's the one on top of me, having broken my holds through sheer unnatural strength alone.

Pinned on the ground, I try one more time to break away, but only manage to snap some object off a chain around his neck. The tiny keepsake dings on the floor and rolls under the sink. What it is, I don't know. I hear it roll, but it's too late to turn and look. Tyson's fingers are now around my throat.

Only then do I understand that I have lost, that no savior is coming through the door behind us at the last minute, that no rescue is imminent, that no reprieve from the darkness of human nature is to be granted. Perhaps the only thing I can be thankful for is that he's now so provoked, so angry at my resistance, that he stops going for my pants. I see it in his frenzied gaze. All he wants now is to crush the life out of me with his bare hands. His grip tightens.

I rake and claw but my defenses are useless. My arms aren't long enough to reach his face, which hovers over me like a demonic mask of rage, his eyes piercing me like bloodshot portals into hell. As my strength finally wanes, I drop my arms to my side in defeat. In doing so, my hand falls against my jacket pocket.

There's something there.

I slide in my hand.

I turn the pocket upward.

And I pull the trigger on Old Bessie.

The shot is no louder than a toy cap gun, but the force that the weapon wields is godly. It may have the look of an antiquated pistol, but it's something else entirely. The energy blast blows the back of Tyson's head apart. Chunks of brain material and bits of skull are flung across the walls and mirrors and stalls and ceiling.

His corpse falls to the floor beside me.

I curl up to the other side into a fetal position.

I cry.

For a long time, I cry.

Alone and broken, I cry.

Then, I pass out.

And I hope to never awaken again.

8

There's light all around me, angelic and comforting. Alongside this light is a sweet hum, emanating from somewhere far off and distant. Or perhaps that isn't true. Perhaps the light, the hum, the peace is emanating from within me, from somewhere deep down in my soul, someplace unknown but now remembered. It's pleasant. Beautiful. It's the sort of ambient melody made by the rustling of leaves in autumn or by ocean waves receding over pebble beaches. All my pain has been stripped away.

I want to remain here in this light, float away with it, I want to let go of my attachments to this world and drift off into the promise of oblivion. But there's a hand holding my own, keeping me grounded. The hand is aged like soft, worn leather. The hand squeezes gently and I open my eyes.

"The sleeper has awakened," Careena says with a small smile.

"Oy. Please tell me you're not my angel."

"No, deary, you're alive and well."

I touch my teeth. Despite having seen them shattered, cast out across a cold tile floor, they're all here. Part of me hopes my assault was only a bad dream. But I know it's not.

Careena takes notice.

"Modern medicine. You're as good as new," she says.

I appreciate her support but that's not true, and it never will be. Some small piece of me has been taken, stolen—and something horrible has been put in its place.

I try to fight the fragments, the shards of memory from the washroom, the image of that man's face, the stench of his breath; I try to bottle these memories up and place them in some dark corner of my mind until I can deal with them on my own terms. But it's a fight I'm destined to lose.

Overwhelmed by the memories, I break down and cry. Clinging on to Careena's hand like a life preserver, I cry.

The old woman leans forward and holds me against a comforting shoulder. "Oh, Freckles, you're all right now. You did what you had to do."

How long I cry I don't know. I'm embarrassed to feel so vulnerable, particularly among strangers. I've always considered myself a fighter, a star athlete on the crew team, a disciplined jujitsu student in my free time, a young woman with serious academic chops and the hard-fought drive to succeed. But no amount of pride can withstand the flood of emotions overpowering me now.

Careena says nothing. She only holds me for as long as I need. It's a gesture I appreciate. After a time, I collect myself and wipe the tears from my bloodshot eyes.

"I'm sorry," I tell the old woman.

"Freckles, there's nothing to be sorry for. I should be apologizing to you, for putting you through all this."

"Just tell me the worst is over."

"The worst is over."

I manage a polite smile.

Looking around, the colors and architecture of the room that we're in are different from before. This room is more spartan, more serious than the one where they were observing Careena. We're in a sick bay, but this is not the *Stellar Pearl*.

My voice is hoarse. "Where are we?"

"Safe," she says. "We're aboard the *Ark Royal*, a Tegan battle cruiser. No one will fork with us here. We're escorting the *Stellar Pearl* the remainder of the way to Tegana. I didn't trust those Mahshadi snake charmers to treat you, so I had you transferred over here."

I realize now that we're not alone.

There's another figure standing beside Careena.

"How are you feeling, Isabel?" Story Beckett asks. She's still a projection, experience allows me to recognize that now, but even so —I'm comforted by her presence.

"Terrified," I tell the young officer. "But I'm glad you're back."

"I won't leave you again. I promise."

I turn back to Careena. "I was worried that man was going to kill you. How did you get away?"

"Hah! You hear that, Beckett? She's known me only a day and already thinks everyone in this galaxy is out to off me. I'll have you know, Freckles, he wasn't after me."

"Who was he?"

"They call him the Red Man," she says. "A pirate of sorts. He's rather infamous in some of the frontier mandates, but this is the first time he's ever been in Ghent. All I know about him is what I've read in the news over the years. He's a sellsword. Into theatrics apparently."

I clutch her forearm. "You have to go back. Please. You have to stop what happened."

"I wish that I could, deary. I would break every law in the galaxy to do that for you, I really would."

I nod. Perhaps that's all I wanted to hear her say. After all, I remember what she told me, about the limits on her powers. There had to be some distance between the present and the date she intends to jump, a distance of more than four hundred years. To jump back only a day or two is apparently a wish that physics has chosen to deny me.

She mumbles. "Theoretically, I suppose you could do it."

Story interjects. "Smith, let's not get into any more trouble than we already are."

"Yeah, you might be right."

"What do you mean?" I ask.

Careena waves a hand. "It's just a pet theory of some of our more eccentric physicists."

"I want to hear it."

She raises an eyebrow to Story, who clearly disapproves of this conversation, both in theory and in practice. But the old woman continues anyway. "You'll remember that I told you the stuff in the past has a bond with the stuff in the present. And the closer stuff is to itself in time, the stronger that bond is, until eventually it's so strong that we can't do anything with it. Which is why we can't go back to the attack. But you see, the thing is, that bond only forms when you're here, tethered to this dimensional membrane, which is a fancy way of saying when you're in the normal three-dimensional space that we all know and love."

"So?"

She leans in close, as if someone might overhear. "So when Hecate brought you here to the present, she did so by untethering you from the membrane. You were placed in the same higher dimensional space that I'm placed while I'm jumping. The only difference being, you were left there for a thousand years. You weren't brought back down and reattached to the membrane until you arrived on the *Stellar Pearl*. That makes you a rather unique individual in this universe. As you weren't here in normal space for all that time, there are no real bonds to speak of holding you back. Theoretically, you're sort of free to go wherever you want."

"What Smith is trying to say," Story clarifies. "Is that she reads entirely too much science fiction. Until you, we've never brought anyone from the past forward to the present before, so this free agent theory, as some call it, has never been tested. And there are many reasons to believe it would never work."

"Bah," the old woman says.

"Fine," I say. "But I still want to know, what did those pirates want? If they weren't after you, then why did they attack us?"

"It's not important."

My gaze is fierce. "It's important to me, Careena."

The time agent relents. "I suppose it is. They were after a cargo container. Something very valuable. Very dangerous."

"What?"

"Not now. You should rest."

"I don't want to rest."

Careena lets out a long breath. "Very well. Your clothes are there on the counter. They've been washed. I took Old Bessie, but why don't you keep Hecate for now. She's out of juice, but wearing her might give you a little strength. I know it does me. Get dressed and join me in the officer's lounge. Beckett can show you the way when you're ready. I'll explain everything there."

I nod in affirmation.

Careena turns to Story. "You'll show her down?"

"Of course."

"And how long do we have?" the old woman asks the officer.

"To Tegana? We've just entered the system, so we're on sublight propulsion now. That makes it four hours, give or take."

Careena dwells on this for a moment. "A real forking riot this is going to be," the old woman finally says. "She's probably going to give you a promotion, Beckett."

"You know that's not why I did this."

"Aye, I know. The fickle demands of time were bound to find me eventually."

With that, the old woman leaves.

"What was all that about?" I ask Story.

"Agent Smith has not been home in many years."

"Why?"

"There was something of a disagreement with our portreeve, who is, shall we say, also rather stubborn. But I should not gossip. Get dressed and I'll show you the way."

Half an hour later I find myself in the officer's lounge of the *Ark Royal*. It's similar in some ways to Rear-Ten aboard the *Stellar Pearl*; this lounge is also nestled at the rear of the ship. But the design is much more functional and the windows are only rows of narrow slits. The truth is I prefer these new windows. The smaller openings are a better barrier between myself and whatever dark forces lurk out there in the beyond.

Standing in the entranceway, I realize I'm hugging my chest. I used to be full of naive confidence. Now I feel like an injured flower, a frightened mouse. I don't like it. But I can't seem to fight it. The harder I push the feelings down, the harder they push back up.

Careena is at the bar, alone, her own face masked in troubled thoughts. Her stool faces the windows, those portals into the emptiness, that abyss that stares back, that sees all for who they truly are. Many fear that prospect, to see themselves in the reflection of a mirror that strips away all the pretty little lies that we tell about ourselves. But a few long for it, long to be finally known, truly known, by someone, anyone, even if that someone is only the void. Is this what Careena seeks?

I join the old woman.

At first, we say nothing.

It's enough not to be alone.

"Want a drink, deary?" Careena eventually asks.

"What are you having?"

"Cognac."

"From where?"

"From France."

"The real France?"

"What other France is there?"

"Sounds expensive."

"Took over seventy bloody years to get here, you bet it is!" The time agent turns to the bartender. "Soldier boy, get Freckles here a drink. Something strong. And make it something Tegan. There's no reason to waste the Earth liquor on an Earth girl. Let her have a taste of the frontier."

The drink arrives.

Neither of us talk much at first.

Company doesn't always need to be shared in words.

After a while, Careena asks, "So where's Beckett?"

"Called away," I tell her. "They caught a traitor in your ministry."

Careena takes a sip.

"Nice to know they told you before they told me."

"To be honest, I get the impression that they don't trust you very much. Maybe that made sense on the *Stellar Pearl*. But I thought we were with your people now?"

"We are. But a lot has happened over the years. Anyway, my troubles aren't why you came down here. I promised I'd tell you about the attack. What do you want to know?"

"Everything."

She takes another sip. "Well, I don't know everything. I don't even know much. As you've just so astutely pointed out, I'm not privy to all the goings-on at the moment. But that Red Man you saw, he's a mercenary. He doesn't work on his own. Which means someone hired him to hit the *Stellar Pearl*. And don't ask me who, because I don't know."

"What did they want?"

"That cargo container. The one we were supposedly checking on when we arrived."

"You mean they planned that whole attack for a bunch of earthworms?"

"It wasn't worms, you tart. That was a cover story. In the container were RGMs, *rare galactic minerals*. They power the tachyon distortion technology used in time travel. As you can imagine, they're dangerous, particularly if they end up on the black market. There's a universal embargo against their mining, trade, and transport. Which is why they were being transported in secret."

"The Mahshadi are smugglers?"

"Hah! Those goody-two-shoes? No. Absolutely not. I hate to admit it, but it was our government doing the smuggling. You see, as you may have noticed, we happen to have an entire ministry dedicated to time travel, so we sort of need the RGMs as much as the bad guys. Thing is, the embargo applies to us too. In fact, we're singled out by name. Call it payback for not sharing our toys. Outside inspectors are allowed to search our ships whenever they like. As such, we've found it best to sneak them in aboard other people's ships. But please don't go telling your buddy Gernsback that."

"You knew they were there?"

"No," she says. "Not my department. It was just a coincidence we were on the same ship. Truthfully, there are only so many ships running between worlds each month, so it's not even that surprising. What's worrisome is that those shipments are super top secret."

"Like your location in the field."

She raises her glass to me. "Bingo."

"It must be the traitor that Story mentioned."

"Sounds about right to me."

"So what happened to the Red Man?"

"He got away, sorry to say. And worse than that, this was no ordinary shipment of RGMs. It was the largest we've ever had, unprecedented really. In any given year, there's rarely enough RGMs discovered to make more than one or two jumpvests. A lack of raw material has always been our greatest ally."

"And this shipment? How much was there?"

Careena slides a napkin over to me. She'd already done dozens of calculations on it before I arrived. "By my quick math, enough for around a hundred vests. That's a small army of jumpers. Gernsback tried her best to stop the heist, but as you know, they had hostages. She also didn't know how valuable the cargo was. Anyway, I can't blame her. Her hands were tied. For what it's worth, the only shot fired during the entire attack was yours."

An anger rises up inside me.

"I'd have shot them all if I could."

"I know."

"They don't deserve to get away."

"They won't."

There's a long silence. The old woman attempts to change the topic. "We'll be at Tegana soon. You'll be able to go home. You can put all this behind you then."

"Can I?" I ask. "After everything I've seen, Careena? Everything I've gone through? I'm not sure I'll recognize home anymore. And if I do, will it still recognize me?"

She takes a sip of cognac. "You're wiser than your years, Freckles. I honestly can't answer you."

"Story told me you've been avoiding your own home."

The response comes quickly. "Beckett should keep to her own damned business, yeah."

"But it's true?"

"Aye, it's true." She looks up toward the window and into the stars. Some thoughts can't be vanquished by cognac. "I'm a very proud, revengeful, and ambitious woman, deary, with more offenses at my back than I have thoughts to put them in or imagination to give them shape. I won't be made to regret the things that I've done. But I can't run from them either. As much as I wish that I could."

She elaborates no further and I do not push her.

Later, after another round taken in silence, Story returns.

"Captain Beckett, so good of you to join us," Careena says, with a touch of liquor in her voice. "I'd offer you a drink if you weren't a projection. Or such a bore."

"I apologize. There's been a lot of activity here, as you can imagine."

"So I've heard," Careena says. "So, who was the traitor? And before you tell me, just know that I plan to shoot the forker in the face."

"Captain Arulo."

The old woman seems surprised. "That's unsettling. You sure about that?"

"Without a doubt."

I ask, "Who is this person?"

Story answers. "A temporal lead, like myself. We assist the agents in the field."

"Speaking of agents," Careena says. "Where are those schnitzel-heads? Why didn't anyone come rescue the damsel in distress when I was in Brooklyn? Heaven knows they'd love to brag about it."

Story's face is serious. "Smith, they're all dead."

"What?"

"Two were killed in the field. Same assassin that went after you. The hits were minutes apart. You were his third and final target. The other four were killed here in the ministry. A bomb went off at an early morning meeting. Several leads and staff were killed as well. It's been chaos here since then, to be honest."

"I don't believe it." Careena looks down at her glass. "And you're saying it was Arulo? I've known that man for forty years. He's been my lead on a dozen missions. Bit of a wide-eyed idealist, though that's just about everyone over there these days. He was into yoga and spinach and all that healthy nonsense. Still, I certainly never took him for the turncoat type."

"It was a shock to all of us. The portreeve actually suspected you for most of this time. She would have hauled you in, had anyone been left to do it."

"Of course she did," Careena mutters. "So what did they get out of Arulo?"

"Nothing," the officer says. "He smuggled the bomb on his person into the meeting. It was the only way to get it through security. He died in the blast."

I watch as Careena considers all this. The politics and logistics of what has happened is beyond me, but I can see it greatly troubles the old woman. "It doesn't make any damned sense," she says. "They had something on him, maybe? They were threatening his daughters? This is exactly why they don't allow us agents to have families, and I've always said they should expand that rule to you lot."

"You're not one to talk, Smith," Story responds. I wonder what she means by that. But then she continues before I can inquire more. "We did have the same thought, though. We went immediately to his family. His wife passed some years ago, but he has two young daughters, Bell and Doria. Unfortunately, they're very young, three and five. But they were able to give us something. Their father had told them about a man named Patmos. Apparently, this Patmos was the leader of a small group, some sort of secret society. We believe Patmos hired the Red Man to steal the RGMs from the *Stellar Pearl*."

"Why?" I ask. "He's a terrorist?"

"We're still not sure," Story says. "But I doubt it. Our computers can detect unnatural levels of stress, even ill intent, but Arulo was never flagged. To have evaded our security protocols, he must have believed, and believed sincerely, that what he was doing was for the greater good."

"Great," Careena says. "So we're dealing with nutters."

"Perhaps more than you know," Story confirms. "Arulo told his daughters that Patmos had promised to take them to a better world. It's been... difficult to parse everything from a five-year-old. But the girls were already packed for a trip when we arrived. It seems likely to me that Arulo betrayed the ministry, and even sacrificed himself, in order to book passage for Bell and Doria. The girls called the place they were going to the World to Come. Which unfortunately will wash away the World that Was."

"That doesn't sound promising," I say.

Careena agrees. "No, it doesn't. We've seen these types of lunatics before. They think they can get God's attention by going back in time and instigating a paradox. Or prove we're living in a simulation managed by a supercomputer somewhere in the multiverse. Who the hell knows. If they aren't stopped, they'll rip apart the fabric of the cosmos, and then it's lights out for everyone. These schemes aren't new, but normally these types can't even put on their shoes straight. We've never dealt with anyone this sophisticated before."

"So what are you thinking?"

The old woman puts a finger to her nose. "That it's safe to assume two things. First, Patmos is not planning to go back in time alone. He intends to bring all his of followers with him, which is why he needed all those RGMs."

"And second?" I ask.

"Second, he doesn't want the time police intervening. He must know we have a few tricks up our sleeves that could prevent whatever he's trying to do. So he went to a lot of trouble to kill everyone in a position to stop him."

"Not everyone," Story interjects. "We still have you."

"Then you haven't got schnitzel." Careena finishes her cognac to prove the point. "You think our wonderful portreeve is going to let me fly again? Not on your life, luv. Enjoy these last moments while you can." She points her glass toward the windows. "Speaking of which, you two haven't even noticed. We're here."

I look up. There on the horizon is a world both beautiful and regal, a blue-green orb of brilliance, an Earth drawn in different borders.

Tegana.

The hair on the back of my neck stands as we enter orbit and more of the planet fills our view. There's a halo on the horizon, as bright as the light of heaven, angelic, a roof of golden fire cast from a nearby sun.

I glance over at Careena. She is lost in the view, lost in thought, lost in regret. This is a sight that she has denied herself for too many years. Her eyes are uncharacteristically wet.

She whispers.

"I've eaten the bitter bread of banishment too long."

It was time.

Time for the prodigal daughter to finally return home.

9

areena and I are escorted to the hangar of the *Ark Royal* where we are met by the stoic captain of the ship, Captain Hamid Bashir. He strikes me as a proud man and somewhat larger than life, a movie character with a neatly trimmed beard left to age naturally with salt and pepper grey. His most striking feature, however, is a black eye patch, a sentiment to some event suffered as a young soldier, one that he likely never speaks of. In a world where any wound can be healed, this statement is not lost upon me.

"Smith," the captain greets us, though his demeanor is hard to read. "What have I told you about using my ship as a damned taxi service?"

"Good to see you too, Hamid."

The two embrace hands in genuine camaraderie and some of the seriousness of the moment evaporates.

"Is it as bad as they say?" the captain asks.

"I think it might be."

The captain nods. "You can accompany me down to port but after that, you're on your own. I've learned my lesson. I don't get involved with those sharks over at Temporal Affairs. And rumor has it, they're gunning for you. Watch yourself."

Careena shrugs. "Eh, what else is new."

Beside us in the hangar are rows of fighters, each a futuristic super jet, slick and intimidating. I'd touch one, but they're so polished and beautiful, I fear I'd leave grubby fingerprints all over them. I know some boys at school who'd lose their minds if they could be this close to such amazing weapons of aerial, or perhaps I should say, stellar, combat. I'm more meh myself. "Will we be taking one of these down?" I ask.

"No," the captain tells me. "We have a diplomatic transport aboard which we'll be taking down. It's far more comfortable, I assure you. The *Ark Royal* is the flagship of the Tegan Navy. In addition to these twenty-one fighters, we have three recon scouts, and three hundred dropboxes for planetary assault. Though now that the war is over, we'll probably be replacing those with something more practical one of these days. If you two will follow me, the others are waiting."

We follow the captain down the length of the hangar, passing the neatly aligned rows of fighters. It feels like being on a movie set. I turn to Careena. "You used to fly one of these?"

She glances at me suspiciously. "How did you know I was a fighter pilot? That information is bloody classified."

I wink back. "You're not the only one with your secrets."

"Smith was one of the best," Captain Bashir says. "We were sad to lose her to those loons over at Temporal Affairs."

"Speaking of loons," Careena says, pointing to a fighter kept on display at the end of the hangar. "What is that old tin can doing here?"

Even I can tell that this particular fighter jet is an antique.

"That's *Sexy Sadie*," answers the captain. "We found her drifting while on patrol some years back. She must have made her way all the way from the Sombor Mandate. She's a piece of history, a relic from the First Khelt War. She'd been floating out there for more than six hundred years. She's got manual controls. Nothing like what you and I used to fly, Smith."

Careena keeps her distance. "Looks bloody haunted, if you ask me. You should toss it back out into space."

"Who are these Khelts?" I ask.

The captain looks at me strangely. "They don't teach history where you're from?"

Careena waves her hand. "Ignore her. She's from a nun convent on the frontier, doesn't get out much." She leans toward me. "The Khelts are machines, deary. From the planet Kheltaris. They're the reason we don't put hard drives in our heads. No one wants to end up the way they did. Anyway, it's not important. We have bigger fish to fry at the moment."

"Patmos," I say.

"Aye."

We reach the long, slender transport yacht that will take us down to the surface. Several of the captain's officers and aids are already aboard. The interior is not unlike that of a comfy private jet. Not that I'd know—my transportation experience is generally limited to the New Jersey Transit commuter rail.

"About this Patmos," Bashir says as we take our seats. "Military intelligence doesn't have much at this point. It would be difficult for him and his group to operate on any of the mainline worlds, so we're assuming he's from the frontier. No known groups match the description and capabilities we've been given, but that's not saying much. It takes months to receive updates from the outermost colonies. If he arrived here using jump technology, then he'll be well ahead of any warnings we'd receive from out there."

"And what about the Red Man?" I ask.

I hate to even think of that monster and his men. It brings up memories I'd rather not deal with. But I have to know.

"Him we know more about," the captain tells me. "His rap sheet goes back decades. He's highly modified, well beyond the

2161 Standard, which makes him dangerous, but also severely restricts the places he can access. As Smith mentioned, body modifications are strictly regulated. Ships like this one, important buildings, sometimes even entire city districts, have sensors that will alert the authorities to anyone with illegal modifications. Intelligence has done a psych profile on the man. Patmos may have ideological or religious motives, but they don't believe that to be the case with the Red Man. He's simply a hired gun, though likely one with a strict honor code and a misplaced sense of purpose. We do think he's still working for Patmos, however. So if we can find the Red Man, we believe he can lead us to Patmos."

"I hope you do, captain."

"We will, ma'am. Don't you worry."

Our little ship departs the hangar and drops comfortably toward the surface. I'm fortunate to have a window seat where I quickly become enthralled, first by the continent below us and then by the city of New Harmony as it comes into view the closer we approach.

I saw a poster of New Harmony earlier aboard the *Stellar Pearl*, but that doesn't compare to the real thing. This is the capital of the Republic of Tegana, a city entirely white and circular in form. Circles are embedded throughout its design, large circles and small circles, circles overlapping circles. There's something organic to the design, like the rings of several trees that have grown together over many generations.

The surrounding countryside is a green and open steppe, with rivers and gently rolling hills. A few suburban settlements are scattered about as well; each their own circle, each white, each a tiny droplet sitting at the edge of a beautiful ivory pool. Trains shoot between these settlements at impossible speeds. There are no automobiles here, no sprawl, no tacky billboards or inhumane architecture; only the greens of nature, the yellows of agriculture, and the white simplicity of a humble city.

Careena catches me staring at the city as we descend. "She was a Quaker settlement originally. They used the radial design to stress equality and the simple, white architecture to stress modesty. There are very few tall buildings, only in the city center, and even those aren't as tall as those garish towers all the Mahshadi live in."

"Where did they go?" I ask.

"Who?"

"The Quakers."

"Why, they didn't go anywhere," she says. "They're me! My ancestors anyway. I'm a descendant of the original settlers. But religions from Old Earth were hard to keep going once we started colonizing the stars and finding life on other worlds, cracking the mysteries of physics, that sort of thing. I think at first a lot of religions saw the cosmic frontier the same way sects from Old Europe must have seen the Americas, a world free from the interference of the state. You could start a colony out here and teach your children any ludicrous notion you wanted. And there'd be no cable television or internet to contradict you otherwise."

It made sense.

"So what happened?"

"Time can be cruel, I reckon. Quite a few of the original colonies were spearheaded by religious organizations. They were eager to leave and start up their little utopias. But because they went first, they only ended up in the Inner Core, which wasn't so far from Earth once we had faster ships. That made those worlds prime real estate. They were flooded with immigration, and eventually absorbed back into the very secular culture they had hoped to escape. The Quakers came here later. I guess you could call this region the Midcore now. But after four hundred years, the results have been the same."

"And aliens? Weren't they out here, colonizing worlds too?"

"You'd think so, but no. Last I heard, there are six hundred and forty-eight worlds with indigenous life that we know of. Though that number is always changing. News of discoveries from the other galactic arms is slow to reach us here. Even so, most of those worlds have never evolved beyond anything more interesting than strange bacterial sludge and photosynthetic algae. Only a few, maybe thirty or forty, have fully developed biospheres with complex ecosystems and critters that we'd call proper animals."

"And intelligent life?" I press.

She laughs. "You met them! The Thanes. Those little bark-skinned boogers. Our fellow intelligentsia in the universe. The truth is, they didn't even have nuclear fission when we encountered them. Though they did manage to shoot an astronaut into space, so we figured it wouldn't hurt to stop by and say hello. Scared the piss out of them, I'm sure. But we were lonely exploring the cosmos all alone. And maybe they had some answers about the nature of existence that we didn't. Turns out, though, they were even more clueless than we were. But they can talk. So that's something, I guess. We were excited about that."

I think back to Lieutenant Chimat. I did like him; he had a strange sort of charm and charisma. I almost miss the strange little man and his boundless enthusiasm for felines.

"We've landed," an officer announces.

"Ladies, welcome to New Harmony," Bashir offers as he and his aids depart. "And Smith, good luck."

I disembark with Careena and see there are only one or two other ships on the large circular platform. They look very militaristic, as do all the workers coming and going about their business. This must be a military base—not the civilian landing port.

Story Beckett is waiting for us on the platform as a tram arrives to take us to the main terminal.

"Is that really you?" I ask as we approach.

She extends a hand. "In the flesh."

I take the hand.

It's warm with life.

I can't help but pull her in for a long overdue hug.

Careena looks around with suspicion. "So you're all we get for a welcoming committee? I thought that hag would have sent a whole battalion here to drag my arse back."

"Oh, she did," Story answers. "They're waiting for you over at Port Central. They still think you're aboard the *Stellar Pearl*."

Careena raises an eyebrow. "A lie, Beckett?"

"A clerical error."

"Bless your damned heart, girl."

The young officer goes on, "I thought you might want a little time to enjoy the city on your own."

"Thank you."

"I'll meet you back at headquarters?"

The old woman nods. "Of course, I won't take too long."

Story welcomes me again to Tegana and then takes her leave. I look out at a horizon, a sky, a sun that is not the one I've known my entire life. To imagine, that I'd be standing on another world, in another arm of the galaxy, and that it would be so beautiful, with a calm breeze and the gentle scent of morning.

A few birds pass by overhead. What is their story? Were they imported from Earth centuries ago? Would they still know their terrestrial cousins were they to ever meet them? I have so many questions, but Careena simply takes my arm and pulls me along.

My tour, it seems, has only just begun.

10

With the excitement of a schoolgirl, Careena shows me as much as she can. Her normal bitterness, that wall she always has up, that barrier between her and the world, has come down, if only slightly. There's even, dare I say, a twinkle in her eye.

We walk through some very beautiful neighborhoods. The homes are stone with simple bleached facades, reminiscent of the white painted houses of the Greek Aegean Sea, yet it's clear they have all the amenities befitting a city perched at the edge of the universe; they're simply disguised as something modest and unassuming.

"I grew up on this street," she tells me at one point. The street she shows me is charming, with cobblestones below and occasional grape vines growing overhead, offering shade and the green of nature. The doors of the white houses are painted different shades of blue, with the occasional red. It really is quite lovely. Where streets intersect, there's sometimes a small stone plaza with a fountain and some benches, a sort of neighborhood square where children play and couples sit.

We continue on toward the heart of the city, where the buildings become taller, though rarely more than five or six stories, and never do they lose their humble aesthetic.

The city center surrounds a great circular space of botanical gardens, small lakes, and running paths known as Prospect Park. One side of the park climbs up a low hill; it seems half the city sits a few hundred feet above the other. On the edge of that hill, overlooking the park, are many official-looking white buildings. Careena tells me that is our destination, the district known as Parliament Hill. One of those buildings is the Ministry of Temporal Affairs.

But before we get there, we pass a pub at the edge of the park.

"Let's just pop in for a pint, shall we?"

"Really, Careena? Is this the time?"

She seems offended. "When isn't it the time?"

"Fine."

We enter the quiet pub, which is named McCoy's. A handful of patrons sit around tables, though few seem to have much to say. The place seems more like a sort of limbo, where souls come to avoid the chores of daily life, the demands of nagging family members; here one can be alone with their thoughts, and yet not alone at all.

The bartender sports a thick, curly mustache and suspenders. Like nearly everyone else I've seen in the future, he looks to be somewhere in his early thirties, though his eyes betray a much older spirit.

Careena scans the patrons, recognizing a few. "Hell must be empty, all the devils are here."

The bartender looks up. "Well, well. Lock up your sons, lads. Trouble just blew in."

The two exchange smiles and a handshake that seems to have been many years in the waiting. Many of the patrons mumble a salute before returning to the contents of their glasses.

"How you been, Smith?" the bartender asks.

Careena and I take a seat at the bar.

"Good enough," the old woman answers.

"We've missed you 'round here. Still doing them secret missions for the Navy?"

"That's classified."

The bartender winks at me. "That would be why they call them secret, I reckon. You on a secret mission as well, lass?"

"Something like that," I tell him.

He pours three liquors into shot glasses. "This one's on the house, ladies. To Captain Smith. For saving my arse more times than I have fingers to count."

We down the liquid together.

My nostrils flare and my eyes water.

But I try my best to play it cool.

"So what's with the wrinkles, Smith?" the bartender asks. "You aging out on us?"

"Has to come sometime," she says.

"Ain't that the truth," he replies. "I'll probably get the nerve one of these days. I mean running a bar forever? Your soul just gets old. You can feel it. Inside. Part of me wishes I'd never come back from that damned war. At least then there wouldn't be a choice in it. It's the choice that drives you mad."

With that, he moves down the bar to attend to another patron.

I turn to Careena. "What does he mean *age out*?"

"It's the 31st Century, Freckles. Old age was solved long ago."

That does explain why so many people look so young. Though I still don't understand this concept of aging out. Or why anyone would want it. Since the beginning of time, hasn't humanity dreamed of the fountain of youth, of the keys to immortality? And now they just toss them away? I can't believe it.

Careena attempts to explain. "Living forever is a dreadful thought. You don't think so when you're young, you can't even imagine, but take my word. You tell yourself, *that will never be me*. But then at some point, you've done everything you've ever wanted to do, seen everything you've ever wanted to see, and you've accepted existence for the mystery that it will always be. You come to understand that no answers will ever be forthcoming, no matter how long you wait around for them. And you grow tired. Some before others, but eventually the feeling takes hold of everyone. Then you want to break the cycle. It's almost like a calling."

"And then what?" I ask. "You just pull a trigger?"

"No, of course not. No one wants that. We just... turn off the magic. We give ourselves back to nature. We let ourselves grow old. And if you get second thoughts, you can always go back to how you were before. But you'd be surprised how many people stick with it, once they've decided, that is. There's a relief in it. I guess you just know when it's your time."

I let all of this sink in.

"So, what are you saying? The bartender isn't thirty?"

"Oh, heavens, no. He's older than me."

I'm afraid to ask. "And how old are you?"

"Hah! How old am I she asks! Didn't anyone ever tell you it's impolite to inquire a woman's age, deary? I'd give up Tegan state secrets before I ever give up that information. Now come on, it's time to get you home."

We leave the pub and head across Prospect Park to Parliament Hill. We pass children at play, couples out for walks, workers on breaks; it couldn't be a more beautiful day. Part of me wishes I could stay longer and explore this new realm, but I have to admit, I'm starting to miss my friends and my family.

I still haven't decided what I will tell everyone. Careena said a day in the past is also a day in the future, but I'm not sure if the reverse is true or if they can simply reinsert me at the moment I left Shira's rooftop. Though, if they could send me back to Oradell instead of Brooklyn, they'd be saving me three train transfers, so maybe I'll ask about that.

I want to tell my dad about everything I've seen, that his stupid sci-fi shows got it all wrong, well a few things right, but mostly I just want to blow his mind. I wish I had a camera, some way to capture these memories, but I left my phone in Shira's room. Stupid. On a normal day I can't even go to the toilet without that thing.

Not that it matters, I guess. I suspect they're going to make me swear an oath of secrecy. Or, who knows, maybe they'll even delete my memories. That would be a shame. Though not entirely. If I never have to remember that attack on the *Stellar Pearl* again, I won't protest. But I'd like to remember Careena and Story, my friends from this other time.

We make our way up the hillside, with its terraced staircases, until we're in the streets of Parliament Hill, the city's centermost district. It's a stately neighborhood, with a series of stone plazas and Greek-inspired buildings facing one another at odd but interesting angles. There are fountains at busy intersections as well. I have a feeling this is not a reproduction of an ancient city, but simply the logical continuation of thousands of years of city planning evolution, the culmination of best practices discovered by centuries of trial and error.

As my dad often likes to complain, American planners sadly threw most of this received wisdom out the window at some point in the 1950s. I'm unsurprised to see that little of their influence has survived into the present day. Unlike back home, here the roads have not been engineered as little more than sewers for noisy cars. The streetscape has not been hacked to pieces just to make room to shoehorn in parking lots for automobiles. We're in the middle of a major city, and all I hear around me are the songs of birds nesting in the many sidewalk trees.

We finally reach our destination, the Ministry of Temporal Affairs. It's white, of course—white marble. A grand stone staircase leads up to portico columns the size of redwood trees. I'm made to feel dwarfed and insignificant by the building, though perhaps that is by design. For what is humanity and all her endeavors compared to the oceans of time that will one day wash it all away?

No one prevents us from entering the great hall of the building. The doorways are open and seemingly made for giants. The ministry feels even larger inside, like a cathedral cut from a block of marble, with occasional skylights above allowing in beams of light. Lining either side of this massive hall are the marble statues of several men and women, seven in all. They must be at least twenty feet tall.

"It's like a temple," I whisper, my voice becoming lost in the mighty chamber.

Careena seems less impressed. "Wait until you meet the crackpot who runs the place."

"And who are they?" I ask of the statues.

"The original temporal agents," she tells me. "The founders of the ministry. That one there is Jonathan Baker, the pioneer of the technology. Around here he's a damned hero. Maybe I used to think that myself when I was younger. But now I think there are some corners of reality that humanity was never meant to discover."

I don't know if I agree with that entirely, but I'm willing to defer for now. I look around at the statues, one of which, a woman, is draped in a grey cloth, covered. "What's her story?" I ask.

"That's Herla Vox. She was Baker's most trusted confidante. She killed him."

"Why?"

"Because power corrupts, luv."

I wonder if maybe there's an admission in that statement.

Before I can ask any more questions, several figures come to greet us in the great hall. They are dressed in strange robes, like futuristic acolytes. They all wear tiny caps, save the lead woman, who has a silk headdress that's round like the rings of Saturn. She is tall and formidable, with straight black hair and narrow eyes. And while she looks to me to be only in her late twenties, I now know not to trust my eyes. In her youthful face is great age, of that there is no doubt.

I don't need to be told that she is the portreeve.

The woman has her gloved hands folded at her waist. There's something aristocratic about the pose. "Sister Smith, you were ordered back here years ago. Where you have been?"

"Doing my job. What the fork have you been doing?"

"Your job," the woman says in a way that conveys particular cynicism. "Some would say you've been on the run. It was out of courtesy that I allowed you to finish your final assignment, sister. To allow you that dignity. To avoid hauling you back here in chains like a common criminal. And you made us fools. Tell me, did you ever find that jumper in Sumeria? Heaven knows you had ample time."

"I was close, but then I got shot. Because you let a mole slip right passed you, Sister Soolin."

"Was that the reason?" The woman approaches and wrinkles her nose at the scent of whiskey to make her point. "You used to be such a good agent. What happened to you?"

There was a biting sincerity in the question.

And Careena has no answer to give.

"I suppose it no longer matters," this woman, Soolin, says. "Careena Jane Smith, as portreeve of this institution, and by the power vested in me by the Republic of Tegana, under the Amended Codices of Time, I am placing you under arrest for the violation of your sacred oath to the Laws of Nature. You will be charged with temporal treason, for the willful corruption of the natural timeline for personal gain, and if found guilty, the punishment will be excommunication from this plane of existence forever."

Only now do I realize Soolin's aids are all armed with silver pistols.

So there's that.

Captain Gernsback had warned me about the lion's den. And she wasn't wrong. I have the sudden feeling of being that awkward third wheel on someone else's date, one going very poorly at the moment. My presence is being ignored, but I truthfully think it's better that way.

Careena raises a finger. "You know you can't do that, Soolin. This man, Patmos, he's not just another tosspot with a jumpvest. He intends to turn the universe into swiss cheese. Now, I could have run off. For good. I could have done that years ago when you first accused me of all this hogwash. You know I could. But I came back because you need a field agent with experience. I can stop him. You need me."

Soolin's stare is harsh. She holds out her hand. "What I need, sister, is your Quantum Distortion Device."

A battle of wills is waged. Silence fills the great hall for many long moments as everyone present watches the two women, waiting to see which side will be the first to break.

Perhaps to my surprise, it's Careena who relents. She slides off her QDD, the ring known as Hecate, and hands it over to Soolin. The portreeve slips the ring into a pocket in her robe.

Careena is powerless now, her status as a demigod absconded. She's been reverted back into mortal form, a mere civilian, a bystander to the passage of history. She's been defeated by Soolin, Portreeve of the Ministry of Temporal Affairs. She's been defeated by time.

Or so one would think.

I try to hide my confusion as I fold my hands behind my back as professionally as possible, like they do in all those military movies. I do this not out of any formal sense of obligation—it's simply that there was one detail about the ring exchange between the two women that has me a little baffled.

Which is that Hecate is still on *my* hand.

I've been wearing her ever since the rooftop on Brooklyn. Careena had never asked for her back. Indeed, she'd even suggested I wear her a little longer, that she might bring me some comfort after all I've been through. I'm wondering now if the old lady didn't have some ulterior motive for leaving the ring with me. Which does raise another question.

What did she just pass off to Soolin?

I jump when the portreeve addresses me.

As much as I want to be afraid of her, there's genuine compassion in her voice. Whatever bad blood exists between her and Careena, the elegant woman is no witch.

"Dear child," she says. "I'm so sorry you had to be involved in all this. I am the portreeve of this ministry and please know that I consider your well-being my personal responsibility while you're here. Captain Beckett has already explained to me the series of unfortunate events that brought you to be with us. I offer you my apology on behalf of the Republic of Tegana. I will see that you are returned home most immediately."

"Thank you, portreeve." I fiddle with the ring for a moment behind my back. I'm aware that if I don't mention it to her now, that makes me complicit in Careena's schemings.

And what do I really know about the old woman? Not much, other than she has an uncomfortably close relationship with whiskey and that she's apparently some sort of time criminal. What if I'm choosing the wrong side? Soolin just wants to get me home—she might *actually* care about my personal well-being. No plots. No tricks. No schemes.

I look over to Careena one last time, thinking that I'm likely about to give her up. I mean, there's that ridiculous quilted overcoat, the hair tied up in a wild mess of a bun. Even her socks are two different shades. This woman is supposed to be a protector of time and space? I can smell the fricken booze from here.

No, I should trust the professionals.

But that doesn't mean that I have to trust *these* professionals.

Story Beckett risked her career to help Careena. Captain Bashir held the old woman in genuine esteem, and I doubt that man gave his respect to many. A pub full of war veterans was willing to give her a deserved nod, a raised glass. If they're all willing to vouch for her, well, it's enough for me.

I keep my mouth shut.

Soolin motions to two of her aids. "Priors Grimalkin and Paddock will escort you to the Chronos Imperium. It's a chamber of this ministry, built into the very heart of Parliament Hill. This chamber has the power to send you home."

The two priors are also dressed in strange robes, though they have sashes and sidearms. Seems the Ministry of Temporal Affairs enjoys their cosplay.

Careena butts in. "I should take her down there."

The portreeve looks impatient.

"And why on Old Earth would I allow that?"

"She knows me. Hell, she saved my life. I'd like to see her off. You and I both know this is no ordinary jump."

Something about that last part causes Soolin pause. Maybe I should be picking up on the subtext, but I don't.

"Fine, I'll allow you in the Imperium to say your farewells, but no tricks," the woman says.

"Wouldn't dream of it."

"Every console in this building has been coded against your DNA. Don't think for one moment that you can escape through the Imperium."

"I got it, I got it. Sheesh."

With that, Careena grabs my arm and leads me toward the rear of the hall while the two priors follow close behind, their hands never far from the pistols at their sides. Careena has been allowed this final courtesy, but she takes it under guard.

As Soolin had mentioned, much of the ministry is built into the hillside of Parliament Hill. This main hall is only the public face of the institution. Behind it are two wings, the Hall of Yugas and the Hall of Saros, each housing the ministry's many offices and research facilities.

I'm told both wings meet again at the base of the hill, at a large room called the Ananke, a sort of foyer that leads into this mysterious Chronos Imperium. I find all these strange names to be oddly esoteric, more superstition than science. But as long as these people get me home, I can forgive the role-playing elements of their ministry.

Speaking of which, the corridor we follow reminds me more of a national museum of culture than a ministry tasked with defending the arrow of time. There are large alcoves along the walls, each stationed with different gods of antiquity, some Greek, some Roman, but many others of indigenous origins that I don't recognize.

Beyond the alcoves we start to pass some offices. One is a conference room, sealed off, the walls inside scorched and blackened, the long table splintered and overturned. I shudder. The attack. The traitor. Careena does her best not to look inside. I know that she lost many colleagues there.

Along the opposite wall of the hallway is an inner courtyard garden, a meditative space not unlike a cave, with light coming down through skylights far above. It's peaceful, contemplative. I hear birds chirping. The secrets of this building, the purpose to its many designs, leave me with many questions.

"So what is this Chronos Imperium anyway?" I ask as we near the end of the massive and elegant hall.

Careena answers, "You asked once why we weren't affected by paradoxes and temporal loops the same way other jumpers are. Well, it's because of the Chronos Imperium. The Imperium is spherical chamber that generates a very unique energy field inside, a sort of osmotic tachyon well. Anyone jumping from within such a well becomes immune to future changes in the timeline. We call it tachyon-grounding."

I think I get it.

She goes on. "Once you're grounded, if someone goes back in time and shoots your grandmother, it won't affect you like it would a normal person. To use the movie analogy, it's like now you're from an entirely different film, being spliced into this one with special effects. That's what we are, luv. We're the special effects."

"I see. So why is Soolin grounding me?"

"That's not why she's doing it this way," Careena tells me. "It's just she can't well send you back with a jumpvest, and any of the agents who could take you back with a QDD are dead. In fact, I think all the other QDDs were destroyed in the attacks. And those things take some time to engineer. So at the moment, she's kind of neutered. But the Chronos Imperium has been set up to send a person back without a vest or QDD. We use it on our computers all the time."

"A computer? Why?"

"You'll see."

The corridor ends in a large foyer, which Careena calls the Ananke. We're deep under Parliament Hill now. To our left, the other wing of the building arrives here. The entire space has an odd design and is poorly lit. Once perhaps it was a cavern, but now the walls are covered in geometric paneling that is black and uncomfortable. Opposite us is the portal into the Chronos Imperium, a round doorway glowing brightly with gold light, the stage to this darkened audience.

To either side of the portal are two white trees, also oddly geometric, like low resolution computer renders of real oaks. Their branches reach up into the shadows, vanishing into the cavernous darkness above us.

"What are the trees for?" I ask.

"You'll have to ask Soolin. She designed them. For aesthetics, you know. She was a sculptor before she took this job. Can you forking believe that? My God. Maybe if these nutters would just stick with their art, there'd be a lot fewer genocides in the world."

The two priors, Grimalkin and Paddock, take up positions outside the entrance to the chamber, each standing beside one of the white trees. As he takes his post, Grimalkin eyes me for the briefest moment, not in disdain, for he seems polite and professional enough. I'm not sure what it is.

"They're not coming in?" I ask Careena.

"They're not allowed. The secrets held in this room are too consequential to ever be known by more than a handful of people. It's a great honor to be allowed in here, one they haven't yet earned."

So Grimalkin is jealous. I suppose I can't blame him, to spend your whole life in pursuit of a near divine cause, protecting the very sanctity of the timeline, only to have to stand by and watch a nobody from New Jersey get to enter your futuristic Holy of Holies before you do. That's got to sting a little.

Careena leads me inside.

The room is about the size of a classroom, though perfectly spherical. There's flooring under our feet so that we're standing pretty much in the center of this strange orb. At the back of the room is a raised platform. Floating above it is what looks like an umbrella, spinning slowly, connected to nothing. My impression is that it's from this platform, under the umbrella, that a jumper is sent on their way.

Curved computer terminals line the walls to the left and to the right of the room. One side has all blue lights while the other has all red. Two technicians are tending them. A freestanding terminal, like an airport ticketing stand, fronts the platform at the back of the room. That one has yellow lights and is likely used for directing jumps. The blue and red computers, though, I'm not sure what they do.

The two technicians, a man and a woman, seem very excited when we enter. "Agent Smith!" one exclaims. "We heard what happened in Brooklyn. Glad to see you got out of there in one piece."

"Did you also hear that I got canned?" Careena asks.

The female technician nods. "That rumor did circulate, yes. In fact, we've been instructed not to let you touch anything. Did you really do it? The long con?"

"Leave her be, Alice," the male technician says. "Smith has been through enough already."

"Fine, Bob."

Careena inspects the airline ticketing computer screen in front of the platform. "So you got everything programmed to send her home, yeah?"

"Yes," Alice says. "Just as the portreeve ordered. Easy peasy."

I look around the room.

"Why are some of the screens different colors?"

"I'm so happy you asked," says Alice, in the voice of one who probably doesn't get to talk about their workday much, given the classified nature to it. "You see, that terminal is Red and that terminal is Blue. They're identical. Completely in every way. Each holds the entirety of human knowledge. Why, there are probably a hundred million hours' worth of uploaded videos from the year you left alone. Plus news articles, television shows, legal documents, books, postcards, company earning statements, love letters, even child artwork from preschools. Anything that survived has been scanned and kept here."

"Why?"

Careena seems impatient. "Is this really important?"

"Come on, Smith," the male technician, Bob, says. "This is the most important department of the whole ministry."

"Damned nerds," Careena mutters.

"To answer your question," Alice says. "Blue has been grounded. Red has not. That means changes to the timeline will affect the records on Red, but not on Blue. So one hundred and eight times per day, Blue cross-references its records with Red."

I'm surprised that I can intuit the purpose of this system so quickly. "So that's how you know if someone has changed the timeline. The entries will no longer match. Red will show the new changes but Blue will show the original history. So with that, you can track down almost exactly where and when a jumper went."

Alice winks at me.

"Are you sure you're not a time agent yourself?"

"Now that you mention it, I did save her," I point out proudly.

Careena shakes her head. "Oh, come now. Bollocks. Enough chatting or these two are going to hand over all our state secrets."

She leads me over to the platform. To think, I'm almost home. But I do have one final question. Well, a million questions, but I don't want to wear out my welcome.

"So how does this chamber work?" I ask. "I know that you don't let just anyone come inside, but aren't you afraid someone else will figure it out on their own? That one day someone else will be able to do what you do?"

"That is always a concern," Alice tells me. "But seeing how we can't even figure it out, we're not too worried."

"How do you mean? You built it, didn't you?"

Bob answers. "Jonathan Baker built it. Not long after discovering tachyon-bond manipulation. But there's some... speculation about where he got the idea to build this chamber."

"Oh, great," Careena mutters. "Now come the conspiracy theories." She's pressing on the yellow terminal, but just as Soolin had warned her, nothing is happening. Mostly, she just seems impatient. I'm not sure why. I mean, I'm a little saddened that this is going to be our last time together. We should at least try to enjoy it.

"It's suspicious, is all," Bob responds with a tone that says he's definitely spent too much time on conspiratorial internet forums, or whatever is the future equivalent. "Baker is gone for a few weeks, jumping to who knows where, doesn't tell anyone where he's going or where he's been, and when he comes back, he's got the idea to build this chamber. And it works. On first go."

"And you don't know how?" I ask.

"Well, there are theories," he says. "I think it likely has something to do with the way he laid strips of RGMs in the walls. He could have layered them like circuit boards, creating a feedback resonance in here, which could then fundamentally alter a particle's tachyon well. That would do it, I think."

I look around the room—all I see is simple white paneling.

"He covered it up, obviously," Bob points out. "So that no one could study the designs or patterns. We're not allowed to remove the paneling to take a look, which tells you something. If you ask me, I think his very first jump got someone's attention, someone who hadn't given the human race much thought before then. I think they gave him the blueprints to this room."

Careena does nothing to hide her skepticism. "They? Who the fork is they?" She turns to me. "This is all new, by the way. Last time I talked to these nuts, they were convinced that we're standing inside the husk of a dead neutron star. So take anything they tell you with a grain of salt."

Bob scratches his temple. "Yes, well, we haven't got all the specifics worked out exactly. Unfortunately, Baker took his secrets with him to the grave. But there's more to the story than we know, that much is for sure. Now, miss," he says to me. "If you'll just stand on the platform."

"All right," I say.

Bob uses a cloth to wipe Careena's fingerprints off the platform terminal with the yellow lights. "You know, I'm really tempted to send you back just a few days, just to see if Alice's theory really works," he tells me as a little joke. "The free agent has always been hypothetical until now. You could save me a thousand credits on last week's poker game."

I remember Careena had also suggested that I was unique somehow, that because of the way I was brought here, I could jump to periods in time that no others could, the *blackout dates* as they were called, which cover the last four hundred years of history.

But I don't care about any of that right now. All I want now is to go home. I'm tired. I'm overwhelmed. My adventure has lasted long enough.

Careena seems to understand the way I'm feeling. "You'll be back in Brooklyn soon, Freckles," she says as I stand on the platform under the spinning umbrella. "It will be like none of this ever happened."

"It did happen, Careena."

And it did, the good and the bad.

"I know, luv."

Bob presses a button and the round doors to the chamber slowly spin closed. It must be required for the chamber to function, to fully form the field.

"I guess this is it then," I tell Careena. I tear up, even though I promised myself that I wouldn't. "I don't know what the hell has happened over these last few days, but I won't ever forget you."

"All right," Careena says, somewhat dismissively. She seems fidgety now that the doors are closing. Some people are bad at farewells, so I decide to forgive her.

"Can you tell Story I said goodbye?"

"Yes, yes."

On second thought, I do find the old woman's abrupt attitude off-putting. "Are you all right?"

"I'm fine, Freckles. Everything is going to be fine."

This is the exact moment I know everything will not, in fact, be fine. On cue, alarm klaxons blare and the pleasant light of the room turns harsh and serious.

Alice turns to her companion. "Bob, what did you do?"

"I didn't do anything."

Both technicians turn to Careena.

"Smith, what have you done?"

"Alice, Bob," she addresses them. "I'm sorry about this."

She fires Old Bessie. The blasts are invisible and knock them back. They fall to the ground and don't move.

I scream. "You killed them!"

"Piglet sticks. Don't be silly, Freckles. I stunned them. They're my bridge partners. I'll never win another game without them. Now quickly. Give me Hecate."

I stare. "I don't know if I should. You just shot your friends. And they were so nice."

Careena is losing her patience. "I shot them *because* they're nice. If Soolin thinks even for one second they were helping us, she'll arrest them both. And then where will my bridge game be? Now the ring, please, or we're going to get shot for real."

"You said Hecate was out of juice."

"A slight exaggeration, now come on!"

I want to hesitate, I do, but already there is a loud banging on the door. A crowbar is making its way into the crack. In a fit of rage, I take off the ring and toss it at Careena. "What is going on? What did you do?"

She jams the ring on her finger. "Nothing! Well, sort of nothing. That dumb hag must have figured out I gave her a fake. Damn thing was supposed to fool her scanner long enough for us to be out of here. Look, I had to power down the real Hecate to avoid tripping the sensors. It'll take her two minutes to respin, then I'll get us out of here."

I look back to the door. The crowbar has wedged it open a crack. There are several soldiers out there, but none of them look as furious as Grimalkin. The man is putting every once of strength into prying the door open. And it's working. "I don't think we have two minutes," I tell Careena.

She sees the situation as well. "Schnitzel. All right, Plan B." She aims Old Bessie and shoots the freestanding terminal computer next to the platform, blowing it into smoldering pieces.

"What the hell!" I shout. "Now we can't go anywhere."

"Don't worry."

My face turns red with anger. "Don't worry? You just shot the computer that's supposed to be taking me home!"

"Yes, I did! Look, it was programmed to transport you. And it still is. It's coded for you. Only now, without the manual controls, it's going to default to your thoughts just like Hecate does. So, well, get us out here, will you? And don't forget to take me along, please."

"So I just think about home?"

"No!" she scolds.

The doors fly open and soldiers start firing energy weapons into the room. They're hesitant, however, to actually cross the threshold, to violate this sacred space. Their hesitancy gives Careena enough time to duck behind the remnants of the computer terminal as I fall to the ground on the platform. Fortunately, they aren't shooting at me—they're trying to hit her. I'm pretty sure, though, as sparks fly in every direction, that no one should be firing at anything inside this room.

Careena yells in-between firing shots back. "Don't think of home! They'll find you there. Think of anywhere but bloody forking New Jersey! Hurry!"

There are more blasts. I'm terrified. I put my hands over my head and try to sink into the floor and disappear. I just want this all to end. My mind is racing. Thinking of a place, any place, should be easy, but it's all a blank, a giant empty void. There's so much confusion, so much screaming, and so much noise coming from every direction.

Finally, a thought comes to me.

The soldiers stop firing.

Because Careena and I are gone.

FIRST INTERLUDE

Here, a little boy and a loving young mother.

"I had the dream again, mummy."

"What dream, my love?"

"About the red monster."

"A monster?"

"Yes, but it looked like a person."

"And what did this person do?"

"They watched me."

"And what did they say?"

"Nothing."

"Nothing?"

"They cried, mummy."

"And why did they cry?"

"Because they had to do something bad."

"And they didn't want to do it?"

"No, I don't think so."

"And this red monster scares you?"

"Very much."

"Well, they can't hurt you. It's only a dream."

"I know."

"I'll protect you."

"I know."

"No one will ever harm you."

"I love you, mummy."

"I love you too, my little angel."

"Will we mend the fences today, mummy?"

"No, we should do your studies."

"But who will mend the fences?"

"Alloy can do it. That's why we bought him."

"But doesn't he get tired working all day?"

"He's a robot, silly. Robots don't tire."

"He looks tired!"

"That's because he's so old. He's all we could afford."

"Was he born here, like me?"

"He wasn't born, my love. He was made, like your shoes. But not here. Maybe he was even made on Earth, the place I come from. He could probably tell you if you ask him."

"Can you show me where Earth is again?"

"Yes, tonight. Your father taught me which star."

"I wish I could remember him."

"I wish that too."

"Do people die on Earth, mummy? Or only on our world?"

Here, a pause.

"They die everywhere, my love. Even on Earth."

"People shouldn't die."

"I know."

"It's not fair."

"I know. Our colonies are hard places, harder than any of us expected. We bear the hopes and expectations of the universe, along with the whips and scorns of time. It's always like that on the frontier. Do you know what frontier means?"

"It means we're on an adventure!"

Here, a laugh.

"Yes, I suppose it does. And like any good adventure, we have to be strong."

"We'll be strong, mummy."

"You're right. You are my strength. And we're lucky to have Alloy now, even if he's old and second-hand. But we'll be able to save a little. You can go to a proper school and a university after that. A university is like a big school for grown-ups. You'll go on to do great things. You won't have to be a farm-maker like me."

"But we need the farms."

"We do, you're right."

"You look sad, mummy."

"It's not sadness. I just have regrets, regrets I hope you never have."

"What's regrets?"

"Regrets are things in the past, things that you wish you could change, but can't."

"But maybe you can."

"Oh? And how could you do that?"

"With science, mummy! Science can do anything."

"Even change time?"

"Yes, why not?"

"Oh, my little Jonathan, you're such a thoughtful little man. Don't ever let the world change you."

"I won't, mummy, not as long as I have you."

Here, an embrace.

Here, a mother's love for her only begotten child.

Here, the beginning.

12

We met in Brampton, on the summer solstice of 1939.

I open my eyes. I'm alone in a field. The breeze is pleasant. The sun is casting down golden rays from a clear blue sky. There's a vista before me, gentle and rolling, a bucolic dreamscape of pastures and fields and the low stone fences that separate them. It's the sort of scene I'd expect to find on a painter's canvas, in a poet's lyric, a songwriter's ballad.

I take a seat on the hillside. The grass makes way for me like a cushion. With a long, deep breath, I take everything in. There are fields of barley and wheat to my left, moving with the breeze like the waves of an ocean. There's rapeseed to my right, bright, yellow, iconic; contrasting sharply with the lines of mature trees that delineate one farmstead from the next. On a neighboring hill are pastures of sheep, though from this distance they look like little more than puffs of cotton.

Then there's the village itself, old and humble. It's not even a mile away, a cute little hamlet surrounded by a sea of green. I pull my knees up to my chest. I could sit here all day, maybe forever, admiring the honesty of this beautiful place, a place where time seems to stand still, where I'm offered a quiet respite from the unforgiving march of modernity.

And yet, modernity is coming.

I'm like the witch's muse, blessed with unnatural foreknowledge and prophecy. Is this how Careena feels each time she slips into the past? Admiring the calm, yet knowing that change is just there on the horizon, threatening to throw it all into chaos?

I can feel it even now. Destiny. Fate. Inevitability. It's perched up in the hills and waiting. Does it see me here? Does it know me to be an outsider, an interloper, a threat to its best-laid schemes?

Because, like it or not, I do know what's coming. The dark tide of history. And it will consume this land before me as surely as a wildfire. This fiery tempest will have no mercy; it will sweep over the face of the entire Earth before it's extinguished, leaving no corner unscathed.

If humanity had ever known innocence before, she was about to lose it in a few short months. And once your innocence is gone, I don't think you ever get it back. I certainly can never reclaim mine.

I choose instead to focus on the beauty all around me. The village of Brampton below is quaint, as if pulled from the pages of an old fable. Or maybe that's just the American in me talking. I've always hated the commercial highways and suburban sprawl that consumes the American countryside like a cancer. Sitting here, seeing the alternative, well, I hate it even more.

But that's not why I chose this place.

We met in Brampton, on the summer solstice of 1939.

That's what my grandmother told me, about my grandfather. It was the sort of fairy tale with just enough magic weaved in to its fabric to have made a lasting impression on a little New Jersey girl. There were darker parts in the story too, of course—darker still because I'd always sensed my grandmother withheld the worst elements, that she had buried them deep in her mind and confronted them privately and alone. I didn't understand why she would do that at the time.

But now maybe I do.

She'd been born in Vienna, to a decent family of entrepreneurs. One night men with sledgehammers came through the streets, smashing windows and burning buildings. They even went into the cemeteries with those sledgehammers.

That's the part that always terrified me most as a child. I imagined these men as faceless shadows, as dark specters smashing everything they saw with their great hammers while the police watched idle. In my imagination, as quickly as they had appeared, the men vanished back into the darkness, leaving behind nothing but rivers of broken glass flowing down the streets.

It was a precursor to greater horrors to come. Fortunately, my grandmother's parents sent her away after that, perhaps prescient of this darker future on the horizon, though they could not immediately join her. It was the last time she ever saw them.

The United Kingdom was the reluctant hero of my grandmother's tale, waiving its immigration policies only a few days following that night of terror and accepting thousands of children from German-controlled lands. Many of those children, not only my grandmother, would never see their families again. But they would always carry the memories of their loved ones in their hearts.

As fate would have it, my grandmother was sent to a foster family in Brampton. The story went that on the summer solstice of the year 1939, only a few months following her arrival in this foreign nation, she met the future love of her life, a young boy who carried around baskets of eggs for delivery, eggs which he accidentally broke on her dress as he ran down the street careless as ever, singing his silly British songs, oblivious to the world.

I can imagine his fright after being yelled at by a little, dark-haired girl who did not suffer fools lightly. That he was dressed down in German probably made no less an impression.

We met in Brampton, on the summer solstice of 1939.

I look off into the distance. I like the sun on my freckles. Great Britain seems to be peacefully slumbering, innocent to the horrors she will shortly endure. A cow rattles her bell somewhere down by the village, the playful highlight of her day no doubt.

A shadow approaches me from behind.

"England?" Careena scoffs. "Of all the terrible places in the forking universe, you chose England. I bloody hate England."

My face goes red. I spring up. It will be a miracle if I don't slug this woman. "What the fuck is wrong with you!"

Careena blows me off, which only makes me angrier. "I did you a favor, freckles."

"A favor? Is that what you call this? They were about to send me home and you started a shootout. You're out of your damned mind. You ruined my life."

"Me? You think I ruined your life? The way I see it, luv, you were doing a pretty brilliant job of that yourself before you ever met me."

I stop for a moment. Not getting into that college program? Is that what she means? How did she even know about that? I really don't care. "You know what," I tell her. "I'm done with you. Soolin is going to be looking for us. I'm going to sit right here until she finds us."

"I thought you were smarter than that, Freckles. Don't be so daft."

"Screw you."

Careena looks up to the sky, like one does when they're begging gods they know don't exist for help. She turns back to me. "What do you think they do over there at the ministry? Huh? Did you not find it a little odd that they were willing to tell you whatever you wanted to know? That they didn't even ask you to keep your mouth shut once you got home? Do you really think we just give people a cup of tea and wave them off on their way?"

I pause.

She goes on. "You think Soolin was going to save you from the mean old lady on your roof, eh? Well, let me tell you about our honorable portreeve. She was going to send you back to Brooklyn all right. Fifty feet above the forking pavement!"

"What? Why would she do that?"

The old woman shakes her head, unsure of herself.

I press.

"Careena, why would she do that? What aren't you telling me?"

"Because..." She hesitates. "Because, she was going to make everything exactly as it was. *Exactly*."

I get a sick feeling in my gut. "I don't understand."

"Freckles, on the rooftop, you fell. I don't know if you jumped or if it was the wind, but that day we met, you were supposed to fall."

My eyes go wide. "And they all knew this?"

"They did."

"Give me your gun," I demand.

"Why?"

"Because I'm going to go shoot that witch Soolin in the face."

"I'd love that as much as you, but you can't blame them, not really, not even that hag. No one wanted to see this happen to you. But they've sworn an oath to protect the timeline at any cost. The consequences of doing otherwise are too dire, too unpredictable."

I'm stunned. "How long did you know?"

"Right from the beginning," she admits. "Emergency protocol. If an operative needs help in the field and none of the other agents are available, the QDD chooses a local from the historical records for assistance. An ideal candidate is someone capable, alone, and about to get hit by a bus. It minimizes any risk to the timeline."

The rooftop. That breeze. I came down from the ledge just in time to save Careena. But what if it had been the other way around? "You saved me..."

"Now don't go getting all mushy on me, Freckles. And let's not get ahead of ourselves. We're not out of the proverbial woods just yet."

"All right," I say. "But I need more. You can't hold back on me any longer. Why are they after you? What did you do?"

"Nothing!" she yells, a little too quickly.

"Careena, they seem to think you did something."

The old woman pauses. "They think I tried to save someone."

"Someone in the past?"

"Aye."

"Someone you knew?"

She's silent a moment. "Aye."

I can see the pain in her eyes.

"I understand if you don't want to talk about it."

"There's nothing to talk about. I lost someone. It's the way the world works, ain't it? Circle of life and all that. I admit, I wouldn't hesitate to go back and change things if I could. Maybe it's that possibility that gnaws at you. When it's not an option, you just accept it and move on. But the truth is, it never was an option, not really. It happened almost twenty years ago, and like I told you, we can't jump into the blackout dates, so there's nothing to be done. We've been given the power to alter the course of human history, yet destiny has forbidden us the power to alter our own lives. Irony, I suppose."

"Still, I don't understand. If no one can jump into those dates, why are you suspected of anything in the first place?"

She shrugs. "You'll have to ask Soolin. All I've been told is that there was a discrepancy in the historical record and that I was the prime suspect. A woman died. A woman I knew. Someone tried to save her. But the attempt failed and she still died. It was enough, however, for Blue to flag Red. Given the unique time period of the incident, it prompted quite an investigation. Not long after that, Soolin discovered I had a relationship with the woman, a relationship I had never disclosed. So I had motive, and it turns out no alibi."

"Maybe you were framed," I suggest.

"It's a plausible theory, though it's no easy task to hack into either Red or Blue, so I'm not sure how I could prove it. Maybe I simply angered God. Wouldn't surprise me at this point."

"I'm sorry, Careena. She must have been very special to you, whoever she was."

"It's not important now. I saved your arse, didn't I? If that impudent strumpet, Soolin, wants to hang me for temporal treason, at least now she can do it with a clear conscience."

"For what it's worth, thank you."

"Don't thank me yet, Freckles. All I've done is make you an exile. Neither one of us can go home now. And worse, every action we take from here on out, no matter how small or seemingly insignificant, becomes a liability. The more we corrupt the timeline, the easier it will be for them to find us."

I try not to consider the ramifications of what she's telling me, that I'll never see my parents again, my friends, I'll never finish school, go to college; I'll never get married or have children, not that I've ever considered that before, but I at least liked having the option. Now even that has been taken from me. Instead, I'll be a fugitive on the run, which truthfully, is only romantic in the movies. In reality, it's terrifying. I never asked for this life, and yet I've been thrust in to it.

And now I've been told I can never go back.

13

I have precious little time to consider the gravity of the situation I've found myself in, before Careena reminds me that situation is even worse than it first seems.

"None of this matter much anyhow," she says a little too casually for my liking. "That nutter Patmos is likely to turn the universe inside out soon. And then it's so long potatoes." She's got her hands on her hips while scanning the surrounding countryside, as if looking for something.

I collect myself. "Okay. So how do we stop him?"

She turns to me like I've told her I've just given birth to an elephant. "Stop him? Deary, we can't stop him. Soolin has an entire ministry trying to stop that turd. And she's got the most advanced technology in the universe. What have we got? Those sheep over there. That's what we've got."

This woman sometimes. Really.

Who is the adult here?

"We can't give up, Careena."

"What do you want me to do? Click my heels three times? We're done, Freckles. Finished. Beaten. The best we can do is live out retirement on some quiet tropical island, preferably one with whiskey sours and foot rubs."

This can't be right. There are moments of discouragement, sure, when you and your team are ready to throw in the towel, when the odds are stacked against you and the chances of success look grim, but that's exactly when you have to press on. You give it your all in that final stretch, because sometimes surrender is not an option.

I put as much passion into my voice as I can. "We can't let the world just end, Careena. Not now, not after coming this far. I heard how everyone spoke of you. It's why I stood by you, even when every impulse I had was to turn you over to Soolin. Don't make me regret that. They said you were one of the best once. I don't know what made you give up, but I need you to be that other woman, the one they all talk about. She's still in there. I know she is. And I need her right now."

My coach would be proud.

Careena, on the other hand, just tries to wave me away with a hand, like I've let out some nasty gas. "Jesus Christ. Fine, fine. You're worse than Beckett. Good lord."

"So we're going to do something?"

Careena puts a finger to the tip of her nose. "Sure. What's the name of that village down there?"

"Brampton. I think."

"You think?"

"Well, I mean, it's not like I've ever been here before. And *somebody* shot the computer, so who knows if it was working correctly."

"Good point," she says. "We'll assume it's Brampton or some reasonable equivalent. We'll head down there."

"For what?"

"This is England, ain't it? There's bound to be pub down there, Freckles."

I want to strangle her.

"A drink. Of course."

Careena starts walking toward the village and calls back to me. "Hey, if I had my way, we'd drink till we drop dead, luv. But I don't want to listen to you harp on me all evening all sanctimonious like, so we'll just drink till I come up with a plan. How's that?"

"Fine."

We march across the fields to Brampton. Hopefully, my grandparents have already had their star-crossed, or perhaps I should say egg-crossed, encounter. Messing that up is the last thing I need right now.

Already in the village, rising from sagging chimneys, are thin spires of black smoke from afternoon cooking fires. The town center is rustic. There's a cobblestone square surrounded by a few quaint shops and an odd clock tower. And just as Careena, wisest of the time-traveling secret agents of the distant future, has predicted, there's also a pub.

The old lady storms in like she owns the place. "Bartender, a pint, please. And one here for my friend."

The bartender is an elderly man with a drooping face and a handle bar mustache bleached orange by tobacco, but only in some parts.

He seems polite enough, though I have difficulty understanding him. Half his words come out like they're strung together like wet soap.

He says something after pouring the two pints, but I can only smile and nod. Apparently Hecate's translation program has been fooled into believing whatever the man is speaking is English, thereby taking the day off. I turn toward Careena, "Why is he asking for a squid?"

"I believe he's asking for a *quid*, dear."

"Oh, right." I ponder this a moment. "What's a quid?"

Careena doesn't answer directly. Instead, she leans in close to me and whispers. "You know, it suddenly occurs to me that I haven't any... money."

That could present a problem. Fortunately, while I may have forgotten my cellphone, I do have my money clip. I reach into my back pocket. "Excuse me, sir. But would you accept payment in United States dollars?"

Careena slaps my hand. "Idiot! You can't give him money with a black president on the note. Don't you know what year this is?"

"Wait, does that happen?"

"A fancy girl like you must have something of value. Some jewelry, yeah?"

"Why my jewelry? What not your jewelry? Those earrings."

I point to her small plastic pearls.

"No good," she says. "These earrings can hijack satellite transmissions. What have you got?"

I shake my head. "Nothing. I took all my jewelry off before my nap. Then I went up to the roof."

"Bollocks. I hate to say it, deary, but we may have to shoot this old geezer."

I can't tell if she's serious. But then I remember something. Luckily no one else is in the pub, or I'm not sure I could do what I'm about to do. I undo my belt and unzip my pants, reaching down under the counter where hopefully the bartender can't see me. I cringe with discomfort. But I have what I need. I hold up a small silver bar, slightly curved, with orbs at either end.

Careena is somewhat slack-jawed. "Where the bloody hell did that just come from?"

"You really don't want to know."

I turn to the old bartender. "It's fourteen karat white gold. Can we pay with this?"

He takes a bite to test the quality of the metal, which causes me to squirm, but then he nods and refills our pints. Afterward, he takes a seat behind the bar, with a paper in hand. The threat of war looms in the headlines.

I lean over to Careena. "I really have to ask, is your first impulse always to shoot people?"

She just shrugs and takes a sip of ale.

I look around. The pub is sparsely decorated with a few odd items here and there. It's comfortable, homey.

Strange to think that in a few decades companies will spend buckets of money on interior decorators to achieve an aesthetic this old barman hadn't even given two thoughts about.

"You must feel right at home," I tell Careena.

"What makes you say that?"

"You're British aren't you?"

She scoffs. "What! Why would you think that?"

"Your accent."

"What about my accent?"

"It sounds so... British."

"Are you taking the piss? I haven't any such thing." She freezes in shocked realization. "My god. Has Hecate been translating me this whole time as a damned Brit?"

"Oh, I'm sorry. I just assumed you were speaking English. I forgot about the translation thing."

"Well, I am speaking English! I'm speaking proper 31st Century English with a sophisticated Tegan accent, I'll have you know. Without the translator, you might as well be speaking Chaucer to me. I'm going to be having words with Beckett about this. This is her doing, believe you me. As punishment. She knows how much I hate England. Makes me wonder what other linguistic schnitzel that forking tart has slipped in there."

I think of Story. "Do you think she'll still be on our side, you know, after you went all Dirty Harry back there?"

"Who's Dirty Harry?"

I try again.

"Annie Oakley?"

A blank stare.

"Rambo?"

Still nothing.

"Never mind." I lift my glass. "Cheers."

"Cheers."

We drink in silence.

I wonder if this will become our routine. Two fugitives, sitting at bars across time and space, looking for the answers to problems in the bottoms of bottles. I see now how easily one could fall into it.

After a while, Careena leaves for the toilet. I try not to think about this new future that awaits me. I had so many dreams before. To go to a top school, to become something important, something people would notice. Maybe some of that desire was motivated by bits of insecurity here and there. Maybe I wanted to prove something. To whom, I don't know. None of it matters now, of course.

And, truthfully, it all seems rather trivial in hindsight. Even if I could snap my fingers or click my heels and return home, I'm not so sure I'd continue down the same path as before, not after all I've experienced. I've seen hints now of the *real* Isabel Mendelssohn lurking inside me.

And I have to say—occasionally she's a badass and I kind of like her.

Fiddling around in my jacket pocket, I notice something.

I pull it out.

A wedding ring.

What the hell?

It takes me a long moment to realize where it came from. My chest tightens. *The washroom.* That vile man. Something was on the chain around his neck. This was that something. I knocked it off during our struggle, but whoever found me in the washroom must have thought it was mine and put it in my pocket so I wouldn't lose it.

I place the ring down on the bar. Part of me wants to hurl it into the trash bin. I close my eyes and take deep breaths, hoping I can prevent the memories and emotions from overwhelming me.

Careena returns to her seat beside me.

Her presence helps calm me.

"You buying us more rounds?" she asks.

"What?"

"That ring. You keep pulling jewelry out of only God knows where."

"Oh, no. This belonged..." The words sticks in my throat. "It belonged to the man that attacked me."

"And you've had that bloody thing this whole time?"

"I guess so. I just found it in my pocket. Honestly, I want to throw it into the deepest pit I can find."

"I understand that," she says with a touch of sympathy in her voice. "But how about we pawn it instead? Next best thing, yeah?"

"Fine."

"May I see it?"

"Sure."

She rubs it in her fingers.

"A wedding ring. Platinum if we're lucky."

"There's an inscription on the inside," I tell her. "I noticed it just before you sat down."

She holds it to the light and reads: "*To my Dearest B, I can express no kinder sign of love, than this kind kiss. Yours, Ian.* Huh. Didn't take those goons as the romantic types."

"I don't think it was his," I say. "It wasn't on his hand. He wore it on a chain around his neck. I assume he stole it."

I see a thought flash across her face. "I wouldn't be so sure. A ring like this doesn't have much value in the future. Unless it's sentimental. And if it's sentimental, it could be..." She trails off.

"Could be what?"

She doesn't answer.

"Careena, could be what?"

She turns to me. "Freckles, I think we just found a clue."

14

F reckles. I really hate it when she calls me that. I've never liked nicknames. Not when Leah started calling me JCVD in fifth grade and not now. The truth regarding my freckles is that when I was younger, and even more insecure than I am now, I used to lather on the foundation to hide them. But some battles you just can't win. Anyway, I can't ignore the light bulbs going off in Careena's eyes. She's thinking. Which is probably dangerous. I'm not sure the gears in her head are as well-oiled as I'd like.

"A clue to what?" I finally ask.

"Well, it's really more of a hunch."

"About what?"

"Maybe nothing."

"Just tell me, dammit."

"All right." She holds up the wedding band. "This ring had a trajectory through time, yeah? It started off somewhere and ended up here. Now imagine we could follow that trajectory backwards, that we could see all the places it's been."

I put on my detective hat. "Assuming you could do that, follow it backwards I mean, and assuming that creep carried it with him everywhere he went, then you'd know where he was prior to the heist."

"Exactly! And that heist took a lot of planning. I'm willing to bet the Red Man has a base somewhere and that this blockhead has been there. We find that base, we find the Red Man. And if we can find the Red Man, he can lead us to Patmos."

I look at the ring. "So how do we follow it backwards?"

"That's the tricky part," she tells me. "We can't. But like everything else, we can cheat a little. Are you familiar with the concept of an isotopic tracer?"

I think back to my AP Biology class with Mrs. Zeitvogel. "I think so. It's when you inject a patient with special radioactive molecules. They're harmless, but as they travel through your bloodstream, machines can record their path. This way you can map out blood flow and stuff like that."

"Aye, now just imagine that on a larger scale. For about twenty years, the ministry has been installing these secret satellites all over the place. It's a big project, all very hush-hush. But these satellites continually scan planets for a particular isotope of a molecule called *illatium phasrex*. When they detect it, they send this information back to Tegana."

"So where do these isotopes come from?"

She pulls a tube of lipstick from her overcoat pocket.

"From here!"

"From lipstick?"

"No, idiot. We're spies, remember? This is a disguise. Point is, with this I can go back in time and mark anything I want with *illatium phasrex*. Then the marked object will continue through time as it normally would. Nothing much happens, until it gets to the era of our satellites. After that, we know where it is. Normally we use this to find where thieves have stashed things like artwork."

"People steal artwork?"

"Oh yes, all the time," she says. "In a world where any luxury can be created at the push of a button, original artwork is one of the few things of real value. And the smarter art thieves know they can't just bring a famous painting into the future, it wouldn't scan as old enough to be authentic. So instead they go back in time, steal the art, stash it somewhere, and collect it centuries later."

"That makes sense, I guess. But we already know where the ring ends up. It ends up here." But then it hits me. Maybe the ale really does help. "Wait, I think I get it. Your satellites won't just tell you where an object is. It will show all it's movements over the last twenty years. It's like you said, we really can follow it backwards. We'll be able to see where that man was just before the heist."

"You got it, kiddo," she says.

I see one problem.

"Isn't all of this assuming that we can find this particular ring in the past and mark it with your lipstick, or whatever that is?"

She takes a deep breath. "Well, that's the tricky part, yes. And we also have to hope that the ring is older than the blackout dates, otherwise this plan is moot. But I have reason to think it is. Both the custom of wedding bands and the use of this type of metal went out of favor centuries ago."

"So how do we find it?"

"We have the inscription to help us. Two names. That's our clue, Freckles! We just need to find these two hapless lovers, tag their ring, and then we can find the Red Man's lair."

She takes a big sip of ale, pleased at her own ingenuity.

I'm a little more doubtful.

"Careena, the names we have are B and Ian. And we don't even know in which century they lived. There must be millions of couples with those names. We'll spend the next five hundred years checking them all out."

"Normally, yes. But let's assume that tosser kept this ring for a sentimental reason, yeah? I saw his file. He was a war orphan. His parents had been killed during the Second Khelt War. It's not unusual for orphans to be given keepsakes from their families. If this is all he had of them, it would have been important to him."

"Don't make me empathize with that monster, Careena."

She holds my hand. "I won't, luv. But follow with me. Maybe this ring is a family heirloom, one of the few things from Old Earth that made it out to the frontier centuries ago. A lot of early colonists couldn't bring much with them, a small box of items at most. So what we do is cross-reference B and Ian with the family tree in his personal records. That really narrows down the search. And if we find a match, then bang! We're in business. Beckett will have no trouble locating the Red Man's base."

"But even if she finds it," I ask. "Isn't all this pointless if he's already given Patmos the RGMs?"

She frowns. "We are under something of a time crunch, unfortunately. The one bit of good news is that those RGMs have to be processed before they can be used in a jumpvest. And that much material will take a week to finish. That's our window, luv. Once Patmos has functional jumpvests, I'm not sure anything can stop him. Hell, I still don't even know what he intends to do, but somehow I doubt it's going back to save the hedgehog from extinction."

"When does that happen?"

The old woman just shrugs.

"If we know all this about the ring," I tell her. "We should inform Story."

"Can't do that without alerting Soolin."

I consider this.

"All right. Then we should tell Soolin. It's irresponsible to keep this to ourselves."

"We can do that if you want, deary. But it's not going to change anything about our situation. She's still going to execute me and send you head-over-heals back to Brooklyn. Is that how you want the story to end?"

"I guess not."

Careena leans into her pint of ale. "Look, how's this. We will tell her. *After* we find the ring. I promise. It'll take an another day or two before the ministry can produce any new functional QDDs, so there's really nothing she can do now anyway, even if we did tell her. Right now, you and I are all the world's got."

I acquiesce. "I suppose you're right. But we don't have any records on this guy. And it's 1939. I don't even think they have the internet yet."

"I might have the records we need." She leans over. "Is that geezer still reading his paper?"

"He's napping."

She swipes her hand over Hecate. A floating screen appears before us—made of nothing but light like a hologram. She keeps it below the bar, waist level, in case the barman looks over at us.

I see the face of my attacker on the screen. My ears go hot. How can there be free will in the universe if I can't even control the anger and terror that takes me at the sight of a stupid photo? I try to calm my nerves. I look at the long rap sheet under his picture, before commenting, "I'm surprised they let you access all this stuff, seeing how you're, like, wanted for treason or something."

She clears her throat. "I may not have acquired all this, shall we say, legally. Remember that fake ring I gave Soolin? When she placed it in the ministry scanners, it hacked the system, sent me all the files they had on the heist, the Red Man, Patmos. I thought they might come in useful."

It dawns on me that Careena is a more skillful spy than I sometimes give her credit for.

"You wanted to get caught. That's why you went back to Tegana without a fight. But there's more to it, isn't there? You didn't go back just for these files. You wanted the files on your own case. About the friend that you lost."

"She was more than friend," Careena bites backs. But then she nods. "I had to know what they know. I had to know what happened. But that wasn't the only reason either. Beckett may have inadvertently given us an ace in the hole. I just had to make sure it would work if we needed it."

I find this comment rather cryptic. "What does that mean?"

"It's not important. Look here." She points to names in a family tree. "Ian and Barbara Hynfol. Our chap's great-great-grandparents. Married 2480 on 51 Kryten b."

"Odd name for a planet."

"It is, now that you mention it." She pauses for a thought, but it doesn't come to her. "Kryten... that name sounds familiar but I can't remember why."

"You can't look it up?"

"No. If I use Hecate to access the mainframe, they'll track us down in half a second. And just because Soolin doesn't have any QDDs, doesn't mean she won't resort to using a jumpvest to bring us in. All I have is the biographical data I downloaded."

"So what do you think?"

Careena repeats the name of the planet. "51 Kryten b. It's not a colony world. The b denotes a bio-reserve. It's an alien world."

"So maybe they went there on a honeymoon?"

"Doubtful. Alien worlds are off limits. No one should be able to touch foot on one. And certainly no one should be able to get married on one. This is damned peculiar."

"Maybe not," I suggest. "Do they ever have research facilities on these planets?"

"Yeah, I suppose sometimes."

"So there you go. Researchers. Think about it, a pair of scientists on a remote world, studying the exotic flora and fauna, stuck alone in some dreary research base on those cold, cold alien nights. Maybe we have ourselves some romantics."

"Great. I hate romantics."

She reads through what little other information there is. "It seems Barbara and Ian leave Kryten in early 2482. Travel in stasis, for nearly a century and a half, to the Perseus Frontier. Talk about wanting to get away from it all. One child is listed. Born in the frontier. Terrible records out there. Looks like Kryten is our best bet. By the time they reach the Perseus worlds, they're already in the blackout dates."

"Which only I can jump into, because I'm special."

"Something like that."

I rub my hands together. We're making progress. "So what's the plan? I assume we jump to this weird Kryten planet, find our lovebirds, and mark the wedding band with your magic lipstick?"

"Yes, that about covers it. But we won't be able to take this ring with us. I'll have to release it back to the present."

"That's fine." I sort of understand the logic here. I recall that we don't actually travel back in time. All we're doing is temporarily rearranging the molecules in the past to match their configuration in the present. But it's the same molecules, then and now. One is simply controlling the other like puppets on a string. Which means if I take this ring back with me, it will vanish from wherever it was before I arrived and appear in my possession. And once I leave, it will snap back.

No problem, except that our dear Barbara is probably the one wearing the ring, and if she comes to believe that it's haunted—and who wouldn't if it has a habit of vanishing right off your hand for a few moments at a time—then it may not end up where it needs to be in the future. It may end up hurled into the bottom an ocean.

"Careena," I ask. "Assuming our lovers are at a research base a billion trillion zillion miles from civilization, aren't they going to be a little freaked out when we show up out of nowhere? I mean, I doubt we can just disguise ourselves as Mormons and go knocking on their door."

"Aye, we'll need to be stealthier than normal," she says. "I have the coordinates of their departure. I'm going to assume that's the location of the research base. So what we'll do is jump in a kilometer away, sneak in while they're sleeping, and tag the ring. In and out. Stealthy as sour apples. They'll never know what hit them! Now finish your drink. Clocks ticking."

I'm also eager to get this over with, but I'm concerned about jumping in blindly. I ask her, "Shouldn't we check first if we can breathe the air? I don't want to be breathing acid or something, you know."

She seems to dismiss the concern. "Convergent evolution. You'd be surprised just how often nature lands on the same general blueprints for life. Turns out the window for self-replicating molecules is pretty small. They fall into one of four general types. Three of which are carbon based. As I recall, there are around twenty or thirty worlds out there with completely breathable atmospheres."

I find that very interesting, but I also seem to remember that she told me once there were more than six hundred alien worlds currently known. Those don't sound like particularly good odds for us. But maybe she knows something that I don't. "So this is one of them?" I ask.

"No clue."

I want to smack my forehead.

"Maybe this isn't the best thought out plan."

"Bah, all right, here you go."

She reaches into her pockets again, rummaging around. What she keeps in those pockets, I have no idea, but she ends up placing a pair of pliers on the table, a small pouch of candies, two hair scrunchies, an arcade token, a crayon, and finally an eyedropper, which seems to be what she was looking for. "Ah, here we are."

She puts one drop in my ale and then one in her own.

"Drink up."

"What is it?" I ask.

"Nanites. Not as powerful as the babies I had before, God rest their souls, but these'll work a treat. If the air is a little off, they'll do some work in your lungs and compensate."

"And what if the planet is a million degrees?"

"Then obviously it couldn't support life, genius." She pauses. "Unless it's like those things living on Venus. But look, if you're worried, I'll set Hecate to hop us right out of there if there's a problem. But I remember Kryten. I just can't remember why. Maybe from my school days? A documentary on Galactic Geographic that I caught once? I don't remember. But I'm sure it will be fine."

Famous last words.

But all right.

While the old barman is snoozing, we make the jump more than five hundred and forty years into the future, to the alien world known only as 51 Kryten b.

15

I had never considered the possibility of life on other worlds before. Sure, I grew up watching *Star Trek* with my dad, but that was his show, his thing, some bit of nostalgia from his own youth that he wished to pass on to me, an endeavor that netted questionable results.

Not that I minded all that much; I wasn't one of those girls who played down her intelligence or curiosity just to placate the egos of the boys at school. But I did have other, more earthly pursuits than the voyages of some corny TV crew in forehead makeup. One of those earthly pursuits was photography. I gave it up, of course, after only a year of snapping photos. It was another disposable hobby in a long list of throwaway pastimes afforded a girl born to a middle-class family.

I'm hesitant to even think about them all now. Viola, gone. Iguana, gifted to a cousin. Ballet shoes, lost in the closet. Camera, sold. And what I wouldn't give to have that fancy retro camera now—with its silvery steel dials, manual lever, and pop-out film compartment. I'd capture everything I see here. A foreign sky some other color of blue. An impostor sun, burning at the wrong temperature, casting off wrongly-hued rays. A strange air that tastes like cotton. And—

"Peanuts," Careena says, interrupting my thoughts.

"Is that a euphemism?" I ask her.

"No, the ground. Look. It's like walking on bloody peanuts."

I take a few steps and the rocks crumble under my feet. She's right. The pebbles are hollow inside. Looking around, it appears we've materialized at the edge of a mountain range. The peaks behind us aren't tall, but they're sharp, like jagged knives, broken and haphazard. We're high enough on the mountainside to have a view of a landscape below us.

And what a view it is.

There are swaths of forests bisected by several thin rivers. But the trees are unlike any I've ever seen. The trunks and limbs are smooth and white, like ivory, like skeletal fingers reaching up from the earth. Their sinewy branches grow from orbs inside circular sockets. Is that so they can rotate with the sun? Are there cellulose ligaments inside the trunk, acting like muscles? Each of the alien branches ends in a single spherical disc, bluish-green in color, with the same texture as dried moss. Light twinkles through spongy pores. Perhaps to maximize surface area inside? To wick moisture from the air? I have so many questions.

"Told you we'd okay," Careena says.

"I guess so. Strange trees, though."

"Eh? A tree is a tree,."

Despite what she says, I can tell she's as curious as I am. She's surely studied alien worlds in school, just as I was taught about the Galapagos and the Amazon, but I have the feeling this is her first time actually stepping foot on one.

And I suppose something like a tree would end up fairly common throughout the galaxy. I was always a good biology student. I remember Earth was thought to have been covered in simple, single-celled life that didn't require the sun at all for energy. Nor oxygen, of which there was little in the early years of the planet.

But once photosynthetic bacteria evolved, capable of producing energy rich sugars from water and carbon dioxide by cleverly utilizing the energy of the sun, everything changed. This chemical process released oxygen as a byproduct, and these organisms were so successful, and took over so much of the lands and the oceans, that they changed the composition of the atmosphere nearly overnight, filling it with oxygen and leading to the near total extinction of all the organisms that came before them; the old, torn down to make way for the new.

Once the sun became the primary source of the world's energy, an evolutionary arms race emerged. An organism that could stand a little taller than his neighbors got more light, potentially while even casting down some shade on all his rivals. A billion years of this back and forth, of this race to the heavens, and you end up with trees. Apparently even ones with funny looking leaves and rotating arm sockets.

"Should we be worried about wild animals here?" I ask.

"First off, you should be worried about everything. Nothing says a tree can't get its nutrients by spearing you with a branch and sucking out your blood like a forking vampire. Creepy things, trees. But as far as other life, I don't know. The categories we use on Earth start to fall apart in other ecosystems. Nothing says a bush can't have legs and wander around the countryside peacocking for pollen. Or that a space beaver can't do photosynthesis with his tail. Heck, the Thanes have cell walls. Does that make them plants? As far as this place, I still can't remember what was so special about it. But I can tell you that there's nothing intelligent around here."

"How do you know that?"

"Because the only intelligent species we've ever encountered are the Thanes. And they wear cat-themed sweaters to diplomatic conventions, so I'll leave it up to you whether or not you want to classify them as truly intelligent."

I gently step a little further away from the nearest tree. "So where's this research base at, anyway?"

She points to the horizon. "There."

A thin trail of smoke is rising from the other side of the forest below us. It's almost on the horizon. We'll have to hike down the hillside and navigate through miles of woodlands to get there.

"Careena, that looks a lot further than *a kilometer* away."

"Bah. Hecate might need recalibrated is all."

"Is this the right year, at least?"

The woman shrugs.

"And are those cooking fires? A little odd for researchers to be roughing it, don't you think?"

Careena starts climbing down a small ridge toward the forest below. "Do you always ask so many blasted questions?"

I roll my eyes. *Whatever.*

I'm going to at least assume we're in the right year. According to the records, Barbara and Ian were married on this planet in the year 2480 and left in the early months of 2482. So we've chosen the latter half of 2481 to make our move.

It's strange because the difference between the 2400's and the 3000's is entirely lost on me, it's all one big clump of future defined by weird gizmos, space colonies, and impossible cosmic travel.

Yet, for Careena this is practically ancient history, six centuries well into her past. No wonder she has trouble remembering the specifics of this world. What would I see if I went back six hundred years into my own past? Probably Spanish conquistadors terrorizing half the Americas while occasionally crapping themselves to death in wooden buckets...

Let's hope this trip goes better than that.

It takes us over an hour to make it down the rocks and into the woodlands. Fortunately, once there, the land is flat and easy to navigate. The ground is dry and seemingly normal, a mix of sand and loose dirt, no more space peanuts.

There's little ground cover, only small, odd weeds growing in patches here and there. The trees we pass are large and spaced far apart, creating a series of great, outdoor rooms for us to hike through, not unlike a pine forest, where the branches are rarely so low as to be of concern. The stiff, disc-shaped leaves offer us shade from a moderate sun.

We end up following a creek. The only sounds in this woodland is the quiet rush of water over stones in the stream and the echo of our own footsteps. Without birds, without insects, without animals of any kind, this is a silent world.

It's after another hour of hiking that we come across the girl.

Careena is a few steps behind me when we encounter her. The little girl is standing directly before us, as if blocking our passage. She's alone. Her face is dirty, her hair blonde and tangled. Her dress, perhaps once white and pretty, is tattered and filthy. She has no shoes. She stares at us.

I suppose I should make the first move.

I kneel to her level.

"Hey there, little one."

I get a small smile, barely perceivable, in return.

"What's your name?" I ask.

She doesn't say anything.

"Where are your parents?"

Careena steps up beside me and whispers, "Don't go near it!"

"It? She's a little kid."

"Exactly my point! Look how dirty she is. Dodgy characters children are. I've always said it."

"Careena, she's a kid. Kids get dirty. That's what they do."

"Fine. But don't say I didn't warn you, Freckles. Every time I see a tot, I turn tail and run. Those sticky hands, runny noses, always crying about God knows what. It's enough to give you night terrors."

I shake my head. But it does raise a question. Why is a little girl out alone in an alien forest? She looks only to be six or so. Was she born here? Or were researchers maybe allowed to bring their children on these missions? Was that even safe? Did something happen at the science base? Is that why they were using cooking fires? I decide we need more answers.

I take a small step forward. "Don't mind that crazy old lady. My name is Isabel. Is your family near?"

The girl still doesn't answer. Instead, she holds out her hand to show me what she's holding. Her smile is both innocent and mischievous.

Ordinarily, the things a child might hold include a pretty rock, a coin maybe, perhaps a tiny frog. But this looks like none of those things. In fact, I may not know much about the future, but to me the thing in the girl's hand looks an awful lot like a taser.

"Oy!"

That's the last thing I can say before the girl tasers me in the chest. My body goes rigid and I fall sideways onto the dusty ground. Try as I might, my body won't respond. I'm forced to watch the next few moments like a statue.

I see Careena pull out Old Bessie. "Okay, dirt ball, playtime's over. You had your fun. Now it's time for the adults to take charge. And don't think just because you're little that I won't enjoy this, darling."

But before Careena can stun the little girl, a little boy, just as filthy and hidden behind a tree, runs out and tasers the old lady in the leg.

"Forkballs!"

She too locks up and falls over sideways onto the dusty ground.

The little girl approaches and I notice something around her neck. It's a chain twinkling in the light of the sun. And on that chain is a ring, a familiar platinum band. My heart beats like a thunderbolt.

What is going on?

But before I can consider more, she tasers me again.

And everything goes black.

16

There's a hand on my cheek, soft and comforting in the way my grandmother's hand was when she'd feel for my temperature as a child. I open my eyes. I'm in a room, simple and undecorated. It's a cabin, built from logs, from the trunks of those strange ivory trees in the Kryten forest. A curtain on the window catches a breeze. Next to me is a cot. Careena is there, still as stone.

The hand that has awoken me belongs to a woman, perhaps thirty years old, though years of hardship have given her face and hands hard creases. She's brown skinned, some ambiguous mixture from Old Earth, and adorned in a simple white cotton dress buttoned up rather conservatively to her neck.

"Where am I?" I ask the woman. My voice is parched.

"You're safe. You're in our settlement."

"The research base?" I ask the question but somehow I know it's not the right one to pose. The simple cabin, the woman's handmade dress—this place feels more like the old pioneer days than some advanced science station on a forbidden planet at the edge of the galaxy.

"Research base?" the woman says. "No, I've never heard of such a thing. My name is Zipporah. I'm the doctor here."

"And my friend?" I ask of Careena.

"She's just fine. She'll be awake soon. We found the two of you in the woods, just over yonder, not even an hour ago."

I put my hand to my temple. It throbs slightly.

Zipporah is very polite. "May I ask what happened to you?"

"We were jumped. By some children," I tell her.

This doesn't seem to surprise the doctor. "I reckoned as much."

"You know them?"

"Yes, the swampies. They cross the mountains from time to time. They like to sneak into our settlement to steal trinkets and bits of jewelry. They think wearing such silly things will protect them from evil spirits. They're harmless really. We all hope they'll find their way back to us soon."

A teen girl enters the cabin with a tray and pitcher of water. She appears mixed race as well, dressed in the same sort of handmade outfit as the doctor. Cheerful eyes make up for her prominent ears and wide, plain face.

"They're awake," the young girl says.

"Yes," Zipporah answers.

"It was the swampies, weren't it?"

"Yes."

"I knew it! Those scoundrels!"

"Dinah!" Zipporah turns to me. "You must forgive my daughter, Dinah. She does not know her manners. May I ask your name?"

"Of course. I'm Isabel."

The daughter Dinah asks, "And did you come in the ship, Miss Isabel? The one we saw? Are you here to take us with you? I told you it was a ship, mama! We didn't make it up."

I'm not sure what to say. I just really hope Careena wakes up soon. I'm not trained in any of this secret, time travel spy stuff. Not only did the technology that brought us here not yet exist, but these 25th Century women look as if they've just stepped out of an episode of *Little House on the Prairie*.

But I have to give some answer.

"Our ship is, um, hidden," I say. "You wouldn't have seen it. My friend can explain when she wakes up."

Zipporah sees my discomfort and respectfully changes the subject. "If I might ask, how were you bested by the swampies? I don't see any marks on you, and they've never resorted to violence before."

"They zapped us."

"Zapped?"

"Yes, with these little electronic devices."

Zipporah seems troubled.

"That's not normal?" I ask.

"No, not really. They don't have any devices like that. There are no weapons at all on this world. At least, as far I know. You see, the swampies were exiled by the Great Father some years ago when they were barely of walking age. They ain't got nothing. I reckon the Great Father expected them to perish out there all alone, but they're tough little rascals. I have to believe some of the exiled wives have helped them one way or another too. As I know, they all live in the swamplands on the other side of the mountains, near the Lord's Sea."

I'm a little confused.

"You exiled little children?"

"Oh, we didn't do it," she clarifies. "The Great Father did. Though I reckon you could accuse us of standing idle. We've tried since to convince the swampies to come home, and a few of the older ones have, but really they don't trust us much. I can't say I blame them. The Great Father, you see, preached the *Harmonious Ratio of All God's Children*. Back then we believed everything he told us, without question. I reckon you probably think we're quite foolish."

There's some shame in her voice. I can hear it. But I'm still trying to catch up. How did these people get here in the first place? I doubt it was in covered wagons. Did the scientists assigned to this planet abandon their post? Go native? Or had we been wrong to assume there'd been a research base here at all? The only thing I can gather for sure is that Careena and I seem to have stumbled into some sort of cult.

Zipporah continues with an explanation, though it does little to answer my questions. "We were taught that the natural order of life is for one boy birthed for every eight daughters. Yet we wifefolk kept birthing boys and daughters in almost equal measure. The Great Father told us that were because we wasn't faithful enough, that we were having impure thoughts, that we were questioning God. Us wifefolk beat ourselves up over it mightily. As hard as we prayed, we never did reach harmony. So the excess boys either got castrated to be raised as farmhands or exiled over the mountains when they were old enough to pick roots."

I'm stunned. "That's awful."

"We ain't like that no more, Miss Isabel," young Dinah is quick to point out.

"Yes," Zipporah says. "Some of the First Wives, like my mother, were able to recollect things from their old lives, from before they came here. They'd all passed away in the early years, or were exiled themselves when they got too feisty, but we tried to piece together what we could from their stories, the ones they was never supposed to tell us, but sometimes, on cold nights, did. But so much of it was confusing. We couldn't make a hawk from a handsaw over it."

I'm afraid to ask. "What else did this Great Father tell you?"

"A bunch of bull, I'm sure. But my, did I believe it when I was little. We were taught that we fled Earth. That it was a place of great sin. For centuries the Divine Race had sent prophets to help the people of Earth see the light, but those prophets were always killed like common criminals. Our Great Father, he was one of the Divines, you see. And he chose us, to be the mothers of a new solar empire, one that would be good and pure, not wicked like the Earthfolk."

Dinah asks, "You're from Earth, ain't you, Miss Isabel?"

Wake the hell up, Careena!

But I assume there's no harm in an honest answer.

"I am."

"And you're here to save us. To take us back with you?"

"Um, not exactly."

"Cause we would go back with you if you was."

I'm at a loss.

"That's not why we're here, Dinah. I'm sorry."

The girl nods solemnly, her hair bobbing around her ears.

"Zipporah," I ask. "You said the boys were exiled over the mountains. But the one that attacked me was a girl."

"Sapphira, likely. She's a crafty little one, like her mother. But she's got a good heart."

"Why is she out there?"

Zipporah explains. "The Old Law said wives could be excommunicated for disobedience. Excommunication is the same as exile. Worse really, since without a husband a wifefolk can't attain the afterlife. Exiled boys, on the other hand, just end up back in line to be born again at their proper time. When Sapphira's mother was excommunicated, she took little Sapphira with her. That's against the Old Law. You see, Sapphira had already been promised to the Great Father. But her mother took her anyway. She was my sister, you know. She died out there. But the swampies adopted Sapphira, thank goodness. Most of the exiled wives have returned, the ones that survived that is, but the swampies refuse to have anything to do with us."

"And what happened to your Great Father?"

"Dead," she tells me without emotion. "Two or three years back now. He was old and not so immortal as he claimed. There was something of an uprising among the wifefolk after he passed. And we've been trying to rebuild something different now that he's gone. But there's so much we don't know. Most of the older wives, the ones from Earth, have all passed."

"That's why we was hoping that you were from Earth, Miss Isabel," Dinah breaks in. "You could help us. You know, you could teach us things."

"I doubt I could be of much help," I tell the two women. And it's true. This land, this world, this time, was as foreign to me as it was to them. And was I even allowed to interfere? Wouldn't I end up altering the future? Would my good intentions cause more harm than good? It's a question I really don't want to have to face. Particularly since now I understand Soolin was forced to ask the very same question of me.

"Would you like to see the settlement, Miss Isabel?" Dinah asks. She seems so excited. She's only a year or two younger than me, maybe fifteen. She's had a hard a life, but some things about adolescence never change.

I turn to her mother to see if it's all right.

"I don't see why not," Zipporah says. "You seem in good health to me. Everyone will be quite curious about you, but they'll respect your privacy. I'll tend to your friend until she wakes. Dinah, you take proper care of our guest. Don't pester her with all your questions."

"Of course, mama!"

I follow Dinah out of the cabin and into the settlement, which she tells me is called Nyssa. It's a loose collection of frontier cabins wedged between a thick alien forest and an open prairie spreading for miles to badland hills at the edge of the horizon.

Unlike most of the strange vegetation on Kryten, the prairie grass around us looks indistinguishable from grass on Earth. I mention this to Dinah.

"That's because it *is* from Earth!" the teen girl says. "It's blue grama grass from an ancient Earth kingdom called Minnesota. I reckon it must be mighty beautiful there. Have you been?"

"No, not personally."

"What's the name of your kingdom?"

"New Jersey."

"Wow. Must be so amazing there. I'll visit one day. I promise."

"Dinah," I ask. "Why is the grass here?"

"Our grandparents brought all sorts of animals and plants from Earth. Most of it died, but the grass loved it here. Eventually it killed all the native grass and took over the entire steppe. Over there you can see our livestock. We got goats, geese, and llamas. Are those common on Earth? We had piggies too, when I was real little, but they're all in the dirt now. We also grow sweet potatoes, leafy goosefoot, white currant, and cowpeas. Nothing else took to the soil so good. But that's all right cause we harvest some of the native plants now, like Red Forest root and Shiva apples, though I'm told they don't look nothing like real apples. You'd probably know, right?"

Before I can answer, she points to two cats warming themselves in the sun near a shed full of farm implements. "Oh, and there is Retsil and Remmir. They're the last cats. The Great Father brought eight woman cats and one man cat for us, to teach us about the Harmonious Ratio. But they started having too many boy cats, cause, you know, cats are wicked and don't give a hoot about God's plans or nothing. So we had to castrate the boys, all but one, of course. Unfortunately, there was a mix-up on gelding day and they castrated the one they wasn't supposed to. Oops. No more man cats, which I reckon means no more cats. Do you like cats, Miss Isabel?"

"Apparently the entire universe likes cats."

Dinah ponders this a moment, then continues the tour.

There was an innocence to the settlement, one that hid a dark secret that makes me sick and furious. That one man could brainwash so many young women. I can imagine how it all began. A charismatic sociopath, seeking out the most lost and vulnerable girls that he could find, convincing them to sever contact with their families, their lifelines of emotional support.

But how did he pay for a starship to bring them all here? I can imagine that too. He likely used the girls on Earth as drug runners or servants in other illicit activities. Forcing them into criminality only defiled their self worth even further, making his offers of redemption all the more salient.

Once he'd broken their spirits, used their longing for meaning against them, he had total control. Not only did he make them endure the sick perversions of his fantasies and his bed, but he forced them to watch as he mutilated the manhood of their own sons, as he cast out their own children, exiled the most free-thinking of their own sisters to near certain death. The holy scriptures of a cruel cosmic pervert.

"Who runs the settlement now?" I ask.

"The New Council," she tells me. "It's mostly wifefolk and the older eunuchs. We don't believe in the teachings no more. Well, maybe some of the older wifefolk do, but they keep their mouths shut. Mama says the future is up to us now. That's why I work hard on my studies. I know all the good plants. Mama is teaching me to be a doctor one day. But I'm thinking maybe I'll join the Council instead. I betchya I'm a born leader."

I smile. How similar we are, me and Dinah, in some small way. Each of us unsure of our path ahead, only knowing that we want to make it into something meaningful. And more than that, we're both adrift in an ocean that we didn't ask to traverse, thrown into a world we didn't ask to inhabit, searching for truths beyond our means to discover.

We pass several women chopping logs near a large woodpile. They are young, either my age or a little older. They whisper and gossip as we pass.

"What are they saying, you think?" I ask my guide.

She grins sheepishly.

"I reckon they think you're dressed like a boy."

I look down at my outfit, a light olive sweater under a suede jacket. Though it's likely the tight black jeans and Chelsea boots that have made the biggest impression.

"Don't worry none, Miss Isabel," Dinah says. "Next week they'll all go dressing like you. A real Earth lady! The menfolk around here are going to have to hide their trousers!"

I see a few of those men out in the fields. They're pulling weeds and tilling earth. A few wave to Dinah who waves back. Everyone in the community is well acquainted; it's a world with precious few secrets. Some children are being tended to on the porch of a cabin. Goats bleat nearby.

It's a simple, tragically beautiful world.

An old man with a long beard sits on a favorite stump, smoking a pipe. He's blind as best I can tell. I wonder his role in all this. The Great Father surely had acolytes, loyal male followers, tasked with the role of giving him more daughters to marry. Small slivers of power were surely promised in exchange for total obedience. What was their story? These willing collaborators?

Dinah is waving a long stalk of grass and breaks my train of thought. "Might I ask, Miss Isabel, if you ain't here for us, then why are you here?"

I feel a bit old every time she calls me *Miss Isabel*. We can't be that far apart in age. But I let it pass.

"I'm looking for a ring, actually," I tell her. "It's silly."

"What kind of ring?"

"A platinum wedding ring."

She reaches into her pocket. "Like this one?"

My heart jumps a beat.

She hands me a ring, identical to the one from the future.

I turn it over, there's no inscription.

"I was promised to Father Avshalom when I was six," she explains, while lowering her eyes. "He was the Right Hand of the Great Father. You saw the Left Hand sitting back there on the stump. The ring is a symbol of our union. But now I don't have to wear it no more on account of him and the Great Father being big old liars full of turd shit."

"I'm sorry."

"It's all right. I keep the ring cause, I don't know. When we were little, we was taught the rings protect us from evil. It's the opposite, though, I reckon. Still, some habits, it's hard to beat."

Dark memories are lingering in Dinah's eyes. I don't want to push her any further about the ring, but I have to find the one I'm looking for. And now that I know most of the girls have rings, it may mean Careena and I don't have to go hunting for that crazy little hellion in the woods. After all, I'm looking for a girl named Barbara, not Sapphira.

Dinah looks up. "I can show you where we keep the jewelry if you like. It's here in the temple."

She leads me to a simple chapel. There's a padlock on the door. She opens it with a key from her pocket. "I got a key on account I'm in charge of sweeping the place. We have to keep it locked cause this place is like a gold mine for the swampies. They wear sacred objects to protect themselves from Dave."

I'm about to ask who that is, but the doors open and I see long tables littered with knickknacks and baubles, jewelry and odd items. The chapel seems to have once held service, but now the pews have been pushed against the walls and I get the feeling the room is used mostly for storage.

We walk along the tables. I can't make heads or tails out of the collection of items on the tabletops. There's a row of cheap plastic crosses displayed as if they're holy relics, next a heavy gold chalice being used to prop up a poster of David Bowie. I lift a small bronze bust of Chairman Mao.

"He's a Divine," Dinah tells me. "Like Baby Jesus and Elvis."

"Right..."

One object does catch my eye, however, hanging off a stone figurine of Ganesha. It's a small hexagram star on a silver chain. The star is set with dozens of tiny diamonds. It twinkles in the light coming through the stain glass window at the head of the chapel.

Dinah sees my interest and whispers mischievously. "You can take it, Miss Isabel. I won't tell no one. Nobody's gonna miss it anyway, I promise you that. They put all this stuff in here cause they don't want to be reminded of the Great Father and his silly Divines."

I'm drawn to the necklace. But I know I can't take it. It might still have some role to play in the future. And it's not why I'm here, regardless. "No, it belongs here, Dinah. The ring I'm looking for, it had an inscription on it. From Ian to Barbara."

The girl thinks a moment. "Well, there ain't no Barbara here, and I'd know. I know everyone. But there is an Ian, he's out in the field. Oh, wait! You know, he married Big Bithiah, but like a love marriage, just last year. We're doing love marriages now, you know. That's what you do on Earth, ain't it? Some of the old wifefolk still call it false marriage, but let me tell you, them days are over, yes sir. And you know what, some of the younger ladies are taking to giving themselves Earth names, since all our names came out of one of the Great Father's stupid scripture books, and we don't want no connection to that no more. I bet you ten baby ducks that Big Bithiah chose Barbara as her new name."

So there it is.

I've solved the fricken case. Me.

I can't help but smile. Isabel Mendelssohn, secret time detective. I could get used to that. Now all I have to do is tell Careena and we can tag the ring and save the damn future.

Dinah looks at me timidly. "I hate to tell you this..."

Uh oh. "What?"

"It's just..."

"What, Dinah?"

"It's just that I don't think Big Bithiah is going to give you her ring. And they don't call her big for nothing."

I wink.

"I don't want her ring, Dinah. I just want to shake her hand."

"Well, that there I can probably arrange!"

We head back to Zipporah's cabin. Careena is awake and looking particularly disgruntled as she chats with the doctor. But I have news that's going to brighten her day.

I charge in. "Careena, I'm glad you're awake."

"Believe me, Freckles, I wish I could sleep all day. Anyway, Zipporah here was just telling me those little swamp monsters that zapped us have a penchant for nicking rings. We have to go after them."

I smile.

"No, it's all right. I found the ring. It's here."

She doesn't seem as pleased at this news as she should be. "You're not listening. We have to go after them and we have to go right now." She slides out of bed and takes a moment to steady herself. Zipporah holds her by the elbow.

I'm confused.

"Why? The ring is here. We can finish this quickly. Minimal interference. Just like you wanted."

She shoots me the most ominous look I've seen on her yet.

"Because, deary—that little hussy stole Hecate."

17

I have seen Careena's ring in action enough to know that Hecate is more than just a marvel of modern engineering, a device capable of spinning cosmic strings through brane-space at such speeds that it manipulates the very curvature of space-time, producing tachyon-tethers to higher dimensional reality, ultimately allowing the wearer to alter the fabric that forms the universe and thereby transcend the barriers of linear existence; she's more than a sophisticated machine able to interface seamlessly with the human mind, able to scan the composition of nearby objects, store terabytes of historical documents, translate a thousand languages, hack computer and security systems at will.

She's also a work of art.

"And one thing she's NOT supposed to do is pop off my forking finger!" Careena snaps.

"She does seem to have been a bit off lately," I note.

Zipporah and Dinah have given us a moment of privacy in the cabin. I'm using this time to calm Careena down. I'm not sure how well my efforts are going.

"I've seen the settlement," I tell her, hoping a change in topic might do the trick.

"And?"

"And I don't think this is scientific research base."

"Really? And what ever gave you that idea?"

She's mocking me, but I detect a softening in her voice.

I raise my cup of water. "It was the wooden cups, actually."

"Wooden cups..." She shakes her head in defeat. She sighs while putting her wrist to her forehead. "I'm sorry I snapped at you. But you're right. I remember this place now. We learned about it in primary school. It's one of those stories you love as a kid, like the voyages of the Mayflower or the Shackleton Expedition."

"So who are they?"

"Some real unfortunate goobers," she says. "They arrived here on an old, beat-up frigate called the *Star of David*. As I recall, they'd won the charter for a colony planet, which back then wasn't so hard. The Colonial Federate was giving out charters like candy, trying to grab as much of the galaxy as possible before anyone else out there could. Of course, that never ended up being a problem. We have to practically beg the Thanes to populate colonies."

"But why was the *Star of David* allowed to come here, of all places?"

"Oh, it wasn't," she explains. "But these nutters knew that even if they applied for the furthest colony they could, it was only a matter of time before the rest of humanity would catch up with them. You see, worlds are independent, to a point. Mandates function like federal unions, overseeing interplanetary trade, territorial disputes, and so on. They're pretty powerless by design, but that doesn't mean they won't intervene when necessary. And each mandate has a basic constitution granting certain human rights. Earth didn't spend trillions of dollars to terraform hundreds of worlds just so a bunch of abusive cults could flourish outside the reach of the law."

"It's looks like they weren't entirely successful," I point out.

"In this case, I suppose not. These blockheads slipped some code into their ship computers, which the inspectors must have missed before letting them leave Sol System. From what I remember, around twenty years into their sixty-year flight, the autopilot jettisoned a bunch of cargo into space. It was all designed to read on long range sensors as the debris of a destroyed ship. They left behind their black box as well, sending out a distress call and some bogus data about an explosion. As far as Earth or the Colonial Federate knew, the *Star of David* was lost en route. It wasn't unheard of at the time."

"So no one thought to come looking for them," I venture.

"Exactly. They banged a course change around some star and shot off this direction. It was a cute trick, but what they didn't consider is that alien worlds are the subject of a lot of research. They got detected not long after they established their colony here. Problem is, this planet is really, really far from anywhere. It's not like the authorities can just drive by and pick everyone up and take them home. The Colonial Federate realized that from the nearest starbase, they'd have to send a ship and a crew eighteen years *each way* to get these schnitzelheads. Who wants to volunteer for that mission?"

"So they decided to leave them here?"

"Maybe at first they thought they might," she tells me. "But videos started going around in the media. Interviews with women who had escaped the Great Father's cult before he left Earth. Once his predilections were known, it wasn't so easy to just ignore all those girls he'd taken with him. Their families advocated for their rescue. There was political pressure as well. Leaving them out here might encourage others to attempt the same trick. So something had to be done. The Japanese Star Navy drew the short straw. They have a ship on the way right now. The *Yamato*, as I recall. Been en route for nearly two decades. It will be here in a few months, and then all this..."

"Comes to end," I realize.

It seemed as if Dinah was going to get her rescue after all, whether she wanted it or not. The way of life here, the future these colonists were forging for themselves, it was all going to be taken from them soon. Perhaps that was for the best.

But I'm still pained at the thought of how hard it will be for them to adjust to a brave new world beyond the stars that they know nothing about, particularly after having only just recently shed their chains of bondage in order to pioneer a destiny of their own. Instead, they were about to become novelties, something schoolchildren like Careena will read about in books one day. It saddens me.

Careena calls out the doorway to the front porch. "Zipporah, we're ready. Can you tell us where to find these swampies?"

Zipporah and Dinah come back inside. It's Dinah who answers with her cheerful enthusiasm. "I can take you. We can trade for your ring back. It shouldn't be no problem. We got things the swampies would give a left arm to have. Like China Jesus."

Zipporah is less enthusiastic. "Dinah, dear, you can't head over the mountains. It ain't safe. And you wouldn't know where to find them. The lands beyond the mountains are vast."

"I'll take Hagen. He knows the way."

"Who is Hagen?" I ask.

Dinah answers. "He was a swampie, but he came back to us. He's older now, my age there abouts. He'll know where to find the others."

Zipporah is still shaking her head. "Hagen can take them if they need it, but I can't let you go. I need you here."

Dinah stomps her foot. "To do what, mama? Pull roots? Milk them old smelly goats? It's the same thing every day. This is my chance to do something important."

"Dinah..."

"I'm going and that's that!" Dinah turns to me. "Meet me at the old shed, the one with the cats. I'll get us food and some spears."

She marches out.

Zipporah attempts a smile. "It's almost enough to make you miss the old fathers. I'm not so sure I can survive this new generation of girls."

I'm still stunned. "Did she say spears?"

"The mountains are home to a few dangerous creatures," Zipporah says. "Hagen will know how to deal with them. You can trust him. Look out for Dinah, will you?"

Careena peers out the doorway. "From the look of that girl, these creatures of yours best watch out for her."

A little while later, Careena and I meet Dinah and Hagen at the shed. Hagen is tall and lanky, perhaps sixteen, with rust-colored hair and red freckles from chin to hairline. He and Dinah both have backpacks filled with bread, flasks of water, a bedroll and a spear each.

Careena declines her own spear. "If we run across any monsters, luv, just let me and Old Bessie here do the talking."

We set out almost immediately, hoping to reach the base of the mountains, which Dinah calls the Spine of the World, before nightfall. Whole crowds of settlers have come out to see us off. The rumor has spread that Careena and I arrived on a small ship and that the swampies stole our keys, which isn't so far off from the truth. But that doesn't explain why so many of them are here, at the edge of the village, waiting for us.

My heart breaks as I come to understand. Women come up to me, they fall on their knees, they cry and they plead. They've heard where we're going and they're begging us to bring back the swampies.

These are the mothers.

In anguish they try to hand me small toys and old blankets, anything they still possess that might prove to their sons that their mothers never failed in loving them, even while they stood silently by and watched as the Great Father sent them away into exile.

I try to cover my own tears as I'm forced to decline the objects.

I want to blame them for what they have done, but I can't. Most were children themselves at the time, brides at six or seven, mothers at fifteen. This way of life was all they ever knew and they were promised it was righteous and pure, that they had been saved from the salacious and sinful cultures of Old Earth.

Knots form in my stomach knowing how these women were shamed by the very people entrusted to care for them, how they were told it was a religious obligation to abandon these little boys, and how, even worse, it was their fault, it was their dereliction of faith, that had caused them to birth too many males to begin with.

I can't imagine the crushing burden of that guilt. And now all that these women want is for their sons to return and to hope beyond hope that they can be forgiven.

It is with a heavy heart that we depart Nyssa.

18

The first leg of our journey brings us back through the woodlands Careena and I encountered earlier, before our untimely ambush. Hagen keeps a quick pace, which I know Careena appreciates. It's strange to see her like this, defrocked and powerless, turned anxious and irritable. For most of the hike, I can pull little more than a stray grumble out of her.

We reach the foothills of the mountains by evening. We climb a small ridge, where Hagen brings us to a stop. It's too dark to continue any further. Ironically, this is the very clearing where Careena and I had first arrived. I can still make out my footprints in the soil, my first steps on an alien world. The universe has a funny way of bringing you full circle sometimes.

Our redheaded boy leader addresses us. He points his spear upward toward the jagged peaks, which in the evening light of a setting sun appear more like the silhouettes of shark teeth than mountains.

"The pass through the mountains starts right up there," he tells us. "But we'll never manage in the dark. We'll camp here for the night and head up first thing in the morn."

"What's up there?" I ask.

He's much too young to be leading an expedition, but he hides it very well. "Stinging vines and skinroot for one. But what we really got to watch out for are the claw bush. That's why we got the spears. With any luck, we won't run into any of them."

"And beyond the mountains?"

"Beyond the mountains is the swamps," he tells me. "And beyond the swamps is the Lord's Sea. Ain't really nothing bad for us in the swamps. That's why the swampies live there. The sea is another matter, but I reckon we won't need to go that far."

My questions answered, I help Dinah clear a patch of ground for a fire. She tells me to make sure we sweep all of the hollow pebbles away. She says they fall from the trees. And apparently they have a habit of exploding when heated. Once we get the fire going, all four of us crowd around it for warmth.

For dinner, Dinah shows me how to cut the native roots she brought and boil them. From her pack, she produces a clay jar of sugary jam, from the Shiva apples.

"Put the jam on the daggit roots," she tells me. "It's better that way. Otherwise, they taste like smelly cat butts."

I do as she suggests and smile at myself—my first foray into extraterrestrial cuisine.

Careena continues her brooding, but after our dinner of roots and jam, she asks a question that must have been on her mind for a while. "Dinah, dear. Where is your ship? Where is the *Star of David*?"

"I ain't never seen it myself," the girl says. "Storms took it before I was born. As the story goes, our original settlement was on the Lord's Sea. But in winter the storms came. Nobody was ready for those. Folks had to run into the hills for shelter. Lasted a month, they say. When they came back down to Old Nyssa, the whole town was gone. Looked like it got clawed right out of the earth. Ship too.

The Good Lord must have dragged it to the bottom of the sea. Anyway, if them storms was going to come every season, then they couldn't hardly stay there, so they packed what they had left and crossed the mountains and that's where we been ever since."

Careena still isn't satisfied. "So, your ship is gone and your people have no electronics?"

"Nope. We live the simple life. Like the Good Lord intended."

I understand what she's getting at. Sapphira and her little highwayman cohort were both armed with some rather fancy tech. "You're wondering about the tasers? Maybe they floated up from the wreck," I suggest.

It's Dinah that answers. "Well, I don't rightly know. But even if something did float up from that old ship, I was told we never brought no weapons here in the first place. That wasn't the type of community we were going to build. If you want my opinion, I think them gadgets you saw came from the other ship."

"Other ship?"

"Yeah. I seen it a month back or so. Mama says I just got an overactive imagination, probably saw a falling star or something. But I swear, it flew right over the clouds, clear as day can be. I thought maybe they was come to rescue us. I thought maybe you was from that ship."

"It wasn't us," I tell her before turning to Careena. "The *Yamato* maybe?"

Careena touches her nose. It's a habit I'm getting used to. "No, the records are pretty clear. The *Yamato* doesn't arrive for another few months. Besides, they'll want to get home as soon as possible. They'd have no reason to hide from the settlers. If it is a ship, then it's something else. And what's more, it's something that's not in the history books. I don't like things that aren't in the history books, Freckles."

That's all she has to say on the matter.

I sleep that night better than expected, despite the fact that Careena and I have only a single handmade blanket to share between us. But there are no dreams. No haunting revelations from my subconscious. And fortunately, no alien critters eat me while I'm sleeping.

As soon as there's enough morning light, we trek up a ridge that cuts through the aptly named Spine of the World. At their highest peaks, the mountains are silver with snow and ice. Here along the pass, the vegetation is sparse, mostly bushes and strange stalks of grass.

By midday the forest and steppes of Nyssa are gone from view completely. From here on, in all directions, there are only unending rows of rock and peaks, the rivets between colliding tectonic plates. Though we're heading east, I have a feeling the mountains likely go on for hundreds of miles to the south. I'm worried how long it will take to bisect such a formidable mountain range.

"How many days to cross?" I ask our guide Hagen.

"Two," he says. "If we're lucky."

The march quickly becomes tedious and punishing. The air is light and difficult to breathe, despite the nanites supposedly aiding my lungs. Hopefully Hagen and Dinah, having both been born on this strange world, have adjusted better than I have. Our direction seems to be ever upward, which tests the limits of my thighs. My left leg begins to itch at the ankle. My shoes maybe? I'm not sure if Chelsea boots are the best footwear for mountaineering.

As the hours pass, little changes to denote our progress. That's the most frustrating part of the journey. I keep having the dreadful feeling that no progress is being made at all, or worse, that we might again arrive at the clearing where we began. I must not be the only one who feels this way. Conversation has fallen to a minimum. No one has the strength to keep up a dialogue, not even young Dinah who is ordinarily as chipper as a songbird.

Night comes for us on the second day, and we make camp in a rocky clearing surrounded by small shrubs. They are twisted, old, and sparse of leaves. Hagen breaks their limbs to set a fire. Everyone is glad to have the crackle of flames in which to lose themselves.

The stars come out and greet us one by one, until there are too many in the night sky to count. Is Earth visible from here? From the edge of eternity? We cook more daggit roots and divvy them up more conservatively than before, hoping to stretch our rations until we reach the swamps.

Dinah comes to sit next to me by the fire. At first, I don't even realize she's there. Some combination of exhaustion and wayward thought has me lost in the dancing flames. She joins me in silence for as long as she can, but finally she has to fill the void. It's simply her nature.

"You're very pretty," she tells me. She says this like a statement of fact, a simple expression of admiration, but I feel it's hiding an insecurity, a comment more on herself than on me.

"Thank you, Dinah, you're very pretty too."

She places her chin on her knees and stares into the flames. "No, I don't think so. Some of the other daughters make fun of me. They say my face is too round and my chest is too small and my nose is too flat."

It seems that teenage girls are the same everywhere in the universe.

"People used to make fun of me too," I tell her. "I had braces, like, practically my whole life. And crazy hair. But you know what? Those other daughters, they're just jealous. You're smarter and have more potential in your little toe than any of them have put together. There's a reason that you're here and they're not. Putting you down is just their way of feeling good about themselves."

"Maybe you're right. I mean, it's got to really be tugging on their skirts that they weren't invited." She changes the topic, though only slightly. "Do you think you'll get married one day?"

"I don't know, it's a bit early to think about that. I'm only seventeen."

"Why, Miss Isabel, that's so old! But I think you're right. I was already married, like I told you. I don't think I want it again. Truth is, if we see the Lord's Sea, I'm going to throw my ring in there. The Good Lord can have his stupid sacrament back if it means so much to him."

I put a hand on her arm. "Don't write off falling in love too soon. Some boys, they can surprise you."

"I reckon they can."

Her gaze has drifted over to Hagen and I smile to myself. He's busy setting a pot of water over the fire. I yell out, "Hagen, come join us. We're bored."

Dinah blushes with anxiety and terror.

But also with a touch of excitement.

Hagen joins us. He's a bit awkward, it's true, but there's no denying the honesty in his eyes. He was exiled very young, lived a hard life in the swamps, and returned to Nyssa not long after the Great Father had died. It was obvious that he still felt adrift between these two very different worlds. A child of both, a child of neither.

"Dinah and I want to hear more about the swamps," I coax him.

"Oh, I don't know if I'm good with the storytelling."

"Try us," I say, while scratching my ankle again.

"All right. It's really quite lovely once you get used to it. There's plenty of fruits and nuts to munch on. Shade too when it's hot. We built a little village actually, out of leaves and such. Was kind of fun now that I think back to it, making something with all your friends. The only thing you got to watch out for is Dave—" He's noticed my scratching. "Are you sure you're all right, miss?"

"I'm fine," I tell him. "Probably just a shin splint from all the hiking. Though it feels sort of hot, now that you mention it."

I don't like the worry on his face.

"Might I see?" he asks.

"Sure."

I pull up my pants to the knee, which requires some work. That's when I see the grey lines under my skin, slightly raised. They start at my ankle and crawl up my shin, looking like the branches of a tree. *Or roots*, I shriek in horror. Now that I see them, the burning sensation intensifies.

"What the hell is that?" I shout.

"Skinroot," he tells me calmly. "We must have walked by some earlier. It's quite far along. I'm very sorry."

I look at him with suspicion.

"Sorry? Sorry for what?"

Without answering, he takes the pot of near boiling water off the fire and dumps it on my shin. I scream as the scalding liquid turns my leg red and tender. I'm about two moments away from punching this kid in the face, but I end up biting down on my lip instead.

"That'll kill it, miss," he tells me as if it was just a pesky weed in the garden, no big deal, as opposed to what it really was—a freaky alien root monster trying to eat me from the inside out!

"I'll go dig up some wetroot," he says. "Good for healing."

I let out a breath. "All right, but hey. Take Dinah with you."

No reason to let a romantic opportunity go to waste.

"Are you sure?" Dinah asks.

I wink. "Don't rush back on my account."

They leave the camp, using the moonlight as a guide.

I hobble over to sit next to Careena.

"Time travel is fricken dangerous," I tell her.

The old woman doesn't respond. Her thoughts are lost in the flames of the fire. She's not the same without Hecate.

"We'll get her back, Careena."

Dinah and Hagen return sometime later and stay up chatting into the early hours. I hope I haven't altered the timeline too much by prompting the two, but I really don't care if I have. After all, what has stupid history ever done for me? Ever since we started this adventure, I feel like I've been thrashed and throttled every step of the way, tossed into one wildfire only to be booted into another. And something tells me this is not a pattern that is going to end any time soon.

I curl up on the hard soil to sleep, my leg still smarting but honestly feeling a little better now that I have Hagen's root to chew on.

But like Careena, I worry.

I worry what awaits us on the other side of these mountains.

On the other side of time.

19

The following morning a greyness takes to the skies and it doesn't let go. A light drizzle sets in, making our trek all the more unpleasant. My leg aches with every step, but Hagen tells me I'll be fine. We pass through canyons and dried river beds, occasionally forced to skirt large boulders that have fallen from their perches ages ago.

By midday, we reach a sweeping valley nestled between two tracts of mountains, a place that looks more like a painting on a canvas than reality. The mountain edges bleed together in the distance like the strokes of oil brushes, while the colors could have been stolen from the mixing board of an artist. If I were told a small moon like a bowling ball had rolled across these mountains eons ago and created this wide and beautiful place, I would not question it. I see a cheer in my companions' eyes and know the same spark has lit up my own face—we are all happy to see something, anything, other than more narrow ravines and outcroppings of rock.

"This is the Valley of Flowers," Hagen tells us.

Dinah's eyes widen. "Really? Everyone speaks of them, but I've never seen the flowers before!"

As we enter the valley, I see no flowers, only leafy balls, not unlike heads of lettuce. They're everywhere, each spaced a foot or so from their neighbor. They fill the length and breadth of the valley.

"We have to cross to the other side," Hagen says as we walk. "From there it's only a short hike through those hills opposite. Then we're at the foot of the swamp."

I'm pleased to hear our journey is almost complete.

We're halfway across the valley when the horizon to our north flashes brightly. Strangely colored lightning jumps between the clouds, never touching the earth. The clouds darken, bringing with them crashes of thunder. A storm is barreling toward us with astonishing speed. Already the wind is picking up. The hairs on my arm rise.

"We need to hurry," Hagen tells us stoically.

We push on as quickly as we can, knowing that we're exposed, hoping to reach the cover of the foothills ahead, but they're still half a mile away. We don't make it. Those ominous clouds roll overhead and blot out the sun, turning the world to night. They bring with them such heavy rains that I can barely see Careena a foot or two ahead of me.

But we don't stop. We march on, hunching our shoulders in a vain attempt to protect ourselves from the heavy droplets that beat on our backs like stones. With each bolt of lightning hurled from one cloud to the next, the world is lit up in reds and purples and yellows. It's a thunderous battle being waged by warring gods in the heavens. I can't say that it doesn't fill some part of me with awe.

Despite the danger, I feel so very alive in this moment. Perhaps I should feel insignificant in the face of nature's raw power, perhaps I should feel minuscule as she tries to pound us out of existence. But the harsh rain beating against my face, the claps of thunder sending shudders down my spine, my legs fighting the mud trying to foil our escape, I love every second of it. To test my mettle, to brush up against my limits, to know who I am and what I can accomplish—I was born for this.

Dinah slips in the mud, and I help her to her feet. Her laughter in that moment, louder than the rain, louder than the storm, drowning out the very gods themselves above, tells me she feels just as I do. It's a moment of camaraderie shared between us. Two girls against the fricken world. We howl together in defiance of the cosmos.

I'm almost saddened when, as quickly as it had arrived, the storm breaks and biblically the heavens open, casting down the gold rays of the sun. We've crossed maybe three-fourths of the valley. The smaller mountain range is just ahead. Hagen brings us to a halt. There's something he wants us to see.

No, I realize with a smile.

There's something he wants *Dinah* to see.

It starts as a small vibration in the ground. At first, I can't place the source, then I see it's those strange heads of lettuce. They're shaking in response to the fresh rainwater and bright sun. It's as if, after years of imprisonment, they're ready to explode, as if, having survived the destruction of the storm, something deep inside them is ready to break free. To be reborn.

With furious explosions, they do just that.

They eject handfuls of butterflies high into the air, a confetti of tiny wings, some blue, some green, others yellow, others red—until the entire valley is filled with these fluttering colors catching the light of the sun.

I pluck one from the air, only to find that they're not butterflies at all. They have no heads, no legs, no eyes, no antennae. They're simple, like colorful string beans with maple leaf wings. *They're flowers*, I gasp in surprise.

Evolution, that splendiferous mother of all design, has found a way to spread their germ far and wide. The winged seeds flutter around the valley like dandelions in the wind. What I wouldn't give for my camera right now.

"We shouldn't linger," Hagen says after allowing all of us our moment of amazement. "The claw bush likes to roam the valley after a storm."

Having already encountered the skinroot, I'm fine with skipping the part of the tour where we discover just what exactly a claw bush is. So we continue our hike and exit the valley, entering a pass of low hills. There's more flora on this side of the mountains and already I taste a wetness in the air.

By nightfall we make camp under a cliff wall. There are hand prints here, child sized, made with ochre pigments, no doubt the playful markings of the swampies. In ten thousand years, archaeologists from other civilizations will find these stampings. What will they make of them, I wonder? Religious art? Sacred ceremony? Or the truth—just boys being boys.

The next morning we clear the mountains at last. We arrive at a ledge overlooking a vast terrain that rolls out before us like a green carpet, a foreign jungle, or more aptly, an alien swamp. To either side of us, waterfalls flow out of the rocks, feeding rivers that bisect the swamplands, turning the lands below into a scattering of puzzle pieces. Far beyond, on the horizon, is a strange blue sea.

Careena is all business.

"The swampies are down there, I take it?" she asks.

"Yes," Hagen tells her. He points to a stretch of forest halfway between the mountains and the sea. "In the drier parts over yonder."

We follow a trail down into the swamps. As we enter this new wetland forests, the world shrinks under dense canopies. Trees grow from standing water. Vines dangle everywhere, connecting everything. To me, the swamps look impenetrable, but Hagen knows paths that link together like a labyrinth through the marshes.

Without birds and without insects, it's an eerily silent sort of jungle. After an hour of hiking, Hagen lifts his hand for us to halt. He looks worried. He's put a finger to his lips. My pulse quickens.

I want to shake the boy. *What is it!* What's out there? Claw bush? Spear trees? Face-eating orchids that slurp down your intestines like spaghetti noodles? Who knew the idea of a vegetable world could be so terrifying? I'll never look at a carrot the same way again.

And then I see them.

From behind several trees and bushes, children materialize, little boys, each holding a spear pointed in our direction.

The swampies.

We're surrounded.

Careena has Old Bessie in hand.

Fortunately, the standoff lasts only a moment.

One boy shouts, "It's Hagen! Hagen's come back!"

Another boy, less pleased, responds, "But he's brought wifefolk with'em!"

Hagen lowers his spear.

"They ain't wives, Alberich," he says. "They're visitors."

This boy, Alberich, the stoutest among them, is suspicious.

"We know all about the visitors, man. They up to no good."

"Not these visitors. I can vouch for them."

"Fine," Alberich concedes.

Everyone lowers their spears.

"Why you back, Hagen?" the first little boy asks.

"We're looking for Sapphira," he tells them.

"Whatch'you want her for?"

He points to us. "She's got something these folks need. And before you say nothing, we're fixing to trade. We brought some crack'en good stuff."

"China Jesus?" one of the littlest boys asks in a squeaky voice.

I first I wonder if he means Chairman Mao, but Hagen reaches into his satchel and produces a small porcelain statue of Jesus. No doubt the words *Made in China* are stamped on his feet. "I got China Jesus right here, bud."

The tiny boy looks excited. "Oh boy, oh boy. Spoons and firecrackers! China Jesus is real mighty good luck, you know."

I look around at the boys. There are about seven in all. They're dirty and unkempt, though not as wild as I had feared. Slowly they come out of the bushes to present themselves.

Their clothes are tattered, but there's a youthful innocence in their eyes. Each wears a necklace with various trinkets attached, often haphazardly so. On those twine chains are all sorts of things; rings, bracelets, crucifixes, old pocket watches, in one case even a medallion of the Hindu goddess Kali and a tiny bust of Darth Vader. It's obvious the children have ascribed special meaning to these items.

"First things first," Hagen says, as he puts Jesus back in his satchel. "We need to see Sapphira."

The tiny boy, who I overhear being called Gunther, steps forward. I'm not sure, but now that I see him more closely, I'm pretty sure that he's the one who tasered Careena. I hope for his sake that the old woman didn't get a good look at the little rapscallion during our last encounter.

"Sapphira ain't here, Hagen," he says.

"Where is she?"

Gunther explains, "The other visitors got her. Almost got Fasolt too. But don't worry, man. We got one of them! Got her down at camp right now. Tomorrow we was fixing to offer them the big trade. We give them their meanie in return for Sapphira."

Careena cuts in, "Excuse me, but what the hell is a *meanie?*"

Gunther looks up to the old woman like she's an idiot.

"A person that is mean," he explains.

Another boy calls out from the back, too afraid to show himself. "You look like a meanie!"

"Yeah!"

"Yeah, man!"

"Right on!"

"Yeah!"

I smirk. I like these boys.

A lot.

Careena is unfazed by the accusation. "And what do these meanies want exactly?"

Gunther answers. "I reckon I don't rightly know. They set up a space temple near the Lord's Sea and run us off anytime we come near. As best we can tell, they're digging in the sea, but if they keep that up, they gonna upset Dave something mighty."

Another adds, "And they took our fishing spot! Spit on'em!"

All the boys spit into the dirt and chant, "Spit on'em!"

Careena seems more worried now.

"Just what does this meanie you got look like?" she asks.

"We might could show you. We got her locked up down in the Hole. Just watch out. She's dangerous. Strong as a hammer."

"And she's got silver bones!" another little boy yells out.

"Silver bones?" I ask.

"Yeah! Yeah!" a boy says. "She tried to run off but she fell down Muffit Cliff, she did. Broke her arm. Bone came right out of her elbow! We all saw it. I almost hurled my guttiwuts."

Careena's eyes furrow. "And the bone was silver?"

"Yes, ma'am, no lie. Silver as silver can be. And not just that, but this morning her arm was halfway healed. That ain't natural! Not even a prayer to Mister Chairman Mao can do that for you. And believe us, we've tried asking him. By now we've rubbed all the paint right off his bald head."

"I'd like to see this meanie you got," Careena says.

The tribe of boys, rather excited to show off their prisoner to someone who might appreciate the effort it took to catch her, lead us to their camp, which is a surprisingly well-constructed village of grass tents under alien trees, complete with straw beds, fire pits, and benches for games.

The hole where they kept their prisoner was aptly named. It was nothing more than a muddy hole in the ground with a bamboo covering tied down with twine.

Down in this hole sits a girl. She looks almost exactly my age, seventeen or so. Her gaze is pensive and angry, though she's looking at nothing in particular. She's in a black leather jacket with an insignia that I can't read on the shoulder.

I'm not sure what to make of her. She has sharp, attractive features, naturally tanned skin, and jet-black hair straight as an arrow, quite the contrast to my own crazy waves and curls. She's athletic, with the posture of a ballerina. And those eyes. They're like dark hazel crystals under midnight eyebrows.

After a moment, we all back away from the hole to be out of earshot of the girl. I turn to Careena, but the old woman's face is a mask of worry. She knows who this girl is, that much I see in her eyes.

"Who is she, Careena?"

"The worst kind of trouble."

"Military?" I ask.

"No, too young. She's some cadet or trainee. Unless I miss my mark, that space temple the kids told us about is a mining operation."

"So they're illegal miners?"

"Aye, but that's not what makes them dangerous."

What is she not telling me?

There is something, I know it. The old woman looks like she's seen the face of the Lucifer himself. I think back to the girl in the hole. How could a teenage girl scare Careena? Unless, maybe, the girl with silver bones wasn't a girl. Maybe I'm not asking the right question.

"Careena, *what* is she?"

The old woman answers.

"Deary, she's a Khelt."

I will admit—I'm a little confused. I know little about these mysterious Khelts, other than the small tidbits I've picked up here and there. By the time of Careena's era, I know that humanity will have already waged two terrible wars against this wicked enemy, wars of such profound sacrifice that they will leave deep psychological wounds on the collective soul of humanity, scars that will last for centuries and generations to come.

Yet, I was led to believe, rightly or wrongly, that the Khelts were machines, some sort of artificial life-forms, a nightmarish foe that had terrified the human race so completely that they all but abandoned the steady march of evolution toward more technologically integrated forms. Perhaps I should be thankful for that. After all, it's likely the only reason I'm able to relate at all with the people of the 31st Century.

But this girl down in the hole, she doesn't look so different from me either. A tad bit more athletic than most girls my age, but then again, so am I.

She's pretty, if you're into the tall, dark, and handsome types. A little aloof maybe, but otherwise a normal girl, as far as I can tell. It never occurred to me that humanity's greatest villain would look so... ordinary.

I need answers.

"Careena, you told me the Khelts were machines."

"They are machines," the old woman shoots back. It's clear she's upset by this recent development. "Don't let that tin can down there fool you. Her skin and blood cells are entirely synthetic, like a damned rubber sex doll. And as these lads already found out, her bones are a specialized titanium alloy. You couldn't break her if you tried. I bet you two Burnt Sienna crayons that she broke her own arm."

It still makes little sense to me.

"So why does she look like a human girl?"

"I am a human girl."

We both turn at once toward the hole. I thought we were far enough away not to be heard, but apparently not. Careena takes my arm and pulls me even further away while whispering in a low voice. Yet, something tells me not even this distance is good enough to have a private conversation. "Look, deary, I know it's strange."

"It's more than strange," I whisper back to her. "You made it sound like these Khelts were killer alien robots from another galaxy."

"No, not exactly. We never encountered any intelligences out in space. Well, no real intelligence anyway. The Khelts were of our own making."

I suppose I can imagine that. Plenty of science fiction has predicted a day when humanity creates military robots that go out of control, or armies of android slaves that rise up against their masters. Not for nothing, even during my own time, plenty of bright people have warned that artificial intelligence will be the single most worrisome existential threat that humanity will ever face.

Still, something doesn't seem right.

"So why does she *think* she's a girl?"

Careena does some math in her head. "Let me see, it's 2481, yeah? So she probably still has a mostly organic brain, they haven't figured out how to completely replicate that yet. But they will, in a few decades from now."

This keeps getting more confusing.

"So what you're saying is that she is a real girl, then?"

The old woman answers coldly. "Don't think of her that way. They gave up the right to call themselves human."

"You'll have to do better than that, Careena."

"Look, fine. They used to be human. But at some point, we had to decide what we wanted to be, how far we wanted to go. We had everything available to us, computer-brain interfaces, virtual realities, genetic engineering, replicated organs, artificial enhancements. We were in danger of becoming an entirely different species. And maybe that's fine. Maybe we've always been the cocoon, meant to emerge one day as the butterfly. I admit, even now, I'm a little different from you. My genes have been polished and cleaned up a bit. But in the early years, we were spiraling completely out of control. Very quickly, we were becoming something we couldn't recognize. And worse than that, different folks were choosing to go off in different directions. We were becoming a lot of different things, splitting off into a multitude of differing branches, with no thought as to the ramifications."

"So what did you do?" I ask.

She explains. "A universal standard was adopted. We call it the 2161 Standard, named for the year it was ratified. We weren't against progress, not at all, but we decided there should be some direction to it, that it should be somewhat uniform, and that it should be slow and steady, so we'd always have the option to hit the brakes if things started to get out of control. So in 2161 they took the averages of the top quartile of all of humanity, in areas of intelligence, strength, height, and so on, and they made that the starting point. Then, using some complex algorithm, they decided how much humanity could improve itself every twelve years. Having a universal standard, one that was legally enforced, worked very well. It prevented an arms race between parents to engineer the smartest kids possible, while still allowing for incremental increases over time; this way parents could know that their little Ollies and Olgas would still be a tad brighter than the generation before them. Which is all most of them wanted. This is sort of ancient history to me, so I may not have all the details right, but it's been considered a success and is still in use in my day."

"Then who is she?"

"Well, there were always individuals who violated the standard, but as long as every world enforced the law, doing so effectively meant exile. Your children could never be enrolled in school, you'd never be able to apply for a job, or even board a starship. For a long time, that was pretty much all the deterrent needed. Which brings us to the colony on Kheltaris V. They'd been founded by a Scandinavian academy of philosophers and scientists. Their mission was to build the ideal secular society, based on science and reason, sort of the opposite of all those religious colonies that got founded out here early on. And they did a lot of good in the early years. Amazing achievements. They were attracting all the best researchers from across the human diaspora. We called it the Kheltaris brain drain. But with great minds came great ambition."

I can see where this is going.

"They weren't too happy about the speed limit placed on human evolution."

"No, they weren't," she says. "The way they saw it, they could do humanity even more good with a little extra pep in their step. And maybe that was their sincere motivation. To help everyone. I don't know. But they started violating the 2161 Standard. And you know what happened after that? Their bloody immigration tripled overnight! Parents are the most corrupt lot in the universe. Shameless. All for super babies. Well, the planet was embargoed, but they were self-sufficient enough for it not to do much good. The Colonial Federate tossed around the idea of a full on invasion, but no one had the stomach for that. Really, what right did we have to impose our will on them? They weren't hurting anyone, after all. No one needed rescue. So we did nothing. Historians have long debated that decision. We could have enforced their charter, arrested their ministers, installed a new government; they were a nation of academics, they couldn't have done anything to stop us. But we did nothing. Just an embargo."

She goes on. "I guess, after that, we sort of forgot about them. Over the decades, isolation created a cultural rift between us. They continued unfettered in all their endeavors. Over the next century or two, their children grew up never having known their less evolved cousins. From what I heard, they were taught we were Luddites stuck in our ways, fools to be pitied, religious bumpkins who denied our children their full potential. It would have remained like that, but at some point they weren't content to be confined to just one solar system, not when there was an entire galaxy to be explored. Fifty years from now, their excursions will lead to the First Khelt War. I've only read about it in the history books, but humanity is going to start off thinking we're about to clean their clocks and set things right once and for all. After all, it will be almost two hundred worlds against one colony of arrogant nerds."

"I take it, it doesn't go as well as planned?"

"Not in the least. By the time an armistice is finally declared, the Khelts will have gained control of half an entire mandate. They'll go from controlling one system to more than a hundred, including seven with former colonies. That will create a massive refugee crisis with downstream effects. Anyway, after that, we never had relations with them again, diplomatic or otherwise."

I'm afraid to ask about the second war, the one she fought in. But I have to know. "And the second war?"

Careena's thoughts go somewhere else. "I don't know, luv. I really don't. By the time of that war, three and a half centuries later, they didn't even look human anymore. The beings I saw... you can't unsee them. Grey humanoids without faces, without clothes, without gender. Without mercy."

I decide not to push her any more on the topic.

That night we're offered beds of moss under leaf roofs. The swampies are excited to cook for us, an array of native vegetables and goose eggs from their one resident goose, snatched in the dead of night from Nyssa, a particularly talkative little fowl named Beetlegoose.

The boys sing songs around a fire, laughing together, creating and strengthening the bonds that have served them well in exile.

Gunther, the little one that shot Careena, stands up before the fire. "Tomorrow we make the big trade for Sapphira!" There's optimism in his voice. Or perhaps naive innocence. He'd seen the evil that can lurk in dark hearts before; indeed, he was exiled by it. But this evil that the boys will face tomorrow, I fear it will be something entirely different. I'm worried his enthusiasm is misplaced.

Someone else chimes in. "Maybe we'll even get a look inside their space temple!"

There's no holding back the boys now.

"We'll show 'em who's boss!"

"Spit on 'em!"

"Spit on 'em!" everyone yells while spitting on the ground.

I lean over to Careena. "Do they stand a chance?"

"Not a snowball's chance in hell," she says. "But the Khelts might take the trade regardless. I can't imagine they care much about this lot."

"I don't think you give the boys enough credit," I say in their defense. "They did manage to capture one of your fearsome Khelts, after all."

She laughs. "Hah! Is that what you think? That toaster oven they got down there has the reflexes of a jaguar and could wrestle a half ton bull to the ground. You think a bamboo gate and a few children with pointy sticks is keeping her here? She was sent to collect intel. And she's only a trainee, so that tells you the priority her bosses put on the mission. No, Freckles, they're just curious why a bunch of feral kids are running around an alien world like some extraterrestrial adaptation of *Lord of the Flies*. I'm sure they weren't expecting that when they arrived here."

"How can you be so sure?"

The old woman takes a sip of swampie tea from a large wooden bowl we've been lent. She slurps a little too loudly. I hate it when people do that. Then she tells me casually, "Because she's transmitting everything she sees and hears back to her people."

"What?"

"She's got some fancy neurolink installed in her head."

I'm shocked.

"So the Khelts know that we're here?"

"Well, not exactly. Not you and I anyway. Remember my magic earrings?" She points to her ears. "I've been blocking her transmissions. Not too hard, really. The Khelts have always been far more advanced than us, but even so, to me her tech is five hundred years old. She might as well be using smoke signals. Now we should get some sleep, deary. Tomorrow is going to a trial for all of us, I reckon."

I suppose she's right. The boys continue their songs around the fire, though in more subdued tones as the later hours arrive. I'm happy to see Dinah and Hagen sitting together with them, joining in with the storytelling and camaraderie, enjoying themselves on this grand adventure.

I wish all evenings could be so lovely, filled with such joy. Such innocence. But dark storms still linger over our heads. I feel them. And I fear them. It doesn't escape my notice that as I finally do fall asleep, Careena is on her side, wide awake, staring off into the distance.

Battling her own demons.

21

The next morning is sunny and bright. The boys pull the bamboo hatch off their hole and order their prisoner out. She follows directions without complaint. The swampies are too young to notice, but Careena was right; it's as clear as day to me that this girl has openly dismissed the boys as any sort of threat. She's simply playing along, like a disinterested babysitter going through the motions of a child's imaginary tea party, even while there are obviously a hundred better things she could be doing right now.

Careena addresses the girl. "You might be wondering why you can't hear your friends, yeah? Well, that's me, hotcakes. And I can do a lot more than just scramble your signals. So if you attempt to hurt any of these little boogers, I'll blow your forking head off. We clear on that?"

The girl says nothing, only nodding politely. She even allows the boys to wrap her wrists together with handmade twine, though I'm pretty sure even I could break the knot they spent five minutes arguing with one another over how to tie.

An away team is assembled to escort the prisoner to the space temple, but I ask Hagen and Dinah to remain behind. Zipporah put their safety in my charge and I want to take that responsibility seriously. Hagen doesn't argue, but Dinah isn't so easy to convince.

"You can't go alone, Miss Isabel. It's dangerous."

"I'll be safe, Dinah."

"But I want to help," the girl protests.

"I know. Which is why I need you to stay here. I need you to do something for me while we're away."

"Anything."

I look over to the swampies, to a row of innocent faces, smudged with dirt and sunburnt as they are. "Talk to these boys," I tell her. "They're too scared and too proud to come home. But they need to. And they want to. Deep down they want to come home. You and Hagen can convince them to come back with us. I know you can."

She agrees and gives me a hug, before pulling something from her pocket and handing it to me. "Take this, Miss Isabel. It will keep you safe."

It's a necklace, the one I saw in the chapel. Hanging from the chain is the small, six-sided star, its tiny diamonds twinkling in the morning light. I don't know what to say. Dinah closes my fingers around it, ensuring that I don't try to give it back. "It wasn't doing no one no good locked up in that musty chapel," she whispers.

"All right, I'll see you soon. And thank you."

I turn to see who will be leading our expedition. Careena told the swampies she wants no more than two guides to join us. It appears Gunther and Fasolt have been selected for the mission. Neither one is much larger than a mouse.

Careena is addressing Fasolt, who has the tallest cowlick I've ever seen on a kid. "What's your name, shortie?" she asks him.

"Fasolt!" he proclaims with pride.

"All right, Fasolt, let's get one thing straight. We're getting your friend back. You can take that to the bank. But under no circumstances are we starting a war with these schnitzelheads. So all these knives you've got, lose them."

"Ah, man!" he complains.

I can't help but laugh. Fasolt and his unfortunate bedhead came with straps and harnesses holding so many knives, forks, and screwdrivers that his tiny frame was nearly lost under all the clanging steel. As he unloads them to his friend Alberich, I realize most were, in actuality, cooking implements stolen from cabin homes in Nyssa. When he's finished, he has only one left, a spatula that he keeps sheathed in his belt like a sword.

His buddy Gunther takes the lead and we head out. We're a company of only five. Me, with some new confidence I've obtained over the last few days. Careena, with her odd quilted jacket and air of eccentric arrogance that so well defines her. In front of us are Gunther and Fasolt, mere boys, unaware of the demands destiny has placed on their young shoulders. And finally the Kheltic girl, who walks a few steps ahead of Careena's tiny pistol.

As we hike through the swamps, following strips of dry land toward what the settlers call the Lord's Sea, at one point I find myself accidentally walking alongside our taciturn prisoner. Before I realize what I'm doing, I strike up a conversation; it's simply a habit one develops on long hikes.

"What's your name?" I ask.

The girl seems surprised. She's a little taller than I am. Her skin and features are flawless. But I can't discount her as human, not like Careena does. I still see something familiar in those dark hazel eyes.

"Rhoda," she says. "Rhoda al-Khansa."

"I'm Isabel Mendelssohn."

"And your friends?" Rhoda asks.

"The boys are Gunther and Fasolt. Her name is Careena."

Rhoda nods toward the old woman. "She is angry with me. Yet I've done nothing to her or these children."

I'm not sure how to respond.

"Apparently, you're not supposed to be on this world."

She looks right through my politeness. "I could say the same about you, Isabel Mendelssohn."

Touche.

She continues, respectful but guarded. "I heard the two of you talking. Your friend speaks of imaginary wars that have never happened. We are at peace with your people, I assure you. I know I was in stasis for some years before my arrival here, but I received a correspondence from my sister only seven days ago."

I should never have started this stupid conversation. "I'm sure your sister is fine," I tell her.

"The old maid claims to know more than mortal knowledge would allow."

Oh boy.

"She's just prone to exaggeration and fantasy is all."

"Clearly."

There's a stretch of silence as we walk. This time it's Rhoda who picks the conversation back up. "I know what else she told you. It is also not true."

"What's not true?" I ask.

"That we're not human."

"But you have a plastic body," I point out.

"Synthetic, yes."

"That doesn't seem very human to me," I tell her.

"Would you condemn your parents were they to require an artificial hip or synthetic heart? I'm sure you'd agree they're still the same person afterward. That has always been our philosophy; improve the body but preserve the person. We simply don't wait for the heart to fail. Or the kidneys. Or the liver. I've never understood why your Earth unions don't take the same approach. It's most illogical."

I really have no answer. It's all science fiction to me. And if I'm being honest, her argument sounds pretty solid. But I've also been given the gift of foreknowledge. Or the curse, I've come to believe. So I know that the path Rhoda's people are heading down, so rational, so analytical, will ultimately lead to the abdication of their human soul.

I can imagine how it will happen. With a synthetic body like Rhoda's must also come synthetic hormones, designed to mimic the effects and desires of their organic counterparts. But for better or worse, my hormones are completely outside the realm of my control, and therefor, to some extent, so are my emotions. The same can likely not be said about the Khelts.

At some point they must realize that while hormones and emotions are required for human bonding and the experience of joy, there are darker consequences to them as well. Millions of years of evolution have left a long shadow of impulses and instincts that are now painfully obsolete in the modern age. These are the hormones and neural wiring that drive irrational jealousy, fear and xenophobia, greed, unrequited lust, uncontrollable anger. Even the unfortunate habit of gorging ourselves on sugar and desserts can be traced back to the evolutionary demands of prehistory.

So how tempting would be it be to have an on-off switch for these spigots of emotion? We could rewrite the human experience, make reading a book as pleasurable an endeavor for a child as eating ice cream. It makes me wonder what else we could do, what other unsightly parts we could crop out of the human experience.

After all, how often have our ancestral instincts led us down a path of self-destruction? To drive a little too fast on a rural road? To cheat on a spouse? Or dare I admit it, to attend a party the night before an important test for a lab program, all because of the fear of missing out?

Would Rhoda fall for such trivial emotional hijinks? Could she still be swayed by the smile of a pretty face? Would she shoplift from a bodega or high dive off a dangerous cliff, just for the thrill of it? Or had her thrills been remapped onto more productive and logical endeavors?

I find myself very curious about her.

"What's your sister's name," I ask the enigmatic girl.

"Fareena."

"It's a pretty name."

She confides in me. "She was only six when I left. Now she's almost finished with youth academy. Yet for me it feels like only a few weeks have passed. I hardly recognized her face. And to think, she'll be older than me by the time I'm back home. I'd share a photo of her with you, but I don't think you do this, with the mind."

"Me? No, just by email."

"It doesn't matter anyway," she says. "I can't share thoughts, not while your friend is doing whatever she's doing."

"She thinks it's for the best."

"Perhaps later I can show you," she tells me.

"I would like that."

By nightfall we reach her ship. It's a great mining facility, sitting on the beach with arms like sewer pipes reaching horizontally over the sea before dropping straight down into the ocean bed. I understand why the swampies believed it to be a temple. The command module of the ship is cone-shaped, sitting upright like some religious pyramid, ominously dark at this hour save a few lit windows.

The moonlight is creating an eeriness along the shore that I don't particularly like. Silver light glimmers on the waves of the sea. The sandy beach is endless, broken only by the ship, an intruder that is clearly unwelcome.

"Should we wait until morning?" I ask Careena.

"No, I want to get this over with as soon as possible. Either they'll make the trade or they won't. I don't give a fork if they're in the middle of reading their bedtime stories."

Gunther whispers from behind me. "A storm is a'coming."

"A storm?" I ask.

"Yeah, you see it? Gonna be a big one, man."

I strain my eyes. In the darkness are clouds like rolling balls of angry cotton spilling out over the horizon of the sea. Already a low hanging fog is seeping onto the beach. There's a stillness in the air, one that says very soon the world was going to be turned upside down.

"Great," Careena mutters. She turns to Rhoda. "You, the walking toaster, why don't you go first."

Rhoda leads us out onto the open beach. The distance we have to cover is greater than I first thought, meaning by the time we reach the cone-shaped vessel, it's far larger, and more intimidating, than I imagined.

A wind and drizzle have arrived as well. I'm thinking that even if the Khelts do accept our trade, they won't be so friendly as to board us for the night. Our journey home is not going to be a pleasant one.

Two soldiers meet us at a ramp leading up into the ship. They are dressed in the same black outfits as Rhoda. They never raise their weapons. Instead, they lead us up several floors on a freight elevator. We're deposited into a large waiting room. We're given no instructions other than to wait.

There are several couches, which Gunther and Fasolt immediately take a liking to. They touch everything, including the paintings on the walls and the lamps.

I walk over to the large window, gazing out onto an alien sea. I'd say we're about thirty floors up. Rain is now beating angrily against the pane, but the full brutality of the storm has yet to arrive. Far in the distance are flashes of lightning.

This won't be like the storm from the day before.

This will be something much, much worse.

Rhoda sits in an armchair under Careena's watchful eye.

"What happens now?" I ask the old woman.

Her answer is simple. "We wait."

Gunther and Fasolt come to join me at the window, their hands pressed against the glass like binoculars while they eye the coming storm with near religious reverence. Their breath makes foggy patterns on the glass. Their silent glances of worry to one another frighten me. I realize they know something.

Something that I don't.

They know what the storm has awakened.

22

I turn away from the windows when the glass doors to the waiting room slide open and a woman enters with two officers. She's tall, with dark hair, high cheekbones, and olive shaped eyes. Rhoda jumps to attention in her presence. I hope beyond hope that these negotiations will go smoothly.

The woman at the doorway addresses all of us. "I am Captain Itoti Nordenskjold of the Kheltaris Mining Directorate. I would like to personally welcome you all aboard the *Ikabeth*. I hope you have been treated well by my staff."

Careena stands. "It's all been fine, captain. But you needn't worry about any pleasantries on our account. We brought back your rubber duck. We just want our girl back, and then we'll be on our way."

Captain Nordenskjold nods. "Very well. Directly to the point. Admirable. I know these two boys from our recon drones. They are Gunther and Fasolt, I believe." The two boys perk up at the mention of their name, but otherwise return their attention to the window and the approaching storm. "I don't believe I know who either of you are, however. An introduction would be in order before we continue any further."

"I'm Careena Smith and this is my travel companion Isabel Mendelssohn."

At the mention of our names, one of the officers searches records on a tablet. He informs the captain that their sensors detected no lie, but that neither of us are in the system either.

Captain Nordenskjold sizes us up. "You're not listed in any of the colonial databases."

"Maybe your records are for schnitzel," Careena says.

Sometimes I really wish this woman could be more diplomatic. Also one of these days we should probably have her translator fixed.

"You must understand my concern, Ms. Smith," the captain says. "You've arrived on this planet on no ship that we have detected. Our internal scanners detect no equipment on you, yet you're jamming Ensign al-Khansa's communicator. Some would call it mysterious, given that it's certainly more sophisticated than any capability the Earth unions are known to possess."

"We're not here to bust up your illegal little mining operation, if that's what you're worried about, captain," Careena says. "Check your lie detector, if you want. We're not supposed to be here anymore than you are. Discretion is as important to us as it is to you. We just want our rugrat back."

The officer nods to Captain Nordenskjold in affirmation.

"All right," the woman says.

I let out an enormous sigh of relief. "We can have Sapphira?"

"Of course," the woman says. "We're not child abductors. The girl was malnourished and needed attention. But you came here to make a trade. That you must still do."

I hold my hand toward Rhoda. "We brought your cadet back."

The captain shakes her head, as if I've said something so obviously wrong as to hardly be worth consideration. "Ensign al-Khansa was never your prisoner, so I can hardly accept her for trade, Ms. Mendelssohn. You must offer something else."

Like a flipped switch, the mood in the room is suddenly very tense. The captain has placed her cards on the table. Her eyes are locked with Careena's. It's a battle of wills now and I have the very unpleasant feeling that this showdown will not end well for anyone.

There's a cry from down the hall behind the captain, from the first door on the right—a little girl demanding to be set free. The sound of her voice is almost lost as winds and rains beat like angry fists against the windows, wailing in violence.

The storm has arrived.

Seconds are starting to feel like minutes.

"What do you want?" Careena manages through her teeth.

"Your jamming device. Give us that and you may all go."

"It can't be done."

I understand why the request is out of the question. Careena can't put 31st Century technology into the hands of the 25th Century, and most especially not into the hands of humanity's future adversary. It might take them decades to understand how the earrings function, it might be like handing a smartwatch over to Sir Isaac Newton; he wouldn't have the first idea how to understand the mechanisms that control it. But given enough time, eventually the Khelts would crack the secrets of Careena's earrings, and it would alter the course of history irrevocably.

"Then no deal," the captain says flatly.

To my surprise, Rhoda jumps to our defense. "Captain Nordenskjold, please, they came here in good faith."

The captain shoots the girl a look both furious and unapproving. She turns back to Careena. "Ms. Smith, how did you arrive on this planet?"

I watch Careena's jaw go tense.

Captain Nordenskjold continues. "Where is your ship? How many forces do you currently have aboard?"

The old woman's hands are clenching into fists.

The captain doesn't stop.

"To which union do the two of you answer?"

Careena growls.

"The girl, captain, or things are going to get real ugly."

"Is that a threat, Ms. Smith?"

"It's a bloody forking promise, you tart."

Oy. I have to teach this woman tact.

Everything happens in a blur after that. With a nod from the captain, the glass doors slam shut, separating us from the Khelts. Rhoda yells for everyone to get down, warning us they're about to stun the room.

I don't even have time to react. With reflexes I wouldn't have believed possible, Rhoda flings an armchair into a freestanding lamp just as it flares up with a stun charge. There's a blast of white light as the chair breaks apart and the young ensign is flung backwards across the room. She's taken the brunt of the stun charge to protect us. She doesn't get back up. She's out cold.

With her own impressive speed, at least for a lady her age, Careena has Old Bessie in hand, pointed directly at Captain Nordenskjold on the other side of a sheet of fortified glass.

"These are specialized blast doors, Ms. Smith," the captain says. "Military grade. You'll never breach—"

Careena fires and the glass explodes, blowing the captain and her officers to the ground as shards of glass fly everywhere.

I want to shake the old woman. "What the hell? Does everything end in a fricken shootout with you?"

She doesn't have time to respond. Gunfire erupts from down the hall as soldiers take up positions and we're all forced to take cover behind the wall. Couches and paintings are blown to bits behind us.

Careena returns fire into the hallway. In all the shooting, pipes are busted and start blowing out streams of smoke. The sprinklers kick in. It's complete chaos.

Fasolt sneaks off into the hallway during a momentary lull in the incoming fire as the soldiers realize they might hit their own captain.

"Fasolt! You idiot! Get back here!" I yell.

But it's too late.

He disappears into the first open doorway.

Looking further down the hallway, Captain Nordenskjold's two aids have dragged her to the safety of a different doorway. She's unconscious, which is unfortunate—it means there's no one of authority who can call a ceasefire.

Worse, it's only a matter of time before the freight elevator behind us arrives with a dozen more armed miners. Careena won't be able to hold off an advance from both front and behind, no matter how powerful Old Bessie is.

We're trapped in the waiting room with no escape. I vow that next time I'm taking a more proactive role in the planning phases of these ridiculous missions.

If there's a next time.

Fasolt's head reemerges from the side door in the hall, but now the gunfire has started up again and there's no way for him to make his way back to us. A second head pops out behind him. It's Sapphira. I don't know how he could have freed her from her guard, seeing how he was armed with little more than a kitchen spatula, but then I remember the swampies likely still had a stolen Kheltic taser at their disposal. Clever boy.

Sapphira looks frightened, but unhurt. More importantly, on a chain around her neck are two rings. One is Hecate. I yell to Careena, "We have to get to them!"

"How?" The incoming fire starts blowing away bits of the wall we're using for cover. "Bloody hell!"

She's right. There's too much crossfire in the hallway to get to the children. I don't know what to do. We need a distraction.

That's when the first moan fills the ship. I can only describe it as a great wailing emanating from somewhere out at sea. Everyone pauses, even the soldiers.

"What was that?" I whisper.

Gunther is crouched low down beside me. "It's Dave! We got to get out of here, man!"

I look over but can't see anything outside the windows. It's dark out there and the storm is brutal.

The moan comes again, only this time much closer.

Careena takes a moment to peer down the hall. It's deserted; the soldiers have all fled. Even the captain is gone. "Hah! Wankers!" the old woman yells in victory.

I'm less certain that we've won the encounter. I can still hear the staccato beats of machine gun fire. The soldiers are still shooting, they're just not shooting at us. They're firing out the windows. They're firing at the sea.

I collect my courage and stand. I look out the window again, into the darkness, into the moonlit sea and shipwrecking storms.

And that's when I see Dave.

I clutch my chest like some old grandmother. The creature out there is the size of a small mountain, marching up the steps of the ocean floor, revealing a little more of its hulking frame with each stride. It has the look of some ancient tree, layered in seaweed and coral.

Vaguely there's a head, though in truth it's just knotted roots, the crevices of which trick the human mind into seeing deep, sad eyes and a massive lopsided mouth, as if the creature's face were frozen in perpetual agony.

Four arms dangle to its side. There are no hands, only long twisted roots like the ends of turnips. Moonlight catches a giant plate of curved steel embedded into the monster's tangled mess of a shoulder, in the same way a young tree might consume a fence post over many long years.

There's red lettering stenciled across the metal. I can make out three letters. DAV. The name of the beast the swampies have taken to be a god.

I scream.

"What is that thing!"

Careena sees it as well. "That's why I never holiday at the beach! But I got a feeling it's also the reason the *Yamato* never finds this rig. I think we're about to get dragged down into hell."

A moment later a giant arm crashes against the ship as the creature lets out a bellowing cry in the storm. We're all knocked off our feet by the force of it.

"What's it want?" I cry.

Careena shrugs. "Probably a new hat."

That's when I realize—the creature is like a hermit crab, one which has outgrown its old shell. It's here for a new home.

DAV

DAVID

This thing was literally wearing the *Star of David*, the ship that had brought the settlers to this world. And soon it was going to be wearing the *Ikabeth*.

With a loud snap, the foundations crack at the base of the ship. Windows everywhere shatter. The entire rig turns sideways. We all tumble toward the wall, barely avoiding being crushed by couches and other debris that falls with us.

My stomach does a loop as the *Ikabeth* hits the ocean sideways. The room fills with ocean water, dark and black. Careena's right. We're being pulled down into the underworld.

She's also right that the Khelts don't survive this encounter. Which means we won't either. That's one gift of foreknowledge I'd rather not have. It means I can't even hold on to hope.

As the room floods and the ship sinks deeper, it's all any of us can do to stay afloat and not be sucked out in a vortex of frigid water. The boys are crying. I find myself holding the broken door frame, trying not to choke and drown. But I have only a few seconds before that will become my inevitable end.

And then I see her. Sapphira, only a foot away, clutching a pipe. Blood is running down the side of her face, but she's still alive. I reach out to her. Her shoulder is just close enough. But I don't want her shoulder. I propel myself forward, letting go the frame, snatching what I need as the black currents of icy water pull me under to throttle me, to drown me, to end my life.

But I don't drown, not today.

I slip on the ring.

I will myself off the ship.

I will all of us off the ship.

23

Calm moonlight and the gentlest breeze catch my wet hair. I'm in a field, on my back, looking up toward a peaceful night sky outlined by a beautiful band of stars. Blue grama grass sways lazily to either side of me. I appreciate the softness of this natural bed. I let out a deserved sigh.

Not far away from my feet are Gunther and Fasolt, eyes wide and large as they look around at their new surroundings. You could mistake them for soaked rats. I almost giggle at that thought.

I look over to my right and see Sapphira, nearly invisible in the tall, dark grass. She's pulled in her knees closely with her pencil thin arms. There's blood in her hair from where she's been cut across the forehead. But she's more afraid than injured.

Careena stands up next to her. The old woman's overcoat is sopping wet, leaving a puddle of mud in the dry soil. I catch her coughing up a fair bit of sea water, but it passes. That terrible ocean is gone now. Here there is only the tranquility of the open steppe.

I'll admit, this is not exactly where I intended to have us arrive. But I can see the twinkle of some rooftops further on the horizon; Nyssa is not even three miles away. While it seems Hecate still needs some calibration, we're close enough.

"Bit surprised we survived that one, to be honest," Careena mutters as she attempts to squeeze the water from her coat by twisting portions of it like one would a mopping rag. "Did we all make it out?"

I see her counting heads.

Gunther, Fasolt, Sapphira, me.

I better warn her.

Too late.

She hears the faint moan in the grass a few feet away.

This is not going to be pretty.

"You brought *her?*"

She's got Old Bessie out in a flash.

I finally sit up. This situation needs to be defused. "She stood up for us back there, Careena. We'd all have been knocked out cold if not for her. I couldn't just leave her back there."

Careena is furious. "You could have and you should have, deary. She's not supposed to be here. The *Yamato* can't find a Khelt here when they arrive. If they do, it will fork up the entire timeline. It might even lead to early war. Not to mention you could have killed us all, you dolt! There's a limit to what a QDD can transport. Four people tops. And you just did bloody six! Congratulations, you set a new interstellar record. Lucky for us, most of them are half pints or I don't think we'd all still have our fingers and toes right now."

I can tell she's upset, but I stand my ground. "I'm not going to apologize. I did what was right."

"You better hope so, Freckles. Because this really complicates things."

Rhoda, the girl in question, opens her eyes and I help her up. She uses my arm for balance. I can tell she's dazed. She's trying to make sense of where she is. A field opposite the mountains. Hopefully she assumes we carried her here while she was unconscious. But she's still going to have questions. I tell her gently that we have to hike to the village. She agrees with a nod.

It takes us more than an hour to reach Nyssa. I spend most of it carrying a sleeping Sapphira with her slender arms around my neck. Gunther and Fasolt march like halfling zombies, but they never complain.

It's the dead of night when we arrive and I don't expect anyone to be awake, but someone is on a porch, watching a shooting star.

It's Zipporah.

"You're back," the mother says with surprise. She immediately does a head count and sees that we're two teenagers short. "Dinah?"

"She's safe," I tell her of her daughter. "She's with the swampies."

I hope that's true. I don't mention the storm.

"You came back without her?"

There's an understandable confusion in her voice.

Careena saves me. "We had to, dear. We were attacked by something from the sea. We couldn't risk leading it towards the swampies or your daughter. We'll go back and get them first thing in the morning."

Zipporah seems to reluctantly accept this explanation.

I try my best to comfort her. "The swampies are looking out for Dinah and Hagen. They're good kids. In the meantime, I think Sapphira hit her head."

"Yes, of course, bring her inside."

The doctor goes to work, laying the girl on a cot, cleaning the wound, and applying a bandage. When she's finished, she turns to our two swampie commandos. "And you two? Are either of you injured?"

Both boys shake their heads.

I make the introductions.

"This one is Gunther and that one is Fasolt."

"Yes, I know them." She leans down and takes the battle spatula from Fasolt's belt. "I've been looking for this for quite some time, young man."

She smiles and it lifts some of the shock and fear in young Fasolt's eyes. As brave as he pretends to be, as courageous as he truly was when the moment required it of him, the events of the last hour have shaken him to his core. What he needs now more than anything is the love and support of a caring adult.

"And your other friend?" Zipporah asks of Rhoda.

I don't know how to explain her presence.

Careena, however, doesn't even miss a beat.

"She's our cook. Doesn't get out much."

Rhoda rolls her eyes, but otherwise says nothing.

Zipporah produces blankets and bedrolls for everyone.

Sleep comes easy and fast.

I wake up early, before everyone else. As quietly as I can, I step out into the morning light, which is just now pouring over the horizon. If there were roosters on this world, they'd surely be calling out right now.

I take a seat in the grass not far from the cabin. There's a peace in this place, a harmony I know I will come to miss. I want to soak it all in before we're forced to leave. Two geese wonder by, plump balls of feathers, waddling without a care in the world. To only be them.

Careena comes to join me after a while, taking a seat next to me. We stare at the steppes and say nothing for many long moments. I've come to realize this is a sign of our friendship, of a real sisterhood, that we have this ability to enjoy one another's company in silence.

After some time, I ask, "How have we made it this far, Careena?"

She stares out at the horizon and answers truthfully, "By drunken prophecies, libels, and dreams."

At the center of the village, a few women are lighting candles around a rock. Careena notices them.

"What are they doing?" she asks.

"It's a vigil for Dinah and Hagen," I tell her. "I think they've been doing it every morning since we left."

Careena is silent.

"Do you think they're all right?" I ask.

What she says surprises me. "I was just there."

"What? How?"

"How do you think? I took Hecate and I jumped there before anyone woke up. I owed it to that woman Zipporah. I was going to bring all the children back. We've already blown our cover and dazzled the natives with our magic, so I figured what could be the harm? But they weren't there."

"You mean Dinah and Hagen left without us?"

"No, I mean no one was there. I don't know how to tell you this, deary, but the entire camp has been wiped out by the storm. It looked like the claws of hell themselves reached out of the ocean and tore away the swamp. Whole swaths of trees were gone. The path of destruction was half a mile wide."

"The monster..."

"Aye. The kids are gone, deary. Everything is gone. There aren't even bodies left behind to bury."

I put a hand to my mouth. "Careena, this is our fault."

The old woman says nothing.

Tears fill my eyes. I'm desperate. "We'll go back. I'll go back. You said I could jump anywhere."

"It doesn't work like that," she tells me. "You can't jump where you've already been. The bonds can't be manipulated twice. I'm sorry"

I put my head down in defeat. She doesn't say it, but I know this is how it was meant to be. The creature destroyed the Kheltic mining ship. That was the history we knew. But it killed the swampies as well. Fate was simply unfolding the way it was always meant to. Fate, that cruel and pathetic pendulum. I'm powerless against it. Careena leaves and I sit for a long time by myself.

Later at breakfast we make no mention of our findings. How could we? A large communal meal is prepared, with several long tables carried out into the center of the village.

It could have been a truly wonderful moment, enjoying this feast with the settlers of Nyssa under a clear, unbroken sky, the vegetables before us harvested by hand, the soups stewed with care.

A few animals wander by. Part of me believes this is the way humans were meant to live, not as drones in a consumerist, artificial dystopia of plastic bottles and constant distractions, but as families bonded around heavy wooden tables.

But I can't enjoy what's been offered, not now. I can't contain the anxiety in my heart. I promised Zipporah I'd bring her daughter back, that talkative, awkward girl full of promise and potential.

Instead, I led her to her death. I don't know if I'll ever be able to forgive myself for that. I want to run away. I know we could. We've already done what we came to do; Careena marked Bithiah's ring with her fancy, invisible isotopes not even five minutes ago during an introduction before we all sat down for our meal.

We're free. The two of us can escape.

Yet I owe it to Zipporah to tell her the truth.

I just don't know how.

Several women, in their prairie outfits, ask me all manners of questions about Earth during breakfast. They had been raised to believe it was a wretched pit, the old country, a harsh land their ancestors had abandoned and not without good cause. But with the passing of their spiritual leader, they've started to question those teachings, those stories, and now they want to know more.

I'm afraid I'm in no mindset to give them honest answers.

Looking over, I wonder what must be going through Rhoda's head. She sits mostly silent, but this is likely her first encounter with her Earth-born cousins. If she thought we were backwards before, I can only imagine what she thinks of us now that she's met this lot.

And besides Dinah's fate and Rhoda's presence, there's yet another dark cloud hanging over my breakfast this morning, one that I'd prefer not to contemplate but which I can't force from my mind. It's Bithiah.

The girl is really lovely, cheerful even, and she seems so full of optimism in her new marriage, one of the very first love marriages the settlement has ever performed. It's not her that torments me. It's my knowledge of her future. Or more precisely, the future of her lineage.

I know that eventually she'll adopt the name Barbara, she'll have a son who will go on to be a settler himself, on some faraway world. He'll have a successful and happy family. His own son will serve in the Colonial Federate with distinction and marry a renowned historian. Many generations of the family will go on, living good, honest lives.

Until the Second Khelt War.

That war will destroy dozens of worlds. It's a war I still don't fully understand. Even in Careena's time the nature of the war and the beings that started it will be hotly debated by academics and scholars. But one thing that I do know, a child will become an orphan during that war, he'll be forgotten in the chaos of conflict, and he'll carry a ring around his neck, a token, an ancestral heirloom, the only connection left to him by a proud family lineage that he never had the opportunity to know.

With some irony, I realize that by sitting here, at this table, having breakfast with these good people, I know his family more than he ever will. I've seen now both sides of the man I killed.

Does that make me hate him any less?

After breakfast I go for a walk alone among the cabins. Careena finds me sitting on a stump behind the chapel building. It's time for us to depart. If I'm going to tell Zipporah the truth of what happened to Dinah, I have to do it now. It's a responsibility I'm not looking forward to.

Before Careena can say anything, or even offer a word of encouragement, there's a third figure with us.

"Agent Smith," Story Beckett says. "I see you've been busy."

Careena almost jumps out of her coat. "Jesus Forking Christmas, do you have to creep up on people like that?"

"Well, I'd love to say that you're a hard woman to find, but half a dozen of these settlers just mentioned you in their diaries. By name."

Careena shrugs. "Oops."

I'm more worried.

"Doesn't that mean Soolin knows we're here too?"

"She does," Story says. "But the new QDDs won't be ready for another twenty hours. She'll have four ready for use, and she's already handpicked the new agents to use them, including Grimalkin, who is still quite upset about the little stunt you pulled on him back at the ministry. I suggest you not be here once those QDDs are active."

"All right," I say, "But I have to speak to Zipporah before we leave. I can't just run out."

Careena doesn't say anything. She's as troubled as I am.

Story is looking at a clipboard. "I see here a new isotopic tracer has appeared in the records. I assume that's you, Smith?"

The old woman nods. "Yeah, it's a ring one of the Red Man's soldier boys was carrying. Think you can use it to find his base?"

"I can try. Give me just a second." The young officer scrolls up on her pad. "All right, looks like prior to the attack on the *Stellar Pearl* he was in the Valeyard for six months. Arrived by conventional transport."

"The Valeyard? Should have guessed. Right in our own damned backyard."

Story looks up. "Smith, that's the best I can do for you. If that base were anywhere else, I could pinpoint where this man used the toilet, but the Valeyard is layers upon layers of interference. Without someone on the ground there, I can't get you anything more specific. Do you want me to inform Soolin?"

Careena considers this a moment. "Not yet. You said she hasn't got the QDDs yet, right? If we tell her now, she'll know you're helping us, and I'm not ready to risk you just yet. I'll go scout the Valeyard. If anything comes up, I'll call her myself. I want to leave you out of this if all possible."

Story is suspicious. "You're not thinking about taking on the Red Man alone are you, Smith?"

"Wouldn't dream of it."

Story then brings up our other predicament. "I also couldn't help but notice that those diaries mention there were three of you. Something about a cook?"

"You can blame Freckles for that."

Story asks, "What are you going to do about it?"

Careena doesn't hesitate. "There's only one thing we can do. Shoot and bury her."

"What?" I yell. "You can't do that. She saved us."

"She was supposed to die on the rig, deary. It was her destiny."

"Like my destiny in Brooklyn?" I shoot back.

"Don't ever compare yourself to that machine."

"She's a human being, Careena."

The old lady's face turns red. "She's no such thing! Look, I'm sorry, but there's nothing we can do. She can't stay here. If the *Yamato* finds her, well, that's not an option."

I turn to Story.

"What does the historical record from the *Yamato* say?"

"At the moment, nothing," she tells me. "But it doesn't work the way you're thinking. There's some complicated physics involved—probability clouds, quantum collapse, Hilbert space, the Lefler Paradox of free will. The short of it is, I can't tell you what will happen until you've committed to an action. It's a little like you're upriver from me. Anything you place in the river, I'll receive immediately, but you must first place it in the water. The only reason I could find you now is that some of the young ladies here have already mentioned you in their daily journals. As soon as they did that, it showed up on my end. You have to understand, you're still tethered to the present. For all intents and purposes, this is all happening in real time. So I can't tell you what leaving her here will do to the timeline until you do it, and by then it will be too late."

"Fine," I say. "Then she's coming with us."

Careena nearly chokes. "Oh, that certainly can't happen."

"It can and it will, Careena."

"She's dangerous, Freckles. And who says she'd even agree to join us?"

I merely point. "Why don't you ask her yourself?"

Careena spins around with Old Bessie.

Rhoda is standing at the corner of the chapel.

The old woman lowers her weapon, but only a little.

"Is everyone sneaking up on me today?" she asks. "How long have you been standing there?"

Rhoda answers, "Long enough, old maid. I wanted to come and ask why you saved me."

"I didn't save you."

Rhoda turns to me. "It was you?"

"Yes."

"Then I am in your debt." The girl turns back to Careena. "Shoot me if you must. As improbable as it is, I've gleaned how it is you know so much about the future. And knowing that, I understand why you feel my death is the only option available to you. I wish only to say that I am not the monster you think I am."

Careena is dismissive. "Bah."

"Hear her out," I say.

"You hold me responsible for things I've never done," the girl says. "You judge my people not for what we are, but for what you say we will become. I cannot speak to crimes never committed. And I certainly will not answer for them. But I also heard the way you spoke of my people. You said we lost our humanity. I wanted to refute you. We are not villains. And we've never had the desire to harm you. In fact, we pity you. We'd even help you, if you allowed us."

She goes on. "But meeting you and these children has made me pause. There are those on my world who would look down upon some of the emotions we've inherited from our ancestors. They call them illogical, primitive, even dangerous. And it made me wonder, what if you're right? What if our downfall comes not from some grand mistake made in the moment, but instead from a thousand cuts over a hundred years? What if each cut makes the next all the easier to inflict? Until we become.... something else."

She stares directly at Careena. "It would seem, old maid, that you have already gazed into that orb of premonition. You have witnessed what is to come. I can see it in your face every time you look at me. Tell me, what did we become to terrify you so?"

Careena doesn't answer. She can't answer. Her own memories are too strong. I can see them in her face as well. The war, the friends lost, the things she was forced to do in the name of survival, the nightmarish beings she confronted. Though she tries to hide it, her hand is trembling.

Rhoda finishes. "I owe both of you the debt of my life. You may believe that you must kill me—but if you would take me, I would fight alongside you. Not out of any foolish sense of honor, but because I've heard what else you've said about what is to come. You are here because you believe the universe to be in peril. Like it or not, old maid, this is my universe too, and I would lay down my life to defend it, to protect my family, my sister, and yes, even my people. I cannot answer for the sins we've yet to commit, but I can promise you this—I'd stand with you right to the gates of perdition if that's what it takes to protect the ones I love and to prevent this end that you fear."

There's a long silence.

"Careena?" I ask.

"I don't like it," she mutters.

"Careena!"

"Fine, fine, whatever. She can tag along."

"Thank you," the Kheltic girl says. "I'd like to offer something else as well, a way to repay you for your kindness. As you've noticed, I can hear many things that you cannot. And I hear something even now. Over there, near the forest."

I don't understand. "What do you hear?"

The girl gives a soft, honest smile. "Your redemption, Isabel."

Without another word, I run past her, past Careena—I run into the fields, I run toward the forest. At first, there is nothing, only the steppes and the treeline beyond. The woodlands appear quiet. What could she have heard? Was it the storm? I see rain clouds on horizon, grey and soft, but they are so far away.

And then I fall to my knees.

Because I see them.

Emerging from the forest, I see them.

All of them.

The swampies.

Some walking with sticks, others carrying on their backs every possession they own. They are haggard, tired, thin, and famished. They are bruised and rough and exhausted. But they march with heads held high. They march with purpose. For they are marching home. They have come to find again the loving embraces of their mothers.

At the head of this wayward pack of scrawny boys is Dinah and Hagen, each now seeming a little older, each standing a little taller. I can't fight my tears as I run to them. I hold them both tightly. Already there are shouts in the settlement behind me, joyous calls, as villagers toss aside their chores and come to join me in the fields.

Dinah smiles as she tugs on the star around my neck.

"You see, Miss Isabel. I told you it would protect you."

She winks at me.

I wipe away my tears of joy and squeeze her again.

A community has finally been reunited.

SECOND INTERLUDE

Here, a young man.

He awakes with a start, covered in sweat, his sheets soaked, his breath short. Triple moons peer down through open windows. A light breeze catches the curtains.

"Was it the dream again?" the woman next to him asks.

"Yes."

"Who is this person, John? This figure in red that so haunts your dreams?"

"I wish I knew."

"Someone from your past? From your childhood?"

"I don't know."

"Come back to bed, John. Hold me. I'll protect you."

Here, an embrace.

"My mother used to hold me like this."

"You must miss her very much."

"I don't know what's wrong with me, Niyanthi."

"It's just nerves, John. Stress. It's the investigation at the university. You can't blame yourself for Davison's death."

"I know. But he wasn't only my colleague, he was my friend. I should never have let him talk me into those experi-ments. We were violating university rules, probably breaking interstellar treaties. But I thought our discoveries could change the world. We were so close."

"Will they prosecute you?"

"No. The Federal Procurator's Office decided there wasn't enough evidence of a crime. The tachyon disruption destroyed the lab. They have no means to prove what we were attempting."

"So you were exonerated. The Circle of Deans will leave you be now."

"Niyanthi, the deans expelled me today."

"They can't do that."

"They can and they did. I'm sure they know I meant no harm, but they fear who might follow in my footsteps. Dean Troughton compared my actions to those of the Khelts. Ambition was their downfall as well. It turned their world into that nightmarish Great Pearl. It destroyed them."

"I fear to ask. What will happen to you now, John?"

"My visa will be revoked. I'll have to leave Chilatmatoic"

"Where will you go?"

"Home. I have nowhere else I can go."

"Is there anything for you there?"

"Only my mother's grave. I sold our farms to study here."

"Your parents were from Earth, were they not? You could claim birthright. You could transfer to Harvard or Tsinghua, continue your studies."

"No university will ever take me now, Niyanthi. This stigma will haunt me for all my days. And would I even know Earth? I've heard it's as foreign to us colonists as the Thanish homeworld. And I'll know it even less after the five decades it will take me to reach it. By that time, I'll be an antique, useful to no one."

Here, Niyanthi's comforting smile. Without her the young man would be lost. This he does not yet understand.

"What if there was somewhere else, John? Somewhere that accepts with open arms the tired, the poor, the huddled masses of this universe?"

"You mean the new colonies? The Kush Mandate?"

"Yes."

"We're already at the edge of the universe, Niyanthi. To go further is exile."

"No, John. It's freedom. You're a colonist at heart. The frontier is in your blood. Out there will be others like you."

"Out there, Niyanthi, are desperate souls, convicts, and naive fools. And besides, I couldn't go alone. I haven't the strength in me anymore. I wouldn't know where to begin. I wouldn't know anyone out there."

"You'd know me."

Here, a surprise.

"You're leaving?"

"Yes. I was afraid to tell you. I know we've only known one another for a semester, but I feel we have something, John, something I've never had before."

"When do you leave?"

"Soon. I've accepted a teaching position on Amleth III. My launch will be the first wave of settlers. Think of it, John, a virgin world, ours to sculpt as we will. If you come with me, we'll be together at the edge of the known galaxy, just like your parents when they arrived on your world. No one will care about what you have done, only what you can contribute to the future. It would be a new beginning."

"Even if I wanted to, Niyanthi, I'd never make your launch. The work assignments will have all been taken and I'm sure the next launch is years away."

"Then don't come as a worker."

"Then how?"

"John, I love you so very much. I know I don't say that enough because we like to pretend what have is still so very casual. But I know that's not so anymore. I was afraid to ask before, but tonight I can't be afraid. Jonathan, for better or for worse, for richer or for poorer, will you join me at the edge of the universe? I guess what I'm asking is, will you marry me?"

Here, a moment of joy, a moment of hope.

Here, a yes, an unwavering and absolute yes.

Here, the curious hand of fate at play.

24

I am saddened to say my farewells to the settlers of Nyssa. In some small way I feel I've made a connection with this strange community, that it's not so much different from myself, a place out of time, a people soon to confront a world beyond everything they know. While I do not envy the existential seas and direful billows they will soon be forced to navigate, I do understand them better than most. I ride them even now.

And so it is, after a tearful goodbye to Dinah and her mother Zipporah, I'm transported to the mysterious city known as the Valeyard. The year is again 3021, the cosmological present as Story Beckett once called it. It's Careena and myself, a rather inseparable duo at this point, but we are joined now by a third temporal interloper, the enigmatic Rhoda al-Khansa.

I still don't know exactly what to make of our new companion. But I've decided that I like her. And as fun as it is to bounce around the cosmos with a gun-toting, whiskey-drinking, foul-mouthed old crone like Careena, it's also refreshing to be around someone my own age.

The Valeyard. We've popped into existence on a busy urban street—so busy in fact, with crowds pushing past us in every which direction, that I'm unsurprised no one seems to have noticed three strange women materialize out of nowhere.

The transition for me personally, however, is bewildering; no longer are there the open, windswept steppes of Kryten. Here instead are claustrophobic towers and skyscrapers piled on top of one another without rhyme or reason, boxing in mobs of passersby, funneling crowds past street vendors shouting and hawking their wares. There are no cars, thank goodness, only the occasional trolley cutting through the mass of people like a knife through warm butter —but even so, it's a dizzying and chaotic metropolis that could easily dwarf ten New Yorks.

The entire city sits within a massive impact crater, making it roughly circular in shape, not unlike Careena's hometown of New Harmony. The similarities, however, start and end there. For beyond those steep crater walls, surrounding the Valeyard for as far as the eye can see, is nothing but lifeless rock. This is a dead world. I'd call it inhospitable and Martian, but I'm willing to bet that in this day and age, Mars is an absolute paradise.

Looking up, there's not even an atmosphere. The entire planet is a frozen rock of perpetual night, freely exposed to the abyss and vacuum of space. This is, I realize, a world that waits with eager anticipation to consume the mortal invaders who have so arrogantly colonized it.

All that protects us from those appetites is a glass dome covering the city, conforming roughly to the walls of the crater in which the city sits. Ships are forced to land in a flat ravine several miles away; passengers are brought in by underground trains.

The city is horrid, with smells like a gymnasium locker room. It's noisy. Old men and women dressed in little more than rags are washing clothes in tubs in alleys behind posh martini lounges filled with fashionable couples.

On every corner I look are dancing billboards, holographic ads, and junky, half-functional robots beckoning us into shops and stores. It all feels rather sleazy, like a shabby red-light district; one the size of Cairo.

I'm a little embarrassed that, once again, Rhoda is not getting to see the best humanity has to offer. When this is all over, I'm taking the girl to Florence.

"Why would anyone choose to live here?" I ask Careena.

"They aren't here by choice, deary," Careena tells me and Rhoda. "This is the Ghent Mandate's dirty little secret. Long ago it was a mining outpost, nothing special. When the mines dried up, smugglers took over the old tunnels. That was back when this was still the real frontier. The smugglers buried all sorts of jamming equipment into the mining tunnels, a lot of which is still functioning to this day, making this place a black market paradise."

"Fine, but everyone here can't be a smuggler."

"They're not," Careena says with some shame. She looks to Rhoda. "You want to know why I hate your people? Look around. This is what you did. During the second war you obliterated worlds, without warning. We had to evacuate entire planets, sometimes with as many as a billion people on them. Colonists piled into any ship they could, but many of those ships weren't equipped for long distance travel. The fighting never came to Ghent, thank goodness, but we were close enough that we were on the front lines of the refugee crisis. They arrived by the hundreds of millions. Sometimes they got deposited in places like this, so that the ships could go back and get more. Back then there was no city here. Refugees were placed in makeshift camps down below in the mining tunnels. It was meant to be only temporary. The Inner Core worlds agreed to draw lotteries and start taking their share of the people here, because our worlds were overwhelmed. No one was ever meant to remain on this rock."

"So what happened?" I ask.

"Lots of things, I suppose. The most obvious being that humanity lost the bulk of her fleets. And, believe it or not, we can't just snap our fingers to make more ships, even in the 31st Century. Reginald drives on starships require years to spin up. On the big ships you've seen, it takes almost a decade. So ships were at a premium for a long time after the war, and we needed them to rebuild our own systems. The refugees out here became a lower and lower priority. It was easy to rationalize, given we were still attempting to deal with the hundreds of millions of refugees we'd already absorbed on our worlds."

She sighs before going on. "So I guess it's easy to forget about people when they're tucked away on some forgotten rock like this. And we kept expecting the Core Worlds to rise to the occasion and to do their part and help us out. Fat chance of that. Eventually the refugees here on the Valeyard got tired living down below in those cramped mining tunnels. They got ingenious."

She points up. "They retrofitted the old mining microbots to build this dome. Took only six months. They were able to move to the surface after that. When rescue still didn't come, they built this city. Necessity breeds invention, as they say. Now an entire generation has grown up here. They've never known any other way of life."

Rhoda asks a question that I've been wondering as well.

"Old maid, how did the war end?"

What she's really asking is what happened to her people.

Careena looks almost saddened to give the answer. "All I can tell you is that the first war was over territorial disputes and embargoes, and I can't say either side was blameless. But that second war came centuries later, when we thought we were at peace. You started it without provocation, without a word of what you wanted; you never responded to a single message we sent you. You just came for world after world. We defended ourselves as best we could, but after a few years it was clear you had us over a barrel. Then one day your people just... left."

"Left?"

"Aye. Your people abandoned every world they had taken, including all those systems they'd captured from the first war four centuries earlier. It was a mystery to us. Your people had removed all evidence of human habitation from the planets they conquered, leaving behind only unspoiled forests and wild animals, but never so much as a single road or building. We never trusted what you may have done to those worlds, which is why the refugees were never allowed to resettle them."

"And Kheltaris?" Rhoda asks of her homeworld.

"That was the strangest part of it all," Careena says. "Your entire race went back there. All your ships, all your people, all your own colonists. Something had happened on Kheltaris. Something tragic. Something we still don't understand. Maybe we never will. All we know is from what we've seen on long range telescopes. Your homeworld turned itself into a silver orb."

Rhoda is unflappable, but even she can't help but be affected by this news. "What are you saying?"

"I'm saying your world is gone, luv. I'm sorry. Something consumed your entire civilization. Our scientists believe it was a type of self-replicating nanite. We know your people relied heavily on them, but these must have gotten out of control. And maybe since your people are connected, something hacked your minds like a computer virus, called you all back home. Some have theorized it was a resource gathering algorithm gone mad, yet one so sophisticated that your people were unable to defend against. I don't know. All I can tell you is that Kheltaris is just an ocean of silver now, smooth as a sheet of steel. We've come to call it the *Great Pearl*."

"It cannot be," Rhoda whispers.

I'm shocked as well.

Careena does her best to explain. "Our best guess is that the entire planetary surface, every molecule, organic or otherwise, has been broken down and rebuilt into copies of those nanites. How deep they go, or what their purpose is, if they even have one, we really don't know. The planet is inert, as far as we can tell. But the truth is, your solar system, along with all the systems your people have ever touched, are quarantined. Because if it was some sort of malfunction that destroyed you, some sort of self-replicating mechanical virus, then it's possible that if even a single nanite escaped, it could start a chain reaction on our worlds, and we'd suffer the same fate you. And given how far advanced your people were, if you couldn't stop what was happening, what chance would we have?"

I see the shock and disbelief in Rhoda's eyes. Perhaps she had hoped that her sister would still be alive, even after five hundred years. That sort of technology, to prolong life, had to have already been well under way on her planet. But now there was nothing, not even the pride of a civilization that had gone on to achieve great things.

Worse, it means Rhoda is the last of her kind.

I put a hand on her arm. "I'm so sorry, Rhoda."

She wants to say something, but she holds off. I can tell she's hurting inside. Stoically, she looks up to Careena. "It changes nothing of our mission. If this Patmos can destroy history, then he can still destroy my loved ones, even if they're no longer alive today. I won't allow him to rob me even of their memories." She looks around at the dirty, noisy, chaotic city we've all found ourselves before adding, "Besides, it would appear as if your own people can use all the help they can get."

Careena shrugs at the comment. "This place will grow on you. But all right, we shouldn't dillydally here in the middle of a busy road. So, first things first."

"Find shelter," I suggest.

And it's true, I'm exhausted.

"And weapons," Rhoda adds.

Not a terrible option either.

Careena scoffs. "No, you blockheads. What's wrong with you two? Drinks, dammit! Drinks!"

I want to complain, but given the heavy news Rhoda has just received, perhaps it's not such a bad idea. We follow Careena into a massive tower of questionable construction standards. The foyer is dirty, the security guard is asleep, and there's a constant stream of strangely dressed people coming and going from the many tiny elevators lining the back wall. We all squeeze into one, along with a few other visitors.

There's one hundred and eight floors to choose from. Careena presses the button for seventy-nine, though as far as I can tell, she pressed it entirely at random.

As people get on and off various floors on our way up, I'm offered a small window into life inside this extraordinary tower. Like a vertical city, each floor is its own neighborhood, the tightly packed halls filled with low-priced hostels, barbers, residential apartments, tiny gyms, sex clubs, dentistry clinics, second-rate law firms, spiritual temples, luxury hotels, corner bodegas, massage parlors, off-world visa agencies, export and import companies, fly-by-night entrepreneurial headquarters of every stripe, and on the fifty-fourth floor, even a cafe where patrons pay to dine with kittens.

The proprietors of that one were a Thanish couple.

Our floor opens not into a hallway like the others, but directly into a lounge. It's windowless and smaller than the other floors, which makes me think we're on a level dedicated mainly to building infrastructure. The occasional clanging and whirling from beyond the walls confirms this theory.

The vibe in the lounge is dreamlike, with soft electronic music and even softer neon lights hanging over the tables and sofas. This is the type of place I imagine people go after leaving the clubs, when the body demands sleep but the mind refuses to comply.

A place hidden between the layers of time.

Careena orders us three whiskeys from the counter and we take a booth in the corner. When the drinks arrive, she takes a hard long look at her glass. When she speaks, it's not to us. "Oh, dear friend, how long has it been?"

I really don't know what to do with this woman. "Careena, it's been, like, three days. Tops."

"Three days! Crikey, even worse than I thought!"

She downs the drink and orders another.

I turn to Rhoda. "How are the drinks on Kheltaris?"

"We have no drinks like this," she says matter-of-factly. "There would be no point."

Careena chimes in. "The point is to have fun, girl."

"No. You don't understand," Rhoda responds. "My body will treat this like poison. It will be processed only as a fuel source."

I'm amazed. "So you can't, like, get drunk?"

"No."

Careena has her own thoughts on the matter. "Good lord, no wonder your people went off their trolleys."

"Careena!"

"Bah."

Rhoda slides her whiskey to me, but she turns her attention to Careena. "What made you this way, old maid? You're a soldier deep down, I can sense that. But it was not the war that broke you. It was something else."

Careena holds both hands on her glass of amber tightly. She doesn't answer the question, not directly at least. "It's irony, ain't it, that just as the world is about to come to an end, I'm brought back here. Back where it all started. The wheel has come full circle."

I'm confused. "How do you mean?"

"I mean this is where I met her, Freckles. My Samus."

The sadness in her eyes is likely as close to a tear as she'll ever allow herself to give. I try to put it all together. "Samus was the friend that you lost, the one you were accused of trying to save. You told me it was a setup."

"It wasn't a bloody setup. I was just incompetent. Not only did I fail to save her, but I got caught in the process. I'd have tried again, I'd have tried a thousand times over, but I was kneecapped by Soolin. She revoked most of my privileges. I was to turn myself in after completing the assignment I was on. Somehow I managed to draw that mission out for years. And during that time I guess I got a wee, shall we say, *friendly* with the bottle. Now I'm nothing. A washed-up, irritable has-been too afraid to face the consequences of her own actions."

I tell her truthfully. "You're not that to us, Careena."

"Who was she?" Rhoda asks. "This Samus?"

"Someone special," the old woman says. "To me at least. She begged me to leave the ministry, to put all this behind me, so we could start something. A bloody family. Can you imagine that? Me? Around babies, dirty diapers, and all that schnitzel. But I'd give anything for the chance now. I was a different person back then. Sometimes, I think it may have even worked..."

"I don't know what to say, Careena."

"You don't need to say anything. What's done is done." She finishes her drink. "Well, now. Aren't we a sad trio of ladies? Here. I've booked us private rooms on eighty-six." She slides us each key cards she must have gotten from the bartender. "We meet back here in seven hours. Then we find the Red Man and beat the bloody answers out of him."

"You told Story we were just going to scope this place out."

She stands to leave. "I say a lot of things, kiddo. Now I'm going to get some sleep."

Rhoda and I are left alone at the booth.

"Can you tell me what we face?" the Kheltic girl asks.

I lean back in my chair. "I don't exactly know myself. The Red Man stole some minerals used to go back in time, but they're not for him. They're for a cult or something, led by a man named Patmos. That's who we're really after. Careena believes if we find the Red Man, he'll lead us to Patmos. From what she told me, she can detect these minerals with her ring, but only if we're close enough. So I don't know what she plans. Hiking up and down every street in this godawful place doesn't seem too appealing. Not to mention we're short on time. These minerals need to be refined before they can be used, but I think that won't take but another day, maybe two. I really don't know."

Rhoda is very perceptive. "Something else is bothering you."

"Yeah, I guess Careena's story got me thinking. Your story got me thinking. I've tried so hard to push my past life out of my mind. But now I'm thinking about my parents. I think the reality of all this is finally sinking in. I can't go back to them. And the worst part is, I just vanished. Into thin air. What must they be thinking? That I was murdered? Kidnapped? They're probably putting up posters right now, crying themselves to bed at night. That's what I see when I close my eyes. I see them crying. And it's all my fault."

My voice cracks as I speak.

"Look at me, I'm in tears."

Rhoda reaches over and comforts me. "We should do something fun. To get our minds off this."

Coming from a girl who I've only ever seen be as serious as a heart attack, this surprises me a little.

She asks me, "What do you Earth girls do for fun?"

I look around the lounge. There's only a handful of patrons, most with half-empty bottles. There's the bartender, who I realize is a malfunctioning robot on a dolly. And there's a small stage.

I smile while wiping away a tear.

I turn back to my new friend.

"We call it karaoke. And you're going to love it!"

25

The following morning brings the same din of neon lights piercing perpetual darkness as the day before. My room has a window offering a remarkable view of this terrifying mega-city, a metropolis hiding under a dome on a dead rock. I'm seduced by the colors, by the lights, by the sounds emanating from below. The city pulsates. It breathes.

Eventually I force myself to turn away; I brush my teeth, dress, and head down to yesterday's lounge to meet the others.

Rhoda is already there at a table, having a breakfast of toast and vegan eggs. The barbaric necessity of animal consumption has been vanquished in the 31st Century, not that there would be many animals on the Valeyard available to consume regardless.

It looks like the girl has been here a while, despite our late night together and the early hour. I have to ask, "You don't sleep?"

"Some nights maybe an hour," she says matter-of-factly.

"Must be nice."

My own breakfast arrives. The quality is questionable. It looked so much better from a distance.

"So you've been up this whole time?" I ask.

"Yes."

"Doing what?"

"Thinking."

"About?"

"My people."

I can't imagine how hard that must be on her. I wish I knew what to say. But then she tells me something rather surprising.

"I heard them, Isabel."

"Heard them? How do you mean?"

"Yesterday, I heard them," she explains. "I wanted to tell you, but I was afraid how the old maid might react. And I wasn't even sure if what I heard was real, or just some wishful thinking on my part. But when I meditate, I can hear them. The old maid believes that this Great Pearl they created destroyed them. But that's not what happened. The pearl *is* them."

"They told you this?" I ask.

"In a way. It's not words that I hear. It's a sort of song, but not one of music or language. To be honest, they've transcended my comprehension. But I can hear my sister's voice among the chorus. At least, I like to believe that I do."

"Are we still a danger?"

"No, I don't believe so. Ironically, their song isn't meant for me. It's meant for you, for humanity. It's an apology for what they did, for their arrogance. They know you can't hear them, not yet. But one day you will. And maybe on that day the human race can be reunited. Their wisdom is great. They hope to share with you all that they've learned."

I'm wide-eyed at the revelation. "Can they do anything to help us now? Because, we may not be around much longer if they don't."

The girl shakes her head. "No. I can't speak to them, only listen. And they've lost all sense of ego. Their concerns are no longer as earthly as ours. It's like they're in a state of meditation now, exploring the depths of consciousness. I think they may have come to know all there is to know about the physical universe. All that's left, the final frontier to reality, is understanding the nature of experience itself."

I can't say I know what that means, but I can guess the implications. "So you're saying that we're on our own?"

"It would be appear so," she tells me. "But we will find the Red Man. Don't worry. We are hunters at heart, you and I."

Despite being the same age, sometimes I feel so much younger than this enigmatic girl. And comments like that really don't help. "Maybe you, Rhoda," I say. "But I spent an hour this morning drying my hair and plucking my eyebrows. Look, I even painted my nails. Would a hunter do that?"

She grins. "A pretty one might."

Careena appears next to us. "So what are you tarts up to?"

"Waiting for you, old maid."

It's me who says this, because it's funny.

"Bah," comes the response. I notice she doesn't order a whiskey with breakfast. So either she's suddenly turned a new leaf, or today is going to be a truly dangerous one. I'm not sure which of those two options I prefer.

"Look, you two," she goes on. "This is the plan. Hecate can detect the RGMs, but only if we're close enough, a hundred meters or so. In a city this big, that's going to be a problem. So we're going to have to do this the old-fashioned way. We ask around, hunt for clues. Try to narrow down the possibilities."

"So we're using our detective hats."

I'm hoping this means no gunfights.

"Exactly. And I think I know a good place to start. It's unlikely the Red Man can refine all that product on his own, at least not in any reasonable amount of time. There are a few black market outfits in the city he could partner with. He's going to try to avoid drawing attention to himself, but word is definitely going to get around. So we'll start with a contact I know. He's got his fingers in a bit of everything, and he owes me a favor."

With our plans decided and our breakfast finished, Careena takes us back into the crowded streets of the Valeyard. We board a double-decker tram heading roughly east.

The tram is silent as a ghost, levitating an inch above the ground; as such it has to make constant and annoying warning dings as it crisscrosses busy streets and crowded neighborhoods. The sea of people part for us, only to reform in our wake.

Our ride is roughly forty minutes. When we alight, I have to immediately put my hand over my nose. "Oy. It smells like rotten cabbage here."

Careena scolds me. "Get your hand off your face, you dolt. You're going to make us look like bloody tourists. This district is home to the city's main food processing facilities. That smell is protein. I think. Anyway, they say it grows on you."

"I hope they don't mean literally."

She only shrugs.

After navigating a large boulevard, she leads us down a long back alley, paved in historic cobblestones, which is odd for a modern city at the edge of an expanding universe. We're behind what once was a ritzy theater, now left in ruination and despair. There's trash everywhere. The walls are covered in torn and faded posters, advertisements mostly. Even in death a few of them try to show moving images as we pass.

The alley is empty save for us. It's dark, creepy, and I feel we're unwelcome. "Are we safe here?" I ask.

Careena looks up. "Probably not. One good meteor crack on that dome and there goes the atmosphere. This city is a forking humanitarian crisis just waiting to happen, believe you me."

"I meant this alley."

"Oh, right. Doubtful."

She leads us further down.

We come to a large iron door.

I can feel someone watching us.

Careena knocks.

There's a sketched drawing of a face on the center panel of the door. It's drawn in white marker with hard angles. Ordinarily, I'd think it was a graffiti tag, but graffiti generally doesn't move. Or talk, for that matter.

"What do you want?" the face on the door asks.

Careena answers. "We're here to see the Tinker."

"What makes you think he wants to see you?"

"We're old friends."

The face looks Careena up and down. "You don't look like his type." It looks me over the same way. "Her maybe."

"Just tell him we're here," Careena demands.

There's a pause. Then the face responds, "The Tinker says he remembers you."

"See, like I said, old friends."

"The Tinker says last time you were here you shot him in the leg."

"It's a... rocky sort of friendship."

The face's eyes narrow. "The Tinker says I should flood this alley with fendahl gas."

Careena's tact is now on full display. "Listen here, you rusted doorknob, tell that tosspot he owes me this visit. And he's lucky it was only his leg. Because I was aiming for his goddamn bollocks!"

A green mist rises out of the cobblestones, clinging to our ankles. I try to kick it away, to little effect. "Um, Careena."

She ignores me. Instead, she raises her hand to the door, exposing her ring. "All right, ask that perverted chipmunk if he knows what this is."

There's another pause.

"You a damn timecop?" the door finally asks.

"I am. I'm also the reason no one from Tegana has ever been here kicking down this door, which is to say *you*. That should at least get me an audience, don't you think?"

The mist pulls back into the stones.

"You got five minutes," says the door.

He opens and we're all hit by a sudden blast of dance music. After passing through a long, dark hallway and a defunct coat check, we walk up some stairs and through a velvet curtain.

What I see amazes me, a dance club, filled with revelers grinding and dancing with fancy cocktails in their hands as laser lights shoot through generated fog. There's a stage to the left, designed to mimic the Roaring Twenties. Which makes the electronic club music all the more out of place.

A woman cuts through the crowd toward the stage. She's petite, with high cheekbones and the aura of a starlit from the early days of cinema. Wavy blonde hair covers one eye. Or it would have been blonde, where the woman in color.

Unlike everyone else, she's entirely in greyscale, from her lipstick right down to her gorgeous evening gown; it's as if she's just stepped out of an old-time, black-and-white television. Once on stage, the dance music is shut off and she sings something befitting of her time period, jazzy and slow.

My mouth hangs open as the revelers' outfits morph to match this older style of music. Women sitting on bar stools grow decorative feathers from the buns in their hair. Tacky club shirts seamlessly meld into period vests. Cigarettes grow into pipes, sneakers morph into loafers. I look down, expecting my own clothes to change, but nothing happens.

I'm sort of disappointed.

The black-and-white woman finishes the song and the lights go up. The fog vanishes. The music stops. The revelers fade out of existence. They'd been a crowd of holograms this entire time. If the world were a stage, it feels like all the actors have gone home, and that we've been left standing behind the curtain of reality, a netherworld both quiet and lonely. The black-and-white woman remains up on stage, though.

She smiles down at us kindly but otherwise doesn't move.

"Did you like the show?" This comes from someone else, a man walking down a grand spiral staircase leading to the dance floor where we're waiting. He's short with unkempt hair, pudgy fingers, and a face that reminds me of a mole.

"Put that on just for us, did you?" Careena asks.

He joins us. "You didn't like it?"

"I recognized your cartoons from last time I was here. When you going to get some real bloody friends?"

The strange man points to the black-and-white woman on stage. "Oh, no. Not her. She's new. That's Veronica Lake. Besides, friends are unreliable." He eyes me and Rhoda. "Speaking of friends, who are these bumpkins you've brought? More agents from the Tegan Ministry of Evil?"

Careena is very casual. She walks over to the bar, looking for a drink. "If we were here on behalf of the ministry, do you really think we would have knocked?"

"Then why are you here, timecop?"

"Information."

"That doesn't come cheap," says the little man.

"Neither does keeping your operation from my bosses."

The Tinker puts a hand to his chin in thought. "I am curious why you've done that. But I'm not stupid enough to ask. What is this information you're looking for?"

"Someone has come through recently with an awful lot of RGMs. They'll want to process it. And fast. Unless I miss my mark, they'd come to you."

"I'm not involved in that anymore," he says. "I found it wasn't good for one's personal wellbeing. Too many ladies with tiny guns aiming for you netherbits."

Careena pushes. "With what these people would be paying, you'd come out of retirement."

The Tinker considers this a moment. "The information you want comes with some personal risk."

"I'll take my chances."

"Not for you, you old witch. For me! Honestly, I'd rather face the Tegan secret police than the wrath of the people you're after."

"I can make it worth your while."

"With what?" he asks. "Money? Do I look like I need money?"

Careena reaches into her pocket for her gun. "Fine, it's the bollocks then. This time I won't miss."

"Wait, wait. There may be one thing you could barter."

Careena's answer is sharp. "These two girls are off limits."

"No, not that. Your QDD. Five minutes in the Veeger."

"Out of the question."

"Then no deal."

Careena stands her ground as long as she can. "Fine, three minutes and it never leaves my hand."

The little man smiles. "Fair enough. I only need two minutes, anyway." He turns to the black-and-white woman. "Veronica, be a doll and go fetch the Veeger."

I can't help but ask. "I thought she was another hologram."

He eyes me with disdain. "Are you from a farm?"

Careena cuts in. "Ignore her. Tell us what you know."

"Very well. Your friends had enough material for three-hundred and twenty-four vests. That was the order. I didn't believe it until I saw it. I mean, I didn't even know that much timecrack existed in all the Milky Way. Someone on your end obviously sucks at their job."

"That can't be right," Careena says. "They only stole enough RGMs to make a hundred jumpvests at best."

The Tinker almost laughs. "A hundred good vests, sure. But you cut it the right way, with the right filler, and you can nearly double your yield. We do it all the time now. But it's not just that. Most jumpers want to be able to, you know, come back. Your friends were able to get three hundred vests because half of those vests are capable of only a single jump. Wherever they're planning to go, it's a one ticket for most of them."

"And you have these vests?"

"No. I sold them all the vests I do have, which wasn't more than thirty. I assume they cleaned out everyone in town. But the actual programming and installation, they're doing all that in-house. They don't trust anyone. They got a man who apparently knows a thing or two about jumps. Patmos is his name, I think. Never heard of him, so I can't tell you if he's any good. There's a lot of hacks out there these days, promising the sky to your grandma, so who knows. And before you ask, I don't have the RGMs either. It's all been processed and delivered. I'm fast. You should have stopped by sooner."

Careena doesn't give up. "I need to know where they are."

This time the Tinker does laugh. "I definitely don't know that. If I did, I assure you, I'd be dead."

I'm suddenly anxious. The Red Man has his vests and now he has the material ready to power them. There's little holding Patmos back now. For all we know, the universe might end at any moment. If that's even what he intends to do; it's absurd that we still haven't the slightest idea what his actual intentions are. He might want to crack the cosmos open like an egg to summon Satan. Or he might have some nobler aim. But if he accidentally creates a paradox, the result will be all but the same. The end of everything.

Veronica returns holding a clear glass orb with a hole large enough for a hand to fit in its center. The Veeger.

Careena eyes the device. "I'm not putting my hand in there unless you give us something else. Nothing you've given us so far has been very helpful."

The Tinker nods. "All right, how's this—two of their technicians came by the other day to drop off the timecrack to be processed. I realized they were both noobs, so while they were here, out of the kindness of my heart, I suggested when they came back to collect the finished material, that if they wanted to bring a vest with them, I could show them how to install a power matrix. After all, this Patmos guy couldn't do all three hundred vests himself, and maybe if they showed some initiative, and a little skill, they'd get a promotion."

"That doesn't help me," Careena says.

"That's because you're not as clever as I am," he points out. "I can't tell you where they went after they left here. I couldn't take the chance they'd find a tracer on any of the vests I sold them. And my new life philosophy involves avoiding getting shot. But I might be able to tell you where they're planning to go. You see, the vest they brought back for a demonstration had already been programmed with jump coordinates, as I thought it might be, given this was a rush job and they seemed in a bit of hurry. It's the one thing Patmos could have gotten out of the way while waiting the several days it would take to process all that timecrack."

"And?" Careena asks.

"And I may have taken the liberty of downloading those coordinates while I was so kindly giving my demonstration."

"And?"

"The data was encrypted."

"How bad?"

"A Hartnell-polytope quantum encryption."

Careena shakes her head. "Impossible to break."

The mole-faced man smiles. "For you fools on Tegana, maybe."

Careena is dubious. "Codswallop and piglet sticks. You're telling me you can break that level of encryption?"

"Veronica can," he says, nodding to the petite woman, who I still don't know if she's an android or a hologram or something entirely new that I can't even comprehend. He continues. "She's been working on it all night. Come back later this afternoon and I'll have your answer for you. I'll tell you exactly where they're going. That way you can be there waiting with the cavalry when they show up."

"Fine, you'll get your fancy scan of Hecate then."

Uncharacteristically she adds, "And, Tinker..."

"Yes?"

"Good work."

He beams. Having few equals in the galaxy, praise from those who could truly appreciate his accomplishments was welcomed, even when it came from the institutions chartered to thwart his endeavors. Or perhaps, especially when it came from those institutions.

We leave his theater to break for lunch and to plan out the rest of the day. I'm relieved once we're out of that creepy back alley and in the bustling crowds of the city again, even if the streets continue to smell like soggy potatoes everywhere we go.

As we walk Rhoda asks, "Old maid, I take it your ring is beyond anything that strange man can produce?"

"A tachyon-string accelerator that can fit in the palm of your hand? You better believe it, hotcakes."

"And if he scans it, he'll be able to reproduce it?"

"Yeap. Pretty much."

"So is it wise to give up your secrets to a man such as that?"

Careena takes off Hecate and hands it to her.

"Here, you can have it."

Rhoda gives a look of confusion.

Careena winks. "It's a fake, luv. I got a whole a pocket full of them. Most are rejects, from back when I was dating one of the engineers. It'll fool the Tinker's scanners, though."

Now I have to ask. "Is this the same sort of fake you gave Soolin back at the ministry to fool *her* scanners?"

"Yeah, why?"

I want to smack my forehead with my palm. Something tells me I should be very worried about how the rest of today is going to turn out.

26

With a few hours to kill until the Tinker has his findings ready, I convince Careena to take us shopping. First, because Rhoda's outfit is too suspicious; I doubt a refugee colony is the best place for a Kheltic girl to be outed. And second, because my own is starting to see quite a bit of wear and tear, which I suppose is to be expected when you're a time-traveling Indiana Jane who has been shot at, assaulted, thrashed around on a sinking ship, and forced to camp out under the stars on faraway alien worlds. A new wardrobe seems like the least the universe owes me.

I admit that while I've never been the type of girl to have closets full of designer shoes or anything, I do enjoy a fresh outfit from time to time. Today is my chance. I indulge in a long sleeve blouse, taupe in color. The fit is nicely tailored with a somewhat conservative cut to the shoulders. There's even a short, ruffled, faux tie. I also grab some black pants, almost identical to my old ones, because in this department I'm not very original. Go with what works. To finish it off, I take a handsome white blazer.

Rhoda is practical to a fault. The best I can convince her is to replace her military jacket with a moto jacket. At least there's no Kheltaris Mining Directorate badge on this one.

She also swaps out her white undershirt with a steely grey blouse. Finally, her army boots she replaces with a slightly more fashionable version of... army boots.

Careena keeps her tacky wardrobe, which never seems to soil or smell, no matter how much she puts it through. The only thing she buys is a handful of new hair scrunchies which, given the number she goes through in a day, I can only assume she eats. I decide not to ask how she affords everything we buy. Sometimes it's best not to know.

"Time to head back," she tells us as we leave the shopping promenade. "That little troll should have what we need by now."

I remark offhandedly, "You'd think with all the money he has, he'd fix his teeth or something."

She looks at me like I've sprouted horns. "What are you talking about, Freckles? No one today is born with genes that would let you get that ugly even if you tried. You have to pay out the arse to get yourself shortened like that, believe you me. And to get one eye slightly above the other! Well, that tells everyone you're absolutely made of money."

I shall never understand the future.

We head back to the theater. As soon as we enter the cobblestone alley, I sense something is wrong. This feeling is confirmed once we reach the talking door, which now hangs crooked from busted hinges, that strange graffiti face twitching and unresponsive.

Careena does not waste a second. With Old Bessie in hand, she slips into the building. It's at moments like this that I remember she is not just some kooky old lady with a drinking problem; she's a former soldier and a world class super spy. She's trained and she's lethal. Rhoda and I follow cautiously behind.

In the main hall, the first thing I notice, besides the eerie quiet, is that Veronica is on stage, standing like a statue, with a listless, dead look in her eyes. I smell burning rubber; to my left is a smoldering jukebox.

It isn't much of a leap of logic to realize the jukebox housed Veronica's mind, her digital soul, developed over years by a man whose social phobias so dominated his life that he'd rather create artificial friends than open himself up to real ones.

"Forkballs," Careena curses. "Stay here, you two."

She runs up the grand spiral staircase. Both Rhoda and I ignore her instructions and follow after. On the second floor is a doorway into a master bedroom. The scene in that room will haunt me for all my days.

First, there's the sound. While standing in the room, some sort of neural projector is filling my mind with the rhythmic moaning of a woman in ecstasy, as if mental porn is being beamed directly into my soul. It's revolting.

But more disturbing is the Tinker himself. He's on his back on his bed. His pants are pulled down to his knees. I don't want to judge, but it looks as if he may have been in an act of self-pleasure. With that neural projector beaming God-knows-what into his head, he was likely too engaged in this *activity* to ever notice his assassin enter the room. I have to cover my mouth. Chunks of his face and skull lay everywhere. His killer went at him with a hatchet.

This wasn't just murder; it was psychopathy.

The combination of sex and violence on display is too much for me to take. It triggers memories of my own assault in the washroom aboard the *Stellar Pearl*. Fearing I might vomit or breakdown, I leave the room and stand over the balcony for air, only to be confronted by the dead-eyed stare of Veronica below.

"The Red Man did this?" I hear Rhoda ask from inside the room. She seems unfazed by the scene. Perhaps having synthetic chemistry isn't so bad after all.

"Aye," I hear Careena answer. "No loose ends, I reckon. Or Patmos realized what the little weasel was up to."

"So what now?" Rhoda asks.

"Now? Now, we have no leads. We have no time. Now we're proper forked."

We all walk back downstairs into the main hall. Careena goes behind the bar. She's muttering to herself as she surveys the various bottles of whiskey. She kicks open a hidden door on the floor. "Jackpot," she says to herself.

I know it's too much to hope for that she may have found a clue, that the Tinker may have hid his findings in a secret compartment.

Sure enough, she lifts a bottle of Woodford Reserve, a simple but elegant bottle that has made its way trillions of miles across space, from the Sol System in the Orion Arm of the Milky Way Galaxy to here, today, this moment, in the loving hands of one Careena J. Smith.

She shows us the bottle as if it's a consolation prize. "Kentucky bourbon, ladies. One shot of this is worth more than most people in the Valeyard will make in a lifetime. So enjoy it. It's probably going to be your last."

Maybe she's right.

Maybe it's time we finally admit defeat.

"Old maid," Rhoda asks. "How will you know when you're in proximity to some of these RGMs?"

"I've set Hecate to glow blue. Why?"

Rhoda nods toward Careena's hand.

The bottle of Kentucky bourbon falls from the old woman's grip. The glass shatters across the floor as a fortune bleeds away into oak floorboards, themselves worth more than gold on a world without trees.

A small piece of Earth history has just seeped into oblivion.

Careena gives the crime not a second thought. She jumps over the bar counter with surprising spryness and charges toward the exit with Old Bessie in hand.

I call out after her. "Where are you going?"

"The assassin is still here, you idiot! They're wearing a vest!"

Rhoda and I run after her. We charge out into the alley and then down toward the main street. There are crowds of people here, filling the width of the boulevard as they come and go, parting only when a trolley passes through.

Careena is desperately looking to her left and to her right. There are hundreds if not thousands of people here. Not to mention street vendors, hawkers, child beggars. There's the din of commerce. The stench of the processing plants.

We'd never find the assassin, if not for Hecate. But the closer we are to whoever it is, the brighter the ring glows. Careena uses her like a dowsing stick, leading us to our quarry.

Finally she points. "That's her."

I see a red-headed woman in a white biker jacket. She hasn't yet noticed us trailing behind her. I doubt she could in this mess of people. We weave through the crowds in pursuit.

"We can't spook her," Careena warns. "She must have brought a jumpvest in case she's caught. If she sees us, she'll be gone quicker than the hedgehogs."

It's a clever fail-safe for an assassin, I'll admit. But unfortunately for her, it also allows us to track her. We may have a few cards left to play yet.

At first, I wonder why she's on foot at all, why not just jump away once the crime is done? After all, the Valeyard has no fancy shields like Tegana preventing such a thing. But then I remember what we learned earlier, that Patmos is trying to stretch out the stolen RGMs to allow for as many jumpvests as possible, even if that means many of the vests will be capable of only a single jump. His ultimate plan must depend on it. Which means our assassin will only use her vest as a last resort.

I'm a little disturbed by the notion of assassins able to jump across time and space in the blink of an eye, arriving like phantoms in the shadows, snuffing out their victims with ease before vanishing back into the void from which they came, their scent on the breeze all that would remain behind as evidence that they had ever existed at all.

This is precisely why so many of the wealthier worlds do now have their special energy shields; it's the reason I couldn't jump Careena directly back to Tegana when we were on my rooftop in Brooklyn. But what of the poorer worlds, like the Valeyard? The ones who can afford no such protection?

I push those questions aside and instead focus on the mission at hand. I've never done this sort of cloak and dagger routine before, but I find that I oddly enjoy it; the hunt keeps my adrenaline going. I feel alive, like when I'm on the water with my crew team, which I've come to miss. The stakes here, however, are so much higher than they are during competition. There's no ribbon for second place in this tournament. Second place here means the end of the world.

Not even thirty minutes later, we're huddled out of sight behind a massive glass tower. Unlike most of the city's towers, this one is cylindrical and uncharacteristically clean. It's also not alone; I count a dozen rows of towers behind it at least three deep, all identical to this one. There are no people around either. This is not a normal district. It's something else.

The assassin goes inside the nearest tower and vanishes.

"What is this place?" I ask.

"Vertical agriculture," Careena says. "These greenhouse towers grow most of the food for the city. They're filled with vine plants that produce custom-made seed pods the size of watermelons. Easy to transport. Looks like tofu when you crack them open. Very nutritious. High in protein. Tastes like proper garbage."

"And why does it smell so bad?"

Careena explains without irony. "Sewage gets pumped in and sprayed down like rain in there. Those genetically modified plants are actually a fungus, and they've been designed to soak it right up for nutrition. They love that schnitzel. Remember that next time you're having your vegan omelets."

"Oy vey."

"But I can tell you something else," she adds. "This is the wealthiest industry in the city. And these buildings are almost entirely automated. They don't allow people to just come and go. Not the police. Not even city inspectors. Hell, these syndicates probably own the city inspectors."

I'm still wearing my detective hat. "Which means if you paid off the right people to set up shop here, one of these towers would make for a perfect hideout."

"Bingo."

"So what's your plan, old maid?" Rhoda asks.

"We get in there, we destroy the vests, we take out Patmos."

"Wait," I protest. "Shouldn't we call the authorities?"

"You can't trust the authorities in a city like this, deary. And even if you could, he'll have people in the police department on his payroll. They'll alert him that he's been found and then he'll be gone. He's got an exit plan, believe me."

"Then Soolin," I push. "You promised Story you'd only scope things out."

I know this is a useless argument, but I try it anyway.

"Soolin's a damned bureaucrat now," she says. "Look, even if she does believe me, she's going to have her hands tied. Tegana has been in hot water lately, more than you know. The interstellar community is looking for an excuse to come down hard on us, to come take away our toys. She can't afford another international incident. So she'll want to put this place under surveillance, make sure it is, in fact, the Red Man's base before she goes in. And we don't have that sort of time. They killed the Tinker. They're ready to do whatever they got planned. This is our only chance."

I turn to Rhoda for help, but the Kheltic girl offers none.

"The old maid may be right."

"It's settled then," Careena says. "We go in guns blazing."

"I don't even have a fricken gun!"

"It's an expression, Freckles. Just stay behind me."

I collect as much composure as I can, surprised by my lack of fear. But I know it will come for me sooner rather than later. I can't keep it buried and locked away forever. When it does show up, I only hope it's not during that moment when I need my courage the most. Because one way or another, this is all coming to an end soon. We're approaching the final stretch.

And with that thought in mind, we head toward the door.

27

We approach the side entrance of the great cylindrical tower carefully. Careena was right that it's some sort of vertical garden. Through the windows I see hundreds of vines, each nearly half a mile long, hanging down from rafters within. Thousands of food pods grow and dangle like fruits up the entire length of each vine. Every few seconds one of the pods matures completely and falls into an automated collection bin on the ground floor. It takes only a few minutes for a new tiny bud to sprout in the place of a fallen pod.

It's an efficient system. Remarkable really, given that the vines are a genetically engineered superorganism capable of transforming nearly any raw organic material into nutritive compounds not just fit, but precisely balanced, for human consumption. Still, now that I know they're sustained on vats of toilet excrement mixed with dirty asteroid ice water, I doubt I'll be enjoying my dinner much tonight.

Once we reach the door, Careena waves Hecate at a security camera. She chants the word *scrambled*, as if it's a magic spell. She's a strange woman. She performs this bit of theater again while passing her hand over the door lock, which clicks open. She smiles because she thinks she's clever. I roll my eyes because I think she's ridiculous.

We enter the tower. We're a floor beneath the vines and therefor, hopefully, safe from any random excrement showers. We're in some sort of service hallway leading us to corporate offices on a lower promenade at the front of the building. Those offices, however, all seem to have been emptied out some time ago, likely moved to another tower or even another part of the city. There are a few pictures still up on the walls though, portraying beautiful agricultural locales on Old Earth. Some show terraced rice farms in Asia, their patties full of standing water reflecting the colors of the sunset. Other photos show giant combines on fields of corn driven by proud Midwestern farmers. What would they make of these towers?

Staring at the poster, I never see the attack coming.

A sentry has been posted to this hallway, but he's cloaked in some sort of special suit that makes him invisible to the human eye. Nor do I see his weapon, a short kodachi blade, slightly curved, fast as lighting. Were I afforded the time, I'd wonder why he didn't simply shoot us. Why the theatrics involving a sword? I wondered the same thing regarding the Tinker's assassin and her hatchet. The answer, I'd find out later, is that there are security satellites orbiting the colony, capable of detecting gunfire and alerting the authorities. And that would be bad for business.

So it's a sword then, silent as the wind, making a clean arc for my neck. I'd have lost my head, if not for my Kheltic companion. Rhoda's reflexes are godlike. And, fortunately for me and Careena, her synthetic eyes can register parts of the electromagnetic spectrum that I wasn't even aware existed.

Rhoda catches the blade in her fist mere inches from my throat. The shimmering sword cuts into the flesh of her palm but stops dead once it strikes neo-titanium bone.

I still have no idea what's going on, honestly; it's like she's fighting with a ghost. Her free hand strikes the air, which causes a bone-cracking crunch. The sentry's body falls to the floor.

I only know this because I hear him collapse and now see streams of blood running down the sides of his invisible head, making something of an outline. Rhoda has flattened his nose, forcing the cartilage into his brain. Part of me is glad I can't see this.

She casually reaches down and takes the cloaked sword from the dead man's hand. It becomes visible once it's no longer in contact with his suit. The weapon is black, from hilt to blade. I don't even want to look at it. It almost killed me. It's evil.

She lays the weapon against her back and it sticks there, like she's a magnet or something. I'm not sure if that's some body modification of hers doing that, or if it's part of the technology of the sword. I'm too much in shock by what just happened to even ask.

I look over. Careena is as stunned as I am.

"You know, for a tin can," she says. "You're starting to grow on me."

"We should wrap your hand," I tell the girl.

"No need." She shows me her palm. There's no blood. Amazing. Her body knows which blood vessels and capillaries to close off until the healing is complete. It won't even take a full day for the synthetic tissue to repair itself. It's a marvel of science that I can't comprehend.

Nor do I understand why human society would so willingly want to reject such remarkable technological sorcery. But, then again, I didn't fight two horrific wars over what it was to be human either.

We continue on, more carefully this time.

We check each office along the hallway, one by one, but most are empty and vacant. It's not until the fifth room that we finally encounter our enemy.

Four men are working around a long conference table. They're binding stacks of jumpvest into neat bundles, for ease of transport, no doubt. That means they haven't finished the hand-over to Patmos.

There's still time.

When they see us, I expect them to attack, to defend their vests at all costs, after all, what else could they do? But I'm still thinking like a country bumpkin from the 21st Century. Instead, the men lurch forward onto their piles, hugging them dearly, each man pressing a trigger on the shoulder of his own vest to vanish away to safety with his stash. I watch as they blink away, one after the other.

Careena yells. "Rhoda!"

Again, that girl's speed dazzles me. I hardly see her arm move as she reaches behind her back and her new sword goes flying across the room like a bullet, striking the slowest man squarely in his chest before he can hit his trigger. He stumbles backwards and collapses. His companions, unfortunately, have all escaped.

Careena runs to the fallen man and grabs him by the collar.

His heart has been pierced, he's bleeding out. She shakes him. "Where were you taking these? Where is Patmos!"

But he dies in her hands.

"Forkballs!"

I look down. There are eight or nine jumpvests scattered on the floor. His bundle. The most important vest, however, might be his own. "Can you check his vest to see where he was going?"

"No," she tells me. "The Tinker claimed he could break a vest's encryption, but the ministry has never been able to. Though, maybe we can do the next best thing."

She takes out her tube of lipstick, the one with the fancy tracing isotope. She draws a big smiley face on the vest and then presses the trigger up near the shoulder. The man vanishes before our eyes.

Careena stands up.

"Now we just need Beckett to tell us where he went."

At least all hope isn't lost.

"How long will that take?" I ask.

"It shouldn't take more than—"

She's interrupted as the walls rattle. There has been an explosion somewhere far off, not from within the building. It felt like a slight earthquake. A photo falls from the wall.

"What was that, old maid?" Rhoda asks.

"I really don't know," the other says as she looks around cautiously. "A meteor? Wouldn't surprise me with our luck."

Alarm sirens blare citywide.

Though muted, I hear them through the walls.

"This can't be good," Careena whispers.

A conference screen at the end of the room comes on, some sort of emergency broadcast. A calm newswoman is speaking. Eerily calm. I think she might be a computer generation.

She informs us, "Citizens of the Valeyard, an act of terrorism has compromised the dome. All residents are instructed to shelter indoors. Atmosphere will deplete in one hour, forty-eight minutes."

The broadcast is on repeat. Only the timer changes.

"It's the Red Man," I say in panic. "It has to be."

"Yes, but why attack the dome? What is he planning? Unless..." Without finishing her thought, Careena grabs one of the jumpvests left behind by the dead jumper. From her pocket she produces a pair of pliers and places them in a fold of the vest. From her other pocket she pulls out a ring, one of her supposed fake QDDs. She holds it down on the jumpvest's trigger.

"What are you doing?" I ask.

"I can't break the encryption, but I can wipe the memory clean. This little baby, Hellcate, can then program new jump coordinates." She's referring to this second ring. "She was a nice prototype. Can do all sorts of cool stuff. Too bad if you jump with her, she spreads your atoms across three galaxies. But one bloke's rubbish is another's treasure, I always say."

When she's finished, she places Hellcate back in her pocket and hits the trigger on the vest. Both the vest and her pliers vanish. I don't know to where or even why she'd jump a pair of pliers. All she'll tell me is that it's an insurance policy.

"What's going to happen to the Valeyard?" I ask next.

"Nothing good. The city is supposed to be ready for this sort of thing. The towers are designed to lock down with their own life support, food processors, all that stuff. But you know how burdensome regulations can be on corporations. I doubt even half the towers are up to code. And most are over capacity, regardless. It could take months to repair the dome and restore the atmosphere. Many of these towers won't last that long."

A pit forms in my stomach. "So everyone's going to die?"

"No, I don't think so," she says. "It's ironic, really. This planet will finally have to be evacuated. For good. Every world in the Ghent Mandate will pitch in since we're the closest. Tegana, Cawdor III and IV, New Mahshad, the New Thracian Republic, Ka Lai Prime. They'll send every ship they've got for the rescue. Our guilt over the neglect of these people will finally have to be answered for. We'll shelter them, and when it's over, we won't send them back."

"What are you saying, Careena? That the Red Man just did these people a favor?"

"Maybe you could see it that way. No more lotteries for citizenship. No more excuses. We always said it wasn't fair that the Outer Colonies should be burdened by the refugee crisis while the Core Worlds squabbled over the quotas they'd have to take. It was us, after all, the front lines, that sacrificed the most during the war. We should have been granted some reprieve afterwards. And that's true. But it's also true that our planets are large and bountiful. On Tegana we have entire continents used only as national parks. So if the Core Worlds want to be cowards, fork them. Maybe it's time we do what we should have done all along."

Sometimes your old foundations, your old identity, have to come down in order to build yourself back up again, as the better version of yourself. Could the same be true for society? Did the Valeyard have to be destroyed in order for her people to have a better life? And isn't that exactly what Patmos promised to do? Tear down the old world to create one better?

Was this his plan all along?

No. A man like that doesn't stop at just one colony. And saving the Valeyard didn't require three hundred jumpvests, regardless. Whatever he's planning is bigger. If Careena is right, that a lot of people are going to die before rescue can arrive, then all Patmos has shown us is that he's willing to sacrifice thousands in pursuit of his utopia. But what are those aims? Why this distraction?

"Careena," I ask. "How many ships will Tegana send here?"

The old woman pays little attention to my question. She's busy waving her hand over the jumpvests on the floor. She's destroying them. I see smoke and smell burnt plastic rising from their internal controls. But it's less than a dozen vests. I doubt this shortage will be enough to foil Patmos's plans. Without looking up, Careena answers, "Every ship she's got, deary. And then some."

I nod and let her get on with her work.

Looking over, I notice Rhoda has left the room. I can't hear anything over the alarm klaxons, but that doesn't mean the Kheltic girl didn't. I exit the conference room to find her. Careena is going to be a few more minutes and she hardly needs my help. Maybe Rhoda found something of interest.

She's not in the hallway, which means she must be around the next intersection. I walk down the hall, turn, and that's when I see her. It's also when I see *him*.

The Red Man comes out of an office at the end of the hall, unaware of our presence. Having seen him once before, he's a figure I could never forget, a titan among mortals, a mythic-like figure with the gaze of a lion and the air of a silverback gorilla in the prime of his life.

Like last time I saw him, he's wearing that long, black trench coat with the shoulders of red fur, all pomp and show. His orange-red beard, pulled into tight curls, may as well have been forged from steel. In his hand is a satchel, something important, no doubt.

Rhoda slides down the hall as silent as a shadow, short sword in hand. He still hasn't turned to see us. His head is cocked to the side. He must be talking to someone, someone who isn't there, like when I speak with Story.

I know I should do something, that I shouldn't just stand here. I should go back and get Careena. But I'm frozen. It's the sight of this red barbarian. This is the moment I feared, where I lock up, a help to no one.

Rhoda's almost upon the Red Man when another mercenary comes out of a doorway behind her. He's armed with a pistol and now that the city is already in turmoil, he's likely unafraid to use it. Rhoda's too focused on her target—she doesn't realize he's right behind her.

"Rhoda!"

I manage to get the words out, I only hope it was in time.

She spins around. With two slices, she takes off the mercenary's arm, followed by his head. She's back facing the Red Man before either body part hits the floor. But he's seen both of us now.

Rhoda shows no fear. "Red Man," she says. "It's over."

Their eyes lock in that moment, fierce gazes, either of which would have struck terror into the hearts of ordinary mortals. They certainly do me. But both Rhoda and the Red Man are anything but ordinary.

Indeed, the Red Man seems to welcome this challenge. For too long had he felt without equal in the universe. His quest for purpose and meaning could no longer be satiated by simple heists and thievery alone. He needs something more. I see it his eyes.

A god among peasants, the truth is he desires, as we all desire, to know his limits, to test his ambitions, to understand his role in the galactic puzzle of existence. It's the question that secretly burns deep in the hearts of all human souls—is this all that I am? Is there nothing more?

He tosses down his satchel and pulls free a sidearm.

I'm worried Rhoda won't be fast enough to reach him before he fires. But then I come to understand that he is bound by a code of honor that his compatriots lack. He is the product of an origin story I'll never know, one both epic and sorrowful. He casts the pistol to the floor and pulls out a long knife from his belt. This is to be a battle of equals—the way the cosmic filaments always intended this moment to be.

While the two gladiators face one another, I sneak ahead and grab the pistol from the dead mercenary's hand. I'm only slightly ashamed to admit that I'm not above firing at the bastard and ending this duel the old-fashioned way, but I'm worried I might hit Rhoda. All I can do at this moment is watch.

They charge.

The rules of the match are simple, kill or be killed. The blades move with such speed I can't even follow them. There's a lot of blocking and deflection.

I'm worried for Rhoda, she's so svelte and willowy compared to the monster she faces, yet in only two or three moves she's disarmed him. His long knife goes skidding down the hallway.

My relief, however, is short-lived.

Though he is not entirely synthetic as she is, his enhancements are still legion, and they are centuries more advanced than hers. He sidesteps one of her swings and slams her against the wall, pounding on her with fists that land like blocks of stone.

She loses her own blade; I see it fall and stick upright in the floor. Thankfully, she manages to break away and return her own swings. Though her arms are lithe, her punches are no less punishing than his. In quick moments each are covered in blood and violent bruises. It's an eerily silent confrontation, all I can hear are the bone-cracking blows. Neither screams nor grunts. Even their breathing is superbly measured.

Just as I think Rhoda might have the upper hand, the Red Man forces her back against the wall again. I watch in horror as he knocks her sideways for a moment, giving himself enough time to pull her sword free from the floor and skewer her through the chest with it, pinning her against the wall. He leaves her hanging there, a few inches above the ground, the blade plunged to its hilt, her body hanging like a decoration.

Her head has dropped.

She's unmoving.

I scream.

Whatever fear froze me before is gone. Not even the sight of the Red Man hovering only a few dozen feet away can paralyze me. I stand with the pistol in hand. He turns to look at me. Does he recognizes me from the *Stellar Pearl?*

I really don't give a damn.

I pull the trigger.

The blast should have torn him apart, should have blown his rip cage across the hallway. But he vanishes and all that happens is the back wall explodes into a smoldering hole.

He had a jumpvest, I realize in rage—one more sophisticated than the others. His can be triggered by thought, much like Careena does with her ring. He's escaped to safety.

I've failed.

I'm overtaken by such fury that I hurl the useless pistol into the poster of a smiling farmer.

I run to Rhoda's hanging body.

Careena comes around the corner, Old Bessie in hand. She must have heard me screaming.

"What's happened?"

I don't know what to say.

I'm crying.

I tell her.

"He's killed Rhoda."

Careena is about to say something. Whether it's meant to be comforting, I'll never know—because she trails off and ignores me completely once she sees the satchel the Red Man was forced to leave behind during the scuffle. She runs over to the abandoned bag, dumping the contents out onto the floor. First, I could hardly contain my tears.

Now I can hardly hold back my anger.

"Did you hear me? He killed her!"

She's on her knees, going through the mess she's created, and hardly looks up. "What? Oh, her? I'm sure she'll be fine."

I scream. "Careena, he staked her through the heart!"

She snaps back. "Then it's a bloody good thing she's not a vampire. Now do you mind?"

I want to punch the old lady's eyes out.

"Pull her down if you're so worried about her," she says while rooting around. She holds up what looks to me like a silver torpedo, about as long as a wine bottle. "I was right, you devil," she whispers to herself.

I ignore whatever she's doing.

I pull the sword out of Rhoda. It slides free easily. The Kheltic girl falls to the floor. I kneel beside her and cradle her head. There's very little blood, but her body is limp and lifeless. I didn't know her that long, but I still considered her my friend. We were both outcasts —she and I. And she saved our lives, more than once.

I hold her hand in my own and think of a prayer to say, a way to thank her. Yet before I can start, I feel tiny spasms in her palm, like beats, faint, nearly imperceptible, but rhythmic—one every minute or so. "I think her heart is still beating," I say in astonishment.

Careena doesn't seem surprised. "The injustice."

"But how can that be?"

I realize that without her heart, Rhoda's muscles are constricting in unison to continue pumping blood to her brain. The pores on her face have widened as well, possibly taking in oxygen. In re-engineering the human form, her people considered every contingency. Neither evolution nor God could compete with the intelligent designers on Kheltaris.

I should be grateful for this, and I am, I truly am.

Yet, I also now understand everything Careena has told me.

Why does Rhoda even have a heart? Why is her brain localized in her head? The truth is, these choices were made only because her generation felt some nostalgia for their ancestral form, nothing more. Her parents had grown up in Iran before immigrating to Kheltaris, I remember her telling me that the night we were singing karaoke. No one among their generation would have wanted a child completely alien to them. But a *little* alien? A *little* better? That was fine. And so it would go for each successive generation, until one day the Khelts would be something else, something other than human, without ever realizing it. A death by a thousand subtle changes.

I wipe away strands of Rhoda's dark hair, happy that she's still on our side of that great coming divide.

She opens her eyes.

"Isabel," she whispers.

"I thought we lost you."

"I couldn't stop him."

Surprisingly, it's Careena that responds. "You did just fine, hotcakes." She holds up the silver torpedo. "You got us this. Without this, that bastard's plan is deader than the hedgehogs."

I'm still angry at her earlier callousness.

"Yeah, well, it looks like a dildo."

"Hardly, Freckles. This here is a—"

It vanishes from her hand, blinking out of existence.

The old woman screeches.

"Is there no pity sitting in the clouds!"

"Where'd it go?"

She's too busy cursing. "Dammit, dammit, dammit. The jump mechanism was remote controlled. He's just sent it off."

"It's a weapon?"

She nods. "Of a sort. It's the Tinker's handiwork. Ingenious really. It's how he's stayed ahead of us all these years. He calls it a time-shot. He sends it back four hundred years, just before the blackout dates. There it buries itself into the planetary crust, deep enough to avoid detection or being disturbed by future construction. Then it waits, hundreds of years, until a timer goes off and it sends a quick message. He can communicate with his earlier self this way, sending himself warnings, stock prices, anything he wants. He used it sparingly because he knew it might draw the attention of the ministry. And it did. I was sent to investigate. But when I saw what he had built..."

I understand immediately.

"You realized you could use it to save Samus."

There's a pause before she answers. "Aye. My moment of weakness, I suppose. I tried sending her a message to avoid going in to work that day. But we were having a fight and she never read it. Not in time, anyway. Obviously, I made sure the message couldn't be traced back to me, and since I was the agent assigned to the Valeyard, I thought I could cover up all the evidence. No one had to know. But Soolin's investigation was more thorough than I expected. This new sort of technology, capable of influencing events within the blackout dates, was particularly troubling to the ministry. I should have realized that, but I was too blinded by the possibilities to think critically. I was taken off the case once my relationship with the intended target was discovered. I never had the opportunity to try again."

"I'm so sorry, Careena."

"Well, it doesn't matter now. What matters is Patmos. And I think I know what he's planning."

"A message to himself?"

"No, that time-shot was different. It wasn't equipped with a transmitter. It has an explosive charge on its head powerful enough to knock out a planetary field generator. Those generators are buried miles down under the earth precisely so they can't be easily taken out. If you tried to access one, you'd trip a hundred alarms."

I see where this is going. "Unless your bomb was already there. Before those alarms were ever installed. Then it just sits there for hundreds of years, waiting for the right time to go off. No one will have thought to look for a bomb that's even older than the colony itself. But how does this help us? We don't which planet he's going after." My first concern is Earth. After all, if you wanted to create a new human civilization from the ashes of the old, that seems the most likely target.

But Careena confirms my other suspicion.

"Don't we?" she asks.

She's right. I do know. And it's not Earth. It's no coincidence that the Valeyard is in Tegana's backyard. He's orchestrated this act of terrorism not to save the residents of this world, but to draw Tegana's forces away from theirs, to leave the planet vulnerable and open to attack. With no wars, no enemies to speak of, the Tegans won't hesitate to send every available ship they have, along with a relief force of thousands of soldiers. The planet will be left virtually undefended when Patmos arrives with the Red Man and a small army of jumpers.

Obviously they could never hope to take the entire planet, or even a single city. But that's not what they're after. They're going for the Chronos Imperium, the throne of the temporal gods. Without it, Tegana would just be another colony world, no more or less remarkable than a hundred others.

But with it, Patmos can ground himself, can free himself from the consequences of his actions. He isn't a fool; he doesn't want to create a paradox, one that could inadvertently rip apart space-time. No, he's planned all this precisely to avoid doing such a thing. When he alters history, he wants it to be absolute, unconditional. Final.

"We have to warn Tegana," I say.

Our one saving grace is that he can't blow the planetary shield yet. The news of the disaster on the Valeyard is only now reaching Tegana. It will take, what, a day, maybe two, for the planet to organize its relief efforts and send her ships?

Patmos will have to wait until they've cleared the solar system to make his move, otherwise his jumpers will be forced to confront the Tegan Defense Force. So we have a small window of time. We can devise a plan to protect the Chronos Imperium. Patmos is going to find himself facing a full battalion of Tegan marines, the bastard.

I don't want to sound too optimistic, but by anticipating his scheme, we may have out maneuvered our enemy.

Then Story Beckett appears out of nowhere.

And everything falls apart.

Before Careena can berate the girl for missing-in-action, Story raises a hand to stop her, saying only, "Smith, they're here."

Careena must realize who she's referring to. Without a word, the old woman dives into me, knocking the air from my chest as we both fall on top of Rhoda. But she's not fast enough. Four of Soolin's newly appointed time agents appear all around us. They've been tasked with apprehending the fugitive Careena J. Smith, and I suppose by extension me, her accomplice.

Knowing their target would attempt to jump away the moment she's found, they've already rehearsed this raid a dozen times. They've appeared with weapons drawn, firing their stun blasts the moment they have visual confirmation on us. Their captain is Prior Grimalkin, now promoted to commander, and it's clear from the unpleasant scowl on his face that he's still upset by the stunt we pulled on Tegana—it's also clear that he is intent on atoning for this failure.

Story's warning gave Careena just enough time to initiate our jump, but not enough to complete it before we're hit by a distortion wave meant to neutralize Hecate and prevent our escape. We're stuck in the in-between as something goes terribly wrong and we blink out of existence. It feels as if my particles have been scattered across the firmament into oblivion.

There's only blackness and I am sure I'm dead.

After some moments, the blackness turns to white.

I'm on my back, exposed. There's a bright and punishing sun above me, presiding over a cloudless sky. I can taste the dry heat in the air. I'm too weak to turn my head, but from the corners of my eye I see miles of dried dirt and cracked soil to my left. To my right is the same. It goes on forever. I'm in a desert, a world burned into a lifeless shell.

I have to close my eyes to block out the sun. Already my skin is sizzling. Soon I'll become just another barren and scorched husk on this barren and scorched world. After some time, a shadow falls over me—shielding me from the sun. I pray it's Careena, come to shelter me from the brutal heat, but when I open my eyes, there's a silhouette in the bright light. And it's not an old woman.

It's some foul demon, a squat monster with hoofed feet and a chin beard of harsh bristles. The beard of a trickster. The creature smiles, revealing rows of crooked teeth crammed together in a small and pathetic mouth. It leans in, no doubt to tear out my throat.

I'm too weak to fight. What does it even matter now, anyway? The Red Man has escaped. Patmos has won. When she finds me, Soolin can throw my half-eaten carcass off the Brooklyn rooftops if she wants. I surrender.

I accept my fate.

Curiously, I find relief in this act, in letting go my obligations to this world, my responsibilities. So many of them, I realize, were foolishly self-imposed, manifesting themselves as anxieties and bad habits. My ego had convinced me I was special, but I'm just an ordinary girl. It was unfair of the universe to ask me to be anything more than that. I let go my ego. And in doing so, I let go my burdens.

I let it all go.

I'm ready.

End me, foul beast.

I do wonder in these final moments, however—why exactly this vicious monster smells like juiced celery.

24

The demon-creature licks my cheek with a long, slimy tongue. Disgusting. So, he's not actually a servant hound summoned from the lowest gates of hell—but in my defense, I'm surely not the first person in history to conflate goats with demons. Seriously. Look at this guy. The tacked-on ears. The ridiculous jaw that can't decide if it wants to hang to the left or to the right. And those eyes; those creepy, unnatural eyes. How anyone can relate to creatures with horizontal pupils and the musty odor of my grandmother's couch is honestly beyond me.

Goats are the worst.

He's hovering over me like a total creepster. I gather why—he wants to know if I'm dead or alive. Not out of any sense of compassion, mind you. It's just that in his mind, if this is the sort of grazing pasture prone to dead girls from New Jersey inexplicably falling from the sky, it's probably a pasture best avoided in the future. When he starts chewing on my bra strap, however, I decide it's time to put my foot down.

"Scram, you vile monster," I bark.

He nods and wanders off. Apparently I've been given a clean bill of health. As he walks, he occasionally flings his floppy ears back and forth to ward off gnats. A tiny bronze bell around his neck rattles each time he does this.

Looking over, I see that he's part of an entire flock, a motley crew of stubby-legged goats of various colors, all a little disheveled from life in the desert, all a little bored.

The discovery of a teen girl has no doubt been a particularly exciting highlight to what were ordinarily very drab wanderings for this gang of freakish-eyed hoofsters.

I sit up and dust myself off. I cough in surprise when I realize one of the goats is not a goat at all, but is a little boy. A goat herder! I don't think I've ever actually seen one before—granted it's not exactly the most common profession in the wonderful state of New Jersey. This little boy certainly looks the part, though. He's dressed in the simplest tunic and twin belt, armed only with a walking stick. He has deep, charming eyes, chestnut colored skin, and perfect dark hair.

He's staring at me with an oddly blank expression.

"Are you in charge here, little boy?" I ask him.

I get nothing in return but that stare of childhood fascination. After a moment he runs over to me, touches my curly locks of black hair, and then hops back among his crowd of goats for protection. Likely he saw me materialize from nowhere. Whether I'm demon or angel, he's apparently not yet sorted. But at least now he knows I'm not a hallucination.

"I use avocado oil," I tell him about my hair while getting up. "But that's our secret, all right?"

I smile.

Nothing.

The boy whispers gently to himself, "*Ishtar, summa awil-um lu immer-am.*"

I look around. For all my detective skills lately, I can't venture a guess as to where I am. One sun. A big desert, a lot of craggy rocks. Mars maybe? The heat makes me think it may be Venus.

Do people live on Venus in the future?

And if so, why did they bring so many goats?

"What planet is this?" I ask the boy.

Nothing but his wide-eyed stare.

"*Summa awil-um lu*," he whispers to himself again.

"I'm sorry, kid. I seem to have lost my magic translation ring."

Someone calls from just over the next rise.

"No, you haven't, deary."

"Careena?" I call back in relief. "Is that you?"

She and Rhoda both come over the rise. They're covered in even more dust than me. Rhoda looks weak and tired, but she's standing on her own. She's zipped her jacket to hide the large gash wound underneath.

"Careena," I ask. "Where are we?"

The old woman looks around. From atop her rise, she has a much better view than I do. "A desert of some sort, by the look of it."

"Really?" I say with a bit of teenage derision.

She studies the landscape harder. "Well, perhaps more of a river delta. I can I see the river just there."

"But you don't know which river?"

She puts her hands on her hips as if insulted. "Of course I know which river. What sort of time traveler do you take me for? It's the lower Euphrates." She hesitates. "Or is it the Tigris?"

I'm surprised. "This is Earth?"

"Aye."

"And the year?" I ask.

"2233."

Rhoda scans the landscape now as well. "The Euphrates. So then we are in Iraq? My grandmother was Iraqi. She'd have born around this time. Tell me, old maid, are we far from the city of Basra?"

Careena is noticeably vague. "Yes and no."

"What does that mean?" I ask. "And I thought Earth was rich in the future. Why can't that little kid afford pants?"

He's whispering to himself again. I can only make out the words *Inanna* and *Enlil*. Maybe those are the names of his goats?

"Well, you see—" Careena begins.

Rhoda turns to the little boy and poses a question in Arabic. She gets the same blank stare I got. She tries again in Farsi.

Nothing.

"Are you sure this is Iraq, old maid?"

Careena throws up her hands.

"Look, I never said this was bloody Iraq."

Rhoda and I are both confused. "But you said—"

"I said it was 2233."

"Yeah?"

"And it is. It's 2233 *BCE*," she says.

"Oy."

She clarifies. "Iraq won't be founded for a few thousand more years. This is the Kingdom of Sumer."

It takes a while for that to sink in.

"Why the hell did you bring us here?"

"It wasn't by choice, Freckles. I tried to get us back on the *Ark Royal*, but those wankers got a blast off just as we jumped. We're lucky to even be alive. Hecate got all kinds of scrambled."

Rhoda observes, "Yet, from nothing more than a desert and a goat, you know precisely where and when we are."

"Aye, we didn't end up here completely at random," she tells us. "This was my last assignment, the one I was dragging my feet on while trying to avoid Soolin's firing squad. Hecate must have defaulted to here in all the confusion. And good thing she did. The alternative was to scatter us across all of oblivion."

"Great. So send us back."

She gives me a long, serious look.

"I'm afraid I can't, deary."

"Why not?"

"That blast, it fried the RGMs that power Hecate. She's deader than a hedgehog. It's the reason you can't understand that little boy. My earrings can work as a backup translator, but they're fried too."

"But wait," I argue. "I can understand you just fine. And Rhoda speaks Persian. Without Hecate, I shouldn't understand either of you."

"Yes, well about that," Careena sort of mumbles. "You see, I may have scrambled your all's brains a bit when I brought you two to the Valeyard. So, um, congratulations. You're both speakers of 31st Century English, with sophisticated Tegan accents no less."

"Who gave you permission to do that! Also, why would you do that?"

Careena is losing her patience. "So we wouldn't have another incident like the one on the *Stellar Pearl*. You remember how well that turned out, don't you?"

I realize she still believes we were outed aboard the *Stellar Pearl* because of my Jersey accent.

"How do we fix the ring, old maid?" Rhoda asks.

"We don't. The ring is fine. But the RGMs are burned out. And there are none on Earth, never have been. So unless you can mine dark matter density clusters inside nova remnants to get us a femtogram of the rarest mineral in existence, I'd say we should start teaching ourselves Sumerian and take some goat herding lessons from that tot. The good news is, it will be hard for Soolin to find us here, since not a lot of the historical record from this century survives into the future. And the ale ain't bad either. I know some nice brewers in Uruk."

I shake my head. "That's not good enough, Careena. I'm not spending the rest of my life here with these creepy, fricken goats. You understand me? No goats."

Careena's look is solemn. "You're asking me to work a miracle, luv. I'm not giving up on you, I'm really not, but we're out of options."

I poke a finger at her chest.

"No, you're getting us out of here."

"We can't, not without RGMs."

"Fine," I tell her. "If that's all you need, then I'll get them for you."

This confuses her.

"And just how on Old Earth are you going to do that?"

I smile. "Easy. I'm going to finish your assignment."

She looks at me curiously.

I explain. "I assume you were sent here because of a jumper, right? And a jumper needs a vest to jump, right? And a vest is powered by these stupid RGMs, right?"

I watch as the light bulb goes off in her head.

"You may be onto something."

"Of course, I am." I say proudly. "So. I'm going to find this dirt-bag jumper of yours, I'm going to kick the crap out of him, and then we're going to use his vest to get the hell out of here. Because, I'm serious, Careena. I've been exploded, I've been shot at, infected by alien vines, held hostage, and forced to eat *literal* shit pancakes for breakfast. But I'm drawing the line at goats. You got that? No goddamn goats."

Rhoda nods in agreement. "I also do not like ungulates."

"See," I say. "So, what was your assignment?"

"It was a tough one," the old woman admits. "In this era there's little in the historical records to go on. As I recall, Blue flagged Red over some changes in a Cuneiform tablet piece that ended up in a national museum in Baghdad. I suspected an archaeologist type, they're common offenders in this period. Unfortunately, I was too busy drowning my sorrows to ever go have a proper look for him."

"Well, it looks like the universe is giving you a second chance."

"Great. Just what I wanted. More work."

"Careena!"

"Fine. Fine."

The old woman turns to the little goat herder, who isn't much taller than his goats. "Hey, goat boy, which way to Isin?"

"Isin?" the boy repeats.

It's a word he appears to know.

"Yes, Isin."

He points toward the river to the south.

"Good, lad. Here, have a ginger sweet."

She tosses him an unwrapped candy from her pocket.

He sticks it in his mouth and smiles with amazement.

I make a face.

"How long has that been in your pocket?"

"Does he look like he cares? Now come, if you're not going to let me drink the rest of my life away on Sumerian ale, we should go have a crack at saving the world."

30

We make our way down to the river. Along the way we pick up a shadow. Or thirty shadows, to be more accurate. The boy and his army of bearded goats follow behind. I have a feeling he's trying to be stealthy, still perhaps believing us mystical beings and therefore not wanting to draw our ire. But with all the bleating and tiny bells, it's hard to miss him only a dozen yards behind us.

As we hike along the riverbanks of the Euphrates, it dawns on me where we are, where we truly are—the heart of ancient Mesopotamia, the southern tip of the Fertile Crescent of antiquity. The lands to either side of the river are moist, fertile, covered in grass, and stretch for as far as the eye can see. They are wedged between other rivers, other tributaries, snaking through what must be a delta pouring out into the Persian Gulf. It is from these bountiful waterways that some of the earliest civilizations ever known have arisen. This isn't Mars or Venus as I had first suspected. This is the Garden of Eden.

We follow a well-trodden trail and eventually pass a small village on the river banks. This is as far as the little boy can follow, for the village, it turns out, is his own, the name of which I'll sadly never know. The homes are all mud structures fortified with stone. The hamlet appears neither rich nor poor. It simply is.

We take the briefest break here. The sun is punishing and the rest welcomed. We're offered tea and fresh bread. Before departing, Careena trades with one of the local women. She's perhaps a cousin to the boy, or an older sister. I dare not imagine that she may be his mother; she can't be much older than me or Rhoda. Careena is showing her a crayon, drawing figures on a stone, much to everyone's joy. The trade comes easily after that.

"Put these on," she tells us. She's procured three shawls, long enough to wrap one's entire body. All are red, though mine is the most rich and beautiful.

"These will help hide our outfits. It's strange enough for the locals to see three ladies in trousers," Careena explains. "But if our time bandit recognizes us, he'll be gone in a heartbeat."

I do as she suggests.

"Old maid," Rhoda asks. "You carry crayons in your pocket?"

I chime in, "You should see all the junk she has in those pockets."

"Silence, you tarts. That was my last Razzle Dazzle Rose. I loved that color."

As we leave the village, our business here finished, the little boy runs up to me one final time. He hands me a bone token, with carvings on either side. I think he may have etched them himself. Before I can react, or even give a thanks, he runs back to the safety of his flock, watching us go with those large, dark eyes.

"Looks like someone's got a crush," Careena says.

I smile.

The gesture was sweet.

We pass a few more settlements as we follow the river. Each is tied in some way to the fertile offerings of the Euphrates, like babes attached to teats. Though rustic, they are not at all as harsh or filthy as I would have imagined the Bronze Age to be. Flower patches are lovingly placed alongside homes. Stone streets are well maintained. Children play while parents perform chores.

And though those chores are manual, they could be completed with a certain sort of leisure. For here in this world there were no deadlines from head office, no quotas to accomplish, no calls from corporate department heads, no boards of directors requesting piles of progress reports. The only nagging executives here were the simple necessities of life.

An hour or two later and I see Isin on the horizon. It is a sight no less awe-inspiring than the futuristic towers of the Valeyard or the ivory tranquility of New Harmony. I wasn't sure how a Sumerian city would be, but now that I've seen this one, I can imagine in my mind's eye nothing else.

Defensive walls rise like cliffs against the river, a river filled with boats, human activity, and the flurry of commerce. A canal, which Careena tells me is named the Isinnitum, forms a moat, before shooting off straight as an arrow into the countryside, feeding an extensive network of irrigation channels, the fruits of which have allowed for the rise of civilization.

Much of Isin itself is sandstone and hard edges; square towers rise over rectangular gates. But there is color here too, the green of hanging vines and treetops, the reds and yellows of tapestries and banners blowing triumphantly in the winds.

The jewel on the crown of this mighty metropolis is visible even from outside the city; it is the central temple, a sort of massive ziggurat, a leveled pyramid the ambition of which is so staggering that it causes the hairs on my neck to rise. Entire levels of the ziggurat are manicured with orchards, like gardens in the sky. On the highest level, placed at the very footsteps of the gods, is a small temple of marble.

"Welcome to Isin, ladies," Careena says.

We line up with what must be hundreds of others waiting to pass under the main gate. They are travelers and merchants, farmers and peasants, pilgrims and seekers; some arriving by foot and others by boat; some coming with goods on carts to sell, others carrying with them offerings for Nininsina Bau, Goddess of Healing, patron deity and divine protector of the city.

Once inside the great walls, the urban chaos is no less mesmerizing. Everywhere I look there are carts and stalls selling fruits and vegetables. Small animals and lizards are fried openly on sticks. Incense and prayer are being offered on nearly every corner. Sculptors in temple gardens are hard at work carving the busts of great protective beasts, creatures with the heads of bearded men, the wings of eagles, and the bodies of lions.

Rhoda is the first to ask.

"What exactly are we looking for, old maid?"

"Anything that might give away our jumper. If he's an academic, as I suspect, he'll be better than most at fitting in. But you'd be surprised what can give away a person from the 31st Century. Posture. Gait. A Rolling Stones tee-shirt. I generally look at people's teeth."

I shake my head.

"Really? Dental hygiene? That's the best you got for us?"

"I admit, we haven't got much to go on," she says. "The tablet that got flagged was a treasury ledger. Very little of it survived, so there were no names, unfortunately. But Forensics believed it likely belonged to a money changer. All the cities around here mint their own coins, so exchanging them is a common business. I suggest we start our search in the main markets."

Our first day passes with little luck. Once night comes, we rent a room of straw mats from an old woman kind enough to prepare us a dinner of warm soup. We don't stand out nearly as much as I feared we would. It's a large, cosmopolitan city, attracting arrivals from all over the Middle East, so the fact that we cannot speak Sumerian, or dress a little odd, is of little suspicion to our host.

We continue our second day moving from market to market. It's amazing all the things that I see. Hideous turtles the size of bicycle wheels. Live goats and birds tied to posts. Farming implements. Hand-crafted cookware. And a disproportionate selection of religious and magical paraphernalia. The crazy preacher on the street corner is not a modern invention. Not by a long shot.

The temples here do, however, fascinate me. Besides the patron goddess Nininsina, there are several temples to lesser gods as well, each offering their own divine favors. Careena informs me that each of these temples has been placed at very specific points within the walls. Were one able to view the city from above, they'd see that the temples map out a constellation, one the Sumerians call the *Steer of Heaven*. And which I know in my time as Taurus the Bull.

I also learn from Careena a little about the politically divisive era that we've entered. The Sumerian city-states, long proud and autonomous, have only recently fallen under the control of the powerful Akkadian dynasties to the north. The two powers, now interwoven, will constitute the largest and most powerful empire humanity has ever known to this point.

Unfortunately, their destiny will end like all great empires. They'll reach too far across too many lands, claim too much of the shared Earth as their own; in the end their decline will be violent, unheroic, and final.

By the third day, we start losing hope. Though I don't fully understand all the mechanics, I know that we're invariably tied to the present even now, that time passing here means time is passing for us there too. Tegana will have dispatched her fleet to the Valeyard by now. Whatever Patmos has planned, he can't be far away from achieving it. And there's no way to warn anyone.

"Old maid," Rhoda asks during a lunch break. "Is it wise to focus so heavily on the markets?"

Careena shrugs. "I'm open to anything at this point. While you two were sleeping last night, I left half a dozen messages for Beckett on clay tablets, warning her about the attack. I buried some, I sold some, I even gave some to those religious freaks as offerings. They really took a fancy to the Latin letters. But the chances that anything I write will survive five thousand years into the future is just about impossible. This city might look impressive now, but by your all's time, it's going to be nothing but a field of rock and sand. Even the river will be gone."

I think for a moment.

"What about the temples?"

They both look at me.

"What about them?" Careena asks. "You think our blockhead is the religious type?"

"No, but don't you guys have the Bible in the future?"

Again, I get only blank stares.

I explain.

"In the Christian Bible, there's that story about the temples. Jesus says they've become dens of thieves and he runs out the money changers with, like, a whip or something. And it occurs to me that we're looking for a money changer, right? And then I look around and there's, like, thousands of pilgrims arriving here every day from every corner of the world, but the gods only take payment in local dollars."

"So?"

"So, somebody's got to be changing all that money for them, right?"

Careena touches the side of her nose.

"All right, can't hurt to look."

The first temple we visit is to that of the goddess Ninlil. A great many old women fill the grounds and gardens here, some with flowers, some with tears. It's my impression they must be praying for sons lost to war, but the truth is I'll never know the complexities of these ancient sects. And that saddens me.

What I do know is that the stories and creation myths being told here today will be passed down to children. And those children will pass them down to their children and their children's children. The stories will change over the centuries, some will vanish entirely, swallowed by the currents of time. But some will endure.

True, they'll evolve. Names will be adapted to accommodate linguistic and cultural trends. Details will be altered as the beliefs of the conquered come into contact with the beliefs of the conquerors, each influencing the other. But the core of these fables will remain largely the same, for perhaps, in some small way, they contain truths universal to the human condition. Perhaps these allegories have helped humankind, generation after generation, better understand their place in a chaotic and indifferent cosmos.

Here in Isin those stories are being passed down orally. Yet I know one day, many centuries from now, they'll be penned to paper. From then onward they'll be frozen in time, taken to be infallible, unalterable; the final say of the last god standing among the many contenders of the ancient pantheon.

I wonder if something might not be lost when that happens, when the fluid river of spiritual exploration is turned to stone and paved over with the static asphalt of dogma.

I push all those thoughts aside for the time being. As I predicted, there's no shortage of money changers just outside the temple of Ninlil, lining the walkway to the first atrium, no doubt preying on those who have come only to seek answers, to seek hope.

The changers are shouting out prices and rates to the many pilgrims who have arrived today. Some shout in Sumerian. Others are yelling in Akkadian. To me, who speaks neither, it's all just noise, really. Occasionally, out of habit, I blurt out a *sorry* or *excuse me* as I try to make my way through the crowds, though to little effect.

As I near the end of the row of stalls, a money changer in rather fine clothing calls out to me from behind his table.

He offers a polite smile before saying, "Sister in the red shawl, such beauty. Like a rich jewel teaching the torches themselves to burn bright. Have you come to make a tithe and receive a blessing today?"

I turn.

I stare.

At first, I think it's just my imagination. But then I ask, "What did you just say to me?"

This man is distinguished, perhaps in his late fifties, with salt and pepper hair, a goatee, and the wise eyes of a professor. "I meant no disrespect," he says. "The compliments are a habit. But you'll need local coinage to tithe. I can offer you excellent rates as an apology for my forwardness. Tell me, are you one of our northern sisters? From Urusalim perhaps?"

"No," I say flatly. "Actually, I'm from New Jersey."

His smile drops immediately.

Probably due to the fact that I'm already jumping across his table and grabbing him by the collar.

Because like I told Careena.

No goddamn goats.

31

Were I able to grapple the man, I could have brought him down. Unfortunately, all I have is the collar of his robe and like a ballerina, he spins himself free of the garment, leaving me holding a useless stretch of cloth. Rather rudely, he then pushes me to the ground and I end up on my ass—but not before he takes a swipe at the bowl of coins on his table, sending them raining down on my head.

A mob of pilgrims descends after the coins, leaving me helplessly pinned under the arms of old women and their long shawls. Remarkably, they aren't trying to pocket the coins, only rescue them for the money changer. Who—unfortunately at this point—is already dashing away.

A familiar hand reaches through the jungle of old lady arms and pulls me free. It's Rhoda. Careena is standing next to her.

"What the hell was that bloke's problem?" she asks.

I'm still trying to catch my breath. "He said I was pretty."

"Well, Jesus Christ, Freckles, you didn't have to cause a scene about it. This place isn't exactly a feminist utopia, you know."

"He said it in English!" I shout.

I'm met with a blank stare.

"He's using a translator!"

I see the click in her brain. "Ah, right!" She pulls Old Bessie from her pocket and fires into the sky. Instead of the normal toy gun pop sound, this time there's a crack of thunder. The pilgrims fall back in fear and awe, giving us a line-of-sight straight to the fleeing money changer, who is jumping the wall of the temple.

Careena looks to me and Rhoda.

"Well, what are you waiting for? After him!"

We pursue him out onto the streets. He causes havoc at every turn, overturning fruit carts and spilling burning pots of religious oils to the ground. Our major disadvantage is that he knows the city better than we do. He charges down alleys that lead into busy markets. He cuts across gardens. But he is our only chance home. So despite the dust in my eyes, the city sounds assaulting my senses, and the strain on my legs, I don't give up the chase.

But I lose him at a busy intersection.

"Dammit!" I curse.

Careena comes up beside me. She leans over, putting her hands on her thighs. She's out of breath and panting. How she's supposed to be some sort of elite time cop is really beyond me.

"I saw you back there, Freckles," she says between huffs. "You went straight for the jugular, no hesitation. Gave me goosebumps. I'm proud of you."

"Yeah? Well, it doesn't matter now. We've lost him."

"Nah," she says after a pant. "I saw him go in there. I just needed to catch my breath. Come on."

She points to a simple squarish building of sandstone, typical of the city though well-kept. There are intricate designs carved around the doorway. The door itself is thick and solid.

I try it. "Locked."

"Rhoda," Careena orders.

"I'm not a dog, old maid."

"Just kick in the damn door, will you, girl?"

Rhoda breaks down the door with ease and Careena storms in, Old Bessie drawn. The building appears to be a private residence, sparsely but beautifully decorated around a large open interior. There is the memorabilia of a long and well-lived life hanging on the walls and sitting in the alcoves. Colorful blankets accentuate simple furniture. A few antiques sit on end tables.

The money changer is on his knees at the far side of the room, lifting a small hidden floorboard.

"Freeze, ya'muppet," Careena yells.

From inside the hidden compartment, the man grabs a futuristic pistol and spins around to fire at us. Careena is the quicker of the two. Her blast blows him backwards against the wall.

Rhoda and I run to him.

It's clear he's dead.

"You didn't have to kill him," I protest. "You could have just stunned him."

Careena, for once, looks remorseful. "Believe me, Freckles. It's better this way."

I can't accept that. "You don't get to decide that."

"It's what he wanted."

"How do you know that?"

She points to his pistol. "See that red meter? No charges left."

I'm stunned. It wouldn't be until much later that I'd come to reflect on the encounter and understand the man's reasoning. It wasn't only that his crimes were unforgivable in the eyes of the Ministry of Temporal Affairs, that he'd find no leniency or mercy there. It's that he himself understood what he had done. He'd betrayed humanity. He'd violated his sacred covenant to time itself. And in a moment, I would learn just how deeply those transgressions went.

In the man's hidden compartment, Careena finds his jump-vest, covered in dust. She lays it out on a table.

Rhoda looks around the abode. "Old maid, what was this man after? Why would a thief take time to decorate a home? He must have lived here many months to have collected so many things." She lifts a tribal mask before putting it back down.

"More like years," Careena tells us. "Judging from the model of his vest, I'd say he's been here at least thirty."

"Thirty years? But why?" Rhoda asks.

"Not by choice, luv. You see this circuit here, the Barclay node? Fried to hell. Probably happened on the initial jump. Black market vests were notoriously unreliable in the old days. Without the tools to fix it, assuming he'd even know how, this ended up being a one-way jump for the old chap."

"But can you fix it?" Rhoda asks.

"Don't need to. We just need the RGMs used to power it. It will take a few minutes. I have to jury-rig a few things to get Hecate going. Lucky for us, these old vests were quite inefficient. There's enough material here to power three modern vests. I'll store the left-over in Hellcate. It's not safe to leave that sort of stuff just lying around."

I take a seat on one of the couches. There's a hint of modernity to the layout of the room. Meticulous care was taken to convey the character and soul of the man that lived here. I find myself curious about him.

Why had he come to ancient Sumer? What drew him to this time and place? Had he only wanted to taste a little of the sounds and smells of the Bronze Age, to peak into the roots of his own civilization? Perhaps he wanted to steal an artifact or two for his study back in the 31st Century. He certainly struck me as a collector. A professor of antiquities, perhaps. A historian.

Was his original plan only to stay here a week? Maybe two? What happened when he realized he was shipwrecked? Surely he spent the first few months of his exile in denial. Surely in those first few years some piece of him secretly prayed for a miracle as he tinkered endlessly with the vest until his fingertips bled, aware that he lacked the knowledge to save himself, but trying, in spite of the odds, nonetheless. At some point, he must have come to accept his fate here.

This home is a testament to that.

Ironically, his knowledge of science could have made him a god in this world, yet he always knew—step too far off the path of obscurity, dazzle the natives a little too much, and truer gods, the gods of time, the Tegan agents sworn to protect eternity, would arrive. And unlike the Sumerian deities worshiped in the temples of Isin, these gods could not be swayed with offerings of fruit, flowers, or coin.

Nothing that I see in this man's life suggests that he was evil. Sumer was not the type of land one would descend upon in an attempt to thwart history or grow rich. It was instead a world that a young professor, too long trapped behind mountains of books, seduced only by the love and respect of an era long since gone from memory, might strive to see just once in life, to taste and touch just once. It was a crime as innocent as it was selfish.

But it was a crime.

And it did not end there.

The young Sumerian girl enters the home with a reed basket in her arms stuffed with vegetables. She is so taken by her daily routine that at first she doesn't even notice the three of us. When she does, she only stares with eyes dark and beautiful. Then she sees the historian, lifeless and limp on the floor.

Her basket falls. Vegetables roll across the floor. She runs to the historian and falls to her knees with such an outpouring of grief that I will come to be haunted for many years by the wailing of this young widow. By the genuine pain of genuine love lost.

"*Nam nij si iri lah! Nam nij si iri lah!*" She is screaming to the heavens, but whether she is making pleas to the gods or curses against the three of us, I do not know.

Careena is working at the table and can't look away, lest she lose focus and blow half the Persian Gulf off the map. "Someone get her out of here!" she snaps.

The young widow continues to wail in anguish.

Rhoda, though sensitive as I am to the young woman's plight, strikes her on the back of the head. The Sumerian girl slumps to floor. Rhoda picks her up and carries her into the bedroom, placing her down gently.

Quiet returns to the house.

I stare at the widow for a long time. I could berate the historian for taking such a young wife, a girl of perhaps not even twenty, and yet, as a 31st Century man, born of an egalitarian society, who took the equality of the genders as granted, had he not afforded her more respect than her own culture would bestow upon any woman for thousands of years to come?

Resigned to his fate, to the fact that he would never again see his own family, did he not wish to seek an equal to share with his life? And perhaps in finding no equal, he had instead found an idealistic young woman and, with respect, taught her the value of her own thoughts, so that she might become the liberated soul he so longed for in a partner.

Careena would consider this to be his greatest sin of all. In the long and calamitous river of history, ideas could spread further, could wreak more havoc than any single act ever could.

What ideas, hopes, and forbidden dreams had the historian gifted to this young woman? And would she in turn pass them down to her children? And they down to their children's children? These were the painful questions Careena's profession demanded be asked.

I do not envy the old woman.

Nor do I envy the widow, not now. What awaits this poor girl when she wakes and is forced to confront alone the bitter reality that she had been shown a better future, had seen possibilities unthinkable in her own time, had felt the warmth of being valued as an equal, only to have it all ripped away, with nothing left to look forward to now but the harsh patriarchal dogmas of the Bronze Age. Could she still find happiness in that world?

I hope that she can.

"I'm finished," Careena says flatly. "It's time for us to go."

Never once before we jump does the aging time traveler look over to the young woman on the bed.

I have a feeling that she can't bring herself to do so.

FINAL INTERLUDE

Here, a little girl with ribbons in her hair.

"Look! I picked these flowers for you, Alloy."

"Thank you, Miss Tatev. I'll put them in my hair, just like you."

"You don't have hair, silly! You're a robot."

"Oh, yes, the misses is correct. I must have forgotten."

"I don't believe that! My friend Nina says you look like a rusted upside down rubbish bin with arms. But father says you never forget anything."

"I suppose I don't, Miss Tatev. In fact, I even remember when your father was your age. I was a little less rusted back then. Storage will do that to a robot. Fortunately they took me back out when you were born."

"Yes! So you could be my old pear."

"I believe the term is *au pair*, Miss Tatev."

"Nina says you're just a clunky old farm bot."

"I don't think I like this Nina very much, Miss Tatev."

"Neither do I. She's the worst!"

Here, a chuckle between two friends, a little girl and her bot.

"Is it true they made you on Old Earth?"

"What does the plate on the back of my head say?"

"It says—proudly made in the United States of Amer... Ameri-ik..."

"America."

"Yes, proudly made in the United States of America. You knew that! You just wanted to show off. What does Payoolee EYE EN mean?"

"That's where I was made, Miss Tatev. Paoli, Indiana."

"I'd like to go there."

"Why is that?"

"To see where they made you."

"Maybe they could give me hair."

"Hah! You'd look funny with hair. I think you're too old for hair. Old people don't have hair. How old are you anyway?"

"I'll be six hundred and forty-eight next month."

"Hurlyburly!"

"And how old are you, Miss Tatev?"

"You know that, silly! I'm five. Unless you count the time I was in mommy's belly. I was in there for ten years! So really, I'm fifteen."

"I don't think they count years that way, Miss Tatev. When they put your mommy in stasis for the flight, you didn't grow. But if you want to count the years that way, we can. However, it means you'll have to start Grade Nine next week."

"With the big kids? No way! I'm only five! I'm only five!"

"Look, here come your parents, Miss Tatev."

"I hope they're in a better mood today. Everyone has been strange lately."

"Must be grownup stuff, Miss Tatev."

"Must be, Mister Alloy."

Here, a father and mother approach with loving smiles.

"Hello, little one."

"Hello, mommy."

"No hello for me?"

"Of course! Hello, daddy!"

"That's better."

"Come now, little one, it's time to wash up before dinner."

"Do I have to wash, mommy?"

"Yes, you have to wash. We may be settlers, but we're not heathens."

"What's heathens?"

"Actually, I don't know, but I know that you don't want to be one. Now come along. There's only room for two in our cart, so your daddy and Alloy will have to walk home."

"All right, bye, Mister Alloy."

"Bye, Miss Tatev."

Now, only a father and his bot remain.

"That girl sure does love her walks, Alloy. Any further and I think you two would have ended up on the other side of the planet."

"She's quite like you were, Mister Jonathan, at that age."

"You remember. I suppose I was like that, wasn't I."

"She's quite perceptive as well. She's aware something is wrong. Something is wrong, isn't it, Mister Jonathan?"

"Maybe. I don't know. We've lost contact with Gravesend on Amleth IV."

"Why, that could be anything, Mister Jonathan. They're a small settlement. Likely they have only a single transmitter. If it went down, they would be unable to communicate. And might I speculate that their repair bots are not as well versed in transmitter mechanics as I am."

"Or farming. Or child rearing. You're quite the renaissance bot, Alloy."

"I do my best. Speaking of which, I found your unpublished thesis while cleaning the house. Extraordinary work, if I might say so, Mister Jonathan. Temporal mechanics are one thing my processors could never master."

"You found that? I told Niyanthi to destroy that years and years ago. I should have known she'd squirrel it away somewhere. Well, that was another life, my friend. I prefer my life here. It's simple but meaningful, and I can share it with those I love. You included."

"As an inanimate object, I greatly appreciate the sentiment."

"I thought you might. Now let's start back or we'll never be home in time for dinner. I also want to check the radio tower and see if there's been any news from Gravesend. The Colonial Federate sent a security frigate to investigate. They should have arrived there by now."

"It's a forty-minute walk, Mister Jonathan. If you're truly concerned, I could intercept any transmissions."

"They'd be encrypted, Alloy."

"Well, as you say, I'm a bot of many trades."

"So not only are you an expert on transmitter repair, but you can function as one as well? Good to know you have hobbies, Alloy. Well, it would technically be illegal, but I suppose this one time wouldn't hurt."

"Parsing."

Here, a pause.

"Mister Jonathan, we should get back to the settlement immediately."

"What's happened?"

"Gravesend has been destroyed by raiders. The Colonial Federate believe these raiders to now be en route here, to Amleth III."

"Raiders? This far into the frontier? There's nothing to raid."

"That's all the information I have. The Colonial Federate is on their way. We've been asked to arm ourselves and go into hiding until they arrive. They've sent the *Virginia Dare*. She's the fastest ship in the mandate."

"She's the only ship in the mandate, Alloy. The Colonial Federate has always been spread thin. But it's never mattered before. We're a peaceful colony. Why would these raiders wish to resort to violence? I don't understand. Human society is rich beyond imagination. We've accomplished feats beyond wonder. Why are there still those with so much hate and anger?"

"I can't say, Mister Jonathan. Unfortunately, my algorithms have difficulty engaging in philosophy. I can only give you practical advice. And that advice is that we hurry. I'm detecting activity in the upper atmosphere."

"The Colonial Federate?"

"Impossible to determine from this range."

"Stars have mercy, Alloy. I can see them. Two ships in the sky, locked in mortal combat. Oh, thank goodness, the *Virginia Dare* has destroyed the raiders."

"Mister Jonathan, it's not over. The raiders sent down dropboxes before the engagement. I'm receiving reports of fighting on the outskirts of the settlement, just ahead."

"Tatev is up there! We have to hurry."

Here, the hurried footsteps of a worried father.

He arrives to a scene of black smoke and fire.

Colonial Federate soldiers secure the area.

"Soldier, what happened here?"

"We believe they were after your settlement's power generator. Or perhaps just sport. It's hard to say. This is my first combat engagement, to be honest. But rest assured, the enemy has been neutralized."

"Soldier, your eye is missing. You're bleeding."

"Yes, we encountered several marauders just now. I took a piece of shrapnel in the eye. But don't worry about me. I'm so hyped on stims I can hardly feel a thing. And the medics will tend to me soon enough, after they tend to your own people."

"So some of our settlers were injured?"

"Yes."

"I must find my family. I didn't see them on the road."

"The road? What's your wife's name, sir?"

"Niyanthi."

"Your name is Jonathan?"

"Yes, how did you know that?"

"Sir, I don't know what to say. She asked for you just before..."

Here, a father runs to the bodies of wife and child, both charred and lifeless. He grieves as he holds the most precious thing to him in the world, a little girl with ribbons in her hair.

"No, this can't be!"
"I'm so sorry, sir."
"I must go back."
"Sir..."
"I must change this."
"That's not possible, sir."
"It is. I can change this."
"Sir, please come with me."
"No, I can change this."
Here, a father rocks on his knees.
"I *must* change this."
Here, a vow.
"I must go back."

32

I recognize immediately where Careena has brought us. I've been here once before—the officer's lounge aboard the flagship of the Tegan Navy, the *TDF Ark Royal*. This was the ship that rescued me my very first day in the future. It would appear that the arc of time has brought me full circle. Those events seem so long ago now. Back then I'd been lost, confused, frightened; a temporal refugee spirited away from her rooftop in Brooklyn and hurled across the very fabric of time and space.

And now? Now that I've survived alien landscapes? Rode across the stars on magnificent ships such as this one? Tasted the colors of ancient Sumer? Now I feel warranted to hold my head a little higher. Ironic as it sounds, in a few short days I've become one of the most experienced time travelers in all of mortal history. The question still remains—will it be enough to save the universe?

The lounge around us is empty, eerily quiet, and dark.

"Where is everyone?" I ask.

There are piles of emergency cots stacked against one wall and boxes of supplies set against another. I have to imagine the scene in the ship's hangars is no different. Likely even the halls are lined with makeshift beds and food goods. Captain Bashir is under no illusions as to the scale of the coming rescue operation. Every inch of the ship will be used to house refugees.

The journey between Tegana and the Valeyard is nineteen days. I'm worried how far along on that course we may already be. If we're too far out, we won't have time to reverse course and be of any use. Once the Red Man takes out the planetary shield, his mercenaries will be able to jump right into Parliament Hill, right onto the footsteps of the Ministry of Temporal Affairs. Soolin had armed guards, including Grimalkin who she sent after me and Careena—but against hundreds of jumpers? They'll stand no chance. Patmos will take the Chronos Imperium within minutes of his arrival.

Careena is whispering to herself. "Three, two, one..."

Alarm sirens blare.

"Hah!" she howls. "I was right on that, weren't I?"

Soldiers appear at two different entryways. All are armed with rifles. They scream, "Hands in the air! Down on your knees!"

We do as told. A few moments later Captain Bashir enters the mess. He's exactly as I remember him. Tall, formidable, with the aura of one who has faced a great many trials during a long and storied life. His hair is greying, his beard is crisp, and his iconic eye patch gives his face a seriousness, an intensity.

When he sees who it is that has breached his security, he becomes visibly irritated. "Smith, I thought we got rid of you. Why are you back on my ship?"

"Good to see you too, Hamid."

He's not finished. He looks at a scanner an officer is showing him, then barks, "And did you bring a Khelt aboard a Defense Ministry ship? Is that young lady there a Khelt?"

"What, her? No, never mind her. Just an unfortunate medical condition is all. We have more pressing matters to attend to."

Bashir has little patience. "You mean like the fact that you shot up the Ministry of Temporal Affairs? Yes, I heard about that. Or how about the fact that I have reports you were on the Valeyard just prior to their dome being breached? I'd call that damned suspicious."

"Well, I'd call it libel," the old woman counters.

The captain orders his men and women to stand down their weapons. I breathe a little easier once they do.

"The three of you might as well get up," he tells us. "You should know, however, that your portreeve has given us orders to shoot you on sight, Smith. And I'm seriously considering it."

He beckons for the three of us to follow him down a hallway. A holographic officer walks beside him. She's a projection—I'm getting better at recognizing those now, but there's still something... different about her. I can't quite put my finger on it.

Bashir turns to Careena. "So what's this all about, Smith? What really happened on the Valeyard? It's a damned humanitarian nightmare over there, you know."

"Has the fleet already left then?" she asks with worry.

"Of course they left," he says. "Most of them left early yesterday. We've also enlisted every passenger ship that could be found. I saw the reports this morning. Hundreds of those towers have faulty ventilation systems. Two thousand people have already died from asphyxiation, but as many a million more are in immediate danger. Their oxygen could go at any moment. Our corps of engineers haven't surveyed the damage yet, but rumors are the entire city will need evacuated. Sixty-four million people. There are not enough ships in the entire mandate for that. We'll be making runs back and forth for months."

"And, Hamid," Careena asks lightly. "If I might be so bold as to inquire, are we with the fleet?"

"Funny you should ask that." The way he phrases this tells me he doesn't think it's humorous at all. "As the flagship, we're supposed to be heading the rescue efforts. Yet we haven't even been able to leave the Tegan System. I had to put Admiral Pertwee aboard the *Hayashi*. A damned embarrassment."

"Most unfortunate," the old woman agrees.

"Aye," the captain says. He pulls a pair of rather familiar-looking pliers from his pocket. "Somehow these fell into our Reginald Drive. Blasted things tore a hole in the Preon-sheath when we fired up the engines. I've given the Engineering crew a good dressing down for their carelessness. The damage took three days to repair."

An insurance policy.

Careena, that clever hellion.

The old woman snatches the pliers from the captain's hand. "Curious. I'll be sure to look into these for you. But believe it or not, it may have been a good thing."

"How could the crippling of my ship be a good thing?" the captain asks with suspicion.

"Well, you see," she starts. "I rather sort of need to commandeer your ship. We have to return to Tegana immediately."

"We're not a damned limo service, Smith. Besides, I'm fairly certain your authority was revoked when they gave me orders to shoot you."

Careena is serious. "The Valeyard is a diversion, Hamid. They're going after Tegana."

The captain stares at her with his one good eye. "Nonsense. How could they? There's not a single ship unaccounted for this side of the mandate."

"They're not coming by ship."

"Jumpers?"

"Yes."

He dismisses the threat. "Then it's a police matter. Let the constables handle it. This is a navy ship."

Careena stands her ground. "They have three hundred jumpvests, Hamid. And I've seen some of these forkers. They're ex-military, well-trained. You and I both know the constables spend all day giving directions to Cawdorian and Mahshadi tourists. I'd be surprised if many of them even know which end of a gun fires the bloody bullets."

He's still not buying it. "Three hundred jumpers, Smith? There's not enough RGMs in the known systems for that many vests. Military Intelligence says we'll never see more than four jumpers in any given year."

"That's always been true," Careena agrees. "Until the heist aboard the *Stellar Pearl.*"

He pauses. He knows he shouldn't believe her, but it's clear he's been suspicious about that heist ever since the day it happened. And not only because the infamous Red Man was involved—but because, despite even his high-level security clearance, he was never informed the contents of the stolen cargo. Only now does he finally have a grasp on the magnitude of what happened that day.

He turns to us. "All right, let's say I believe you. Tegana is protected by a tachyonic shield. No one can jump in."

"They've got a way to blow it," she tells him. "They're just waiting for the fleet to move off so you won't be able to respond in time. So like I said, it's a bit fortuitous luck that your engines went out when they did, or the attack would already be underway."

"Are you sure about this?"

"I am."

The decision weighs heavily on him. "Then there's something you should know. I received a report this morning of a prison break at a high security facility on Iskender Bay. Iskender is three years away in the Prizren Mandate, so ordinarily, I wouldn't even give it a second thought. But something caught my eye. The break was orchestrated with the aid of three jumpers. That should have been impossible. Like everywhere these days, the prison is protected by a tachyonic shield. Yet somehow, they were able to bring down the shield and make the jump. No one knows how they did it yet. But it would seem that you do."

Bashir turns to the female holographic officer. "Abi, show me that report on Iskender Bay again."

She hands him a small tablet, which he quickly skims.

Careena, meanwhile, is lost in thought. She's second-guessing herself. She was positive the Red Man was going to use the time-shot device against Tegana, but it appears he's used it against this prison world instead. Was that what this was all about?

A jail break?

Bashir asks, "How many vests did you say they have?"

"I destroyed a few," Careena tells him. "But they could still have as many as three hundred."

The captain rubs his beard.

His jaw is tight.

"What is it, Hamid?"

"You say they have three hundred vests, but these recent updates say no one has left the planet yet. Nearly a thousand prisoners have fled into the jungles, but they all have trackers and they have no where to go. The prison is on an island surrounded by hundreds of miles of toxic ocean. The local authorities will have no problem picking them up soon. So if what you say is true, why are they still there? Why haven't they jumped to freedom?"

"Because they can't," I blurt out.

Everyone turns to me.

"Not yet, anyway." I try my best to explain, despite the pressure I suddenly feel from so many sets of eyes. "Think about it. The Red Man has a few loyal soldiers at his side, but I bet he doesn't have enough for an invasion force. And he believes he's going to need one to get Patmos into the Chronos Imperium. So where does one recruit several hundred desperate mercenaries on such short notice?"

"From the prison," Careena says.

"Exactly. He's probably promised them those jumpvests in exchange for this mission. He's promising them not just freedom, but the power of the gods. They'll do anything for him now. But he's lying. The Tinker told us that to make as many vests as they did, most of them are good for only a single jump. The prisoners don't know it, but once they jump, that's it, their vests are useless after that."

I can tell Careena is impressed.

Captain Bashir nods knowingly as well. "So if you're right, they'll have to jump from Iskender Bay directly to New Harmony. Which means they must have a second explosive device ready to take out Tegana's shield."

"They're just waiting for you and your ship to get out of the way, sir."

He's as serious as stone. "Well then, Miss Mendelssohn, let's not do that for them." He turns back to the female officer. "Abi, full reverse. Yellow alert. Prep the dropboxes for a planetary incursion. Notify TDF Command of possible inbound hostiles. We haven't much time."

I ask Careena, "If they blow the shield, what stops them from just jumping directly into the Chronos Imperium?"

"There's a secondary shield around Parliament Hill," she tells us. "Soolin had it installed ages ago. As far as I know, only two or three people know where the generator is. And I ain't one of them."

"But Patmos might know. His mole was good."

"He doesn't know," she assures me.

"How can you be sure?"

It's Captain Bashir who answers. "Because if he did, Miss Mendelssohn, he wouldn't need to jailbreak a small army of mercenaries to take the building. Smith, how far out does this second shield extend?"

"I'm not sure exactly. The generator is small. Rumor is it's a proto-type being designed to protect ships in space. My guess is it can't cover a radius of more than a few dozen blocks. Still, it should give us some breathing room. The Red Man will have to jump in at the perimeter of the field and fight his way in."

"And surely your planet has ground forces," Rhoda asks.

Again the captain answers, "We do. We maintain a very small, but effective, defense force. Unfortunately, our troops are currently on Great Southern setting up camps for when the refugees arrive. It's a beautiful continent, and we've decided that it's theirs if they want it. We're certainly not going to force anyone to return to that Valeyard hellhole. The problem is any ship that could ferry our soldiers back to New Harmony was commandeered for the evacuation efforts. The *Ark Royal* is all that there is."

I ask with worry, "And you have soldiers aboard?"

"Yes. We're running a skeleton crew, but I still have sixty combat-ready marines. Once we're back in orbit, we'll send them down in dropboxes. They'll set up a perimeter around Parliament Hill. Patmos and his Red Man won't get through, I promise you that."

"How long until we're back?"

"Unfortunately, while in the system, due to the stellar bodies, we're limited to conventional speeds, which brings along some minor issues of time dilation," he tells me. "So that puts us roughly two hours out from Tegana. I'll contact the planet on secure channels and let them know we're on our way back. But we don't want to give away our hand just yet. If our enemy sees us coming, they'll initiate the attack. So I'll deploy a false transponder and send it toward the Valeyard. For anyone watching, it will appear our course hasn't changed. In the meantime, why don't the three of you wait in the forward observation deck. There are couches down there. You can rest until we arrive. I'll have food brought to you. Your work in all this is finished. The Navy will handle it from here."

I'm so very relieved that the end to all this is so close at hand. I know I've thought that before, several times in fact, but Captain Bashir and his staff are some of the most competent people I've ever encountered. And they know the threat. I have no reluctance handing the reins of this task over to him, his women, his men, and his ship.

So with that finished, Careena, Rhoda, and I do as he suggests and make our way to the observation deck. It's a beautiful room, slightly more esoteric in design than the mess hall. This is where soldiers and staff come to read or watch the stars or meditate.

In this time of crisis, however, there's no one here but us.

I take a seat on a couch and stroke the edges of my red shawl. Both Careena and Rhoda have discarded theirs, but I decide to keep mine. It represents something to me. But what? That like it, I'm a backwards bumpkin a thousand years behind the times? No, something deeper. I've stolen this shawl from antiquity. Someone else was meant to wear it. It was meant to play some other role in history. But now it will play its part here, like me.

I turn to Careena. "What happens to us when this is all over?"

"I really don't know, Freckles. Maybe Soolin will pardon us, you know, for saving all of forking time. But given how she's taken to dressing in those ridiculous robes and treating everything like a damn religious procession, I can't even venture a guess. Whether she forgives us or not, you can't go home."

I suppose this I should have understood. I can't go back to my old life because there's no life to return to. There never was. The girl I was before, little Izzy Mendelssohn, the overly ambitious, occasionally anxious, but otherwise generally ordinary teenager, died; she fell off a ledge.

I'm someone else.

I could try to slip back into the 21st Century and live out my days quietly in Jersey. I won't deny that some part of me has considered it—but with wisdom and maturity comes a sense of responsibility. And I know now that if I went back, I'd end up accidentally pulling too many levers, altering too many of the life paths of those around me. I'd leave too many marks on the flow of time, like scratches of graffiti on the sandstone pillars holding up the cosmos; until the grooves become so deep that the stones crumble.

No, the best I can do is live a worthy and meaningful life here, to make that my small way of honoring that lovely and innocent girl I used to be. It is for her I push on.

Careena seems to read my mind.

She has her own regrets.

"I'm sorry I took you out of Brooklyn, luv."

"Could you have gotten this far without me?" I ask.

"Probably not."

"Then don't be sorry."

More than an hour passes. Food is brought in. I nap. Conversation comes to us in only small pieces. The waiting brings with it an anxiety that eats away at us. A storm is brewing, a confrontation is coming, a battle between the forces of good and evil. And yet, regardless of which side wins, the three of us will have no place in either of the worlds to come.

At some point I open my eyes and look out the windows. Coming into focus is the blue-green marble I know to be Tegana. From here, perched so high above in the heavens, like gods gazing down from the top of Olympus, the planet looks peaceful, like a sleeping child cradled in the loving embrace of his solar mother. Perhaps we're not too late. Perhaps we've succeeded and the world will be saved.

My hopes are dashed, however, when the lights in the lounge turn red, when thick blast shielding falls over the windows, and alarm klaxons blare.

A voice over the speaker orders all crews to battle stations.

New Harmony has fallen under attack.

33

We make our way to the bridge. In the halls marines are strapping themselves into rectangular dropboxes, sized for about a dozen soldiers each. These men and women are ready to shoot down to the surface at breakneck speeds the moment we reach the upper atmosphere. I envy their commitment. In a world where I've never known what I wanted to do, what I wanted to be, not before and especially not now, it's encouraging to see individuals of such singular conviction. They could have been anything, and they chose to be the guardians of their homeworld.

On the bridge is Captain Bashir, stoic as ever, barking orders.

"How bad is it?" Careena asks.

"It's just as you predicted, Smith. A seismic blast in the mantel took out the primary shield generator. But they couldn't jump directly into the city center, so they've appeared around the perimeter. It's a war zone now. The constables are spread thin, forced to defend streets coming in from every direction. They're being overrun, pushed back block by block. Causalities are already in the hundreds, including a fair number of civilians caught in the crossfire."

There's worry on Careena's face.

"How long till we can deploy?"

"Six minutes forty-eight seconds to drop range," an officer at a command station answers.

"There's something else, Smith," the captain says while pointing to a map of the city on a display. "Take a look at this. The attackers appeared in ten teams of twelve. All strategically chosen points." Displayed on the map are little red dots that must indicate the movement of the Red Man's forces. They're converging from different directions on Parliament Hill. And they're not far away now.

But what Bashir is pointing to next are blue dots behind the red ones. He goes on, "Then there's these. Fifty-four pairs of jumpers, each comprised of a man and a woman. They arrived with the fighters, yet none of them have penitentiary identifier tags. Which means this second group didn't originate from Iskender Bay. And one more thing. They're unarmed. It's damned curious."

"It's Patmos," I venture. "It has to be."

"Aye, my guess as well," Careena agrees. "So it's true then, he has a group of followers. The Red Man's job is simply to get them into the ministry."

I ask, "Even if they succeed, Careena. Couldn't you still stop them? Story told us a jumper has to commit an action before it will have an effect. Couldn't you track them down with those fancy computers before they do any harm?"

She shakes her head. "Me? Alone? There are more than a hundred of them, deary. I don't know how I could. And are they all even going to the same place? Or a hundred different places? We still don't know what they're bloody planning," she says in frustration. "And I didn't want to mention this, but there's a bigger problem if they jump. If they do something radical, and they do it quick enough, then it's possible they'll alter time to such a degree that Tegana never gets colonized. If that happens, the planet will transform right before our eyes, back into the lifeless rock it was before humanity ever showed up."

The implications are not lost upon me. "Which also means the *Ark Royal* will have never been built. But since you and I have been grounded, the changes won't affect us. We'll continue flying through space... only without a ship."

The old woman turns her attention back to the captain. "Hamid, I should jump down there and have a look."

"You won't be able to," he tells her.

"Why the hell not?"

"The EMP blast they used knocked out the shield only temporarily. It's respun and back online now."

She stomps her foot. "Then tell those blockheads to shut it off, yeah? I can ferry your marines down there two at a time. We can get the city constables the reinforcements they need."

Again the captain gives her a grave look. "Two of their teams went straight for the radio relays. They're using them to jam our communications. We can't get through to the surface."

"Forkballs!"

On the main viewscreen, we all watch as Tegana grows in size. Continents take shape. Moons begin to stand out in contrast to the mighty world they orbit. The mood among the bridge staff is tense. The ship is rattling. We're approaching as fast as we can— any faster and I think we'd fly apart.

A minute or two later we hit the upper atmosphere. The impact is brutal but everyone manages to keep their footing. I don't know what sort of technological magic manages the ship's gravity, but I'm thankful our sudden near stop didn't splatter our bodies across the walls of the ship.

Just as I think we might be in the clear, just as I can see the clouds a few miles below us, the entire ship shakes violently at the sound of an explosion. Red warning lights start beeping at consoles all over the bridge.

"Report," the captain demands.

"Unclear, sir."

"Perhaps we struck a satellite," an officer guesses.

Another bridge officer replies, "There's no satellites that large."

A pilot is desperately trying to correct for our descent. We're dropping rapidly. I'm not entirely sure, but I don't think the *Ark Royal*, a battle cruiser nearly a kilometer long, is the type of ship designed to land on a planet, or even enter the lower atmosphere, for that matter.

"Stabilizers offline," the pilot says. "We're losing altitude."

The ship shakes again at another explosion.

"Captain, direct hit. Decks four and five have been compromised."

The first officer shouts, "It's Planetary Defense, sir. They've locked on to us. Anti-spacecraft batteries are firing from the ground."

"Why the hell is your planet shooting at us?" I cry.

Bashir seems to be wondering the same thing. "They must have taken over the Defense Ministry. We were so damned concerned about Temporal Affairs that we left our ass wide open. They're turning our own weapons against us."

"The Defense Ministry is only a few blocks from Temporal Affairs," Careena points out. "He's almost there."

None of that really matters if we get shot out of the sky.

"Incoming," an officer warns.

Bashir yells into his wrist. "All hands brace for—"

This third strike is the most violent. The tail of the *Ark Royal* begins to spin around. We've lost all ability to hold a course or our altitude. I feel the g-forces as we spin, the invisible tug pulling me toward the walls of the ship as we go round and round like an amusement park ride. Through the view screen I see a trail of smoke forming like a coiled snake as we drop lower and lower toward the planet below.

Captain Bashir takes only the briefest moment to make up his mind. He knows indecision and delay often cost lives. He knows this better than most. He barks at an officer. "Van Sessen, prepare the bridge for evacuation." He speaks back into his sleeve, "All quarters, abandon ship. Repeat, all hands, abandon ship."

The officers begin leaving their stations.

"Abi," the captain calls. The holographic woman from before appears. I realize she *is* the ship; she's the ship computer in interactive form. Her name is an acronym—*Automated Bridge Interface*.

"Here, sir."

"Abi, take over ship functions. Employ all countermeasures. They're going to be shooting us down in our dropboxes. Use the unoccupied boxes as decoys to draw their fire. Cover our drop into New Harmony as best you can."

"Understood, sir."

He takes a long, last, nostalgic look at his bridge. "And Abi..."

"Yes, sir?"

"Scuttle the ship somewhere meaningful. I want future generations to remember the name *Ark Royal*."

"It was an honor serving with you, captain," the hologram says.

In his otherwise taciturn eyes is the look of a long and storied relationship coming to an end. Bashir was smart enough to know that Abi was nothing more than a script, with programmed responses, and yet even he was not beyond a heartfelt connection to her. How many battles had they survived together during the Second Khelt War? How many years had she been his ship, his savior, his steadfast companion through the stars?

And now it was all coming to an end.

Much was said in his polite nod goodbye.

We follow the captain and his bridge crew to an emergency dropbox, a small rectangular vessel with seats and harnesses. Once we're all seated, I feel like I'm going to vomit in anticipation. Or maybe it's just because we're still spinning so goddamn fast.

Bashir speaks again into his wrist, to give one final message to his soldiers divided among the many dropboxes as they ready themselves to drop into combat. Though he is not far from me, I hear him over the speakers.

"Crew of the *Ark Royal*. As you know by now, our homeland is in peril. It is without exaggeration that I tell you the very existence of our world is at stake. In a moment, we will be launched into battle. I cannot tell you what you will face when our ships land and those doors before you open. How could I ever describe to you, the men and women who must face it, the ugly guise of war? I can tell you only this—fortune has offered us and us alone the privilege to answer this call. And answer it we shall. Our enemy is guile, but our courage, our conviction, *will* win us this day. So, brave soldiers of Tegana, if it's a war they want, then by God, it's the fire-eyed maid of smoky war, all hot and bleeding, that we shall offer them. Let us now show these lily-livered cowards just who we are."

Our dropbox releases without warning. The sudden pressure of the fall causes me to black out momentarily. My body is pressed against my harness with such force I'm sure that it's crushing my bones. I'm nauseous. I'm scared.

I'm falling to my destiny.

Surely, I'm falling to my death.

And was that not, despite the temporary reprieve granted over these previous few days, always what the fates had intended for me?

34

Half the dropboxes launched from the falling *Ark Royal* are shot down by Planetary Defense cannons before they ever reach the ground. Most were empty, thank goodness. They were decoys used to fool the enemy targeting systems. But I see in Captain Bashir's face that not all his men and women survived the landing. How many soldiers were lost, I don't know. It's only by the grace of the cosmos that we ourselves were not blown into oblivion.

We hit the ground with bone-jarring force. The doors fall open. We've landed in the center of Prospect Park, that great green emerald at the heart of New Harmony. Ahead, on the northeastern edge, are the white and stately government ministries of Parliament Hill. I hope we're not too late.

Marines in front of me charge out into the green, weapons at the ready, only to be cut down by sniper fire from rooftops far away. An officer next to me is killed instantly, even before she's unbuckled her harness. Her blood is sprayed across the pod walls.

Across my face.

Captain Bashir grabs my shoulder and half pulls, half throws me out of the pod and into the bright sunlight as his soldiers return fire. He presses me down against the rear of the dropbox for cover. As my eyes adjust, I see Rhoda and Careena are both with me.

Our soldiers return fire, blowing the rooftop to pieces with powerful rifles, killing the enemy snipers. But already it's clear how precarious the situation is. Several buildings on Parliament Hill are on fire and there's the constant staccato of gunfire echoing from the streets. Black smoke is rolling into the sky. The last line of city constables has taken cover behind the great marble columns fronting the Temporal Affairs building. They're being overrun even as we watch.

Bashir gives the order and his men and women charge up the gently sloping hillside of the park. To their credit they never hesitate, even while they have the inferior ground and are taking heavy fire with heavy losses. I start to follow, but the captain holds me back with a hand.

"You should remain here, Miss Mendelssohn. You'll be safe here until this is over."

"With all due respect, captain," I say. "If this is how the universe ends, I have no desire to be remembered as a spectator."

He understands.

We follow behind the front line marines and enter the urban blocks and plazas of the ministry buildings. A brutal shootout ensues as the battle is fought block by block. We've easily already lost two-thirds of our soldiers, but the Red Man's forces have been heavily depleted as well.

As we round a corner, I'm unprepared for the scene on the streets. Bodies are strewn everywhere, and not all are combatants. In such a busy district, it was inevitable that there would be collateral damage. Glass from windows litter the sidewalks. Children, who only an hour ago were bored on educational school trips, are now crouched in alleys, tears streaking their young faces.

The anger boils inside me like a tempest. I can't explain it; I should be afraid. I should want to run away, to flee. But the only thought going through my mind right now is that Patmos will pay for this, that I'd march into the very forges of hell for the opportunity to strike him down, to pass judgment on his soul, whether or not such a right was mine to pass. A wiser version of myself may have been more careful what she wished for.

We reach the foot of the ministry. No one is here. They must already be inside. Several of the facade columns have been blasted apart and the bodies of the defenders lie on the steps, some of whom I remember from my last visit. The lifeless form of Prior Grimalkin sits only a few meters away from me, his blood spilling step over step over step down the ivory staircase.

I know Bashir would prefer to regroup before storming the building, to lay out a plan, but there's no time; Patmos need only reach the Chronos Imperium and all our fighting, all our sacrifice, and the sacrifice of the city constables who laid down their lives to buy us the time we needed to get here, will have been for nothing.

We rush in.

There are scorch marks everywhere in the giant domed hall that had previously reminded me of a cathedral. The bodies of several slain constables and ministry guards lay on the floor, along with many of those of the enemy. Three or four of the great marble statues that encircle the room, the seven pioneering agents of time, have been shot to pieces, some now resting on their sides on the floor. The room no longer feels like a sacred place of worship.

It feels like a tomb.

There are the two arched portals facing us, the two wings of the building, the Hall of Yugas and the Hall of Saros. Either leads to the Chronos Imperium, that mysterious chamber under Parliament Hill, built by Jonathan Baker centuries ago.

Captain Bashir splits his forces in two. He takes the Hall of Yugas with half his marines while Careena, Rhoda, and I take the other hall with the remainder. We follow behind. Careena is armed with Old Bessie. Me, only with my wits.

At first, the hallway is quiet, peaceful almost. It's the same corridor I was brought down before. There are large alcoves with gods and goddesses of antiquity displayed. Further ahead are columns on the right side, opening into that meditative, cave-like courtyard with the skylight sun.

It's from that garden the gunfire erupts. The three of us take cover in an alcove as the marines return fire. It's impossible to tell what's happening as bits of stone and dust explode from every direction. After a moment, the noise and chaos dies down.

Careena peaks into the hallway. "Come, ladies."

No one is left moving, neither in the hallway nor in the courtyard adjacent. Either the marines we were with continued ahead without us, or they're all dead. Given the number of bodies on the floor, I'm very afraid it's the latter.

We're not far from the Chronos Imperium now. I grab Careena's shoulder. "What do we do once we get there?"

"I really don't know," she says honestly.

We come to the large foyer fronting the chamber, that strange dark space called the Ananke, designed by Soolin who placed two white, geometric trees to either side of the chamber's entrance. I don't see anyone, but I hold out hope that at any moment we'll encounter Bashir and his marines approaching from the other wing of the building. Perhaps the Red Man's forces have already been neutralized. Perhaps we've already won.

Careena decides not to wait and find out. We follow her into the foyer, into the open, heading toward the doorway of the Chronos Imperium, which glows with golden light like a portal.

That's when everything goes wrong.

There's a blast out of the darkness from the other side of the room and half the wall near us explodes. I'm thrown to the ground as bits of stone and marble rain down. Careena returns fire, but I can see almost nothing of what's happening. Smoke stings my eyes. I hear Careena scream. Everything goes silent.

I'm still on the floor, waiting for my ears to stop ringing and for the smoke to clear when I see the figure approaching. All I can make out in the fog and filthy air is a silhouette—huge, fearsome, hovering over me. But a silhouette is all I need. I'd know the shape of this foul devil anywhere.

The Red Man.

He takes another step toward me, his hefty frame lumbering like a giant. I can see his eyes now, smeared with dark mascara, the intent in them all too clear. There's no question that he recognizes me. And he means to extinguish my life.

I grab a shard of marble and clutch it like a dagger. In response, his knotted hands pull free a blade from his belt. No sound is made in the act. Another step forward and that red beard hangs over me like the pendulum of death.

His knife sweeps down.

35

I expect my life to flash before my eyes, to relive cut scenes of my youth, brief as it was, in my mind's eye. That's how it always happens in the movies, after all. But before any of that can happen, a hand is on my shoulder and I'm skidding backwards across the floor.

The Red Man's dagger strikes nothing.

And in my place now stands Rhoda al-Khansa.

As her nemesis looks up in surprise, she throws her first punch, which lands squarely in his throat. He instinctively grasps for his windpipe. She strikes again, this time going for his knife, which flies out of his hand and vanishes into the darkness.

Her slight frame continues to deliver impossible shockwaves of force. She breaks his nose, fractures his eye socket. She doesn't hold back, not this time, not after what he'd done to her before. She reaches deep into her genetic code, into the part of her brain that is still human, and pulls forth the most feral shards of her primal DNA.

There's a moment, as the Red Man staggers, when the two opponents lock eyes.

"You," the giant curses.

They hover like this for only a moment before he comes back at her. He's no stranger to pain and her attacks only momentarily caught him off guard. His swipes are fast and calculated. It takes every ounce of Rhoda's speed and concentration to avoid being completely pummeled. Each lands horrible blows upon the other. But neither offers an inch of ground.

Behind me, lining the hallways of the Ministry of Temporal Affairs like a museum, are the statues to the gods of ancient fancy. But here, in this foyer, I watch as two authentic gods do battle, locked in mortal combat, the fate of humanity the prize in which to be awarded the victor.

The Red Man gets Rhoda by her arm and swings her skidding across the floor, into the Chronos Imperium chamber itself. He charges in after her. Before she can stand, he's on her, bringing down blows of terrible wrath. One, then another, then another.

He lifts her like a rag doll and throws her up against the computer terminals lining the wall. Sparks fly. He rakes her body over the consoles, the sharp edges ripping the flesh off her back. I flinch at the amount of blood left behind, streaking across the computer screens.

He hurls her back to the ground, his rage and eagerness on full display as he rips a panel off a terminal, holding it in both hands over the Kheltic girl like a guillotine. Piercing her heart before was not enough. The only way to end her is to take off her head. The sharp edge of the panel is ready to do just that. A heavy boot on her chest holds her down helplessly.

I scream. But what can I do? This is not my fight. Every challenge these two warriors have ever overcome, every hardship and obstacle they've ever conquered—it has all led them to this moment, to stand against one another there, inside that esoteric chamber.

The Red Man seems to know this. It's visible in his eyes. Even though his face is bloody and busted, for the first time in many decades, he feels alive again. He feels purpose; something that was robbed from when he became an immortal being that could not be slain, a demon who could not be conquered.

Rhoda is the adversary he's sought his entire life.

Her death will be his greatest accomplishment.

Well, screw that. His knife landed only a foot away from my hand. Part of me dreams of yanking it off the floor like Excalibur and plunging it into that pathetic hobgoblin's heart. Instead, I do the next best thing—I send it flying across the floor to Rhoda. She catches it just in time to deflect the sheet of metal coming down on her, slicing the Red Man's calf in the process.

He staggers back in pain—but now Rhoda is on her feet and she's armed. He's forced to use the metal panel like a shield, desperate as each of her strikes cause a flurry of sparks. In another instant he loses his grip and the panel goes skidding across the floor. Rhoda charges forward with his knife.

Knowing he's been defeated, he wills himself away, just as he had done on the Valeyard, jumping away in the same moment that Rhoda tackles him with the knife.

Coward, I scream!

Worse still, intertwined in that instant—both warriors are teleported away. To where I don't know. But he's inadvertently taken Rhoda with him. They're gone and the chamber is quiet.

I'd worry—I'd worry that their battle is now destined to continue across time and space, across the heavens, like the ancient myths of gods locked in combat for all of eternity; but the truth is I know that she's already won. I know because left behind on the floor of the Chronos Imperium, discarded in the heat of battle, abandoned in the escape—is the Red Man's severed head.

"Freckles," someone coughs.

I turn. "Careena!"

I almost forgot about the old woman in the melee. She's sitting propped up against one of the fallen statues in the hallway we came down. Near to her are the lifeless bodies of two mercenaries she shot moments ago, each in a jumpvest. Such wicked technology. I'd burn it all if I could.

Her voice is weak as she tries to talk. I see her wound and am filled with sudden dread. I've seen this sort of wound once before, a glowing crater of black ash. Those tiny nanites are eating her away from the inside. And this time she doesn't have any fancy defenses to fight them off.

"I haven't much time," she whispers.

"We can save you."

"Not this time, deary. All things come full circle."

"You've cheated death before."

She touches my cheek. "Maybe I don't want to. Not anymore. At least now I can say it meant something."

My eyes tear up. "Careena..."

There is the echo of steps coming from down the other hall. I'm no longer so optimistic or naive as to believe it might be Captain Bashir and his marines come to save us. We crouch against the wall of our hallway, out of sight, obscured by a fallen statue of the goddess Parvati.

What I see I almost don't believe. Pairs of men and women, dressed in simple white tunics and brown slacks, each carrying a canvas bag of belongings on their shoulders. There must be around a hundred in all. A few mercenaries escort them.

On the faces of these men and women I see innocence, and no small amount of horror at the carnage they're forced to pass as they walk. They enter the Chronos Imperium without ever noticing us.

Looking back to Careena, her wound has already nearly doubled in size. Next to her is an empty eye dropper, the nanites she gave us before we left for Kryten. They'll slow the growth a little, but they won't save her.

"Who are they?" she asks of the men and women. She's too weak to look over the statue and see herself.

"I don't know," I tell her. "This is the end, isn't it, Careena?"

She takes my hands in hers. She speaks with great strain. "Do you remember once, Freckles, that I told you we had an ace in the hole? I think it might be time we use it. Look, I need you to do something for me."

When she pulls her hands away, I realize she's place Hecate in my palm. I know what she wants. For how long I've known, I don't know. *But I know.* In a strange way, it feels like I've always known, that I've been running from this moment my whole life.

As children we believe the world can be easily divided between good and evil, between black and white, between noble people and bad people. But this moment, this is the greyness in-between. This is the real world. The adult world. The world of only hard choices. Where sometimes there are no good answers.

There's only what's necessary.

"I can't do it," I tell her.

"Then you don't have to," she says. "You don't owe this world anything, deary. It took everything from you. And it kept on taking. And now it wants to take all that you have left. You can tell it to fork off. Heavens knows for a long time, I did."

She takes a deep, difficult breath and then continues. "But you won't do that. Because you're you. And I wish it wasn't like that. I'm sorry, Freckles. I'm sorry this responsibility falls to you. I'm sorry for everything. I tried to protect you from this. I really did..."

"Careena..."

I can't hold back my tears.

The old woman whispers.

"You remind me of her, you know."

"Who?" I ask.

"My Samus. You would have liked her. She wasn't at all like me. So miserable. I wish you could have met her. But even we gods can't defy our destiny. Now go, luv. Go save this forking world, whether it deserves it or not."

I nod.

I stand.

I go and confront my destiny.

36

The one hundred and eight mysterious newcomers have already filed into the Chronos Imperium. I slide along the wall of the darkened foyer to get closer to the chamber's entrance, but I'm forced to take cover behind one of the white trees standing at the entrance. A mercenary guards the doorway.

Still, I have a view into the chamber. I see the men and women in their white tunics and over those tunics are jumpvests, also painted white. Most are adults, though there are two little girls in the group.

I recall that the man who started this all, who betrayed Tegana to Patmos, had two daughters, Bell and Doria—it was for their passage that he had sacrificed himself and sold out his world. Were these his girls? Was Patmos the type of man to keep his word?

Who are these people?

What destination could be so important to them?

Where do they intend to go?

"Isabel."

I turn at the sound of my name; it's Story Beckett.

"Story! You're safe!" I'm immediately worried that the guard will have heard me, but then I remember that as long as I'm careful, I'm speaking to her only in my mind. A trick of the 31st Century.

"For now," she says.

"Where are you?"

"Not far. A few of us are in the mess hall on the other side of the building. We're trying to reactivate the building's security measures, or at least open the doors, but Patmos has a hacker tapped into the system. They've locked us in here."

"I can come get you out."

She shakes her head. "You won't have any more luck with the door than we do. And there's probably a guard down that way, regardless. Where's Smith?"

Until now I've refused to look behind me, to see what has become of my friend and mentor. But I can't help it now. I nod in Careena's direction.

All that remains is the woman's frumpy overcoat. She's been reduced to nothing, erased from existence. Not far from her are the bodies of the two men that killed her, one wearing a vest and the other not. I don't believe in Hell, but had I the power, I would create one. Just so they could burn in it.

Story looks down. "I'm sorry, Isabel."

I don't say anything. There will be time enough for tears later. I've promised not to let Careena's death be in vain.

I look back toward the acolytes in white. "Story, who are they?"

"I don't know."

"Which one is Patmos?" I ask. There's an edge to my voice. "Tell me his name."

Did my question tip my hand? If Story knew what I was planning, would she attempt to stop me? Was she, like Soolin and the others of the ministry, so beholden to the institution she served that it had become a religion, the violation of which was unthinkable? Unforgivable?

"I don't know that either," she tells me. "Assuming that's his real name, which is unlikely, there are 2.16 million men with that surname registered in the database. I would need more information. A first name. Or a planet of residence to cross-reference it with."

"Then you need to go in there," I tell her. "I need to hear what they're saying."

"It doesn't work that way. I can only hear what Hecate hears... unless."

"Unless what?" I ask.

"Soolin is in there," she says with some surprise. "I can use her communicator to let us hear what she's hearing. We can see what she sees."

I can't explain my sudden double vision, a consciousness overlaid upon my own—but in my mind's eye, I'm seeing from inside the Chronos Imperium. I see the disciples in their white tunics. They are crowded together. The looks on their faces range from purpose to anxiety to fear.

Why haven't they jumped yet?

Something is in my hands, only it's not my hands. They must be Soolin's. She's holding a small rod with a blue a light. I start to understand what's going on. The rod is creating a distortion field— it's negating the effects of the chamber!

Patmos and his people can jump away should they wish, but they'll lose the benefit of the room if they do. And they fought very hard to be here.

An older man, tall with the imperfect posture of an academic, steps forward. He could have been a loving grandfather, his face so gentle and his eyes so caring. He's not at all what I had imagined.

"Patmos, I presume," Soolin says in her dignified voice.

He addresses her politely. "Portreeve. Please, there's been enough bloodshed this day. Put down your device. If you do, we will leave and harm no one else."

"Harm no one?" she scoffs. "Sir, you ask for the powers to end the world. You can't expect me to grant you that."

He motions to his mercenaries to lower their weapons. "We've come to end nothing," he says. "We only wish to start again. And the path before us is not an easy one. Come with us, Doctor Soolin. Help us."

To her credit, the woman is defiant.

"I won't help a gang of petty butchers."

"It's regrettable what had to happen today." He says this as though he believes it. It makes my blood boil. He goes on, "But my friends here are not responsible for any of this. I planned this attack. Me alone. They are blameless of my sins."

"If that is true," Soolin says. "Then I would ask them to leave. The door is just there."

"Some of them may wish that, having now seen today's savagery. Given your second shield, it was not something that I could hide from them. But what they will build for us is too important to turn back now."

"And what is that?" Soolin asks. The same question is in my mind, as well. Who are these people? What could be worth so much death and destruction?

There's pain in his voice as he answers. "Have you not seen the rot in humanity? I know you have. You and your agents have dedicated yourselves to fighting it across all of time and space. And for that I commend you. But our weapons have grown too powerful, our ambitions too great. It's only a matter of time before we destroy ourselves. That is why I'm here. That is what I hope to prevent. A lone madman today can accomplish more destruction than entire states could have dreamed of just a few generations ago. We can no longer simply cut the weeds as they appear. We must pull up their roots. Once and for all. Before they strangle us."

He motions toward the foyer outside. "I've seen from your halls, that you are a student of the classics, the fables, our shared mythologies. You know then that there are truths sometimes hidden in those allegories. Truths about our nature. Let me tell you of one. Since the first bite of the apple, we've allowed the darker demons of our nature to hold us back. True, we've tried to outgrow our barbarism. We tell ourselves our generation is more enlightened than all those who came before. But you need look no further than the refugees left forgotten on the Valeyard to know this is not true. You need only consider our outer colonists, left abandoned to suffer at the edge of nowhere, to know this is a shameless story—a lie that we tell ourselves in vanity."

The way he says this last part gives me pause.

Soolin does not back down. "So you would condemn us for our mortal failings? You believe you have that right? To throw that first stone?"

"I'm not seeking stones, portreeve. I'm seeking salvation. The salvation of our race. It's not merely an idle promise told in old stories. We *can* start again, and without the sin of the apple to haunt us, without the cancer lurking in the heart of humanity."

Soolin gives a warning. "So you wish to remake us then. The Khelts too had aims such as yours. They too wished to improve humanity, to conquer the darker shadows of our nature, to remake ourselves in a better image. What you offer, sir, is nothing but a repeat of history."

"No," Patmos says with some conviction. "The Khelts attempted to cheat fate. There are no shortcuts. One cannot replace ten thousand years of wisdom with technological convenience. Doing so destroyed them. But I ask you, honestly, is our path now so different? We walk it slower, yes. But it's the same road, regardless."

"And you believe you can do better?" Soolin asks dismissively.

"I do. We've lost our way, our purpose in life. It was easy to do. We came into existence in a world without signposts, forced to find our own meaning without guidance, as an indifferent universe rained thunder and hailstorms down upon us. We drifted. We did horrible things to one another, things that have left wounds in our collective psyche, wounds that fester even now, wounds that will never heal. Our civilization is built on broken foundations, on pillars stained in blood and misery. We are the snake consuming its own tail, growing fat on a banquet of hate, feuds, and greed. Sooner or later, it will end us."

He continues, "My friends here wish to slay that serpent, not with vapid technology but with wisdom, compassion, and perseverance. They know, as you know, that we've learned much about ourselves over the last five thousand years. We conquered the stars and yet realized the most important place for us is simply a welcoming home with friends and family to share it. We've conquered aging and death and realized it brought us no happiness, for it is the circle of life that is the beating heart of the universe. Without that give and take, that push and pull, we live in a stagnant and dead world, one without meaning. My friends are philosophers and healers, farmers and craft-makers. They will take the best of us with them. They will build us a society on a foundation of hope, love, and the wisdom of the ages. And those foundations, Doctor Soolin, will last forever."

"Read your history again," Soolin says. "You speak of utopian madness. A hundred colonies over a thousand years have dreamed your dreams. And where are they now? How many millions are in the ground because of them? If you believe your society will be any different, then you, sir, are guilty of the greatest sin of all. Arrogance."

"No, ours *is* different," he says. "With your chamber, I will cleanse humanity of all her sins. With a single stroke of the brush, all the wars ever fought, all the inequity ever created, every genocide and conquest; they will have never happened. Don't you see, portreeve? Everything we've ever gone through as a species has led us to this moment. The moment we finally step out of the darkness. This is our baptism. In the very rivers of time."

"So you plan to end us," Soolin says, more a statement than a question. "You plan to go back before civilization ever began."

He nods. "Don't we all long that we could go back to our younger selves and create something better? To erase our regrets so they no longer haunt us? To live as the best versions of ourselves?" He points to the acolytes behind him. "They will create a society from all the best lessons from every culture, from every land, from every era. They are diverse, but their society will never have known slavery. Their daughters will never have known submission. Their sons will never have known war. For them, history will begin without original sin. They'll have never left the garden. The rot will be gone. The cancer will have no soil in which to grow."

Soolin's judgment fills her voice. "You forget, sir, that your world will be built on the sin of genocide."

"Then let that sin be mine and mine alone. I will suffer it. I will bear it. And when I die, it will die with me."

Soolin has her own realization.

"You're not going with them, are you?"

There's a long pause. Is it sadness? Regret?

"How I could?" he asks. "I've corrupted my own soul, portreeve, more than you could possibly know. It was the devil's bargain I made so that they would not have to. I'm as deserving of paradise as the vile brute whose head lies there on the floor before us. Though he did not know it, this was always meant to be our last supper."

"And how far back will you send them?" Soolin asks.

"Thirteen million years."

The answer shocks me.

The portreeve bows her head in understanding. "So you truly intend to end us then. Your followers, they will cultivate the lands and build their cities. They will prosper. Of that I have no doubts. In doing so, they will claim the most fertile regions. What then becomes of our primate ancestors? I'm sure your people will be humane to them. But they will be robbed of the niches they were meant to fill, the environments that would encourage them to walk upright, to create language, to realize their place in the cosmos. When you leave this chamber, humanity will have never been."

There's a gentleness in his response. "Birth and rebirth, Doctor Soolin. It's the cycle of time, the very nature of the universe. I can't help but think that this is how it was always meant to be. The realization of all our hopes, all our good intentions, the best part of ourselves placed on an ark and surviving on as the detritus of a thousand unholy wars is washed away."

He asks her longingly, "Surely you've felt it as well, at least once in your life? The tender whisper of what is to come, a sixth sense of destiny. Has it not, so often, found its way into our myths and holy scriptures? Perhaps today we finally understand why."

I listen, unconvinced, but I listen. I know how to defeat him, but there's something I need first.

His name.

Because I too have read the ancient fables. And in the old myths the gods can be summoned by the utterance of their names. Names are power. For this reason the gods tried to hide their names in obscurity, using only titles and aliases, protecting their names, guarding them feverishly. For a thing that can be summoned—

Can also be destroyed.

I hear steps coming from down the hall. A mercenary is leading two Tegan soldiers now into the Chronos Imperium. I crouch behind the white tree as they pass. The two marine prisoners are perhaps the last of the forces from the *Ark Royal* left alive.

One, I realize, is Captain Bashir.

Once inside, they're forced to their knees.

"Should we execute them, sir?" the mercenary asks. I've seen her before. She's the red-haired assassin who butchered the Tinker on the Valeyard. I have the impression that without the Red Man, she's next in the chain of command. Patmos seems oddly drawn to the color red. Wearing my own red shawl from Sumeria, I ponder what the source of his affinity could be.

"No," he tells the woman. "There's been enough bloodshed today. And I fear our friends have no stomach for it. Nor should they." He turns back to Soolin. "You have lost, portreeve. If you were attempting to buy time for a rescue, you can see it was to no avail. I've been as polite as I can. Lower your device. There would no honor in us wrestling you to the ground for it."

I think Soolin might comply.

But then Bashir speaks up.

"I know you," the captain says from where he kneels.

He's looking directly at Patmos with his one good eye.

"I doubt that very much, captain. I've never before set foot on your world."

"No, I remember you."

"You must be mistaken."

Yet, there is a pause in Patmos.

Bashir recalls, "It was my very first posting with the Colonial Federate. I was assigned to the *Virginia Dare*. We received a distress call. Raiders. I lost my eye in the fighting that day. And I remember you. How could I forget? You lost your precious little girl."

The lines of sadness grow on Patmos's face. He has difficulty with his words. "You were... you were very kind to me that day, captain. It seems our destinies are intertwined. I'm sorry that it had to be your ship that answered the call. Both then and now."

"Is that why you're here?" the captain asks. "Is that why you're doing this? To go back and save your little girl? You told me that you would. I remember."

Patmos's voice becomes thin. "I don't deny that my heart longed so very much to change the course of that day. I cursed the heavens, and for many years I cursed this ministry. I cursed them for denying us the powers they so selfishly hoard for themselves. But I came to understand what Jonathan Baker must have understood when he founded this chamber and enlisted those sworn to protect it, that while it may be excellent to have a god's strength, it is tyrannous to use it like a god."

He continues, "I could have risked the universe and everything in it to get what I wanted, but what right did I have to resurrect my loved ones, needlessly taken as they were, over the rights of the millions of fathers before me who lost their own children and their own wives to the cruel whims of humanity's broken soul, to the lecherous trolls of mortal vanity? So instead, I decided to make their loss mean something. I do this for them, captain. So that all the fathers yet to come, while they may still lose their children, for the wheel of time always turns, they will, at the very least, never have to face the evils I was forced to endure —a loss without purpose, a turn without meaning, at the hands of one's very own brothers."

With a nod, Captain Bashir seems to have accepted his fate. "I've always wondered what happened to you," he tells the man. "Your loss affected me, as well. I was so green. I'd never seen death before."

I listen as the captain recalls his youth solemnly.

"For a long time, I blamed myself for what had happened, though there was nothing I could have done. And I blamed the Colonial Federate for arriving in the Amleth system too late to help you. It was our duty and we failed you. I left the frontier after that. I immigrated here. But I found soldiering was the only thing that I knew. I kept the eye patch, though, as a reminder of that terrible day. Your little girl, her name was Tatev, right? I remember that. And you're Jonathan. I remember that too. I've never allowed myself to forget."

I take a deep breath.

Using Hecate, I cross-reference the names.

I find a match.

Jonathan Patmos Samaya. Former colonist of Amleth III.

His entire life is in the records; his university studies, his expulsion papers, his marriage contract, his planet of birth.

It's all there.

I have what I need to save humanity.

And all it will cost me is my soul.

Epilogue

Here, a highway of stars.

They streak above me in the night sky, brilliant and beautiful. Below me on a grassy hill sits a young mother, enjoying the calm of late evening with a tiny toddler, one too young to speak in anything other than giggles and smiles.

He seems so innocent, this boy, so fragile.

Yet, have I not looked into the seeds of time, peered into the celestial filaments? And through that profane lens have I not been granted an unnatural foresight, seen a darker cosmic story yet to unfold?

I hide in the shadows not far from mother and son. For a moment, all three of us look to the heavens. Secretly we yearn for Earth. I believe all souls must long for the homes they can never return—for the innocence they can never reclaim.

I envy the mother. How brave she is, to have fought her way to the edge of civilization, to face impossible odds on an untamed frontier, all to create a better life for her first and only child. I give them this moment together. But only this one. It's all that I can afford them.

The baby giggles.

"Oh, my little Johnny, you silly baby," the mother says. Her voice is soft. It makes me miss my own mother. "You see all those stars up there, Johnny? I'd give them all to you if I could."

The baby reaches out, to touch his mother's lips.

"We're just poor farmers, and we're alone now, but I promise you, my love, I'll make it better for us. Somehow I will. I'll give you a good life. The life your father and I always dreamed for you."

There is recent loss in those words.

"I'll give you all my heart to love, Johnny, and in that heart the courage to make your love known to the universe. You'll do great things. I know you will."

She kisses his forehead tenderly.

"We should go inside, before it gets too cold."

They retire to their small cabin. She places the baby in his crib. For many long moments she cannot look away from her child and I cannot look away from her. He must be the most beautiful thing in the world to her. Will I ever know that kind of love? Will the universe ever offer me such a gift? I try to push those thoughts away.

Finally, the mother dims the lights and leaves the nursery to finish her evening chores.

I enter the baby's nursery as silent as a ghost. It's not so difficult. I enter on bare feet. Indeed, I wear nothing but my necklace and the red shawl from Sumer, pulled tightly around me for warmth and modesty. The clothes I bought in the Valeyard could not travel back with me, not to this year. This year sits at the heart of the blackout dates, a time no traveler from the 31st Century has ever entered. They are forbidden to do so.

But not me.

I belong to no time. Not anymore. When I was spirited away from my rooftop in Brooklyn, my existence was revoked for nearly a thousand years. It was an act of some consequence. Did they know that at the time? That this would be my fate? That I alone would be endowed with powers not even Careena or Soolin could hope to possess?

I'd fancy myself a god of time.

But looking down at this boy, I know I am something else.

He smiles at me from his crib, reaching toward me with tiny fingers. I want to scream. Doesn't he know why I'm here! I've pulled the shawl to cover my mouth and my hair, exposing nothing more than my eyes. I am a coward too ashamed to show her face while she commits her crimes. To him I must be only a silhouette. A shadow.

A figure in red.

Again he smiles.

Stop it! I scream.

My hands are trembling. Moments are still passing on Tegana. Soolin is buying me a few minutes, but no more. The cruel and pathetic pendulum of time does not forgive. I must do what I've come to do.

I take a pillow from beside the little boy.

Can I truly commit this vulgar act? My stomach turns. Sickness fills me. Tears blind me. There is no forgiveness for what I'm about to do. And the truth is, I wouldn't want it even if there were. How can the universe forgive me, when I'll never be able to forgive myself?

I place the pillow over the babe.

I press.

Inside I scream.

I press harder.

It wasn't fair to ask this of me.

I press even harder.

Were I granted my life again, allowed to rewrite the pages of this wretched and unjust tale, I'd choose to fall from that fateful rooftop in Brooklyn—and in doing so, defy the callous schemings of the stars.

Harder!

I collapse. My strength has left me. I cling to the side of the crib with tears uncontrolled. I lower my shawl and rake sharp fingernails across my skin. So much worse I deserve.

I hear no breathing behind me.

The deed is done.

The man one day known as Patmos will never be.

Were I endowed at this moment with the powers to witness the changes I've destined upon the future, I would see a great many outcomes altered.

I'd see New Harmony, crippled by the smoke and chaos of war only moments ago, now serene and peaceful; I'd hear the sounds of children crying replaced instead with their laughter; I'd watch as plazas-turned-battlefields curiously fill with the sweet nothings whispered by young couples out for daytime strolls.

I'd see other things, as well. I'd see the *Ark Royal*, smoldering in a crater, hollow and defeated, vanish in the blink of an eye from her terrestrial grave; I'd see her now on patrol along popular shipping lanes, a tireless Captain Bashir at the helm, his marines—many whose blood I saw spilling into the streets—alive and well, either at their posts or in their mess halls, trading stories, writing love poems to crushes, inhabiting a world more innocent than the one I had ever known.

Not all would be remedied, however.

Soolin's agents, they were like me, grounded; and as such, they will be unaffected by the new currents of time that I've created. Their blood-soaked and limp bodies will still be lying on the steps of the Ministry of Temporal Affairs, much to the horror of school children eagerly arriving for a morning tour.

Soolin, herself a former agent, will still be in the Chronos Imperium, on her knees, awaiting the end, awaiting the inevitable. Her captors, however, will inexplicably vanish; the mercenaries back to their prison cells and the followers of Patmos, the propagators of his brave new world, to places hopefully more peaceful.

I've seen enough violence today that I do not wish them ill. I hope only that they find the meaning and purpose they were so desperately seeking.

Soolin will infer what I've done. She'll know that I alone possessed the power to alter the cosmos so completely. The only question is, will she, in her religious devotion to the arrow of time, forgive me? Or will she continue to hunt me down until the last syllable of recorded time?

Oh, Careena, how I wish you were here.

I can't go on.

I can't do this alone.

And yet I have to.

I stand and wipe away my tears.

First, I decide I must find Rhoda. She is not only a temporal outcast like me, but she is my friend. And having jumped from within the Chronos Imperium, she too has now stepped outside the veil of history; she will have been spared the changes in the timeline I created, the ripples I sent through time. And something tells me that in the future to come, we will need one another.

And what of that future? There are mysteries out there in the galaxy. Dangerous ones. Careena told me that Baker, the architect of all this sorcery, journeyed somewhere unknown, and upon his return he had in his possession the blueprints for the Chronos Imperium.

Some say he traveled only into his own madness, that he was as tortured as he was brilliant. But I don't think so. I think he found something, out there, on the other side of time and space. And whatever it was—if the stories are to be believed—it was enough for his lover and confidante Herla Vox to kill him for it. And wherever she is now is anyone's guess.

As long as this riddle is left unsolved, as long as this black box is left out there on the horizon, someone else may stumble upon it; and they may not be so noble in their intentions as the esoteric agents of the Ministry of Temporal Affairs.

So when those scoundrels come, and come they will, who will stand against them? Because Patmos was right about one thing. There is a darkness lurking in the heart of humankind, an abyss ever threatening to consume humanity.

He believed it was our history that fed this darkness, and that by washing away our past, by placing civilization on new foundations of virtuous and saintly stones, our worse nature would never be born.

But as a traveler through time, I've come to see that the seeds of corruption lay not in our history—they lay buried in each of us. Perhaps Patmos never wanted to admit that, that there can be no good without the pull of evil, no light without the push of darkness. The only choice we ever have is whether to side with the better or worse angels already within us.

And while we cannot excise our demons, we can temper a strength within ourselves to hold them at bay, so that when the moment is called upon us we do not fall to cowardice or temptation, but instead stand strong against the tides of subversion.

I've confronted that darkness now. I've seen the good I'm capable of. But I've also seen the evil. And while I wish, oh how dearly do I wish, that I could remain the innocent flower, never aware of the serpent that lurks underneath, only in acknowledging my darker half can I remain vigilant against its seductions.

And so what now?

Patmos and the Red Man may have been defeated, but I doubt they will be the last enemies humanity will ever face. Someone will have to be there.

And her name will be Isabel Tzofiya Mendelssohn.

I can only hope that going forward my trials and tribulations, my exploits and adventures yet to be known, will inspire others to follow in my footsteps, to raise their own torches.

For perhaps united we can use the guiding lights left to us by generations past, by people like Careena, my dear friend and mentor, to lead humanity to better continents—not by erasing our sins, but by accepting our regrets as the stepping stones on a road to a wiser, worthier, and nobler undiscovered world to come.

Here, I jump.
Here, the beginning.

ACKNOWLEDGMENTS

All my love and appreciation to my parents, who always supported me. Though we came from modest means, they never said no to a new book, a new pencil, or a new notepad. Special thanks to my early readers for their encouragement and suggestions, Marissa D. and Rebekah N.

And to everyone else—thank you for reading this novel (my first!) It means a lot to me. Be well, and may the magic sustain you.

Kind regards, Daniel Andis

Made in United States
North Haven, CT
22 April 2023